P9-BIY-577

QUEEN SHEBA'S RING

Queen Sheba's Ring

BY

H. RIDER HAGGARD

Author of
"Queen of the Dawn,"
"Wisdom's Daughter,"
"The Virgin of the Sun,"
Etc.

GARDEN CITY   NEW YORK
GARDEN CITY PUBLISHING CO., INC.
1926

COPYRIGHT, 1909, BY
H. RIDER HAGGARD

ALL RIGHTS RESERVED

PRINTED IN THE UNITED STATES

CONTENTS

v

QUEEN SHEBA'S RING

Queen Sheba's Ring

CHAPTER I

THE COMING OF THE RING

EVERY one has read the monograph, I believe that is the right word, of my dear friend, Professor Higgs — Ptolemy Higgs to give him his full name — descriptive of the tableland of Mur in North Central Africa, of the ancient underground city in the mountains which surround it, and of the strange tribe of Abyssinian Jews, or rather their mixed descendants, by whom it is, or was, inhabited. I say every one advisedly, for although the public which studies such works is usually select, that which will take an interest in them, if the character of a learned and pugnacious personage is concerned, is very wide indeed. Not to mince matters, I may as well explain what I mean at once.

Professor Higgs's rivals and enemies, of whom either the brilliancy of his achievements or his somewhat abrupt and pointed methods of controversy seem to have made him a great many, have risen up, or rather seated themselves, and written him down — well, an individual who strains the truth. Indeed, only this morning one of these inquired, in a letter to the press, alluding to some adventurous traveller who, I am told, lectured to the British Association several years ago, whether Professor Higgs did not, in fact, ride across the desert to Mur,

3

not upon a camel, as he alleged, but upon a land tortoise of extraordinary size.

The innuendo contained in this epistle has made the Professor, who, as I have already hinted, is not by nature of a meek disposition, extremely angry. Indeed, notwithstanding all that I could do, he left his London house under an hour ago with a whip of hippopotamus hide such as the Egyptians call a *koorbash*, purposing to avenge himself upon the person of his defamer. In order to prevent a public scandal, however, I have taken the liberty of telephoning to that gentleman, who, bold and vicious as he may be in print, is physically small and, I should say, of a timid character, to get out of the way at once. To judge from the abrupt fashion in which our conversation came to an end, I imagine that the hint has been taken. At any rate, I hope for the best, and, as an extra precaution, have communicated with the lawyers of my justly indignant friend.

The reader will now probably understand that I am writing this book, not to bring myself or others before the public, or to make money of which I have no present need, or for any purpose whatsoever, except to set down the bare and actual truth. In fact, so many rumours are flying about as to where we have been and what befell us that this has become almost necessary. As soon as I laid down that cruel column of gibes and insinuations to which I have alluded — yes, this very morning, before breakfast, this conviction took hold of me so strongly that I cabled to Oliver, Captain Oliver Orme, the hero of my history, if it has any particular hero, who is at present engaged upon what must be an extremely agreeable journey round the world — asking his consent. Ten minutes since the answer arrived from Tokyo. Here it is:

"Do what you like and think necessary, but please

alter all names, et cetera, as propose returning via America, and fear interviewers. Japan jolly place." Then follows some private matter which I need not insert. Oliver is always extravagant where cablegrams are concerned.

I suppose that before entering on this narration, for the reader's benefit I had better give some short description of myself.

My name is Richard Adams, and I am the son of a Cumberland yeoman who married a Welshwoman. Therefore I have Celtic blood in my veins, which perhaps accounts for my love of roving and other things. I am now an old man, near the end of my course, I suppose; at any rate, I was sixty-five last birthday. This is my appearance as I see it in the glass before me: tall, spare (I don't weigh more than a hundred and forty pounds — the desert has any superfluous flesh that I ever owned, my lot having been, like Falstaff, to lard the lean earth, but in a hot climate); my eyes are brown, my face is long, and I wear a pointed white beard, which matches the white hair above.

Truth compels me to add that my general appearance, as seen in that glass which will not lie, reminds me of that of a rather aged goat; indeed, to be frank, by the natives among whom I have sojourned, and especially among the Khalifa's people when I was a prisoner there, I have often been called the White Goat.

Of my very commonplace outward self let this suffice. As for my record, I am a doctor of the old school. Think of it! When I was a student at Bart.'s the antiseptic treatment was quite a new thing, and administered, when at all, by help of a kind of engine on wheels, out of which disinfectants were dispensed with a pump, much as the advanced gardener sprays a greenhouse to-day.

I succeeded above the average as a student, and in my early time as a doctor. But in every man's life there happen things which, whatever excuses may be found for them, would not look particularly well in cold print (nobody's record, as understood by convention and the Pharisee, could really stand cold print); also something in my blood made me its servant. In short, having no strict ties at home, and desiring to see the world, I wandered far and wide for many years, earning my living as I went, never, in my experience, a difficult thing to do, for I was always a master of my trade.

My fortieth birthday found me practising at Cairo, which I mention only because it was here that first I met Ptolemy Higgs, who, even then in his youth, was noted for his extraordinary antiquarian and linguistic abilities. I remember that in those days the joke about him was that he could swear in fifteen languages like a native, and in thirty-two with common proficiency, and could read hieroglyphics as easily as a bishop reads the *Times*.

Well, I doctored him through a bad attack of typhoid, but as he had spent every farthing he owned on scarabs or something of the sort, made him no charge. This little kindness I am bound to say he never forgot, for whatever his failings may be (personally I would not trust him alone with any object that was more than a thousand years old), Ptolemy is a good and faithful friend.

In Cairo I married a Copt. She was a lady of high descent, the tradition in her family being that they were sprung from one of the Ptolemaic Pharaohs, which is possible and even probable enough. Also, she was a Christian, and well educated in her way. But, of course, she remained an Oriental, and for a European to marry an Oriental, is as I have tried to explain to others, a very dangerous thing, especially if he continues to live in the East, where it cuts him off from social recognition and intimacy with his own race. Still, although this step of mine forced me to leave Cairo and go to Assouan, then a little-known place, to practise chiefly among the natives, God knows we were happy enough together till the plague took her, and with it my joy in life.

I pass over all that business, since there are some things too dreadful and too sacred to write about. She left me one child, a son, who, to fill up my cup of sorrow, when he was twelve years of age, was kidnapped by the Mahdi's people.

This brings me to the real story. There is nobody else to write it; Oliver will not; Higgs cannot (outside of anything learned and antiquarian, he is hopeless); so I must. At any rate, if it is not interesting, the fault will be mine, not that of the story, which in all conscience is strange enough.

We are now in the middle of June, and it was a year ago last December that, on the evening of the day of my arrival in London after an absence of half a lifetime, I found myself knocking at the door of Professor Higgs's rooms in Guildford Street, W. C. It was opened by his housekeeper, Mrs. Reid, a thin and saturnine old woman, who reminded and still reminds me of a reanimated mummy. She told me that the Professor was in, but had a gentleman to dinner, and suggested sourly that I should call again the next morning. With difficulty I persuaded her at last to inform her master that an old Egyptian friend had brought him something which he certainly would like to see.

Five minutes later I groped my way into Higgs's sitting-room, which Mrs. Reid had contented herself with indicating from a lower floor. It is a large room, running the whole width of the house, divided into two by an arch, where once, in the Georgian days, there had been folding doors. The place was in shadow, except for the firelight, which shone upon a table laid ready for dinner, and upon an extraordinary collection of antiquities, including a couple of mummies with gold faces arranged in their coffins against the wall. At the far end of the room, however, an electric lamp was alight in the bow window hanging over another table covered with books, and by it I saw my host, whom I had not met for twenty years, although until I vanished into the desert we frequently corresponded, and with him the friend who had come to dinner.

First, I will describe Higgs, who, I may state, is admitted, even by his enemies, to be one of the most learned antiquarians and greatest masters of dead languages in Europe, though this no one would guess from his appearance at the age of about forty-five. In build short and stout, face round and high-coloured, hair and beard of a fiery red, eyes, when they can be seen — for generally he wears a pair of large blue spectacles — small and of an indefinite hue, but sharp as needles. Dress so untidy, peculiar, and worn that it is said the police invariably request him to move on, should he loiter in the streets at night. Such was, and is, the outward seeming of my dearest friend, Professor Ptolemy Higgs, and I only hope that he won't be offended when he sees it set down in black and white.

That of his companion who was seated at the table, his chin resting on his hand, listening to some erudite discourse with a rather distracted air, was extraordinarily different, especially by contrast. A tall, well-made young man, rather thin, but broad-shouldered, and apparently five or six and twenty years of age. Face clean-cut — so much so, indeed, that the dark eyes alone relieved it from a suspicion of hardness; hair short and straight, like the eyes, brown; expression that of a man of thought and ability, and, when he smiled, singularly pleasant. Such was and is Captain Oliver

Orme, who, by the way, I should explain, is only a captain of some volunteer engineers, although, in fact, a very able soldier, as was proved in the South African War, whence he had then but lately returned.

I ought to add also that he gave me the impression of a man not in love with fortune, or rather of one with whom fortune was not in love; indeed, his young face seemed distinctly sad. Perhaps it was this that attracted me to him so much from the first moment that my eyes fell on him — me with whom fortune had also been out of love for many years.

While I stood contemplating this pair, Higgs, looking up from the papyrus or whatever it might be that he was reading (I gathered later that he had spent the afternoon in unrolling a mummy, and was studying its spoils), caught sight of me standing in the shadow.

"Who the devil are you?" he exclaimed in a shrill and strident voice, for it acquires that quality when he is angry or alarmed, "and what are you doing in my room?"

"Steady," said his companion; "your housekeeper told you that some friend of yours had come to call."

"Oh, yes, so she did, only I can't remember any friend with a face and beard like a goat. Advance, friend, and all 's well."

So I stepped into the shining circle of the electric light and halted again.

"Who is it? Who is it?" muttered Higgs. "The face is the face of — of — I have it — of old Adams, only he 's been dead these ten years. The Khalifa got him, they said. Antique shade of the long-lost Adams, please be so good as to tell me your name, for we waste time over a useless mystery."

"There is no need, Higgs, since it is in your mouth already. Well, I should have known you anywhere; but then *your* hair does n't go white."

"Not it; too much colouring matter; direct result of a sanguine disposition. Well, Adams — for Adams you must be — I am really delighted to see you, especially as you never answered some questions in my last letter as to where you got those First Dynasty scarabs, of which the genuineness, I may tell you, has been disputed by certain envious beasts. Adams, my dear old fellow, welcome a thousand times" — and he seized my hands and wrung them, adding, as his eye fell upon a ring I wore, "Why, what's that? Something quite unusual. But never mind; you shall tell me after dinner. Let me introduce you to my friend, Captain Orme, a very decent scholar of Arabic, with a quite elementary knowledge of Egyptology."

"*Mr.* Orme," interrupted the younger man, bowing to me.

"Oh well, Mr. or Captain, whichever you like. He means that he is not in the regular army, although he has been all through the Boer War, and wounded three times, once straight through the lungs. Here's the soup. Mrs. Reid, lay another place. I am dreadfully hungry; nothing gives me such an appetite as unrolling mummies; it involves so much intellectual wear and tear, in addition to the physical labour. Eat, man, eat. We will talk afterwards."

So we ate, Higgs largely, for his appetite was always excellent, perhaps because he was then practically a teetotaller; Mr. Orme very moderately, and I as becomes a person who has lived for months at a time on dates — mainly of vegetables, which, with fruits, form my principal diet — that is, if these are available, for at a pinch I can exist on anything.

When the meal was finished and our glasses had been filled with port, Higgs helped himself to water, lit the large meerschaum pipe he always smokes, and pushed

round the tobacco-jar which had once served as a sepul-
chral urn for the heart of an old Egyptian.

"Now, Adams," he said when we also had filled our
pipes, "tell us what has brought you back from the
Shades. In short, your story, man, your story."

I drew the ring he had noticed off my hand, a thick
band of rather light-coloured gold of a size such as an
ordinary woman might wear upon her first or second
finger, in which was set a splendid slab of sapphire
engraved with curious and archaic characters. Pointing
to these characters, I asked Higgs if he could read
them.

"Read them? Of course," he answered, producing
a magnifying glass. "Can't you? No, I remember;
you never were good at anything more than fifty years
old. Hullo! this is early Hebrew. Ah! I 've got it,"
and he read:

" ' The Gift of Solomon the Ruler — no, the Great One
— of Israel, Beloved of Jah, to Maqueda of Sheba-land,
Queen, Daughter of Kings, Child of Wisdom, Beautiful.'

"That 's the writing on your ring, Adams — a really
magnificent thing. 'Queen of Sheba — Bath-Melachim,
Daughter of Kings,' with our old friend Solomon chucked
in. Splendid, quite splendid!" — and he touched the
gold with his tongue, and tested it with his teeth. "Hum
— where did you get this intelligent fraud from, Adams?"

"Oh!" I answered, laughing, "the usual thing, or
course. I bought it from a donkey-boy in Cairo for
about thirty shillings."

"Indeed," he replied suspiciously. "I should have
thought the stone in it was worth more than that, although,
of course, it may be nothing but glass. The engraving,
too, is first-rate. Adams," he added with severity, "you
are trying to hoax us, but let me tell you what I thought
you knew by this time — that you can't take in Ptolemy

Higgs. This ring is a shameless swindle; but who did the Hebrew on it? He 's a good scholar, anyway."

"Don't know," I answered; "was n't aware till now that it was Hebrew. To tell you the truth, I thought it was old Egyptian. All I do know is that it was given, or rather lent, to me by a lady whose title is Walda Nagasta, and who is supposed to be a descendant of Solomon and the Queen of Sheba."

Higgs took up the ring and looked at it again; then, as though in a fit of abstraction, slipped it into his waist-coat pocket.

"I don't want to be rude, therefore I will not contradict you," he answered with a kind of groan, "or, indeed, say anything except that if anyone else had spun me that yarn I should have told him he was a common liar. But, of course, as every schoolboy knows, Walda Nagasta — that is, Child of Kings in Ethiopic — is much the same as Bath-Melachim — that is, Daughter of Kings in Hebrew."

Here Captain Orme burst out laughing, and remarked, "It is easy to see why you are not altogether popular in the antiquarian world, Higgs. Your methods of con-troversy are those of a savage with a stone axe."

"If you only open your mouth to show your ignorance, Oliver, you had better keep it shut. The men who carried stone axes had advanced far beyond the state of savagery. But I suggest that you had better give Doctor Adams a chance of telling his story, after which you can criticize."

"Perhaps Captain Orme does not wish to be bored with it," I said, whereon he answered at once:

"On the contrary, I should like to hear it very much — that is, if you are willing to confide in me as well as in Higgs."

I reflected a moment, since, to tell the truth, for sundry

reasons, my intention had been to trust no one except the Professor, whom I knew to be as faithful as he is rough. Yet some instinct prompted me to make an exception in favour of this Captain Orme. I liked the man; there was something about those brown eyes of his that appealed to me. Also it struck me as odd that he should happen to be present on this occasion, for I have always held that there is nothing casual or accidental in the world; that even the most trivial circumstances are either ordained, or the result of the workings of some inexorable law whereof the end is known by whatever power it is that directs our steps, though it be not yet declared.

"Certainly I am willing," I answered; "your face and your friendship with the Professor are passport enough for me. Only I must ask you to give me your word of honour that without my leave you will repeat nothing of what I am about to tell you."

"Of course," he answered, whereon Higgs broke in:

"There, that will do; you don't want us both to kiss the Book, do you? Who sold you that ring, and where have you been for the last dozen years, and whence do you come now?"

"I have been a prisoner of the Khalifa's among other things. I had five years of that entertainment of which my back would give some evidence if I were to strip. I think I am about the only man who never embraced Islam whom they allowed to live, and that was because I am a doctor, and, therefore, a useful person. The rest of the time I have spent wandering about the North African deserts looking for my son, Roderick. You remember the boy, or should, for you are his godfather, and I used to send you photographs of him as a little chap."

"Of course, of course," said the Professor in a new

tone; "I came across a Christmas letter from him the other day. But, my dear Adams, what happened? I never heard."

"He went up the river to shoot crocodiles against my orders, when he was about twelve years old — not very long after his mother's death, and some wandering Mahdi tribesmen kidnapped him and sold him as a slave. I have been looking for him ever since, for the poor boy was passed on from tribe to tribe, among which his skill as a musician enabled me to follow him. The Arabs call him the Singer of Egypt, because of his wonderful voice, and it seems that he has learned to play upon their native instruments."

"And now where is he?" asked Higgs, as one who feared the answer.

"He is, or was, a favourite slave among a barbarous, half-negroid people called the Fung, who dwell in the far interior of North Central Africa. After the fall of the Khalifa I followed him there; it took me several years. Some Bedouin were making an expedition to trade with these Fung, and I disguised myself as one of them.

"On a certain night we camped at the foot of a valley outside a great wall which encloses the holy place where their idol is. I rode up to this wall and, through the open gateway, heard someone with a beautiful tenor voice singing in English. What he sang was a hymn that I had taught my son. It begins:

"'Abide with me, fast falls the eventide.'

"I knew the voice again. I dismounted and slipped through the gateway, and presently came to an open space, where a young man sat singing upon a sort of raised bench with lamps on either side of him, and a large audience in front. I saw his face and, notwithstanding the turban which he wore and his Eastern robe — yes, and the passage of all those years — knew it for that of my son. Some spirit of madness entered into me, and I called aloud, 'Roderick, Roderick!' and he started up, staring about him wildly. The audience started up also, and one of them caught sight of me lurking in the shadow.

"With a howl of rage, for I had desecrated their sanctuary, they sprang at me. To save my life, coward that I was, I fled back through the gates. Yes, after all those years of seeking, still I fled rather than die, and though I was wounded with a spear and stones, managed to reach and spring upon my horse. Then, as I was headed off from our camp, I galloped away anywhere, still to save my miserable life from those savages, so strongly is the instinct of self-preservation implanted in us. From a distance I looked back and saw by the light of the fired tents that the Fung were attacking the Arabs with whom I had travelled, I suppose because they thought them parties to the sacrilege. Afterwards I heard that they killed them every one, poor men, but I escaped, who unwittingly had brought their fate upon them.

"On and on I galloped up a steep road. I remember hearing lions roaring round me in the darkness. I remember one of them springing upon my horse and the poor beast's scream. Then I remember no more till I found myself — I believe it was a week or so later — lying on the veranda of a nice house, and being attended by some good-looking women of an Abyssinian cast of countenance."

"Sounds rather like one of the lost tribes of Israel," remarked Higgs sarcastically, puffing at his big meerschaum.

"Yes, something of that sort. The details I will give you later. The main facts are that these people who

picked me up outside their gates are called Abati, live
in a town called Mur, and allege themselves to be
descended from a tribe of Abyssinian Jews who were
driven out, and migrated to this place four or five centuries
ago. Briefly, they look something like Jews, practise
a very debased form of the Jewish religion, are civilized
and clever after a fashion, but in the last stage of deca-
dence from interbreeding — about nine thousand men
is their total fighting force, although three or four generations ago they had twenty thousand — and live in hourly
terror of extermination by the surrounding Fung, who
hold them in hereditary hate as the possessors of the
wonderful mountain fortress that once belonged to
their forefathers."

"Gibraltar and Spain over again," suggested Orme.

"Yes, with this difference — that the position is
reversed, the Abati of this Central African Gibraltar are
decaying, and the Fung, who answer to the Spaniards,
are vigorous and increasing."

"Well, what happened?" asked the Professor.

"Nothing particular. I tried to persuade these Abati
to organize an expedition to rescue my son, but they
laughed in my face. By degrees I found out that there
was only one person among them who was worth anything at all, and she happened to be their hereditary ruler
who bore the high-sounding titles of Walda Nagasta
or Child of Kings, and Takla Warda, or Bud of the
Rose, a very handsome and spirited young woman, whose
personal name is Maqueda ———"

"One of the names of the first known Queens of Sheba,"
muttered Higgs; "the other was Belchis."

"Under pretence of attending her medically," I went
on, "for otherwise their wretched etiquette would scarcely
have allowed me access to one so exalted, I talked things
over with her. She told me that the idol of the Fung

is fashioned like a huge sphinx, or so I gathered from her description of the thing, for I have never seen it."

"What!" exclaimed Higgs, jumping up, "a sphinx in North Central Africa! Well, after all, why not? Some of the earlier Pharaohs are said to have had dealings with that part of the world, or even to have migrated from it. I think that Makreezi repeats the legend. I suppose that it is ram-headed."

"She told me also," I continued, "that they have a tradition, or rather a belief, which amounts to an article of faith, that if this sphinx or god, which, by the way, is lion, not ram headed, and is called Harmac——"

"Harmac!" interrupted Higgs again. "That is one of the names of the sphinx — Harmachis, god of dawn."

"If this god," I repeated, "should be destroyed, the nation of the Fung whose forefathers fashioned it as they say, must move away from that country across the great river which lies to the south. I have forgotten its name at this moment, but I think it must be a branch of the Nile.

"I suggested to her that, in the circumstances, her people had better try to destroy the idol. Maqueda laughed and said it was impossible, since the thing was the size of a small mountain, adding that the Abati had long ago lost all courage and enterprise, and were content to sit in their fertile and mountain-ringed land, feeding themselves with tales of departed grandeur and struggling for rank and high-sounding titles, till the day of doom overtook them.

"I inquired whether she were also content, and she replied, 'Certainly not'; but what could she do to regenerate her people, she who was nothing but a woman, and the last of an endless line of rulers?

"'Rid me of the Fung,' she added passionately, 'and I will give you such a reward as you never dreamed of.

The old cave-city yonder is full of treasure that was buried with its ancient kings long before we came to Mur. To us it is useless, since we have none to trade with, but I have heard that the peoples of the outside world worship gold.'

"'I do not want gold,' I answered; 'I want to rescue my son who is a prisoner yonder.'

"'Then,' said the Child of Kings, 'you must begin by helping us to destroy the idol of the Fung. Are there no means by which this can be done?'

"'There are means,' I replied, and I tried to explain to her the properties of dynamite and of other more powerful explosives.

"'Go to your own land,' she exclaimed eagerly, 'and return with that stuff and two or three who can manage it, and I swear to them all the wealth of Mur. Thus only can you win my help to save your son.'"

"Well, what was the end?" asked Captain Orme.

"This: They gave me some gold and an escort with camels, which were literally lowered down a secret path in the mountains so as to avoid the Fung, who ring them in and of whom they are terribly afraid. With these people I crossed the desert to Assouan in safety, a journey of many weeks, where I left them encamped about sixteen days ago, bidding them await my return. I arrived in England this morning, and as soon as I could ascertain that you still lived, and your address, from a book of reference called 'Who's Who,' which they gave me in the hotel, I came on here."

"Why did you come to me? What do you want me to do?" asked the Professor.

"I came to you, Higgs, because I know how deeply you are interested in anything antiquarian, and because I wished to give you the first opportunity, not only of winning wealth, but also of becoming famous as the discoverer of the most wonderful relics of antiquity that are left in the world."

"With a very good chance of getting my throat cut thrown in," grumbled Higgs.

"As to what I want you to do," I went on, "I want you to find some one who understands explosives, and will undertake the business of blowing up the Fung idol."

"Well, that's easy enough, anyhow," said the Professor, pointing to Captain Orme with the bowl of his pipe, and adding, "he is an engineer by education, a soldier and a very fair chemist; also he knows Arabic and was brought up in Egypt as a boy — just the man for the job if he will go."

I reflected a moment, then, obeying some sort of instinct, looked up and asked:

"Will you, Captain Orme, if terms can be arranged?"

"Yesterday," he replied, colouring a little, "I should have answered, 'Certainly not.' To-day I answer that I am prepared to consider the matter — that is, if Higgs will go too, and you can enlighten me on certain points. But I warn you that I am only an amateur in the three trades that the Professor has mentioned, though, it is true, one with some experience."

"Would it be rude to inquire, Captain Orme, why twenty-four hours have made such a difference in your views and plans?"

"Not rude, only awkward," he replied, colouring again, this time more deeply. "Still, as it is best to be frank, I will tell you. Yesterday I believed myself to be the inheritor of a very large fortune from an uncle whose fatal illness brought me back from South Africa before I meant to come, and as whose heir I have been brought up. To-day I have learned for the first time that he married secretly, last year, a woman much below him in rank, and has left a child, who, of course, will take all his property,

as he died intestate. But that is not all. Yesterday I
believed myself to be engaged to be married; to-day I
am undeceived upon that point also. The lady," he
added with some bitterness, "who was willing to marry
Anthony Orme's heir is no longer willing to marry Oliver
Orme, whose total possessions amount to under £10,000.
Well, small blame to her or to her relations, whichever
it may be, especially as I understand that she has a
better alliance in view. Certainly her decision has
simplified matters," and he rose and walked to the other
end of the room.

"Shocking business," whispered Higgs; "been infa-
mously treated," and he proceeded to express his opinion
of the lady concerned, of her relatives, and of the late
Anthony Orme, shipowner, in language that, if printed,
would render this history unfit for family reading. The
outspokenness of Professor Higgs is well known in the
antiquarian world, so there is no need for me to enlarge
upon it.

"What I do not exactly understand, Adams," he added
in a loud voice, seeing that Orme had turned again,
"and what I think we should both like to know, is *your*
exact object in making these proposals."

"I am afraid I have explained myself badly. I thought
I had made it clear that I have only one object—to attempt
the rescue of my son, if he still lives, as I believe he does.
Higgs, put yourself in my position. Imagine yourself
with nothing and no one left to care for except a single
child, and that child stolen away from you by savages.
Imagine yourself, after years of search, hearing his very
voice, seeing his very face, adult now, but the same, the
thing you had dreamed of and desired for years; that for
which you would have given a thousand lives if you could
have had time to think. And then the rush of the howling,
fanatic mob, the breakdown of courage, of love, of every-

thing that is noble under the pressure of primæval instinct, which has but one song — Save your life. Lastly, imagine this coward saved, dwelling within a few miles of the son whom he had deserted, and yet utterly unable to rescue or even to communicate with him because of the poltroonery of those among whom he had refuged."

"Well," grunted Higgs, "I have imagined all that high-faluting lot. What of it? If you mean that you are to blame, I don't agree with you. You would n't have helped your son by getting your own throat cut, and perhaps his also."

"I don't know," I answered. "I have brooded over the thing so long that it seems to me that I have disgraced myself. Well, there came a chance, and I took it. This lady, Walda Nagasta, or Maqueda, who, I think, had also brooded over things, made me an offer — I fancy without the knowledge or consent of her Council. 'Help me,' she said, 'and I will help you. Save my people, and I will try to save your son. I can pay for your services and those of any whom you may bring with you.'

"I answered that it was hopeless, as no one would believe the tale, whereon she drew from her finger the throne-ring or State signet which you have in your pocket, Higgs, saying: 'My mothers have worn this since the days of Maqueda, Queen of Sheba. If there are learned men among your people they will read her name upon it and know that I speak no lie. Take it as a token, and take also enough of our gold to buy the stuffs whereof you speak, which hide fires that can throw mountains skyward, and the services of skilled and trusty men who are masters of the stuff, two or three of them only, for more cannot be transported across the desert, and come back to save your son and me.' That's all the story, Higgs. Will you take the business on, or shall I try elsewhere? You must make up your mind, because I have no time to lose if I am to get into Mur again before the rains."

"Got any of that gold you spoke of about you?" asked the Professor.

I drew a skin bag from the pocket of my coat, and poured some out upon the table, which he examined carefully.

"Ring money," he said presently, "might be Anglo-Saxon, might be anything; date absolutely uncertain, but from its appearance I should say slightly alloyed with silver; yes, there is a bit which has oxydized — undoubtedly old, that."

Then he produced the signet from his pocket, and examined the ring and the stone very carefully through a powerful glass.

"Seems all right," he said, "and although I have been greened in my time, I don't make many mistakes nowadays. What do you say, Adams? Must have it back? A sacred trust! Only lent to you! All right, take it by all means. *I* don't want the thing. Well, it is a risky job, and if anyone else had proposed it to me, I'd have told him to go to — Mur. But, Adams, my boy, you saved my life once, and never sent in a bill, because I was hard up, and I have n't forgotten that. Also things are pretty hot for me here just now over a certain controversy of which I suppose you have n't heard in Central Africa. I think I'll go. What do you say, Oliver?"

"Oh!" said Captain Orme, waking up from a reverie, "if you are satisfied, I am. It does n't matter to me where I go."

CHAPTER II

AT THIS moment a fearful hubbub arose without. The front door slammed, a cab drove off furiously, a policeman's whistle blew, heavy feet were heard trampling; then came an invocation of "In the King's name," answered by "Yes, and the Queen's, and the rest of the Royal Family's, and if you want it, take it, you chuckle-headed, flat-footed, pot-bellied Peelers."

Then followed tumult indescribable as of heavy men and things rolling down the stairs, with cries of fear and indignation.

"What the dickens is that?" asked Higgs.

"The voice sounded like that of Samuel — I mean Sergeant Quick," answered Captain Orme with evident alarm; "what can he be after? Oh I know, it is something to do with that infernal mummy you unwrapped this afternoon, and asked him to bring round after dinner."

Just then the door burst open, and a tall, soldier-like form stalked in, carrying in his arms a corpse wrapped in a sheet, which he laid upon the table among the wine glasses.

"I'm sorry, Captain," he said, addressing Orme, "but I've lost the head of the departed. I think it is at the bottom of the stairs with the police. Had nothing else to defend myself with, sir, against their unwarranted attacks, so brought the body to the present and charged, thinking it very stiff and strong, but regret to say neck snapped, and that deceased's head is now under arrest."

As Sergeant Quick finished speaking, the door opened again, and through it appeared two very flurried and dishevelled policemen, one of whom held, as far as possible from his person, the grizzly head of a mummy by the long hair which still adhered to the skull.

"What do you mean by breaking into my rooms like this? Where's your warrant?" asked the indignant Higgs in his high voice.

"There!" answered the first policeman, pointing to the sheet-wrapped form upon the table.

"And here!" added the second, holding up the awful head. "As in duty bound, we ask explanation from that man of the secret conveyance of a corpse through the open streets, whereon he assaults us with the same, for which assault, pending investigation of the corpse, I arrest him. Now, Guv'nor (addressing Sergeant Quick), will you come along with us quietly, or must we take you?"

The Sergeant, who seemed to be inarticulate with wrath, made a dash for the grizzly object on the table, with the intention, apparently, of once more using it as a weapon of offence, and the policemen drew their batons.

"Stop," said Orme, thrusting himself between the combatants, "are you all mad? Do you know that this woman died about four thousand years ago?"

"Oh, Lord!" said the policeman who held the head, addressing his companion, "it must be one of them mummies what they dig up in the British Museum. Seems pretty ancient and spicy, don't it?" and he sniffed at the head, then set it down upon the table.

Explanations followed, and after the wounded dignity of the two officers of the Force had been soothed with sundry glasses of port wine and a written list of the names of all concerned, including that of the mummy, they departed.

"You take my advice, Bobbies," I heard the indignant sergeant declaim outside the door, "and don't you believe things is always what they seem. A party ain't necessarily drunk because he rolls about and falls down in the street; he may be mad, or 'ungry, or epileptic, and a body ain't always a body jest because it's dead and cold and stiff. Why, men, as you've seen, it may be a mummy, which is quite a different thing. If I was to put on that blue coat of yours, would that make me a policeman? Good heavens! I should hope not, for the sake of the Army to which I still belong, being in the Reserve. What you bobbies need is to study human nature and cultivate observation, which will learn you the difference between a new-laid corpse and a mummy, and many other things. Now you lay my words to heart, and you'll both of you rise to superintendents, instead of running in daily 'drunks' until you retire on a pension. Good night."

Peace having been restored, and the headless mummy removed into the Professor's bedroom, since Captain Orme declared that he could not talk business in the presence of a body, however ancient, we resumed our discussion. First of all, at Higgs's suggestion I drew up a brief memorandum of agreement which set out the objects of the expedition, and provided for the equal division among us of any profit that might accrue; in the event of the death of one or more of us, the survivors or survivor to take their or his share.

To this arrangement personally I objected, who desired neither treasure nor antiquities, but only the rescue of my son. The others pointed out, however, that, like most people, I might in future want something to live on, or that if I did not, in the event of his escape, my boy certainly would; so in the end I gave way.

Then Captain Orme very sensibly asked for a definition of our respective duties, and it was settled that I was to be guide to the expedition; Higgs, antiquarian, interpreter, and, on account of his vast knowledge, general referee; and Captain Orme, engineer and military commander, with the proviso that, in the event of a difference of opinion, the dissentient was to loyally accept the decision of the majority.

This curious document having been copied out fair, I signed and passed it to the Professor, who hesitated a little, but, after refreshing himself with a further minute examination of Sheba's ring, signed also, remarking that he was an infernal fool for his pains, and pushed the paper across the table to Orme.

"Stop a minute," said the Captain; "I forgot something. I should like my old servant, Sergeant Quick, to accompany us. He's a very handy man at a pinch, especially if, as I understand, we are expected to deal with explosives with which he has had a lot to do in the Engineers and elsewhere. If you agree I will call him, and ask if he will go. I expect he is somewhere round."

I nodded, judging from the episode of the mummy and the policemen that the Sergeant was likely to be a useful man. As I was sitting next to it, I opened the door for the Captain, whereon the erect shape of Sergeant Quick, who clearly had been leaning against it, literally fell into the room, reminding me much of an overset wooden soldier.

"Hullo!" said Orme as, without the slightest change of countenance, his retainer recovered himself and stood to attention. "What the deuce are you doing there?"

"Sentry go, Captain. Thought the police might change their minds and come back. Any orders, Captain?"

"Yes. I am going to North Central Africa. When can you be ready to start?"

"The Brindisi mail leaves to-morrow night, Captain, if you travel by Egypt, but if you go by Tunis, 7.15 A.M. Saturday is the time from Charing Cross. Only, as I understand that high explosives and arms have to be provided, these might take a while to lay in and pack so as to deceive customs."

"You understand!" said Orme. "Pray, how do you understand?"

"Doors in these old houses are apt to get away from their frames, Captain, and the gentleman there" — and he pointed to the Professor — "has a voice that carries like a dog-whistle. Oh no offence, sir. A clear voice is an excellent thing — that is, if the doors fit" — and although Sergeant Quick's wooden face did not move, I saw his humorous gray eyes twinkle beneath the bushy eyebrows.

We burst out laughing, including Higgs.

"So you are willing to go," said Orme. "But I hope you clearly understand that this is a risky business, and that you may not come back?"

"Spionkop was a bit risky, Captain, and so was that business in the donga, where everyone was hit except you and me and the sailor man, but we came back, for all that. Begging your pardon, Captain, there ain't no such thing as risk. Man comes here when he must, and dies when he must, and what he does between don't make a ha'porth of difference."

"Hear, hear," I said; "we are much of the same way of thinking."

"There have been several who held those views, sir, since old Solomon gave the lady that" — and he pointed to Sheba's ring, which was lying on the table. "But excuse me, Captain: how about local allowances? Not having been a marrying man myself, I 've none dependent upon me, but, as you know, I 've sisters that have, and a soldier's pension goes with him. Don't think me greedy, Captain," he added hastily, "but, as you gentlemen understand, black and white at the beginning saves bother at the end"—and he pointed to the agreement.

"Quite right. What do you want, Sergeant?" asked Orme.

"Nothing beyond my pay, if we get nothing, Captain, but if we get something, would 5 per cent. be too much?"

"It might be ten," I suggested. "Sergeant Quick has a life to lose like the rest of us."

"Thank you kindly, sir," he answered; "but that, in my opinion, would be too much. Five per cent. was what I suggested."

So it was written down that Sergeant Samuel Quick was to receive 5 per cent. of the total profits, if any, provided that he behaved himself and obeyed orders, and he also signed the agreement, and was furnished with a glass of whisky and water to drink to its good health.

"Now, gentlemen," he said, declining the chair which Higgs offered to him, apparently because, from long custom, he preferred his wooden-soldier attitude against the wall, "as a humble 5-per-cent. private in this very adventurous company I 'll ask permission to say a word."

Permission was given accordingly, and the sergeant proceeded to inquire what weight of rock it was wished to remove.

I told him that I did not know, as I had never seen the Fung idol, but I understood that its size was enormous, probably as large as St. Paul's Cathedral.

"Which, if solid, would take some stirring," remarked the Sergeant. "Dynamite might do it, but it is too bulky to be carried across the desert on camels in that quantity. Captain, how about them picrates? You remember those new Boer shells that blew a lot of us to kingdom come, and poisoned the rest?"

"Yes," answered Orme; "I remember; but now they have stronger stuffs — azo-imides, I think they call them —terrific new compounds of nitrogen. We will inquire to-morrow, Sergeant."

"Yes, Captain," he answered; "but the point is, who 'll pay? You can't buy hell-fire in bulk for nothing. I calculate that, allowing for the purchase of the explosives and, say, fifty military rifles with ammunition and all other necessaries, not including camels, the outfit of this expedition can't come to less than £1,500."

"I think I have that amount in gold," I answered, "of which the lady of the Abati gave me as much as I could carry in comfort."

"If not," broke in Orme, "although I am a poor man now, I could find £500 or so at a pinch. So don't let us bother about the money. The question is—Are we all agreed that we will undertake this expedition and see it through to the end, whatever that may be?"

We answered that we were.

"Then has anybody anything more to say?"

"Yes," I replied; "I forgot to tell you that if we should ever get to Mur, none of you must make love to the Walda Nagasta. She is a kind of holy person, who can only marry into her own family, and to do so might mean that our throats would be cut."

"Do you hear that, Oliver?" said the Professor. "I suppose that the Doctor's warning is meant for you, as the rest of us are rather past that kind of thing."

"Indeed," replied the Captain, colouring again after his fashion. "Well, to tell you the truth, I feel a bit past it myself, and, so far as I am concerned, I don't think we need take the fascinations of this black lady into account."

"Don't brag, Captain. Please don't brag," said Sergeant Quick in a hollow whisper. "Woman is just the one thing about which you never can be sure. To-day she's poison, and to-morrow honey — God and the climate alone know why. Please don't brag, or we may live to see you crawling after this one on your knees, with the gent in the specs behind, and Samuel Quick, who hates the whole tribe of them, bringing up the rear. Tempt Providence if you like, Captain, but don't tempt woman, lest she should turn round and tempt you, as she has done before to-day."

"Will you be so good as to stop talking nonsense, and call a cab," said Captain Orme coldly. But Higgs began to laugh in his rude fashion, and I, remembering the appearance of "Bud of the Rose" when she lifted her veil of ceremony, and the soft earnestness of her voice, fell into reflection. "Black lady" indeed! What, I wondered, would this young gentleman think if ever he should live to set his eyes upon her sweet and comely face?

It seemed to me that Sergeant Quick was not so foolish as his master chose to imagine. Captain Orme undoubtedly was in every way qualified to be a partner in our venture; still, I could have wished either that he had been an older man, or that the lady to whom he was recently affianced had not chosen this occasion to break her engagement. In dealing with difficult and dangerous combinations, my experience has been that it is always well to eliminate the possibility of a love affair, especially in the East.

CHAPTER III

THE PROFESSOR GOES OUT SHOOTING

OF ALL our tremendous journey across the desert until we had passed the forest and reached the plains which surround the mountains of Mur, there are, I think, but few incidents with which the reader need be troubled. The first of these was at Assouan, where a letter and various telegrams overtook Captain Orme, which, as by this time we had become intimate, he showed to me. They informed him that the clandestine infant whom his uncle left behind him had suddenly sickened and died of some childish ailment, so that he was once again heir to the large property which he thought he had lost, since the widow only took a life interest in some of the personalty. I congratulated him, and said I supposed this meant that we should not have the pleasure of his company to Mur.

"Why not?" he asked. "I said I was going and I mean to go; indeed, I signed a document to that effect."

"I daresay," I answered, "but circumstances alter cases. If I might say so, an adventure that perhaps was good enough for a young and well-born man of spirit and enterprise without any particular resources, is no longer good enough for one who has the ball at his feet. Think what a ball it is to a man of your birth, intelligence, record, and now, great fortune come to you in youth. Why, with these advantages there is absolutely nothing that you cannot do in England. You can go into

Parliament and rule the country; if you like you can become a peer. You can marry any one who is n't of the blood royal; in short, with uncommonly little effort of your own, your career is made for you. Don't throw away a silver spoon like that in order, perhaps, to die of thirst in the desert or be killed in a fight among unknown tribes."

"Oh, I don't know," he answered. "I never set my heart much on spoons, silver or other. When I lost this one I did n't cry, and now that I have found it again I shan't sing. Anyway, I am going on with you, and you can't prevent me under the agreement. Only as I have got such a lot to leave I suppose I had better make a will first and post it home, which is a bore."

Just then the Professor came in, followed by an Arab thief of a dealer, with whom he was trying to bargain for some object of antiquity. When the dealer had been ejected and the position explained to him, Higgs, who, whatever may be his failings in small matters, is unselfish enough in big ones, said that he agreed with me and thought that under the circumstances, in his own interest, Orme ought to leave us and return home.

"You may save your breath, old fellow," answered the Captain, "for this reason if for no other," and he threw him a letter across the table, which letter I saw afterwards. To be brief, it was from the young lady to whom he had been engaged to be married, and who on his loss of fortune had jilted him. Now she seemed to have changed her mind again, and, although she did not mention the matter, it is perhaps not uncharitable to suppose that the news of the death of that inconvenient child had something to do with her decision.

"Have you answered this?" asked Higgs.

"No," answered Orme, setting his mouth. "I have not answered it and I am not going to answer it, either by writing or in person. I intend to start to morrow for Mur and to travel as far on that road as it pleases fate to allow, and now I am going to look at the rock sculptures by the cataract."

"Well, that's flat," said Higgs after he had departed, "and for my part I am glad of it, for somehow I think he will be a useful man among those Fung. Also, if he went I expect that the Sergeant would go too, and where should we be without Quick, I should like to know?"

Afterward I conversed with the said Quick about this same matter, repeating to him my opinions, to which the Sergeant listened with the deference which he was always kind enough to show to me.

"Begging your pardon, sir," he said, when I had finished, "but I think you are both right and wrong. Everything has two ends, has n't it? You say that it would be wicked for the Captain to get himself killed, there being now so much money for him to live for, seeing that life is common as dirt while money is precious, rare and hard to come by. It ain't the kings we admire, it's their crowns; it ain't the millionaires, it's their millions; but, after all, the millionaires don't take their millions with them, for Providence, that, like Nature, hates waste, knows that if they did they'd melt, so one man dead gives another bread, as the saying goes, or p'raps I should say gingerbread in such cases.

"Still, on the whole, sir, I admit you're right as to the sinfulness of wasting luck. But now comes the other end. I know this young lady what the Captain was engaged to, which he never would have been if he had taken my advice, since of all the fish-blooded little serpents that ever I set eyes on she 's the serpentest, though pretty, I allow. Solomon said in his haste that an honest woman he had not found, but if he had met the Honourable Miss — well, never mind her name — he 'd have said it at his leisure, and gone on saying it. Now, no one should never take back a servant what has given notice and then says he's sorry, for if he does the sorrow will be on the other side before all's done; and much less should he take back a *fiancée* (Quick said a "finance"), on the whole, he'd better drown himself — I tried it once, and I know. So that's the tail of the business.

"But," he went on, "it has a couple of fins as well, like that eel beast I caught in the Nile. One of them is that the Captain promised and vowed to go through with this expedition, and if a man's got to die, he'd better die honest without breaking his word. And the other is what I said to you in London when I signed on, that he won't die a minute before his time, and nothing won't happen to him but what's bound to happen, and therefore it ain't a ha'porth of use bothering about anything, and that's where the East's well ahead of the West.

"And now, sir, I'll go and look after the camels and those half-bred Jew boys what you call Abati, but I call rotten sneaks, for if they get their thieving fingers into those canisters of picric salts, thinking they're jam, as I found them trying to do yesterday, something may happen in Egypt that'll make the Pharaohs turn in their graves and the Ten Plagues look silly."

So, having finished his oration, Quick went, and in due course we started for Mur.

The second incident that is perhaps worth recording was an adventure that happened to us when we had completed about two of our four months' journey.

After weeks of weary desert travel — if I remember right, it was exactly a fortnight after the dog Pharaoh, of which I shall soon have plenty to say, had come into Orme's possession — we reached an oasis called Zeu, where I had halted upon my road down to Egypt. In this oasis, which, although not large in extent, possesses springs of beautiful water and groves of date-trees, we were, as it chanced, very welcome, since when I was there before, I had been fortunate enough to cure its sheik of an attack of ophthalmia and to doctor several of his people for various ailments with good results. So, although I was burning to get forward, I agreed with the others that it would be wise to accede to the request of the leader of our caravan, a clever and resourceful, but to my mind untrustworthy Abati of the name of Shadrach, and camp in Zeu for a week or so to rest and feed our camels, which had wasted almost to nothing on the scant herbage of the desert.

This Shadrach, I may add here, whom his companions, for some reason unknown to me at that time, called the Cat, was remarkable for a triple line of scars upon his face, which, he informed me, had been set there by the claws of a lion. Now the great enemies of this people of Zeu were lions, which at certain seasons of the year, I suppose when food grew scarce, descended from the slopes of a range of hills that stretched east and west at a distance of about fifty miles to the north of the oasis, and, crossing the intervening desert, killed many of the Zeu sheep, camels, and other cattle, and often enough any of the tribe whom they could catch. As these poor Zeus practically possessed no firearms, they were at the mercy of the lions, which grew correspondingly bold. Indeed, their only resource was to kraal their animals within stone walls at night and take refuge in their huts, which they seldom left between sunset and dawn, except to replenish the fires that they lit to scare any beast of prey which might be prowling through the town.

Though the lion season was now in full swing, as it happened—for the first five days of our stay at Zeu we saw none of these great cats, although in the darkness we heard them roaring in the distance. On the sixth night, however, we were awakened by a sound of wailing which came from the village about a quarter of a mile away, and when we went out at dawn to see what was the matter, were met by a melancholy procession advancing from its walls. At the head of it marched the gray-haired old chief, followed by a number of screaming women, who in their excitement, or perhaps as a sign of mourning, had omitted to make their toilette, and by four men, who carried something horrid on a wickerwork door.

Soon we learned what had happened. It seemed that hungry lions, two or three of them, had broken through the palm-leaf roof of the hut of one of the sheik's wives, she whose remains were stretched upon the door, and, in addition to killing her, had actually carried off his son. Now he came to implore us white men who had guns to revenge him on the lions, which otherwise, having once tasted human flesh, would destroy many more of his people.

Through an interpreter who knew Arabic, for not even Higgs could understand the peculiar Zeu dialect, he explained in excited and incoherent words that the beasts lay up among the sand-hills not very far away, where some thick reeds grew around a little spring of water. Would we not come out and kill them and earn the blessing of the Zeus?

Now I said nothing, for the simple reason that, having such big matters on hand, although I was always fond of sport, I did not wish any of us to be led off after these lions. There is a time to hunt and a time to cease from hunting, and it seemed to me, except for the purposes of food, that this journey of ours was the latter. However, as I expected, Oliver Orme literally leaped at the idea. So did Higgs, who of late had been practising with a rifle and began to fancy himself a shot. He exclaimed loudly that nothing would give him greater pleasure, especially as he was sure that lions were in fact cowardly and overrated beasts.

From that moment I foreboded disaster in my heart. Still, I said I would come too, partly because I had not shot a lion for many a day and had a score to settle with those beasts which, it may be remembered, nearly killed me on the Mountain of Mur, and partly because, knowing the desert and also the Zeu people much better than either the Professor or Orme, I thought that I might possibly be of service.

So we fetched our rifles and cartridges, to which by an afterthought we added two large water-bottles, and ate a hearty breakfast. As we were preparing to start, Shadrach, the leader of the Abati camel-drivers, that man with the scarred face who was nicknamed the Cat, came up to me and asked me whither we were going. I told him, whereon he said:

"What have you to do with these savages and their troubles, lords? If a few of them are killed it is no matter, but as you should know, O Doctor, if you wish to hunt lions there are plenty in the land whither you travel, seeing that the lion is the fetish of the Fung and therefore never killed. But the desert about Zeu is dangerous and harm may come to you."

"Then accompany us," broke in the Professor, between whom and Shadrach there was no love lost, "for, of course, with you we should be quite safe."

"Not so," he replied, "I and my people rest; only madmen would go to hunt worthless wild beasts when they might rest. Have we not enough of the desert and its dangers as it is? If you knew all that I do of lions you would leave them alone."

"Of the desert we have plenty also, but of shooting very little," remarked the Captain, who talked Arabic well. "Lie in your beds; we go to kill the beasts that harass the poor people who have treated us so kindly."

"So be it," said Shadrach with a smile that struck me as rather malicious. "A lion made this" — pointing to the dreadful threefold scar upon his face. "May the God of Israel protect you from lions. Remember, lords, that, the camels being fresh again, we march the day after to-morrow, should the weather hold, for if the wind blows on yonder sand-hills, no man may live among them;" and, putting up his hand, he studied the sky carefully from beneath its shadow, then, with a grunt, turned and vanished behind a hut.

All this while Sergeant Quick was engaged at a little distance in washing up the tin breakfast things, to all appearance quite unconscious of what was going on. Orme called him, whereupon he advanced and stood to attention. I remember thinking how curious he looked in those surroundings — his tall, bony form clothed in semi-military garments, his wooden face perfectly shaved, his iron-gray hair neatly parted and plastered down upon his head with pomade or some equivalent after the old private soldier fashion, and his sharp ferret-like gray eyes taking in everything.

"Are you coming with us, Sergeant?" asked Orme.

"Not unless ordered so to do, Captain. I like a bit of hunting well enough, but, with all three officers away, some one should mount guard over the stores and transport, so I think the dog Pharaoh and I had best stop behind."

"Perhaps you are right, Sergeant, only tie Pharaoh up, or he 'll follow me. Well, what do you want to say? Out with it."

"Only this, Captain. Although I have served in three campaigns among these here Arabians (to Quick, all African natives north of the Equator were Arabians, and all south of it, niggers), I can't say I talk their lingo well. Still, I made out that the fellow they call Cat don't like this trip of yours, and, begging your pardon, Captain, whatever else Cat may be, he ain't no fool."

"Can't help it, Sergeant. For one thing, it would never do to give in to his fancies now."

"That's true, Captain. When once it's hoist, right or wrong, keep the flag flying, and no doubt you'll come back safe and sound if you're meant to."

Then, having relieved his mind, the Sergeant ran his eye over our equipment to see that nothing had been forgotten, rapidly assured himself that the rifles were in working order, reported all well, and returned to his dishes. Little did any of us guess under what circumstances we should next meet with him.

After leaving the town and marching for a mile or so along the oasis, accompanied by a mob of the Zeus armed with spears and bows, we were led by the bereaved chief, who also acted as tracker, out into the surrounding sands. The desert here, although I remembered it well enough, was different from any that we had yet encountered upon this journey, being composed of huge and abrupt sand-hills, some of which were quite three hundred feet high, separated from each other by deep, wind-cut valleys.

For a distance, while they were within reach of the moist air of the oasis, these sand-mountains produced vegetation of various sorts. Presently, however, we passed out into the wilderness proper, and for a while climbed up and down the steep, shifting slopes, till from the crest of one of them the chief pointed out what in South Africa is called a pan, or *vlei*, covered with green reeds, and explained by signs that in these lay the lions. Descending a steep declivity, we posted ourselves, I

at the top, and Higgs and Orme a little way down either
side of this *vlei*. This done, we dispatched the Zeus
to beat it out toward us, for although the reeds grew
thick along the course of the underground water, it was
but a narrow place, and not more than a quarter of a
mile in length.

Scarcely had the beaters entered the tall reeds, evidently with trepidation, for a good many of them held
back from the adventure, when a sound of loud wailing
informed us that something had happened. A minute
or two later we saw two of them bearing away what
appeared to be the mangled remains of the chief's son
who had been carried off on the previous night.

Just then, too, we saw something else, for half-way
down the marsh a great male lion broke cover, and began
to steal off toward the sand-hills. It was about two
hundred yards from Higgs, who chanced to be nearest
to it, and, therefore, as any big-game hunter will know,
for practical purposes, far out of shot. But the Professor, who was quite unaccustomed to this, or, indeed,
any kind of sport, and, like all beginners, wildly anxious
for blood, lifted his rifle and fired, as he might have
done at a rabbit. By some marvellous accident the
aim was good, and the bullet from the express, striking
the lion fair behind the shoulder, passed through its
heart, and knocked it over dead as a stone.

"By Jingo! Did you see that?" screamed Higgs in
his delight. Then, without even stopping to reload the
empty barrel, he set off at the top of his speed toward
the prostrate beast, followed by myself and by Orme, as
fast as our astonishment would allow.

Running along the edge of the marsh, Higgs had
covered about a hundred yards of the distance, when
suddenly, charging straight at him out of the tall reeds,
appeared a second lion, or rather lioness. Higgs wheeled

round, and wildly fired the left barrel of his rifle without touching the infuriated brute. Next instant, to our horror, we saw him upon his back, with the lioness standing over him, lashing her tail, and growling.

We shouted as we ran, and so did the Zeus, although they made no attempt at rescue, with the result that the lioness, instead of tearing Higgs to pieces, turned her head confusedly first to one side and then to the other. By now I, who had a long start of Orme, was quite close, say within thirty yards, though fire I dared not as yet, fearing lest, should I do so, I might kill my friend. At this moment the lioness, recovering her nerve, squatted down on the prostrate Higgs, and though he hit at her with his fists, dropped her muzzle, evidently with the intention of biting him through the head.

Now I felt that if I hesitated any more, all would be finished. The lioness was much longer than Higgs — a short, stout man — and her hind quarters projected beyond his feet. At these I aimed rapidly, and, pressing the trigger, next second heard the bullet clap upon the great beast's hide. Up she sprang with a roar, one hind leg dangling, and, after a moment's hesitation, fled toward the sand-hills.

Now Orme, who was behind me, fired also, knocking up the dust beneath the lioness's belly, but although he had more cartridges in his rifle, which was a repeater, before either he or I could get another chance, it vanished behind a mound. Leaving it to go where it would, we ran on toward Higgs, expecting to find him either dead or badly mauled, but, to our amazement and delight, up jumped the Professor, his blue spectacles still on his nose, and, loading his rifle as he went, charged away after the wounded lioness.

"Come back," shouted the Captain as he followed.

"Not for Joe!" yelled Higgs in his high voice. "If

you fellows think that I'm going to let a great cat sit on my stomach for nothing, you are jolly well mistaken."

At the top of the first rise the long-legged Orme caught him, but persuade him to return back was more than he, or I when I arrived, could do. Beyond a scratch on his nose, which had stung him and covered him with blood, we found that he was quite uninjured, except in temper and dignity. But in vain did we beg him to be content with his luck and the honours he had won.

"Why?" he answered, "Adams wounded the beast, and I'd rather kill two lions than one; also I have a score to square. But if you fellows are afraid, you go home."

Well, I confess I felt inclined to accept the invitation, but Orme, who was nettled, replied:

"Come, come; that settles the question, does n't it? You must be shaken by your fall, or you would not talk like that, Higgs. Look, here runs the spoor — see the blood? Well, let's go steady and keep our wind. We may come on her anywhere, but don't you try any more long shots. You won't kill another lion at two hundred and fifty yards."

"All right," said Higgs, "don't be offended. I did n't mean anything, except that I am going to teach that beast the difference between a white man and a Zeu."

Then we began our march, following the blood tracks up and down the steep sand-slopes. When we had been at it for about half an hour our spirits were cheered by catching sight of the lioness on a ridge five hundred yards away. Just then, too, some of the Zeus overtook us and joined in the hunt, though without zeal.

Meanwhile, as the day grew, the heat increased until it was so intense that the hot air danced above the sand slopes like billions of midges, and this although the sun was not visible, being hidden by a sort of mist. A strange silence, unusual even in the desert, pervaded the earth and sky; we could hear the grains of sand trickling from the ridges. The Zeus, who accompanied us, grew uneasy, and pointed upward with their spears, then behind toward the oasis of which we had long lost sight. Finally, when we were not looking, they disappeared.

Now I would have followed them, guessing that they had some good reason for this sudden departure. But Higgs refused to come, and Orme, in whom his foolish taunt seemed still to rankle, only shrugged his shoulders and said nothing.

"Let the black curs go," exclaimed the Professor as he polished his blue spectacles and mopped his face. "They are a white-livered lot of sneaks. Look! There she is, creeping off to the left. If we run round that sand-hill we shall meet her."

So we ran around the sand-hill, but we did not meet her, although after long hunting we struck the blood spoor afresh, and followed it for several miles, first in this direction and then in that, until Orme and I wondered at Higgs's obstinacy and endurance. At length, when even he was beginning to despair, we put up the lioness in a hollow, and fired several shots at her as she hobbled over the opposing slope, one of which hit her, for she rolled over, then picked herself up again, roaring. As a matter of fact, it came from the Captain's rifle, but Higgs, who, like many an inexperienced person, was a jealous sportsman, declared that it was his and we did not think it worth while to contradict him.

On we toiled, and, just beyond the ridge, walked straight into the lioness, sitting up like a great dog, so injured that she could do nothing but snarl hideously and paw at the air.

"Now it is my turn, old lady," ejaculated Higgs, and straightway missed her clean from a distance of five yards. A second shot was more successful, and she rolled over, dead.

"Come on," said the exultant Professor, "and we'll skin her. She sat on me, and I mean to sit on her for many a day."

So we began the job, although I, who had large experience of this desert, and did not like the appearance of the weather, wished to leave the beast where it lay and get back to the oasis. It proved long, for I was the only one of us who had any practical knowledge of flaying animals, and in that heat extremely unpleasant.

At length it was done, and, having doubled the hide over a rifle for two of us to carry, in turns we refreshed ourselves from the water-bottles (I even caught the Professor washing the blood off his face and hands with some of the precious fluid). Then we started for the oasis, only to discover, though we were all sure that we knew the way, that not one of us had the slightest idea of its real direction. In the hurry of our departure we had forgotten to bring a compass, and the sun, that would have been our guide in ordinary circumstances, and to which we always trusted in the open desert, was hidden by the curious haze that has been described.

So, sensibly enough, we determined to return to the sand crest where we had killed the lioness, and then trace our own footprints backward. This seemed simple enough, for there, within half a mile, rose the identical ridge.

We reached it, grumbling, for the lion-skin was heavy, only to discover that it was a totally different ridge. Now, after reflection and argument, we saw our exact mistake, and made for what was obviously the real ridge — with the same result.

We were lost in the desert!

CHAPTER IV

THE DEATH-WIND

"THE fact is," said Higgs presently, speaking with
the air of an oracle, "the fact is that all these
accursed sand-hills are as like each other as
mummy beads on the same necklace, and therefore it is
very difficult to know them apart. Give me that water-
bottle, Adams; I am as dry as a lime-kiln."

"No," I said shortly; "you may be drier before the end."

"What do you mean? Oh! I see; but that's nonsense; those Zeus will hunt us up, or, at the worst, we
have only to wait till the sun gets out."

As he spoke, suddenly the air became filled with a
curious singing sound impossible to describe, caused,
as I knew, who had often heard it before, by millions
and millions of particles of sand being rubbed together.
We turned to see whence it came, and perceived far away,
rushing toward us with extraordinary swiftness, a huge
and dense cloud preceded by isolated columns and funnels
of similar clouds.

"A sand-storm," said Higgs, his florid face paling a
little. "Bad luck for us! That's what comes of getting
out of bed the wrong side first this morning. No, it's
your fault, Adams; you helped me to salt last night, in
spite of my remonstrances" (the Professor has sundry
little superstitions of this sort, particularly absurd in
so learned a man). "Well, what shall we do? Get
under the lee of the hill until it blows over?"

uppose it will blow over. Can't see anything
: say our prayers," remarked Orme with sweet
Oliver is, I think, the coolest hand in an
of any one I ever met, except, perhaps, Sergeant Quick, a man, of course, nearly old enough to be
his father. "The game seems to be pretty well up,"
he added. "Well, you have killed two lions, Higgs,
and that is something."

"Oh, hang it! You can die if you like, Oliver. The
world won't miss you; but think of its loss if anything
happened to *me*. I don't intend to be wiped out by a
beastly sand-storm. I intend to live to write a book on
Mur," and Higgs shook his fist at the advancing
clouds with an air that was really noble. It reminded me
of Ajax defying the lightning.

Meanwhile I had been reflecting.

"Listen," I said. "Our only chance is to stop where
we are, for if we move we shall certainly be buried alive.
Look; there is something solid to lie on," and I pointed
to a ridge of rock, a kind of core of congealed sand, from
which the surface had been swept by gales. "Down
with you, quick," I went on, "and let's draw that lion-
skin over our heads. It may help to keep the dust from
choking us. Hurry, men; it's coming!"

Coming it was indeed, with a mighty, wailing roar.
Scarcely had we got ourselves into position, our backs
to the blast and our mouths and noses buried after the
fashion of camels in a similar predicament, the lion-skin
covering our heads and bodies to the middle, with the
paws tucked securely beneath us to prevent it from being
blown away, when the storm leaped upon us furiously,
bringing darkness in its train. There we lay for hour
after hour, unable to see, unable to talk because of the
roaring noise about us, and only from time to time lifting
ourselves a little upon our hands and knees to disturb

the weight of sand that accumulated on our bodies, lest it should encase us in a living tomb.

Dreadful were the miseries we suffered — the misery of the heat beneath the stinking pelt of the lion, the misery of the dust-laden air that choked us almost to suffocation, the misery of thirst, for we could not get at our scanty supply of water to drink. But worst of all perhaps, was the pain caused by the continual friction of the sharp sand driven along at hurricane speed, which, incredible as it may seem, finally wore holes in our thin clothing and filed our skins to rawness.

"No wonder the Egyptian monuments get such a beautiful face on them," I heard poor Higgs muttering in my ear again and again, for he was growing light-headed; "no wonder, no wonder! My shin-bones will be very useful to polish Quick's tall riding boots. Oh! curse the lions. Why did you help me to salt, you old ass; why did you help me to salt? It's pickling me behind."

Then he became quite incoherent, and only groaned from time to time.

Perhaps, however, this suffering did us a service, since otherwise exhaustion, thirst, and dust might have over-whelmed our senses, and caused us to fall into a sleep from which we never should have awakened. Yet at the time we were not grateful to it, for at last the agony became almost unbearable. Indeed, Orme told me afterwards that the last thing he could remember was a quaint fancy that he had made a colossal fortune by selling the secret of a new torture to the Chinese — that of hot sand driven on to the victim by a continuous blast of air.

After a while we lost count of time, nor was it until later that we learned that the storm endured for full twenty hours, during the latter part of which, notwith-standing our manifold sufferings, we must have become more or less insensible. At any rate, at one moment I remembered the awful roar and the stinging of the sand whips, followed by a kind of vision of the face of my son — that beloved, long-lost son whom I had sought for so many years, and for whose sake I endured all these things. Then, without any interval, as it were, I felt my limbs being scorched as though by hot irons or through a burning-glass, and with a fearful effort staggered up to find that the storm had passed, and that the furious sun was blistering my excoriated skin. Rubbing the caked dirt from my eyes, I looked down to see two mounds like those of graves, out of which projected legs that had been white. Just then one pair of legs, the longer pair, stirred, the sand heaved up convulsively, and, uttering wandering words in a choky voice, there arose the figure of Oliver Orme.

For a moment we stood and stared at each other, and strange spectacles we were.

"Is he dead?" muttered Orme, pointing to the still buried Higgs.

"Fear so," I answered, "but we'll look;" and painfully we began to disinter him.

When we came to it beneath the lion-skin, the Professor's face was black and hideous to see, but, to our relief, we perceived that he was not dead, for he moved his hand and moaned. Orme looked at me.

"Water would save him," I said.

Then came the anxious moment. One of our water-bottles was emptied before the storm began, but the other, a large, patent flask covered with felt, and having a screw vulcanite top, should still contain a good quantity, perhaps three quarts — that is, if the fluid had not evaporated in the dreadful heat. If this had happened, it meant that Higgs would die, and unless help came, that soon we should follow him. Orme unscrewed the flask, for my hands refused that office, and used his teeth to draw the cork, which, providentially enough, the thoughtful Quick had set in the neck beneath the screw. Some of the water, which, although it was quite hot, had *not* evaporated, thank God, flew against his parched lips, and I saw him bite them till the blood came in the fierceness of the temptation to assuage his raging thirst. But he resisted it like the man he is, and, without drinking a drop, handed me the bottle, saying simply:

"You are the oldest; take care of this, Adams."

Now it was my turn to be tempted, but I, too, overcame, and, sitting down, laid Higgs's head upon my knee; then, drop by drop, let a little of the water trickle between his swollen lips.

The effect was magical, for in less than a minute the Professor sat up, grasped at the flask with both hands, and strove to tear it away.

"You cruel brute! You cruel, selfish brute!" he moaned as I wrenched it from him.

"Look here, Higgs," I answered thickly; "Orme and I want water badly enough, and we have had none. But you might take it all if it would save you, only it would n't. We are lost in the desert, and must be sparing. If you drank everything now, in a few hours you would be thirsty again and die."

He thought a while, then looked up and said:

"Beg pardon — I understand. I 'm the selfish brute. But there 's a good lot of water there; let 's each have a drink; we can't move unless we do."

So we drank, measuring out the water in a little india-rubber cup which we had with us. It held about as much as a port-wine glass, and each of us drank, or rather slowly sipped, three cupfuls; we who felt as though we could have swallowed a gallon apiece, and asked for more. Small as was the allowance, it worked wonders in us; we were men again.

We stood up and looked about us, but the great storm had changed everything. Where there had been sand-hills a hundred feet high, now were plains and valleys; where there had been valleys appeared sand-hills. Only the high ridge upon which we had lain was as before, because it stood above the others and had a core of rock. We tried to discover the direction of the oasis by the position of the sun, only to be baffled, since our two watches had run down, and we did not know the time of day or where the sun ought to be in the heavens. Also, in that howling wilderness there was nothing to show us the points of the compass.

Higgs, whose obstinacy remained unimpaired, what-ever may have happened to the rest of his vital forces, had one view of the matter, and Orme another diametri-cally opposed to it. They even argued as to whether the oasis lay to our right or to our left, for their poor heads were so confused that they were scarcely capable of accurate thought or observation. Meanwhile I sat down upon the sand and considered. Through the haze I could see the points of what I thought must be the hills whence the Zeus declared that the lions came, although, of course, for aught I knew, they might be other hills.

"Listen," I said; "if lions live upon those hills, there must be water there. Let us try to reach them; perhaps we shall see the oasis as we go."

Then began our dreadful march. The lion-skin that had saved our lives, and was now baked hard as a board, we left behind, but the rifles we took. All day long we dragged ourselves up and down steep sand-slopes, paus-ing now and again to drink a sip of water, and hoping always that from the top of the next slope we should see a rescue party headed by Quick, or perhaps the oasis itself. Indeed, once we did see it, green and shining, not more than three miles away, but when we got to the head of the hill beyond which it should lie we found that the vision was only a mirage, and our hearts nearly broke with disappointment. Oh! to men dying of thirst, that mirage was indeed a cruel mockery.

At length night approached, and the mountains were yet a long way off. We could march no more, and sank down exhausted, lying on our faces, because our backs were so cut by the driving sand and blistered by the sun that we could not sit. By now almost all our water was gone. Suddenly Higgs nudged us and pointed upward. Following the line of his hand, we saw, not thirty yards away and showing clear against the sky, a file of antelopes trekking along the sand ridge, doubtless on a night journey from one pasturage to another.

"You fellows shoot," he muttered; "I might miss and frighten them away," for in his distress poor Higgs was growing modest.

Slowly Orme and I drew ourselves to our knees, cocking our rifles. By this time all the buck save one had passed; there were but six of them, and this one marched along about twenty yards behind the others. Orme pulled the trigger, but his rifle would not go off because, as he discovered afterwards, some sand had worked into the mechanism of the lock.

Meanwhile I had also covered the buck, but the sunset dazzled my weakened eyes, and my arms were feeble; also my terrible anxiety for success, since I knew that on this shot hung our lives, unnerved me. But it must be now or never; in three more paces the beast would be down the dip.

I fired, and knowing that I had missed, turned sick and faint. The antelope bounded forward a few yards right to the edge of the dip; then, never having heard such a sound before, and being overcome by some fatal curiosity, stopped and turned around, staring in the direction whence it had come.

Despairingly I fired again, almost without taking aim, and this time the bullet went in beneath the throat, and, raking the animal, dropped it dead as a stone. We scrambled to it, and presently were engaged in an awful meal of which we never afterwards liked to think. Happily for us that antelope must have drunk water not long before.

Our hunger and thirst assuaged after this horrible fashion, we slept awhile by the carcase, then arose extraordinarily refreshed, and, having cut off some hunks of meat to carry with us, started on again. By the position of the stars, we now knew that the oasis must lie somewhere to the east of us; but as between us and it there appeared to be nothing but these eternal sand-hills stretching away for many miles, and as in front of us toward the range the character of the desert seemed to be changing, we thought it safer, if the word safety can be used in such a connection, to continue to head for that range. All the remainder of this night we marched, and, as we had no fuel wherewith to cook it, at dawn ate some of the raw meat, which we washed down with the last drops of our water.

Now we were out of the sand-hills, and had entered on a great pebbly plain that lay between us and the foot of the mountains. These looked quite close, but in fact were still far off. Feebly and ever more feebly we staggered on, meeting no one and finding no water, though here and there we came across little bushes, of which we chewed the stringy and aromatic leaves, that contained some moisture, but drew up our mouths and throats like alum.

Higgs, who was the softest of us, gave out the first, though to the last he struggled forward with surprising pluck, even after he had been obliged to throw away his rifle, because he could no longer carry it, though this we did not notice at the time. When he could not support himself upon his feet, Orme took him by one arm, and I by the other, and helped him on, much as I have seen two elephants do by a wounded companion of the herd.

Half an hour or so later my strength failed me also. Although advanced in years, I am tough and accustomed to the desert and hardships; who would not be who had been a slave to the Khalifa? But now I could do no more, and, halting, begged the others to go on and leave me. Orme's only answer was to proffer me his left arm. I took it, for life is sweet to us all, especially when one has something to live for — a desire to fulfil as I had, though, to tell the truth, even at the time I felt ashamed of myself.

Thus, then, we proceeded awhile, resembling a sober man attempting to lead two drunken friends out of reach of that stern policeman, Death. Orme's strength must be wonderful; or was it his great spirit and his tender pity for our helplessness which enabled him to endure beneath this double burden.

Suddenly he fell down as though he had been shot, and lay there senseless. The Professor, however, retained some portion of his mind, although it wandered. He became light-headed, and rambled on about our madness in having undertaken such a journey, "just to pot a couple of beastly lions," and although I did not answer them, I agreed heartily with his remarks. Then he seemed to imagine that I was a clergyman, and, kneeling on the sand, he made a lengthy confession of his sins which, so far as I gathered, though I did not pay much attention to them, for I was thinking of my own, appeared chiefly to consist of the unlawful acquisition of certain objects of antiquity, or of having overmatched others in the purchase of such objects.

To pacify him, for I feared lest he should go raving mad, I pronounced some ridiculous absolution, whereon poor Higgs rolled over and lay still by Orme. Yes; he, the friend whom I had always loved, for his very failings were endearing, was dead or at the point of death, like the gallant young man at his side, and I myself was dying. Tremors shook my limbs; horrible waves of blackness seemed to well up from my vitals, through my breast to my brain, and thence to evaporate in queer, jagged lines and patches, which I realized, but could not actually see. Gay memories of my far-off childhood arose in me, particularly those of a Christmas party where I had met a little girl dressed like an elf, a little girl with blue eyes whom I had loved dearly for quite a fortnight, to be beaten down, stamped out, swallowed by that vision of the imminent shadow which awaits all mankind, the black womb of a re-birth, if re-birth there be.

What could I do? I thought of lighting a fire; at any rate it would serve to scare the lions and other wild beasts which else might prey upon us before we were quite dead. It would be dreadful to lie helpless but sentient, and feel their rending fangs. But I had no strength to collect the material. To do so at best must have meant a long walk, for even here it was not plentiful. I had a few cartridges left — three, to be accurate — in my repeating rifle; the rest I had thrown away to be rid of their weight. I determined to fire them, since, in my state, I thought that they could no longer serve either to win food or for the purposes of defence, although, as it happened, in this I was wrong. It was possible that, even in that endless desert, someone might hear the shots, and if not — well, good night.

So I sat up and fired the first cartridge, wondering in a childish fashion where the bullet would fall. Then I went to sleep for a while. The howling of a hyena woke me up, and, on glancing around, I saw the beast's flaming eyes quite close to me. I aimed and shot at it, and heard a yell of pain. That hyena, I reflected, would want no more food at present.

The silence of the desert overwhelmed me; it was so terrible that I almost wished the hyena back for company. Holding the rifle right above my head, I fired the third cartridge. Then I took the hand of Higgs in my own, for, after all, it was a link — the last link with humanity and the world — and lay down in the company of death that seemed to fall upon me in black and smothering veils.

I woke up and became aware that someone was pouring water down my throat. Heaven! I thought to myself, for at that time heaven and water were synonymous in my mind. I drank a good deal of it, not all I wanted by any means, but as much as the pourer would allow, then raised myself upon my hands and looked. The starlight was extraordinarily clear in that pure desert atmosphere, and by it I saw the face of Sergeant Quick bending over me. Also I saw Orme sitting up, staring about him stupidly, while a great yellow dog, with a head like a mastiff, licked his hand. I knew the dog at once; it was that which Orme had bought from some wandering natives, and named Pharaoh because he ruled over all other dogs. Moreover, I knew the two camels that stood near by. So I was still on earth — unless, indeed, we had all moved on a step.

"How did you find us, Sergeant?" I asked feebly.

"Did n't find you, Doctor," answered Quick; "dog Pharaoh found you. In a business like this a dog is more useful than man, for he can smell what one can't see. Now, if you feel better, Doctor, please look at Mr. Higgs, for I fear he 's gone."

I looked, and, although I did not say so, was of the same opinion. His jaw had fallen, and he lay limp and senseless; his eyes I could not see, because of the black spectacles.

"Water," I said, and Quick poured some into his mouth, where it vanished.

Still he did not stir, so I opened his garments and felt his heart. At first I could detect nothing; then there was the slightest possible flutter.

"There 's hope," I said in answer to their questioning looks. "You don't happen to have any brandy, do you?" I added.

"Never travelled without it yet, Doctor," replied Quick indignantly, producing a metal flask.

"Give him some," I said, and the Sergeant obeyed with liberality and almost instantaneous effect, for Higgs sat up gasping and coughing.

"Brandy; filthy stuff; teetotaller! Cursed trick! Never forgive you. Water, water," he spluttered in a thick, low voice.

We gave it to him, and he drank copiously, until we would let him have no more, indeed. Then, by degrees, his senses came back to him. He thrust up his black spectacles which he had worn all this while, and stared at the Sergeant with his sharp eyes.

"I understand," he said. "So we are not dead, after all, which, perhaps is a pity after getting through the beastly preliminaries. What has happened?"

"Don't quite know," answered Orme; "ask Quick."

But the Sergeant was already engaged in lighting a

little fire and setting a camp-kettle to boil, into which he poured a tin of beef extract that he had brought with other eatables from our stores on the chance that he might find us. In fifteen minutes we were drinking soup, for I forbade anything more solid as yet, and, oh! what a blessed meal was that. When it was finished, Quick fetched some blankets from the camels, which he threw over us.

"Lie down and sleep, gentlemen," he said; "Pharaoh and I will watch."

The last thing that I remember was seeing the sergeant, in his own fashion an extremely religious man, and not ashamed of it, kneeling upon the sand and apparently saying his prayers. As he explained afterwards, of course, as a fatalist, he knew well that whatever must happen would happen, but still he considered it right and proper to return thanks to the Power which had arranged that on this occasion the happenings should be good, and not ill, a sentiment with which every one of us agreed. Opposite to him, with one of his faithful eyes fixed on Orme, sat Pharaoh in grave contemplation. Doubtless, being an Eastern dog, he understood the meaning of public prayer; or perhaps he thought that he should receive some share of gratitude and thanks.

When we awoke the sun was already high, and to show us that we had dreamed no dream, there was Quick frying tinned bacon over the fire, while Pharaoh still sat and watched him — or the bacon.

"Look," said Orme to me, pointing to the mountains, "they are still miles away. It was madness to think that we could reach them."

I nodded, then turned to stare at Higgs, who was just waking up, for, indeed, he was a sight to see. His fiery red hair was full of sand, his nether garments were gone, apparently at some stage in our march he had dispensed with the remains of them because they chafed his sore limbs, and his fair skin, not excluding that of his face, was a mass of blisters, raised by the sun. In fact he was so disfigured that his worst enemy would not have known him. He yawned, stretched himself, always a good sign in man or beast, and asked for a bath.

"I am afraid you will have to wash yourself in sand here, sir, like them filthy Arabians," said Quick, saluting. "No water to spare for baths in this dry country. But I 've got a tube of hazeline, also a hair-brush and a looking-glass," he added, producing these articles.

"Quite so, Sergeant," said Higgs as he took them; "it 's sacrilege to think of using water to wash. I intend never to waste it in that way again." Then he looked at himself in the glass, and let it fall upon the sand, ejaculating, "Oh! good Lord, is that me?"

"Please be careful, sir," said the Sergeant sternly; "you told me the other day that it 's unlucky to break a looking-glass; also I have no other."

"Take it away," said the Professor; "I don't want it any more, and, Doctor, come and oil my face, there 's a good fellow; yes, and the rest of me also, if there is enough hazeline."

So we treated each other with the ointment, which at first made us smart fearfully, and then, very gingerly sat down to breakfast.

"Now, Sergeant," said Orme, as he finished his fifth pannikin of tea, "tell us your story."

"There is n't much of a story, Captain. Those Zeu fellows came back without you, and, not knowing the lingo, I could make nothing of their tale. Well, I soon made Shadrach and Co. understand that, death-wind or no death-wind — that 's what they call it —they must come with me to look for you, and at last we started.

although they said that I was mad, as you were dead already. Indeed, it was n't until I asked that fellow Shadrach if he wanted to be dead too" — and the Sergeant tapped his revolver grimly — "that he would let anyone go.

"As it proved, he was right, for we could n't find you, and after awhile the camels refused to face the storm any longer; also one of the Abati drivers was lost, and has n't been heard of since. It was all the rest of us could do to get back to the oasis alive, nor would Shadrach go out again even after the storm had blown itself away. It was no use arguing with the pig, so, as I did not want his blood upon my hands, I took two camels and started with the dog Pharaoh for company.

"Now this was my thought, although I could not explain it to the Abati crowd, that if you lived at all, you would almost certainly head for the hills, as I knew you had no compass, and you would not be able to see anything else. So I rode along the plain which stretches between the desert and the mountains, keeping on the edge of the sand-hills. I rode all day, but when night came I halted, since I could see no more. There I sat in that great place, thinking, and after an hour or two I observed Pharaoh prick his ears and look toward the west. So I also stared toward the west, and presently I thought that I saw one faint streak of light which seemed to go upward, and therefore could n't come from a falling star, but might have come from a rifle fired toward the sky.

"I listened, but no sound reached me, only presently, some seconds afterward, the dog again pricked his ears as though *he* heard something. That settled me, and I mounted and rode forward through the night toward the place where I thought I had seen the flash. For two hours I rode, firing my revolver from time to time; then as no answer came, gave it up as a bad job, and stopped. But Pharaoh there would n't stop. He began to whine and sniff and run forward, and at last bolted into the darkness, out of which presently I heard him barking some hundreds of yards away, to call me, I suppose. So I followed and found you three gentlemen, dead, as I thought at first. That's all the story, Captain."

"One with a good end, anyway, Sergeant. We owe our lives to you."

"Beg your pardon, Captain," answered Quick modestly; "not to me at all, but to Providence first that arranged everything, before we were born perhaps, and next to Pharaoh. He's a wise dog, Pharaoh, though fierce with some, and you did a good deal when you bought him for a bottle of whisky and a sixpenny pocket-knife."

It was dawn on the following morning before we sighted the oasis, whither we could travel but slowly, since, owing to the lack of camels, two of us must walk. Of these two, as may be guessed, the Sergeant was always one and his master the other, for of all the men I ever knew I think that in such matters Orme is the most unselfish. Nothing would induce him to mount one of the camels, even for half an hour, so that when I walked, the brute went riderless. On the other hand, once he was on, notwithstanding the agonies he suffered from his soreness, nothing would induce Higgs to get off.

"Here I am and here I stop," he said several times, in English, French, and sundry Oriental languages. "I've tramped it enough to last me the rest of my life."

Both of us were dozing upon our saddles when suddenly I heard the Sergeant calling to the camels to halt, and asked what was the matter.

"Looks like Arabians, Doctor," he said, pointing to a cloud of dust advancing toward us.

"Well, if so," I answered, "our best chance is to show no fear and go on. I don't think they will harm us."

So, having made ready such weapons as we had, we advanced, Orme and the Sergeant walking between the two camels, till presently we encountered the other caravan, and, to our astonishment, saw none other than Shadrach riding at the head of it, mounted on my dromedary, which his own mistress, the Lady of the Abati, had given to me. We came face to face, and halted, staring at each other.

"By the beard of Aaron! is it you, lords?" he asked. "We thought that you were dead."

"By the hair of Moses! so I gather," I answered angrily, "seeing that you are going off with all our belongings," and I pointed to the camels laden with goods.

Then followed explanations and voluble apologies, which Higgs for one accepted with a very bad grace. Indeed, as he can talk Arabic and its dialects perfectly, he made use of that tongue to pour upon the heads of Shadrach and his companions a stream of Eastern invective that must have astonished them, ably seconded as it was by Sergeant Quick in English.

Orme listened for some time, then said:

"That 'll do, old fellow; if you go on, you will get up a row, and, Sergeant, be good enough to hold your tongue. We have met them, so there is no harm done. Now, friend Shadrach, turn back with us to the oasis. We are going to rest there for some days."

Shadrach looked sulky, and said something about our turning and going on with *them*, whereon I produced the ancient ring, Sheba's ring, which I had brought as a token from Mur. This I held before his eyes, saying:

"Disobey, and there will be an account to settle when

you come into the presence of her who sent you forth, for even if we four should die" — and I looked at him meaningly — "think not that you will be able to hide this matter; there are too many witnesses."

Then, without more words, he saluted the sacred ring, and we all went back to Zeu.

CHAPTER V

PHARAOH MAKES TROUBLE

ANOTHER six weeks or so had gone by, and at length the character of the country began to change. At last we were passing out of the endless desert over which we had travelled for so many hundreds of miles; at least a thousand, according to our observations and reckonings, which I checked by those that I had taken upon my eastward journey. Our march, after the great adventure at the oasis, was singularly devoid of startling events. Indeed, it had been awful in its monotony, and yet, oddly enough, not without a certain charm — at any rate for Higgs and Orme, to whom the experience was new.

Day by day to travel on across an endless sea of sand so remote, so unvisited that for whole weeks no man, not even a wandering Bedouin of the desert, crossed our path. Day by day to see the great red sun rise out of the eastern sands, and, its journey finished, sink into the western sands. Night by night to watch the moon, the same moon on which were fixed the million eyes of cities, turning those sands to a silver sea, or, in that pure air, to observe the constellations by which we steered our path making their majestic march through space. And yet to know that this vast region, now so utterly lonesome and desolate, had once been familiar to the feet of long-forgotten men who had trod the roads and dug the wells at which we drank.

Armies had marched across these deserts, also, and perished there. For once we came to a place where a recent fearful gale had almost denuded the underlying rock, and there found the skeletons of thousands upon thousands of soldiers, with those of their beasts of burden, and among them heads of arrows, sword-blades, fragments of armour and of painted wooden shields.

Here a whole host had died; perhaps Alexander sent it forth, or perhaps some far earlier monarch whose name has ceased to echo on the earth. At least they had died, for there we saw the memorial of that buried enterprise. There lay the kings, the captains, the soldiers, and the concubines, for I found the female bones heaped apart, some with the long hair still upon the skulls, showing where the poor, affrighted women had hived together in the last catastrophe of slaughter or of famine, thirst, and driven sand. Oh, if only those bones could speak, what a tale was theirs to tell!

There had been cities in this desert, too, where once were oases, now overwhelmed, except perhaps for a sand-choked spring. Twice we came upon the foundations of such places, old walls of clay or stone, stark skeletons of ancient homes that the shifting sands had disinterred, which once had been the theatre of human hopes and fears, where once men had been born, loved, and died, where once maidens had been fair, and good and evil wrestled, and little children played. Some Job might have dwelt here and written his immortal plaint, or some king of Sodom, and suffered the uttermost calamity. The world is very old; all we Westerns learned from the contemplation of these wrecks of men and of their works was just that the world is very old.

One evening against the clear sky there appeared the dim outline of towering cliffs, shaped like a horseshoe.

They were the Mountains of Mur many miles away, but still the Mountains of Mur, sighted at last. Next morning we began to descend through wooded land toward a wide river that is, I believe, a tributary of the Nile, though upon this point I have no certain information. Three days later we reached the banks of this river, following some old road, and faring sumptuously all the way, since here there was much game and grass in plenty for the camels that, after their long abstinence, ate until we thought that they would burst. Evidently we had not arrived an hour too soon, for now the Mountains of Mur were hid by clouds, and we could see that it was raining upon the plains which lay between us and them. The wet season was setting in and, had we been a single week later, it might have been impossible for us to cross the river, which would then have been in flood. As it was, we passed it without difficulty by the ancient ford, the water never rising above the knees of our camels.

Upon its further bank we took counsel, for now we had entered the territory of the Fung, and were face to face with the real dangers of our journey. Fifty miles or so away rose the fortress of Mur, but, as I explained to my companions, the question was how to pass those fifty miles in safety. Shadrach was called to our conference, and at my request set out the facts.

Yonder, he said, rose the impregnable mountain home of the Abati, but all the vast plain included in the loop of the river which he called Ebur, was the home of the savage Fung race, whose warriors could be counted by the ten thousand, and whose principal city, Harmac, was built opposite to the stone effigy of their idol, that was also called Harmac ——

"Harmac — that is Harmachis, god of dawn. Your Fung had something to do with the old Egyptians, or both of them came from a common stock," interrupted Higgs triumphantly.

"I daresay, old fellow," answered Orme; "I think you told us that before in London; but we will go into the archæology afterwards if we survive to do so. Let Shadrach get on with his tale."

This city, which had quite fifty thousand inhabitants, continued Shadrach, commanded the mouth of the pass or cleft by which we must approach Mur, having probably been first built there for that very purpose.

Orme asked if there was no other way into the stronghold, which, he understood, the embassy had left by being let down a precipice. Shadrach answered that this was true, but that although the camels and their loads had been let down that precipitous place, owing to the formation of its overhanging rocks, it would be perfectly impossible to haul them up with any tackle that the Abati possessed.

He asked again if there was not a way round, if that circle of mountains had no back door. Shadrach replied that there was such a back door facing to the north some eight days' journey away. Only at this season of the year it could not be reached, since beyond the Mountains of Mur in that direction was a great lake, out of which flowed the river Ebur in two arms that enclosed the whole plain of Fung. By now this lake would be full, swollen with rains that fell on the hills of Northern Africa, and the space between it and the Mur range nothing but an impassable swamp.

Being still unsatisfied, Orme inquired whether, if we abandoned the camels, we could not then climb the precipice down which the embassy had descended. To this the answer, which I corroborated, was that if our approach were known and help given to us from above, it might be possible, provided that we threw away the loads.

"Seeing what these loads are, and the purpose for which we have brought them so far, that is out of the question," said Orme. "Therefore tell us at once, Shadrach, how we are to win through the Fung to Mur."

"In one way only, O son of Orme, should it be the will of God that we do so at all; by keeping ourselves hidden during the daytime and marching at night. According to their custom at this season, to-morrow, after sunset, the Fung hold their great spring feast in the city of Harmac, and at dawn go up to make sacrifice to their idol. But after sunset they eat and drink and are merry, and then it is their habit to withdraw their guards, that they may take part in the festival. For this reason I have timed our march that we should arrive on the night of this feast, which I know by the age of the moon, when, in the darkness, with God's help, perchance we may slip past Harmac, and at the first light find ourselves in the mouth of the road that runs up to Mur. Moreover, I will give warning to my people, the Abati, that we are coming, so that they may be at hand to help us if there is need."

"How?" asked Orme.

"By firing the reeds" — and he pointed to the dense masses of dead vegetation about — "as I arranged that I would do before we left Mur many months ago. The Fung, if they see it, will think only that it is the work of some wandering fisherman."

Orme shrugged his shoulders, saying:

"Well, friend Shadrach, you know the place and these people, and I do not, so we must do what you tell us. But I say at once that if, as I understand, yonder Fung will kill us if they can, to me your plan seems very dangerous."

"It is dangerous," he answered, adding with a sneer, "but I thought that you men of England were not cowards."

"Cowards! you son of a dog," broke in Higgs in his high voice. "How dare you talk to us like that? You see this man here" — and he pointed to Sergeant Quick, who, tall and upright, stood watching this scene grimly, and understanding most of what passed — "well, he is the lowest among us — a servant only (here the Sergeant saluted), but I tell you that there is more courage in his little finger than in your whole body, or in that of all the Abati people, so far as I can make out."

Here the Sergeant saluted again, murmuring beneath his breath, "I hope so, sir. Being a Christian, I hope so, but till it comes to the sticking-point, one never can be sure."

"You speak big words, O Higgs," answered Shadrach insolently, for, as I think I have said, he hated the Professor, who smelt the rogue in him and scourged him continually with his sharp tongue, "but if the Fung get hold of you, then we shall learn the truth."

"Shall I punch his head, sir?" queried Quick in a meditative voice.

"Be quiet, please," interrupted Orme. "We have troubles enough before us, without making more. It will be time to settle our quarrels when we have got through the Fung."

Then he turned to Shadrach and said:

"Friend, this is no hour for angry words. You are the guide of this party; lead us as you will, remembering only that if it comes to war, I, by the wish of my companions, am Captain. Also, there is another thing which you should not forget — namely, that in the end you must make answer to your own ruler, she who, I understand from the doctor here, is called Walda Nagasta, the Child of Kings. Now, no more words; we march as you wish and where you wish. On your head be it!"

The Abati heard and bowed sullenly. Then, with a look of hate at Higgs, he turned and went about his business.

"Much better have let me punch his head," soliloquized Quick. "It would have done him a world of good, and perhaps saved many troubles, for, to tell the truth, I don't trust that quarter-bred Hebrew."

Then he departed to see to the camels and the guns while the rest of us went to our tents to get such sleep as the mosquitoes would allow. In my own case it was not much, since the fear of evil to come weighed upon me. Although I knew the enormous difficulty of entering the mountain stronghold of Mur by any other way, such as that by which I had quitted it, burdened as we were with our long train of camels laden with rifles, ammunition, and explosives, I dreaded the results of an attempt to pass through the Fung savages.

Moreover, it occurred to me that Shadrach had insisted upon this route from a kind of jealous obstinacy, and to be in opposition to us Englishmen, whom he hated in his heart, or perhaps for some dark and secret reason. Still, the fact remained that we were in his power, since owing to the circumstances in which I had entered and left the place, it was impossible for me to act as guide to the party. If I attempted to do so, no doubt he and the Abati with him would desert, leaving the camels and their loads upon our hands. Why should they not, seeing that they would be quite safe in concluding that we should never have an opportunity of laying our side of the case before their ruler?

Just as the sun was setting, Quick came to call me, saying that the camels were being loaded up.

"I don't much like the look of things, Doctor," he said as he helped me to pack my few belongings, "for the fact is I can't trust that Shadrach man. His pals call him 'Cat,' a good name for him, I think. Also, he is showing his claws just now, the truth being that he hates the lot of us, and would like to get back into Purr or Mur, or whatever the name of the place is, having lost us on the road. You should have seen the way he looked at the Professor just now. Oh! I wish the Captain had let me punch his head. I'm sure it would have cleared the air a lot."

As it chanced, Shadrach was destined to get his head "punched" after all, but by another hand. It happened thus. The reeds were fired, as Shadrach declared it was necessary to do, in order that the Abati watchmen on the distant mountains might see and report the signal, although in the light of subsequent events I am by no means certain that this warning was not meant for other eyes as well. Then, as arranged, we started out, leaving them burning in a great sheet of flame behind us, and all that night marched by the shine of the stars along some broken-down and undoubtedly ancient road.

At the first sign of dawn we left this road and camped amid the overgrown ruins of a deserted town that had been built almost beneath the precipitous cliffs of Mur, fortunately without having met anyone or being challenged. I took the first watch, whilst the others turned in to sleep after we had all breakfasted off cold meats, for we dared not light a fire. As the sun grew high, dispelling the mists, I saw that we were entering upon a thickly populated country which was no stranger to civilization of a sort. Below us, not more than fifteen or sixteen miles away, and clearly visible through my field-glasses, lay the great town of Harmac, which, during my previous visit to this land, I had never seen, as I passed it in the night.

It was a city of the West Central African type, with open market-places and wide streets, containing thousands of white, flat-roofed houses, the most important of which were surrounded by gardens. Round it ran a high and thick wall, built, apparently, of sunburnt brick, and in front of the gateways, of which I could see two, stood square towers whence these might be protected. All about this city the flat and fertile land was under cultivation, for the season being that of early spring, already the maize and other crops showed green upon the ground.

Beyond this belt of plough-lands, with the aid of the field-glasses, I could make out great herds of grazing cattle and horses, mixed with wild game, a fact that assured me of the truth of what I had heard during my brief visit to Mur, that the Fung had few or no firearms, since otherwise the buck and quagga would have kept at a distance. Far off, too, and even on the horizon, I saw what appeared to be other towns and villages. Evidently this was a very numerous people, and one which could not justly be described as savage. No wonder that the little Abati tribe feared them so intensely, notwithstanding the mighty precipices by which they were protected from their hate.

About eleven o'clock Orme came on watch, and I turned in, having nothing to report. Soon I was fast asleep, notwithstanding the anxieties that, had I been less weary, might well have kept me wakeful. For these were many. On the coming night we must slip through the Fung, and before midday to-morrow we should either have entered Mur, or failed to have entered Mur, which meant — death, or, what was worse, captivity among barbarians, and subsequent execution, preceded probably by torture of one sort or another.

Of course, however, we might come thither without accident, travelling with good guides on a dark night, for, after all, the place was big, and the road lonely and little used, so that unless we met a watch, which, we were told,

would not be there, our little caravan had a good chance
to pass unobserved. Shadrach seemed to think that
we should do so, but the worst of it was that, like Quick,
I did not trust Shadrach. Even Maqueda, the Lady
of the Abati, she whom they called Child of Kings, had
her doubts about him, or so it had seemed to me.

At any rate, she had told me before I left Mur that she
chose him for this mission because he was bold and
cunning, one of the very few of her people also who, in
his youth, had crossed the desert and, therefore, knew the
road. "Yet, Physician," she added meaningly, "watch
him, for is he not named 'Cat'? Yes, watch him, for
did I not hold his wife and children hostages, and were
I not sure that he desires to win the great reward in land
which I have promised to him, I would not trust you to
this man's keeping."

Well, after many experiences in his company, my
opinion coincided with Maqueda's, and so did that of
Quick, no mean judge of men.

"Look at him, Doctor," he said when he came to tell
me that I could turn in, for whether it were his watch or
not, the Sergeant never seemed to be off duty. "Look
at him," and he pointed to Shadrach, who was seated
under the shade of a tree, talking earnestly in whispers
to two of his subordinates with a very curious and unpleas-
ing smile upon his face. "If God Almighty ever made
a scamp, he's squatting yonder. My belief is that he
wanted to be rid of us all at Zeu, so that he might steal
our goods, and I hope he won't play the same trick again
to-night. Even the dog can't abide him."

Before I could answer, I had proof of this last statement,
for the great yellow hound, Pharaoh, that had found us
in the desert, hearing our voices, emerged from some
corner where it was hidden, and advanced toward us,
wagging its tail. As it passed Shadrach, it stopped

and growled, the hair rising on its back, whereon he hurled a stone at it and hit its leg. Next instant Pharaoh, a beast of enormous power, was on the top of him, and really, I thought, about to tear out his throat.

Well, we got him off before any harm was done, but Shadrach's face, lined with its livid scars, was a thing to remember. Between rage and fear, it looked like that of a devil.

To return. After this business I went to sleep, wondering if it were my last rest upon the earth, and whether, having endured so much for his sake, it would or would not be my fortune to see the face of my son again, if, indeed, he still lived, yonder not a score of miles away — or anywhere.

Toward evening I was awakened by a fearful hubbub, in which I distinguished the shrill voice of Higgs ejaculating language which I will not repeat, the baying of Pharaoh, and the smothered groans and curses of an Abati. Running from the little tent, I saw a curious sight, that of the Professor with Shadrach's head under his left arm, in chancery, as we used to call it at school, while with his right he punched the said Shadrach's nose and countenance generally with all his strength, which, I may add, is considerable. Close by, holding Pharaoh by the collar which we had manufactured for him out of the skin of a camel that died, stood Sergeant Quick, a look of grim amusement on his wooden face, while around, gesticulating after their Eastern fashion, and uttering guttural sounds of wrath, were several of the Abati drivers. Orme was absent, being, in fact, asleep at the time.

"What are you doing, Higgs?" I shouted.

"Can't — you — see," he spluttered, accompanying each word with a blow on the unfortunate Shadrach's prominent nose. "I am punching this fellow's beastly head. Ah! you'd bite, would you? Then take that and that and — that. Lord, how hard his teeth are Well, I think he has had enough," and suddenly h released the Abati, who, a gory and most unpleasan spectacle, fell to the ground and lay there panting. Hi companions, seeing their chief's melancholy plight, advanced upon the Professor in a threatening fashion; indeed, one of them drew a knife.

"Put up that thing, sonny," said the Sergeant, "or by heaven, I'll loose the dog upon you. Got your revolver handy, Doctor?"

Evidently, if the man did not understand Quick's words, their purport was clear to him, for he sheathed his knife and fell back with the others. Shadrach, too, rose from the ground and went with them. At a distance of a few yards, however, he turned, and, glaring at Higgs out of his swollen eyes, said:

"Be sure, accursed Gentile, that I will remember and repay."

At this moment, too, Orme arrived upon the scene, yawning.

"What the deuce is the matter?" he asked.

"I'd give five bob for a pint of iced stone ginger," replied Higgs inconsequently. Then he drank off a pannikin of warmish, muddy-coloured water which Quick gave to him, and handed it back, saying:

"Thanks, Sergeant; that's better than nothing, and cold drink is always dangerous if you are hot. What's the matter? Oh! not much. Shadrach tried to poison Pharaoh; that's all. I was watching him out of the corner of my eye, and saw him go to the strychnine tin, roll a bit of meat in it which he had first wetted, and throw it to the poor beast. I got hold of it in time, and chucked it over that wall, where you will find it if you care to look. I asked Shadrach why he had done such a thing. He answered, 'To keep the dog quiet while we are passing through the Fung,' adding that anyhow it was a savage beast and best out of the way, as it had tried to bite him that morning. Then I lost my temper and went for the blackguard, and although I gave up boxing twenty years ago, very soon had the best of it, for, as you may have observed, no Oriental can fight with his fists. That's all. Give me another cup of water, Sergeant."

"I hope it may be," answered Orme, shrugging his shoulders. "To tell the truth, old fellow, it would have been wiser to defer blacking Shadrach's eyes till we were safe in Mur. But it's no use talking now, and I daresay I should have done the same myself if I had seen him try to poison Pharaoh," and he patted the head of the great dog, of which we were all exceedingly fond, although in reality it only cared for Orme, merely tolerating the rest of us.

"Doctor," he added, "perhaps you would try to patch up our guide's nose and soothe his feelings. You know him better than we do. Give him a rifle. No, don't do that, or he might shoot someone in the back — by accident done on purpose. Promise him a rifle when we get into Mur; I know he wants one badly, because I caught him trying to steal a carbine from the case. Promise him anything so long as you can square it up."

So I went, taking a bottle of arnica and some court plaster with me, to find Shadrach surrounded by sympathizers and weeping with rage over the insult, which, he said, had been offered to his ancient and distinguished race in his own unworthy person. I did my best for him physically and mentally, pointing out, as I dabbed the arnica on his sadly disfigured countenance, that he had brought the trouble on himself, seeing that he had really no business to poison Pharaoh because he had tried to bite him. He answered that his reason for wishing to

kill the dog was quite different, and repeated at great
length what he had told the Professor — namely, that
it might betray us while we were passing through the
Fung. Also he went on so venomously about revenge
that I thought it time to put a stop to the thing.

"See here, Shadrach," I said, "unless you unsay
those words and make peace at once, you shall be bound
and tried. Perhaps we shall have a better chance of
passing safely through the Fung if we leave you dead
behind us than if you accompany us as a living enemy."

On hearing this, he changed his note altogether, saying
that he saw he had been wrong. Moreover, so soon as
his injuries were dressed, he sought out Higgs, whose
hand he kissed with many apologies, vowing that he had
forgotten everything and that his heart toward him was
like that of a twin brother.

"Very good, friend," answered Higgs, who never
bore malice, "only don't try to poison Pharaoh again,
and, for my part, I 'll promise not to remember this
matter when we get to Mur."

"Quite a converted character, ain't he, Doctor?"
sarcastically remarked Quick, who had been watching
this edifying scene. "Nasty Eastern temper all gone; no
Hebrew talk of eye for eye or tooth for tooth, but kisses
the fist that smote him in the best Christian spirit. All
the same, I would n't trust the swine further than I
could kick him, especially in the dark, which," he added
meaningly, "is what it will be to-night."

I made no answer to the Sergeant, for although I
agreed with him, there was nothing to be done, and
talking about a bad business would only make it worse.

By now the afternoon drew toward night — a very
stormy night, to judge from the gathering clouds and
rising wind. We were to start a little after sundown,
that is, within an hour, and, having made ready my own

baggage and assisted Higgs with his, we went to look for Orme and Quick, whom we found very busy in one of the rooms of an unroofed house. To all appearance they were engaged, Quick in sorting pound tins of tobacco or baking powder, and Orme in testing an electric battery and carefully examining coils of insulated wire.

"What's your game?" asked the Professor.

"Better than yours, old boy, when Satan taught your idle hands to punch Shadrach's head. But perhaps you had better put that pipe out. These azo-imide compounds are said to burn rather more safely than coal. Still, one never knows; the climate or the journey may have changed their constitution."

Higgs retreated hurriedly, to a distance of fifty yards indeed, whence he returned, having knocked out his pipe and even left his matches on a stone.

"Don't waste time in asking questions," said Orme as the Professor approached with caution. "I'll explain. We are going on a queer journey to-night — four white men with about a dozen half-bred mongrel scamps of doubtful loyalty, so you see Quick and I thought it as well to have some of this stuff handy. Probably it will never be wanted, and if wanted we shall have no time to use it; still, who knows? There, that will do. Ten canisters; enough to blow up half the Fung if they will kindly sit on them. You take five, Quick, a battery and three hundred yards of wire, and I'll take five, a battery, and three hundred yards of wire. Your detonators are all fixed, are n't they? Well, so are mine," and without more words he proceeded to stow away his share of the apparatus in the poacher pockets of his coat and elsewhere, while Quick did likewise with what remained. Then the case that they had opened was fastened up again and removed to be laden on a camel.

CHAPTER VI

HOW WE ESCAPED FROM HARMAC

AS FINALLY arranged this was the order of our
march: First went an Abati guide who was said to
be conversant with every inch of the way. Then
came Orme and Sergeant Quick, conducting the camels
that were loaded with the explosives. I followed in order
to keep an eye upon these precious beasts and those in
charge of them. Next marched some more camels,
carrying our baggage, provisions, and sundries, and
finally in the rear were the Professor and Shadrach with
two Abati.

Shadrach, I should explain, had selected this situation
for the reason, as he said, that if he went first, after what
had passed, any mistake or untoward occurrence might
be set down to his malice, whereas, if he were behind, he
could not be thus slandered. On hearing this, Higgs,
who is a generous soul, insisted upon showing his confidence in the virtue of Shadrach by accompanying him
as a rearguard. So violently did he insist, and so flattered
did Shadrach seem to be by this mark of faith, that Orme,
who, I should say, if I have not already done so, was in
sole command of the party now that hostilities were in
the air, consented to the plan, if with evident reluctance.

As I know, his own view was that it would be best for
us four Englishmen to remain together, although, if
we did so, whatever position we chose, it would be impossible for us in that darkness to keep touch with the line

of camels and their loads, which were almost as important to us as our lives. At least, having made up our minds to deliver them in Mur, we thought that they were important, perhaps because it is the fashion of the Anglo-Saxon race to put even a self-created idea of duty before personal safety or convenience.

Rightly or wrongly, so things were settled, for in such troublous conditions one can only do what seems best at the moment. Criticism subsequent to the event is always easy, as many an unlucky commander has found out when the issue went awry, but in emergency one must decide on something.

The sun set, the darkness fell, and it began to rain and blow. We started quite unobserved, so far as we could tell, and, travelling downward from the overgrown, ruined town, gained the old road, and in complete silence, for the feet of camels make no noise, passed along it toward the lights of Harmac, which now and again, when the storm-clouds lifted, we saw glimmering in front of us and somewhat to our left.

In all my long wanderings I cannot remember a more exciting or a more disagreeable journey. The blackness, relieved only from time to time by distant lightnings, was that of the plagues of Egypt; the driving rain worked through the openings of our camel-hair cloaks and the waterproofs we wore underneath them, and wet us through. The cold, damp wind chilled us to the bone, enervated as we were with the heat of the desert. But these discomforts, and they were serious enough, we forgot in the tremendous issue of the enterprise. Should we win through to Mur? Or, as a crown to our many labours and sufferings, should we perish presently on the road? That was the question; as I can assure the reader, one that we found very urgent and interesting.

Three hours had gone by. Now we were opposite

to the lights of Harmac, also to other lights that shone up a valley in the mountain to our right. As yet everything was well; for this we knew by the words whispered up and down the line.

Then, of a sudden, in front of us a light flashed, although as yet it was a long way off. Next came another whispered message of "Halt!" So we halted, and presently one of the front guides crept back, informing us that a body of Fung cavalry had appeared upon the road ahead. We took counsel. Shadrach arrived from the rear, and said that if we waited awhile they might go away, as he thought that their presence must be accidental and connected with the great festival. He implored us to be quite silent. Accordingly, not knowing what else to do, we waited.

Now I think I have forgotten to say that the dog Pharaoh, to prevent accidents, occupied a big basket; this basket, in which he often rode when tired, being fixed upon one side of Orme's camel. Here he lay peaceably enough until, in an unlucky moment, Shadrach left me to go forward to talk to the Captain, whereon, smelling his enemy, Pharaoh burst out into furious baying. After that everything was confusion. Shadrach darted back toward the rear. The light ahead began to move quickly, advancing toward us. The front camels left the road, as I presume, following their leader according to the custom of these beasts when marching in line.

Presently, I know not how, Orme, Quick, and myself found ourselves together in the darkness; at the time we thought Higgs was with us also, but in this we were mistaken. We heard shoutings and strange voices speaking a language that we could not understand. By the sudden glare of a flash of lightning, for the thunderstorm was now travelling over us, we saw several things. One of these was the Professor's riding-dromedary, which could not be mistaken because of its pure white colour and queer method of holding its head to one side, passing within ten yards, between us and the road, having a man upon its back who evidently was not the Professor. Then it was that we discovered his absence and feared the worst.

"A Fung has got his camel," I said.

"No," answered Quick; "Shadrach has got it. I saw his ugly mug against the light."

Another vision was that of what appeared to be our baggage camels moving swiftly away from us, but off the road which was occupied by a body of horsemen in white robes. Orme issued a brief order to the effect that we were to follow the camels with which the Professor might be. We started to obey, but before we had covered twenty yards of the cornfield or whatever it was in which we were standing, heard voices ahead that were not those of Abati. Evidently the flash which showed the Fung to us had done them a like service, and they were now advancing to kill or capture us.

There was only one thing to be done — turn and fly — and this we did, heading whither we knew not, but managing to keep touch of each other.

About a quarter of an hour later, just as we were entering a grove of palms or other trees which hid everything in front of us, the lightning blazed again, though much more faintly, for by this time the storm had passed over the Mountains of Mur, leaving heavy rain behind it. By the flash I, who was riding last and, as it chanced, looking back over my shoulder, saw that the Fung horsemen were not fifty yards behind, and hunting for us everywhere, their line being extended over a long front. I was, however, sure that they had not yet caught sight of us in the dense shadow of the trees.

"Get on," I said to the others; "they will be here presently," and heard Quick add:

"Give your camel his head, Captain; he can see in the dark, and perhaps will take us back to the road."

Orme acted on this suggestion, which, as the blackness round us was pitchy, seemed a good one. At any rate it answered, for off we went at a fair pace, the three camels marching in line, first over soft ground and afterwards on a road. Presently I thought that the rain had stopped, since for a few seconds none fell on us, but concluded from the echo of the camels' feet and its recommencement that we had passed under some archway. On we went, and presently even through the gloom and rain I saw objects that looked like houses, though if so there were no lights in them, perhaps because the night drew toward morning. A dreadful idea struck me: we might be in Harmac! I passed it up for what it was worth.

"Very likely," whispered Orme back. "Perhaps these camels were bred here, and are looking for their stables. Well, there is only one thing to do — go on."

So we went on for a long while, only interfered with by the occasional attentions of some barking dog. Luckily of these Pharaoh, in his basket, took no heed, probably because it was his habit if another dog barked at him to pretend complete indifference until it came so near that he could spring and fight, or kill it. At length we appeared to pass under another archway, after which a hundred and fifty yards or so further on the camels came to a sudden stop. Quick dismounted, and presently I heard him say;

"Doors. Can feel the brasswork on them. Tower above, I think, and wall on either side. Seem to be in a trap. Best stop here till light comes. Only thing to do."

Accordingly, we stopped, and, having tied the camels

to each other to prevent their straying, took shelter from the rain under the tower or whatever it might be. To pass away the time and keep life in us, for we were almost frozen with the wet and cold, we ate some tinned food and biscuits that we carried in our saddle-bags, and drank a dram of brandy from Quick's flask. This warmed us a little, though I do not think that a bottleful would have raised our spirits. Higgs, whom we all loved, was gone — dead, probably, by that time; the Abati had lost or deserted us, and we three white men appeared to have wandered into a savage stronghold, where, as soon as we were seen, we should be trapped like birds in a net, and butchered at our captors' will. Certainly the position was not cheerful.

Overwhelmed with physical and mental misery, I began to doze; Orme grew silent, and the Sergeant, having remarked that there was no need to bother, since what must be must be, consoled himself by humming in a corner over and over again the verse of the hymn which begins:

> "There is a blessed home beyond this land of woe,
> Where trials never come nor tears of sorrow flow."

Fortunately for us, shortly before dawn the "tears of sorrow" as represented by the rain ceased to flow. The sky cleared, showing the stars; suddenly the vault of heaven was suffused with a wonderful and pearly light, although on the earth the mist remained so thick that we could see nothing Then above this sea of mist rose the great ball of the sun, but still we could see nothing that was more than a few yards away from us.

> "There is a blessed home beyond this land of woe,"

droned Quick beneath his breath for about the fiftieth time, since, apparently he knew no other hymn which he considered suitable to our circumstances, then ejaculated suddenly:

"Hullo! here's a stair. With your leave I'll go up it, Captain," and he did.

A minute later we heard his voice calling us softly:

"Come here, gentlemen," he said, "and see something worth looking at."

So we scrambled up the steps, and, as I rather expected, found ourselves upon the top of one of two towers set above an archway, which towers were part of a great protective work outside the southern gates of a city that could be none other than Harmac. Soaring above the mist rose the mighty cliffs of Mur that, almost exactly opposite to us, were pierced by a deep valley.

Into this valley the sunlight poured, revealing a wondrous and awe-inspiring object of which the base was surrounded by billowy vapours, a huge, couchant animal fashioned of black stone, with a head carved to the likeness of that of a lion, and crowned with the *uræus*, the asp-crested symbol of majesty in old Egypt. How big the creature might be it was impossible to say at that distance, for we were quite a mile away from it; but it was evident that no other monolithic monument that we had ever seen or heard of could approach its colossal dimensions.

Compared to this tremendous effigy indeed, the boasted Sphinx of Gizeh seemed but a toy. It was no less than a small mountain of rock shaped by the genius and patient labour of some departed race of men to the form of a lion-headed monster. Its majesty and awfulness set thus above the rolling mists in the red light of the morning, reflected on it from the towering precipices beyond, were literally indescribable; even in our miserable state they oppressed and overcame us, so that for a while we were silent. Then we spoke, each after his own manner:

"The idol of the Fung!" said I. "No wonder that savages should take it for a god."

"The greatest monolith in all the world," muttered Orme, "and Higgs is dead. Oh! if only he had lived to see it, he would have gone happy. I wish it had been I who was taken; I wish it had been I!" and he wrung his hands, for it is the nature of Oliver Orme always to think of others before himself.

"That's what we have come to blow up," soliloquized Quick. "Well, those 'azure stinging bees,' or whatever they call the stuff (he meant azo-imides) are pretty active, but it will take a lot of stirring if ever we get there. Seems a pity too, for the old pussy is handsome in his way."

"Come down," said Orme. "We must find out where we are; perhaps we can escape in the mist."

"One moment," I answered. "Do you see that?" and I pointed to a needle-like rock that pierced the fog about a mile to the south of the idol valley, and say two miles from where we were. "That's the White Rock; it isn't white really, but the vultures roost on it and make it look so. I have never seen it before, for I passed it in the night, but I know that it marks the beginning of the cleft which runs up to Mur; you remember, Shadrach told us so. Well, if we can get to that White Rock we have a chance of life."

Orme studied it hurriedly and repeated, "Come down; we may be seen up here."

We descended and began our investigations in feverish haste. This was the sum of them: In the arch under the tower were set two great doors covered with plates of copper or bronze beaten into curious shapes to represent animals and men, and apparently very ancient. These huge doors had grilles in them through which their defenders could peep out or shoot arrows. What seemed more important to us, however, was that they lacked locks, being secured only by thick bronze bolts and bars such as we could undo.

"Let's clear out before the mist lifts," said Orme. "With luck we may get to the pass."

We assented, and I ran to the camels that lay resting just outside the arch. Before I reached them, however, Quick called me back.

"Look through there, Doctor," he said, pointing to one of the peep-holes.

I did so and in the dense mist saw a body of horsemen advancing toward the door.

They must have seen us on the top of the wall. "Fools that we were to go there!" exclaimed Orme.

Next instant he started back, not a second too soon, for through the hole where his face had been, flashed a spear which struck the ground beyond the archway. Also we heard other spears rattle upon the bronze plates of the doors.

"No luck!" said Orme; "that's all up, they mean to break in. Now I think we had better play a bold game. Got your rifles, Sergeant and Doctor? Yes? Then choose your loopholes, aim, and empty the magazines into them. Don't waste a shot. For heaven's sake don't waste a shot. Now — one — two — three, fire!"

Fire we did into the dense mass of men who had dismounted and were running up to the doors to burst them open. At that distance we could scarcely miss and the magazines of the repeating rifles held five shots apiece. As the smoke cleared away I counted quite half a dozen Fung down, while some others were staggering off, wounded. Also several of the men and horses beyond were struck by the bullets which had passed through the bodies of the fallen.

The effect of this murderous discharge was instantaneous and remarkable. Brave though the Fung might be, they were quite unaccustomed to magazine rifles. Living as they did perfectly isolated and surrounded by a great river, even if they had heard of such things and occasionally seen an old gaspipe musket that reached them in the course of trade, of modern guns and their terrible power they knew nothing. Small blame to them, therefore, if their courage evaporated in face of a form of sudden death which to them must have been almost magical. At any rate they fled incontinently, leaving their dead and wounded on the ground.

Now again we thought of flight, which perhaps would have proved our wisest course, but hesitated because we could not believe that the Fung had left the road clear, or done more than retreat a little to wait for us. While we lost time thus the mist thinned a great deal, so much indeed that we could see our exact position. In front of us, toward the city side, lay a wide open space, whereof the walls ended against those of Harmac itself, to which they formed a kind of vestibule or antechamber set there to protect this gateway of the town through which we had ridden in the darkness, not knowing whither we went.

"Those inner doors are open," said Orme, nodding his head toward the great portals upon the farther side of the square. "Let's go and see if we can shut them. Otherwise we shan't hold this place long."

So we ran across to the farther doors that were similar to those through which we had just fired, only larger, and as we met nobody to interfere with our efforts, found that the united strength of the three of us was just, only just, sufficient to turn first one and then the other of them upon its hinges and work the various bolts and bars into their respective places. Two men could never have done the job, but being three and fairly desperate we managed it. Then we retreated to our archway and, as nothing happened, took the opportunity to eat and drink a few mouthfuls, Quick remarking sagely that we might as well die upon full as upon empty stomachs.

When we had crossed the square the fog was thinning rapidly, but as the sun rose, sucking the vapours from the rain-soaked earth, it thickened again for a while.

"Sergeant," said Orme presently, "these black men are bound to attack us soon. Now is the time to lay a mine while they can't see what we are after."

"I was just thinking the same thing, Captain; the sooner the better," replied Quick. "Perhaps the Doctor will keep a watch here over the camels, and if he sees any one stick up his head above the wall, he might bid him good morning. We know he is a nice shot, is the Doctor," and he tapped my rifle.

I nodded and the two of them set out laden with wires and the packages that looked like tobacco tins, heading for a stone erection in the centre of the square which resembled an altar, but was, I believe, a rostrum whence the native auctioneers sold slaves and other merchandise. What they did there exactly, I am sure I do not know; indeed, I was too much occupied in keeping a watch upon the walls whereof I could clearly see the crest above the mist, to pay much attention to their proceedings.

Presently my vigilance was rewarded, for over the great gateway opposite, at a distance of about a hundred and fifty paces from me, appeared some kind of a chieftain clad in white robes and wearing a very fine turban or coloured head-dress, who paraded up and down, waving a spear defiantly and uttering loud shouts.

This man I covered very carefully, lying down to do so. As Quick had said, I am a good rifle shot, having practised that art for many years; still, one may always miss, which, although I bore no personal grudge against the poor fellow in the fine head-dress, on this occasion I did not wish to do. The sudden and mysterious death of that savage would, I felt sure, produce a great effect among his people.

At length he stopped exactly over the door and began to execute a kind of war-dance, turning his head from time to time to yell out something to others on the farther side of the wall. This was my opportunity. I covered him with as much care as though I were shooting at a target, with one bull's eye to win. Aiming a little low in case the rifle should throw high, very gently I pressed the trigger. The cartridge exploded, the bullet went on its way, and the man on the wall stopped dancing and shouting and stood quite still. Clearly he had heard the shot or felt the wind of the ball, but was untouched.

I worked the lever jerking out the empty case, preparatory to firing again, but on looking up saw that there was no need, for the Fung captain was spinning round on his heels like a top. Three or four times he whirled thus with incredible rapidity, then suddenly threw his arms wide, and dived headlong from the wall like a bather from a plank, but backward, and was seen no more. Only from the farther side of those gates arose a wail of wrath and consternation.

After this no other Fung appeared upon the wall, so I turned my attention to the spy-hole in the doors behind me, and seeing some horsemen moving about at a distance of four or five hundred yards on a rocky ridge where the mist did not lie, I opened fire on them and at the second shot was fortunate enough to knock a man out of the saddle. One of those with him, who must have been a brave fellow, instantly jumped down, threw him, dead or living, over the horse, leaped up behind him and galloped away accompanied by the others, pursued by some probably ineffective bullets that I sent after him.

Now the road to the Pass of Mur seemed to be clear, and I regretted that Orme and Quick were not with me to attempt escape. Indeed, I meditated fetching or calling them, when suddenly I saw them returning, burying a wire or wires in the sand as they came, and at the same time heard a noise of thunderous blows of which I could not mistake the meaning. Evidently the Fung were breaking down the farther bronze doors with some kind of battering-ram. I ran out to meet them and told my news.

"Well done," said Orme in a quiet voice. "Now, Sergeant, just join up those wires to the battery, and be careful to screw them in tight. You have tested it, have n't you? Doctor, be good enough to unbar the gates. No, you can't do that alone; I'll help you presently. Look to the camels and tighten the girths. These Fung will have the doors down in a minute, and then there will be no time to lose."

"What are you going to do?" I asked as I obeyed.

"Show them some fireworks, I hope. Bring the camels into the archway so that they can't foul the wire with their feet. So — stand still, you grumbling brutes! Now for these bolts. Heavens! how stiff they are. I wonder why the Fung don't grease them. One door will do — never mind the other."

Labouring furiously we got it undone and ajar. So far as we could see there was no one in sight beyond. Scared by our bullets or for other reasons of their own, the guard there appeared to have moved away.

"Shall we take the risk and ride for it?" I suggested.

"No," answered Orme. "If we do, even supposing there are no Fung waiting beyond the rise, those inside the town will soon catch us on their swift horses. We must scare them before we bolt, and then those that are left of them may let us alone. Now listen to me. When I give the word, you two take the camels outside and make them kneel about fifty yards away, not nearer, for I don't know the effective range of these new explosives; it may be greater than I think. I shall wait until the

Fung are well over the mine and then fire it, after which I hope to join you. If I don't, ride as hard as you can go to that White Rock, and if you reach Mur give my compliments to the Child of Kings, or whatever she is called, and say that although I have been prevented from waiting upon her, Sergeant Quick understands as much about picrates as I do. Also get Shadrach tried and hanged if he is guilty of Higgs's death. Poor old Higgs! how he would have enjoyed this."

"Beg your pardon, Captain," said Quick, "but I 'll stay with you. The doctor can see to the baggage animals."

"Will you be good enough to obey orders and fall to the rear when you are told, Sergeant? Now, no words. It is necessary for the purposes of this expedition that one of us two should try to keep a whole skin."

"Then, sir," pleaded Quick, "may n't I take charge of the battery?"

"No," he answered sternly. "Ah! the doors are down at last," and he pointed to a horde of Fung, mounted and on foot, who poured through the gateway where they had stood, shouting after their fashion, and went on: "Now then, pick out the captains and pepper away. I want to keep them back a bit, so that they come on in a crowd, not scattered."

We took up our repeating rifles and did as Orme told us, and so dense was the mass of humanity opposite that if we missed one man, we hit another, killing or wounding a number of them. The result of the loss of several of their leaders, to say nothing of meaner folk, was just what Orme had foreseen. The Fung soldiers, instead of rushing on independently, spread to right and left, until the whole farther side of the square filled up with thousands of them, a veritable sea of men, at which we pelted bullets as boys hurl stones at a wave.

At length the pressure of those behind thrust onward those in front, and the whole fierce, tumultuous mob began to flow forward across the square, a multitude bent on the destruction of three white men, armed with these new and terrible weapons. It was a very strange and thrilling sight; never have I seen its like.

"Now," said Orme, "stop firing and do as I bid you. Kneel the camels fifty yards outside the wall, not less, and wait till you know the end. If we should n't meet again, well, good-bye and good luck."

So we went, Quick literally weeping with shame and rage.

"Good Lord!" he exclaimed, "good Lord! to think that, after four campaigns, Samuel Quick, Sergeant of Engineers, with five medals, should live to be sent off with the baggage like a pot-bellied bandmaster, leaving his captain to fight about three thousand niggers single-handed. Doctor, if he don't come out, you do the best you can for yourself, for I 'm going back to stop with him, that 's all. There, that 's fifty paces; down you go, you ugly beasts," and he bumped his camel viciously on the head with the butt of his rifle.

From where we had halted we could see through the archway into the space beyond. By now the square looked like a great Sunday meeting in Hyde Park, filled up with men, of whom the first rows were already past the altar-like rostrum in its centre.

"Why don't he loose off them stinging-bees?" muttered Quick. "Oh! I see his little game. Look," and he pointed to the figure of Orme, who had crept behind the unopened half of the door on our side of it and was looking intently round its edge, holding the battery in his right hand. "He wants to let them get nearer so as to make a bigger bag. He ——"

I heard no more of Quick's remarks, for suddenly

something like an earthquake took place, and the whole sky seemed to turn to one great flame. I saw a length of the wall of the square rush outward and upward. I saw the shut half of the bronze-plated door skipping and hopping playfully toward us, and in front of it the figure of a man. Then it began to rain all sorts of things.

For instance, stones, none of which hit us, luckily, and other more unpleasant objects. It is a strange experience to be knocked backward by a dead fist separated from its parent body, yet on this occasion this actually happened to me, and, what is more, the fist had a spear in it. The camels tried to rise and bolt, but they are phlegmatic brutes and, as ours were tired as well, we succeeded in quieting them.

Whilst we were thus occupied somewhat automatically, for the shock had dazed us, the figure that had been propelled before the dancing door arrived, reeling in a drunken fashion, and through the dust and falling *débris* we knew it for that of Oliver Orme. His face was blackened, his clothes were torn half off him, and blood from a scalp wound ran down his brown hair. But in his right hand he still held the little electric battery, and I knew at once that he had no limbs broken.

"Very successful mine," he said thickly. "Boer melinite shells are n't in it with this new compound. Come on before the enemy recover from the shock," and he flung himself upon his camel.

In another minute we had started at a trot toward the White Rock, whilst from the city of Harmac behind us rose a wail of fear and misery. We gained the top of the rise on which I had shot the horseman, and, as I expected, found that the Fung had posted a strong guard in the dip beyond, out of reach of our bullets, in order to cut us off, should we attempt to escape. Now, terrified by what had happened, to them a supernatural catastrophe, they were escaping themselves, for we perceived them galloping off to the left and right as fast as their horses would carry them.

So for a while we went on unmolested, though not very quickly, because of Orme's condition. When we had covered about half of the distance between us and the White Rock, I looked round and became aware that we were being pursued by a body of cavalry about a hundred strong, which I supposed had emerged from some other gate of the city.

"Flog the camels," I shouted to Quick, "or they will catch us after all."

He did so, and we advanced at a shambling gallop, the horsemen gaining on us every moment. Now I thought that all was over, especially when of a sudden from behind the White Rock emerged a second squad of horsemen.

"Cut off!" I exclaimed.

"Suppose so, sir," answered Quick, "but these seem a different crowd."

I scanned them and saw that he was right. They were a very different crowd, for in front of them floated the Abati banner, which I could not mistake, having studied it when I was a guest of the tribe: a curious, triangular, green flag covered with golden Hebrew characters, surrounding the figure of Solomon seated on a throne. Moreover, immediately behind the banner in the midst of a bodyguard rode a delicately shaped woman clothed in pure white. It was the Child of Kings herself!

Two more minutes and we were among them. I halted my camel and looked round to see that the Fung cavalry were retreating. After the events of that morning clearly they had no stomach left for fight with a superior force.

The lady in white rode up to us.

"Greetings, friend," she exclaimed to me, for she knew me again at once. "Now, who is captain among you?"

I pointed to the shattered Orme, who sat swaying on his camel with eyes half-closed.

"Noble sir," she said, addressing him, "if you can, tell me what has happened. I am Maqueda of the Abati, she who is named Child of Kings. Look at the symbol on my brow, and you will see that I speak truth," and, throwing back her veil, she revealed the coronet of gold that showed her rank.

CHAPTER VII

BARUNG

A T THE sound of this soft voice (the extreme soft-ness of Maqueda's voice was always one of her greatest charms), Orme opened his eyes and stared at her.

"Very queer dream," I heard him mutter. "Must be something in the Mohammedan business after all. Extremely beautiful woman, and that gold thing looks well on her dark hair."

"What does the lord your companion say?" asked Maqueda of me.

Having first explained that he was suffering from shock, I translated word for word, whereon Maqueda blushed to her lovely violet eyes and let fall her veil in a great hurry. In the confusion which ensued, I heard Quick saying to his master:

"No, no, sir; this one ain't no houri. She's a flesh and blood queen, and the pleasantest to look at I ever clapped eyes on, though a benighted African Jew. Wake up, Captain, wake up; you are out of that hell-fire now. It's got the Fung, not you."

The word Fung seemed to rouse Orme.

"Yes," he said; "I understand. The vapour of the stuff poisoned me, but it is passing now. Adams, ask that lady how many men she's got with her. What does she say? About five hundred? Well, then, let her attack Harmac at once. The outer and inner gates

are down; the Fung think they have raised the devil
and will run. She can inflict a defeat on them from
which they will not recover for years, only it must be
done at once, before they get their nerve again, for, after
all, they are more frightened than hurt."

Maqueda listened to this advice intently.

"It is to my liking; it is very good." she said in her
quaint, archaic Arabic when I had finished translating.
"But I must consult my Council. Where is my uncle,
the prince Joshua?"

"Here, Lady," answered a voice from the press behind,
out of which presently emerged, mounted on a white
horse, a stout man, well advanced in middle age, with
a swarthy complexion and remarkably round, prominent
eyes. He was clad in the usual Eastern robes, richly
worked, over which he wore a shirt of chain-mail, and
on his head a helmet with mail flaps, an attire that gave
the general effect of an obese Crusader of the early
Norman period without his cross.

"Is that Joshua?" said Orme, who was wandering a
little again. "Rummy-looking cock, isn't he? Sergeant, tell Joshua that the walls of Jericho are down, so
there'll be no need for him to blow his own trumpet.
I'm sure from the look of him that he's a perfect devil
with a trumpet."

"What does your companion say?" asked Maqueda
again.

I translated the middle part of Orme's remarks, but
neither the commencement nor the end, but even these
amused her very much, for she burst out laughing, and
said, pointing to Harmac, over which still hung a cloud
of dust:

"Yes, yes, Joshua my uncle, the walls of Jericho
are down, and the question is, will you not take your
opportunity? So in an hour or two we shall be dead, or

if God goes with us, perhaps free from the menace of
the Fung for years."

The prince Joshua stared at her with his great, prominent eyes, then answered in a thick, gobbling voice:

"Are you mad, Child of Kings? Of us Abati here
there are but five hundred men, and of the Fung yonder
tens of thousands. If we attacked, they would eat us
up. Can five hundred men stand against tens of
thousands?"

"It seems that three stood against them this morning,
and worked some damage, my uncle, but it is true those
three are of a different race from the Abati," she added
with bitter sarcasm. Then she turned to those behind
her and cried: "Who of my captains and Council
will accompany me, if I who am but a woman dare to
advance on Harmac?"

Now here and there a voice cried, "I will," or some
gorgeously dressed person stepped forward in a hesitating
way, and that was all.

"You see, men of the West!" said Maqueda after a
little pause, addressing us three. "I thank you for the
great deeds that you have done and for your counsel.
But I cannot take it because my people are not — war-
like," and she covered her face with her hands.

Now there arose a great tumult amongst her followers,
who all began to talk at once. Joshua in particular
drew a large sword and waved it, shouting out a recital
of the desperate actions of his youth and the names of
Fung chieftains whom he alleged he had killed in single
combat.

"Told you that fat cur was a first-class trumpeter,"
said Orme languidly, while the Sergeant ejaculated in
tones of deep disgust:

"Good Lord! what a set. Why, Doctor, they ain't
fit to savage a referee on a London football ground.

Pharaoh there in his basket (where he was barking loudly) would make the whole lot run, and if he was out — oh my! Now, then, you porpoise" — this he addressed to Joshua, who was flourishing his sword unpleasantly near — "put your pasteboard up, won't you, or I 'll knock your fat head off," whereon the Prince, who, if he did not understand Quick's words, at any rate caught their meaning wonderfully well, did as he was told, and fell back.

Just then, indeed, there was a general movement up the pass, in the wide mouth of which all this scene took place, for suddenly three Fung chieftains appeared galloping toward us, one of whom was veiled with a napkin in which were cut eyeholes. So universal was this retreat, in fact, that we three on our camels, and the Child of Kings on her beautiful mare, found ourselves left alone.

"An embassy," said Maqueda, scanning the advancing horsemen, who carried with them a white flag tied to the blade of a spear. "Physician, will you and your friends come with me and speak to these messengers?" And without even waiting for an answer, she rode forward fifty yards or so on to the plain, and there reined up and halted till we could bring our camels round and join her. As we did so, the three Fung, splendid-looking, black-faced fellows, arrived at a furious gallop, their lances pointed at us.

"Stand still, friends," said Maqueda; "they mean no harm."

As the words passed her lips, the Fung pulled the horses to their haunches, Arab-fashion, lifted spears and saluted. Then their leader — not the veiled man but another — spoke in a dialect that I, who had spent so many years among the savages of the desert, understood well enough, especially as the base of it was Arabic.

"O, Walda Nagasta, Daughter of Solomon," he said, "we are the tongues of our Sultan Barung, Son of Barung for a hundred generations, and we speak his words to the brave white men who are your guests. Thus says Barung, like the Fat One whom I have already captured: You white men are heroes. Three of you alone, you held the gate against my army. With the weapons of the white man you killed us from afar, here one and there one. Then, at last, with a great magic of thunder and lightning and earthquake, you sent us by scores into the bosom of our god, and shook down our walls about our ears, and out of that hell escaped yourselves.

"Now, O white men, this is the offer of Barung to you: Leave the curs of the Abati, the baboons who gibber and deck themselves out, the rock-rabbits who seek safety in the cliffs, and come to him. He will give you not only life, but all your hearts' desire — lands and wives and horses; great shall you be in his councils and happy shall you live. Moreover, for your sakes he will try to spare your brother, the Fat One, whose eyes look out of black windows, who blows fire from his mouth, and reviles his enemies as never man did before. Yes, although the priests have doomed him to sacrifice at the next feast of Harmac, he will try to spare him, which, perhaps, he can do by making him, like the Singer of Egypt, also a priest of Harmac, and thus dedicate forever to the god with whom, indeed, he says he has been familiar for thousands of years. This is our message, O white men."

Now, when I had translated the substance of this oration to Orme and Quick, for, as I saw by the quiver that passed through her at the Fung insults upon her tribe, Maqueda understood it, their tongues not differing greatly, Orme who, for the time at any rate, was almost himself again, said:

"Tell these fellows to say to their Sultan that he is a

good old boy, and that we thank him very much; also that we are sorry to have been obliged to kill so many of them in a way that he must have thought unsportsman-like, but we had to do it, as we are sure he will understand, in order to save our skins. Tell him also that, speaking personally, having sampled the Abati yonder and on our journey, I should like to accept his invitation. But although, as yet, we have found no men among them, only, as he says, baboons, rock-rabbits, and boasters without a fight in them, we have" — and here he bowed his bleeding head to Maqueda — "found a woman with a great heart. Of her salt we have eaten, or are about to eat; to serve her we have come from far upon her camels, and, unless she should be pleased to accompany us, we cannot desert her."

All of this I rendered faithfully, while every one, and especially Maqueda, listened with much attention. When they had considered our words, the spokesman of the messengers replied to the effect that the motives of our decision were of a nature that commanded their entire respect and sympathy, especially as their people quite concurred in our estimate of the character of the Abati ruler, Child of Kings. This being so, they would amend their proposition, knowing the mind of their Sultan, and having, indeed, plenipotentiary powers.

"Lady of Mur," he went on, addressing Maqueda directly, "fair daughter of the great god Harmac and a mortal queen, what we have offered to the white lords, your guests, we offer to you also. Barung, our Sultan, shall make you his head wife; or, if that does not please you, you shall wed whom you will" — and, perhaps by accident, the envoy's roving eyes rested for a moment upon Oliver Orme.

"Leave, then, your rock-rabbits, who dare not quit their cliffs when but three messengers wait without with sticks," and he glanced at the spear in his hand, "and come to dwell among men. Listen, high Lady; we know your case. You do your best in a hopeless task. Had it not been for you and your courage, Mur would have been ours three years ago, as it was ours before your tribe wandered thither. But while you can find but a hundred brave warriors to help you, you think the place impregnable, and you have perhaps that number, though we know they are not here; they guard the gates above. Yes, with a few of your Mountaineers whose hearts are as those of their forefathers were, so far you have defied all the power of the Fung, and when you saw that the end drew near, using your woman's wit, you sent for the white men to come with their magic, promising to pay them with the gold which you have in such plenty in the tombs of our old kings and in the rocks of the mountains."

"Who told you that, O Tongue of Barung?" asked Maqueda in a low voice, speaking for the first time. "The man of the West whom you took prisoner — he whom you call Fat One?"

"No, no, O Walda Nagasta, the lord Black Windows has told us nothing as yet, except sundry things about the history of our god, with whom, as we said, he seems to be familiar, and to whom, therefore, we vowed him at once. But there are others who tell us things, for in times of truce our peoples trade together a little, and cowards are often spies. For instance, we knew that these white men were coming last night, though it is true that we did not know of their fire magic, for, had we done so, we should not have let the camels slip through, since there may be more of it on them ——"

"For your comfort, learn that there is — much more," I interrupted.

"Ah!" replied the Tongue, shaking his head sadly,

"and yet we suffered Cat, whom you call Shadrach, to make off with that of your fat brother; yes, and even gave it to him after his own beast had been lamed by accident. Well, it is our bad luck, and without doubt Harmac is angry with us to-day. But your answer, O Walda Nagasta, your answer, O Rose of Mur?"

"What can it be, O Voices of Barung the Sultan?" replied Maqueda. "You know that by my blood and by my oath of office I am sworn to protect Mur to the last."

"And so you shall," pleaded the Tongue, "for when we have cleaned it of baboons and rock-rabbits, which, if you were among us, we soon should do, and thus fulfilled our oath to regain our ancient secret City of the Rocks, we will set you there once more as its Lady, under Barung, and give you a multitude of subjects of whom you may be proud."

"It may not be, O Tongue, for they would be worshippers of Harmac, and between Jehovah, whom I serve, and Harmac there is war," she answered with spirit.

"Yes, sweet-smelling Bud of the Rose, there is war, and let it be admitted that the first battle has gone against Harmac, thanks to the magic of the white men. Yet yonder he sits in his glory as the spirits, his servants, fashioned him in the beginning," and he pointed with his spear toward the valley of the idol. "You know our prophecy — that until Harmac rises from his seat and flies away, for where he goes, the Fung must follow — till then, I say, we shall hold the plains and the city of his name — that is, for ever."

"For ever is a long word, O Mouth of Barung." Then she paused a little, and added slowly, "Did not certain of the gates of Harmac fly far this morning? Now what if your god should follow his gates and those worshippers who went with them, and be seen no more?

Or what if the earth should open and swallow him, so that he goes down to hell, whither you cannot follow? Or what if the mountains should fall together and bury him from your sight eternally? Or what if the lightnings should leap out and shatter him to dust?"

At these ominous words the envoys shivered, and it seemed to me that their faces for a moment turned gray.

"Then, O Child of Kings," answered the spokesman solemnly, "the Fung will acknowledge that your god is greater than our god, and that our glory is departed.

Thus he spoke and was silent, turning his eyes toward the third messenger, he who wore a cloth or napkin upon his head, that was pierced with eyeholes and hung down to the breast. With a quick motion, the man dragged off this veil and threw it to the ground, revealing a very noble countenance, not black like that of his followers, but copper-coloured. He was about fifty years of age, with deep-set, flashing eyes, hooked nose, and a flowing, grizzled beard. The collar of gold about his neck showed that his rank was high, but when we noticed a second ornament of gold, also upon his brow, we knew that it must be supreme. For this ornament was nothing less than the symbol of royalty once worn by the ancient Pharaohs of Egypt, the double snakes of the *uræus* bending forward as though to strike, which, as we had seen, rose also from the brow of the lion-headed sphinx of Harmac.

As he uncovered, his two companions leapt to the ground and prostrated themselves before him, crying, "Barung! Barung!" while all three of us Englishmen saluted, involuntarily, I think, and even the Child of Kings bowed.

The Sultan acknowledged our greetings by raising his spear. Then he spoke in a grave, measured voice:

"O Walda Nagasta, and you, white men, sons of great

fathers, I have listened to the talk between you and my servants; I confirm their words and I add to them. I am sorry that my generals tried to kill you last night. I was making prayer to my god, or it should not have happened. I have been well repaid for that deed, since an army should not make war upon four men, even though, by their secret power, four men can defeat an army. I beseech you, and you also, Rose of Mur, to accept my proffered friendship, since otherwise, ere long, you will soon be dead, a..d your wisdom will perish with you, for I weary of this little war against a handful whom we despise.

"O Walda Nagasta, you have breathed threats against the majesty of Harmac, but he is too strong for you, nor may the might that can turn a few bricks to dust and shatter the bones of men prevail against him who is shaped from the heart of a mountain and holds the spirit of eternity. So at least I think; but even if it is decreed otherwise, what will that avail you? If it should please the god to leave us because of your arts, the Fung will still remain to avenge him ere they follow. Then I swear to you by my majesty and by the bones of my ancestors who sit in the caves of Mur, that I will spare but one of the Abati Jews, yourself, O Child of Kings, because of your great heart, and the three white men, your guests, should they survive the battle, because of their courage and their wisdom. As for their brother, Black Windows, whom I have captured, he must be sacrificed to the god, since I have sworn it, unless you yield, when I will plead for his life to the god, with what result I cannot tell. Yield, then, and I will not even slay the Abati; they shall live on and serve the Fung as slaves and minister to the glory of Harmac."

"It may not be, it may not be!" Maqueda answered, striking the pommel of her saddle with her small hand.

"Shall Jehovah whom Solomon, my father, worshipped, Jehovah of all the generations, do homage to an idol shaped by the hands He made? My people are worn out; they have forgot their faith and gone astray, as did Israel in the desert. I know it. It may even happen that the time has come for them to perish, who are no longer warriors, as of old. Well, if so, let them die free, and not as slaves. At least I, in whom their best blood runs, do not seek your mercy, O Barung. I'll be no plaything in your house, who, at the worst, can always die, having done my duty to my God and those who bred me. Thus I answer you as the Child of many Kings. Yet as a woman," she added in a gentler voice, "I thank you for your courtesy. When I am slain, Barung, if I am fated to be slain, think kindly of me, as of one who did her best against mighty odds," and her voice broke.

"That I shall always do," he answered gravely. "Is it ended?"

"Not quite," she answered. "These Western lords, I give them to you; I absolve them from their promise Why should they perish in a lost cause? If they take their wisdom to you to use against me, you have vowed them their lives, and, perhaps, that of their brother, your captive. There is a slave of yours also — you spoke of him, or your servant did — Singer of Egypt is his name. One of them knew him as a child; perchance you will not refuse him to that man."

She paused, but Barung made no answer.

"Go, my friends," she went on, turning toward us. "I thank you for your long journey on my behalf and the blow you have struck for me, and in payment I will send you a gift of gold, the Sultan will see it safe into your hands. I thank you. I wish I could have known more of you, but mayhap we shall meet again in war. Farewell"

She ceased, and I could see that she was watching us intently through her thin veil. The Sultan also watched us, stroking his long beard, a look of speculation in his eyes, for evidently this play interested him and he wondered how it would end.

"This won't do," said Orme when he understood the thing. "Higgs would never forgive us if we ate dirt just on the off-chance of saving him from sacrifice. He's too straight-minded on big things. But, of course, Doctor," he added jerkily, "you have interests of your own and must decide for yourself. I think I can speak for the Sergeant."

"I have decided," I answered. "I hope that my son would never forgive me either; but if it is otherwise, why, so it must be. Also Barung has made no promises about him."

"Tell him, then," said Orme. "My head aches infernally, and I want to go to bed, above ground or under it."

So I told him, although, to speak the truth, I felt like a man with a knife in his heart, for it was bitter to come so near to the desire of years, to the love of a life, and then to lose all hope just because of duty to the head woman of a pack of effete curs to whom one had chanced to make a promise in order to gain this very end. If we could have surrendered with honour, at least I should have seen my son, whom now I might never see again.

One thing, however, I added on the spur of the moment — namely, a request that the Sultan would tell the Professor every word that had passed, in order that whatever happened to him he might know the exact situation.

"By Harmac," said Barung when he had heard, "how disappointed should I have been with you if you had answered otherwise when a woman showed you the way. I have heard of you English before — Arabs and traders brought me tales of you. For instance, there was one who died defending a city against a worshipper of the Prophet who called himself a prophet, down yonder at Khartoum on the Nile — a great death, they told me, a great death, which your people avenged afterwards.

"Well, I did not quite believe the story, and I wished to judge of it by you. I have judged, white lords, I have judged, and I am sure that your fat brother, Black Windows, will be proud of you even in the lions' jaws. Fear not; he shall hear every word. The Singer of Egypt, who, it appears, can talk his tongue, shall tell the tale to him, and make a song of it to be sung over your honourable graves. And now farewell; may it be my lot to cross swords with one of you before all is done. That shall not be yet, for you need rest, especially yonder tall son of a god who is wounded," and he pointed to Orme. "Child of Kings with a heart of kings, permit me to kiss your hand and to lead you back to your people, that I would were more worthy of you. Ah! yes, I would that *we* were your people."

Maqueda stretched out her hand, and, taking it, the Sultan barely touched her fingers with his lips. Then, still holding them, he rode with her toward the pass.

As we approached its mouth, where the Abati were crowded together, watching our conference, I heard them murmur, "The Sultan, the Sultan himself!" and saw the prince Joshua mutter some eager words to the officers about him.

"Look out, Doctor," said Quick into my ear. "Unless I'm mistook, that porpoise is going to play some game."

Hardly were the words out of his mouth when, uttering the most valiant shouts and with swords drawn, Joshua and a body of his companions galloped up and surrounded our little group.

"Now yield, Barung," bellowed Joshua; "yield or die!"

The Sultan stared at him in astonishment, then answered:

"If I had any weapon (he had thrown down his lance when he took Maqueda by the hand), certainly one of us should die, O Hog in man's clothes."

Then he turned to Maqueda and added, "Child of Kings, I knew these people of yours to be cowardly and treacherous, but is it thus that you suffer them to deal with envoys under a flag of peace?"

"Not so, not so," she cried. "My uncle Joshua, you disgrace me; you make our people a shame, a hissing, and a reproach. Stand back; let the Sultan of the Fung go free."

But they would not; the prize was too great to be readily disgorged.

We looked at each other. "Not at all the game," said Orme. "If they collar him, we shall be tarred with their extremely dirty brush. Shove your camel in front, Sergeant, and if that beggar Joshua tries any tricks, put a bullet through him."

Quick did not need to be told twice. Banging his dromedary's ribs with the butt end of his rifle, he drove it straight on to Joshua, shouting.

"Out of the light, Porpoise!" with the result that the Prince's horse took fright, and reared up so high that its rider slid off over its tail to find himself seated on the ground, a sorry spectacle in his gorgeous robes and armour.

Taking advantage of the confusion which ensued, we surrounded the Sultan and escorted him out of the throng back to his two companions, who, seeing that there was something amiss, were galloping toward us.

"I am your debtor," said Barung, "but, O White Men, make me more so. Return, I pray you, to that hog in armour, and say that Barung, Sultan of the Fung, understands from his conduct that he desires to challenge him to single combat, and that, seeing he is fully armed, the Sultan, although he wears no mail, awaits him here and now."

So I went at once with the message. But Joshua was far too clever to be drawn into any such dangerous adventure.

Nothing, he said, would have given him greater joy than to hack the head from the shoulders of this dog of a Gentile sheik. But, unhappily, owing to the conduct of one of us foreigners, he had been thrown from his horse, and hurt his back, so that he could scarcely stand, much less fight a duel.

So I returned with my answer, whereat Barung smiled and said nothing. Only, taking from his neck a gold chain which he wore, he proffered it to Quick, who, as he said, had induced the prince Joshua to show his horsemanship if not his courage. Then he bowed to us, one by one, and before the Abati could make up their minds whether to follow him or not, galloped off swiftly with his companions toward Harmac.

Such was our introduction to Barung, Sultan of the Fung, a barbarian with many good points, among them courage, generosity, and appreciation of those qualities even in a foe, characteristics that may have been intensified by the blood of his mother, who, I am told, was an Arab of high lineage, captured by the Fung in war and given as a wife to the father of Barung.

CHAPTER VIII

THE SHADOW OF FATE

OUR ride from the plains up the pass that led to the high tableland of Mur was long and, in its way, wonderful enough. I doubt whether in the whole world there exists another home of men more marvellously defended by nature. Apparently the road by which we climbed was cut in the first instance, not by human hands, but by the action of primæval floods, pouring, perhaps, from the huge lake which doubtless once covered the whole area within the circle of the mountains, although to-day it is but a moderate-sized sheet of water, about twenty miles long by ten in breadth. However this may be, the old inhabitants had worked on it, for the marks of their tools may still be seen upon the rock.

For the first mile or two the road is broad and the ascent so gentle that my horse was able to gallop up it on that dreadful night when, after seeing my son's face, accident, or rather Providence, enabled me to escape the Fung. But from the spot where the lions pulled the poor beast down, its character changes. In places it is so narrow that travellers must advance in single file between walls of rock hundreds of feet high, where the sky above looks like a blue ribbon, and even at mid-day the path below is plunged in gloom. At other spots the slope is so precipitous that beasts of burden can scarcely keep their foothold; indeed, we were soon obliged to transfer ourselves from the camels to horses accustomed to the rocks. At others, again, it follows the brink of a yawning precipice, an ugly place to ride or turn rectangular corners, which half a dozen men could hold against an army, and twice it passes through tunnels, though whether these are natural I do not know.

Besides all these obstacles to an invader there were strong gates at intervals, with towers near by where guards were stationed night and day, and fosses or dry moats in front of them which could only be crossed by means of drawbridges. So the reader will easily understand how it came about that, whatever the cowardice of the Abati, though they strove for generations, the Fung had as yet never been able to recapture the ancient stronghold, which, or so it is said, in the beginning these Abati won from them by means of an Oriental trick.

Here I should add that, although there are two other roads to the plains — that by which, in order to outflank the Fung, the camels were let down when I started on my embassy to Egypt, and that to the north where the great swamps lie — these are both of them equally, if not more, impassable, at any rate to an enemy attacking from below.

A strange cavalcade we must have seemed as we crawled up this terrific approach. First went a body of the Abati notables on horseback, forming a long line of colour and glittering steel, who chattered as they rode, for they seemed to have no idea of discipline. Next came a company of footmen armed with spears, or rather two companies in the centre of which rode the Child of Kings, some of her court and chief officers, and ourselves, perhaps, as Quick suggested, because infantry in the event of surprise would find it less easy to run away than those who were mounted upon horses. Last of all rode more cavalry, the duty of whose rear files it was to turn from time to time, and, after inspection, to shout out that we were not pursued.

It cannot be said that we who occupied the centre of the advance were a cheerful band. Orme, although so far he had borne up, was evidently very ill from the shock of the explosion, so much so that men had to be set on each side of him to see that he did not fall from the saddle. Also he was deeply depressed by the fact that honour had forced us to abandon Higgs to what seemed a certain and probably a cruel death, and if he felt thus, what was my own case, who left not only my friend, but also my son, in the hands of savage heathen?

Maqueda's face I could not see because of the thin spangled veil that she wore, but there was something about her attitude suggestive of shame and of despair. The droop of her head and even her back showed this, as I, who rode a little behind and on one side of her, could see. I think, too, that she was anxious about Orme, for she turned toward him several times as though studying his condition. Also I am sure that she was indignant with Joshua and others of her officers, for when they spoke to her she would not answer or take the slightest notice of them beyond straightening herself in the saddle. As for the Prince himself, his temper seemed to be much ruffled, although apparently he had overcome the hurt to his back which prevented him from accepting the Sultan's challenge, for at a difficult spot in the road he dismounted and ran along actively enough. At any rate, when his subordinates addressed him he only answered them with muttered oaths, and his attitude toward us Englishmen, especially Quick, was not amiable. Indeed, if looks could have killed us I am sure that we should all have been dead before ever we reached the Gate of Mur.

This so-called Gate was the upper mouth of the pass

whence first we saw, lying beneath us, the vast, mountain-ringed plain beyond. It was a beautiful sight
in the sunshine. Almost at our feet, half-hidden in
palms and other trees, lay the flat-roofed town itself,
a place of considerable extent, as every house of any
consequence seemed to be set in a garden, since here
there was no need for cramping walls and defensive
works. Beyond it to the northward, farther than the eye
could reach, stretching down a gentle slope to the far-off
shores of the great lake of glittering water, were cultivated fields, and amongst them villas and, here and there,
hamlets.

Whatever might be the faults of the Abati, evidently
they were skilled husbandmen, such as their reputed
forefathers, the old inhabitants of Judæa, must have
been before them, for of that strain some trace pre-
sumably was still present in their veins. However
far he may have drifted from such pursuits, originally
the Jew was a tiller of the soil, and here, where many
of his other characteristics had evaporated under pressure of circumstances — notably the fierce courage that
Titus knew — this taste remained to him, if only by
tradition.

Indeed, having no other outlet for their energies and
none with whom to trade, the interests of the Abati were
centred in the land. For and by the land they lived and
died, and, since the amount available was limited by the
mountain wall, he who had most land was great amongst
them, he who had little land was small, he who had no
land was practically a slave. Their law was in its essen-
tials a law of the land; their ambitions, their crimes,
everything to do with them, were concerned with the
land, upon the produce of which they existed and grew
rich, some of them, by means of a system of barter.
They had no coinage, their money being measures of

corn or other produce, horses, camels, acres or their equivalent of soil, and so forth.

And yet, oddly enough, their country is the richest in gold and other metals that I have ever heard of even in Africa — so rich that, according to Higgs, the old Egyptians drew bullion from it to the value of millions of pounds every year. This, indeed, I can well believe, for I have seen the ancient mines which were worked, for the most part as open quarries, still showing plenty of visible gold on the face of the stopes. Yet to these alleged Jews this gold was of no account. Imagine it; as Quick said, such a topsy-turvy state of things was enough to make a mere Christian feel cold down the back and go to bed thinking that the world must be coming to an end.

Well, the prince Joshua, who appeared to be general-issimo of the army, having, in what was evidently a set phrase, exhorted the guards at the last gates to be brave and, if need were, deal with the heathen as some one or other dealt with Og, King of Bashan, and other unlucky persons of a different faith. In reply he received their earnest congratulations upon his escape from the frightful dangers of our journey.

These formalities concluded, casting off the iron discipline of war, we descended, a joyous mob, or rather the Abati did, to partake of the delights of peace. Really, conquerors returning from some desperate adventure could not have been more warmly greeted. As we entered the suburbs of the town, women, some of them very handsome, ran out and embraced their lords or lovers, holding up babies for them to kiss, and a little farther on children appeared, throwing roses and pomegranate flowers before their triumphant feet. And all this because these gallant men had ridden to the bottom of a pass and back again!

"Heavens! Doctor," exclaimed the sardonic Quick, after taking note of these demonstrations, "Heavens! what a hero I feel myself to be. And to think that when I got back from the war with them Boers after being left for dead on Spionkop with a bullet through my lung and mentioned in a despatch — yes, I, Sergeant Quick, mentioned in a despatch by the biggest ass of a general as ever I clapped eyes on, for a job that I won't detail, no one in my native village ever took no note of me, although I had written to the parish clerk, who happens to be my brother-in-law, and told him the train I was coming by. I tell you, Doctor, no one so much as stood me a pint of beer, let alone wine," and he pointed to a lady who was proffering that beverage to some-one whom she admired.

"And as for chucking their arms round my neck and kissing me," and he indicated another episode, "all my old mother said — she was alive then — was that she 'hoped I'd done fooling about furrin' parts as I called soldiering, and come home to live respectable, better late than never.' Well, Doctor, circumstances alter cases, or blood and climate do, which is the same thing, and I did n't miss what I never expected, why should I when others like the Captain there, who had done so much more, fared worse? But, Lord! these Abati are a sick-ening lot, and I wish we were clear of them. Old Barung's the boy for me."

Passing down the main street of this charming town of Mur, accompanied by these joyous demonstrators, we came at last to its central square, a large, open space where, in this moist and genial climate, for the high surrounding mountains attracted plentiful showers of rain, trees and flowers grew luxuriantly. At the head of this square stood a long, low building with white-washed walls and gilded domes, backed by the towering cliff, but at a little distance from it, and surrounded by double walls with a moat of water between them, dug for purposes of defence.

This was the palace, which on my previous visit I had only entered once or twice when I was received by the Child of Kings in formal audience. Round the rest of this square, each placed in its own garden, were the houses of the great nobles and officials, and at its western end, among other public buildings, a synagogue or temple which looked like a model of that built by Solomon in Jerusalem, from the description of which it had indeed been copied, though, of course, upon a small scale.

At the gate of the palace we halted, and Joshua, riding up, asked Maqueda sulkily whether he should conduct "the Gentiles," for that was his polite description of us, to the lodging for pilgrims in the western town.

"No, my uncle," answered Maqueda; "these foreign lords will be housed in the guest-wing of the palace."

"In the guest-wing of the palace? It is not usual," gobbled Joshua, swelling himself out like a great turkey cock. "Remember, O niece, that you are still unmarried. I do not yet dwell in the palace to protect you."

"So I found out in the plain yonder," she replied; "still, I managed to protect myself. Now, I pray you, no words. I think it necessary that these my guests should be where their goods already are, in the safest place in Mur. You, my uncle, as you told us, are badly hurt, by which accident you were prevented from accepting the challenge of the Sultan of the Fung. Go, then, and rest; I will send the court physician to you at once. Good night, my uncle; when you are recovered we will meet again, for we have much that we must discuss. Nay, nay, you are most kind, but I will not detain you another minute. Seek your bed, my uncle, and forget not to thank God for your escape from many perils."

At this polite mockery Joshua turned perfectly pale with rage, like the turkey cock when his wattles fade from scarlet into white. Before he could make any answer, however, Maqueda had vanished under the archway, so his only resource was to curse us, and especially Quick, who had caused him to fall from his horse. Unfortunately the Sergeant understood quite enough Arabic to be aware of the tenor of his remarks, which he resented, and returned:

"Shut it, Porpoise," he said, "and keep your eyes where Nature put 'em, or they 'll fall out."

"What says the Gentile?" spluttered Joshua, whereon Orme, waking up from one of his fits of lethargy, replied in Arabic:

"He says that he prays you, O Prince of princes, to close your noble mouth and to keep your high-bred eyes within their sockets lest you should lose them"; at which words those who stood listening broke into a fit of laughter, for one redeeming characteristic among the Abati was that they had a sense of humour.

After this I do not quite know what happened, for Orme showed signs of fainting, and I had to attend to him. When I looked round again the gates were shut and we were being conducted toward the guest-wing of the palace by a number of gaily dressed attendants.

They took us to our rooms — cool, lofty chambers ornamented with glazed tiles of quaint colour and beautiful design, and furnished somewhat scantily with articles made of rich-hued woods. This guest-wing of the palace, where these rooms were situated, formed, we noted, a separate house, having its own gateway, but, so far as we could see, no passage or other connection joining it to the main building. In front of it was a small garden, and at its back a courtyard with buildings in which, we were informed, our camels had been stabled. At the time we noted no more, for night was falling, and, even if it had not been, we were too worn out to make researches.

Moreover, Orme was desperately ill — so ill that he could scarcely walk even leaning on our shoulders. Still, he would not be satisfied till he was sure that our stores were safe, and, before he could be persuaded to lie down, insisted upon being supported to a vault with copper-bound doors, which the officers opened, revealing the packages that had been taken from the camels.

"Count them, Sergeant," he said, and Quick obeyed by the light of a lamp that the officer held at the open door. "All correct, sir," he said, "so far as I can make out."

"Very good, Sergeant. Lock the door and take the keys."

Again he obeyed, and, when the officer demurred to their surrender, turned on him so fiercely that the man thought better of it and departed with a shrug of his shoulders, as I supposed to make report to his superiors.

Then at length we got Orme to bed, and, as he complained of intolerable pains in his head and would take nothing but some milk and water, having first ascertained that he had no serious physical injuries that I could discover, I administered to him a strong sleeping-draught from my little travelling medicine case. To our great relief this took effect upon him in about twenty minutes, causing him to sink into a stupor from which he did not awake for many hours.

Quick and I washed ourselves, ate some food that was brought to us, and then took turns to watch Orme throughout the night. When I was at my post about six o'clock on the following morning he woke up and asked for drink, which I gave to him. After swallowing it he began to wander in his mind, and, on taking his temperature, I found that he had over five degrees of fever. The end of it was that he went off to sleep again, only waking up from time to time and asking for more drink.

Twice during the night and early morning Maqueda sent to inquire as to his condition, and, apparently not satisfied with the replies, about ten in the forenoon arrived herself, accompanied by two waiting-ladies and a long-bearded old gentleman who, I understood, was the court physician.

"May I see him?" she asked anxiously.

I answered yes, if she and those with her were quite quiet. Then I led them into the darkened room where Quick stood like a statue at the head of the bed, only acknowledging her presence with a silent salute. She gazed at Oliver's flushed face and the forehead blackened where the gases from the explosion had struck him, and as she gazed I saw her beautiful violet eyes fill with tears. Then abruptly she turned and left the sick-chamber. Outside its door she waved back her attendants imperiously and asked me in a whisper:

"Will he live?"

"I do not know," I answered, for I thought it best that she should learn the truth. "If he is only suffering from shock, fatigue, and fever, I think so, but if the explosion or the blow on his head where it is cut has fractured the skull, then ——"

"Save him," she muttered. "I will give you all I — nay, pardon me; what need is there to tempt you, his friend, with reward? Only save him, save him."

"I will do what I can, Lady, but the issue is in other hands than mine," I answered, and just then her attendants came up and put an end to the conversation.

To this day the memory of that old rabbi, the court physician, affects me like a nightmare, for of all the

medical fools that ever I met he was by far the most pre-
eminent.   All about the place he followed me suggesting
remedies that would have been absurd even in the Middle
Ages.   The least harmful of them, I remember, was
that poor Orme's head should be plastered with a compound of butter and the bones of a still-born child, and
that he should be given some filthy compound to drink
which had been specially blessed by the priests.   Others
there were also that would certainly have killed him in
half an hour.

Well, I got rid of him at last for the time, and returned
to my vigil.   It was melancholy work, since no skill
that I had could tell me whether my patient would live
or die.   Nowadays the young men might know, or say that
they did, but it must be remembered that, as a doctor, I
am entirely superannuated.   How could it be otherwise,
seeing that I have passed the best of my life in the desert
without any opportunity of keeping up with the times.

Three days went by in this fashion, and very anxious
days they were.   For my part, although I said nothing
of it to any one, I believed that there was some injury to
the patient's skull and that he would die, or at the best
be paralyzed.   Quick, however, had a different opinion.
He said that he had seen two men in this state before from
the concussion caused by the bursting of large shells
near to them, and that they both recovered, although
one of them became an idiot.

But it was Maqueda who first gave me any definite
hope.   On the third evening she came and sat by Orme
for a while, her attendants standing at a little distance.
When she left him there was a new look upon her face —
a very joyful look — which caused me to ask her what
had happened.

"Oh! he will live," she answered.

I inquired what made her think so.

"This," she replied, blushing. "Suddenly he looked up and in my own tongue asked me of what colour were my eyes. I answered that it depended upon the light in which they might be seen.

"'Not at all,' he said. 'They are always *vi-o-let*, whether the curtain is drawn or no.' Now, Physician Adams, tell me what is this colour *vi-o-let?*"

"That of a little wild flower which grows in the West in the spring, O Maqueda — a very beautiful and sweet-scented flower which is dark blue like your eyes."

"Indeed, Physician," she said. "Well, I do not know this flower, but what of that? Your friend will live and be sane. A dying man does not trouble about the colour of a lady's eyes, and one who is mad does not give that colour right."

"Are you glad, O Child of Kings?" I asked.

"Of course," she answered, "seeing that I am told that this captain alone can handle the fire-stuffs which you have brought with you, and, therefore, that it is necessary to me that he should not die."

"I understand," I replied. "Let us pray that we may keep him alive. But there are many kinds of fire-stuffs, O Maqueda, and of one of them which chances to give out violet flames I am not sure that my friend is master. Yet in this country it may be the most dangerous of all."

Now when she heard these words the Child of Kings looked me up and down angrily. Then suddenly she laughed a little in a kind of silent way that is peculiar to her, and, without saying anything, beckoned to her ladies and left the place.

"Very variegated thing, woman, sir," remarked Quick, who was watching. (I think he meant to say "variable.") "This one, for instance, comes up that passage like a tired horse — shuffle, shuffle, shuffle — for I could hear the heels of her slippers on the floor. But now she goes out like a buck seeking its mate — head in air and hoof lifted. How do you explain it, Doctor?"

"You had better ask the lady herself, Quick. Did the Captain take that soup she brought him?"

"Every drop, sir, and tried to kiss her hand afterward, being still dazed, poor man, poor man! I saw him do it, knowing no better. He'll be sorry enough when he comes to himself."

"No doubt, Sergeant. But meanwhile let us be glad that both their spirits seem to have improved, and if she brings any more soup when I am not there, I should let him have it. It is always well to humour invalids and women."

"Yes, Doctor; but," he added with a sudden fall of face, "invalids recover sometimes, and then how about the women?"

"Sufficient to the day is the evil thereof," I answered; "you had better go out for exercise; it is my watch." But to myself I thought that Fate was already throwing its ominous shadow before, and that it lay deep in Maqueda's violet eyes.

Well, to cut a long story short, this was the turning-point of Orme's illness, and from that day he recovered rapidly, for, as it proved, there was no secret injury to the skull, and he was suffering from nothing except shock and fever. During his convalescence the Child of Kings came to see him several times, or to be accurate, if my memory serves me right, every afternoon. Of course, her visits were those of ceremony — that is to say, she was always accompanied by several of her ladies, that thorn in my flesh, the old doctor, and one or two secretaries and officers-in-waiting.

But as Oliver was now moved by day into a huge

reception room, and these people of the court were
expected to stop at one end of it while she conversed with
him at the other, to all intents and purposes, save for the
presence of myself and Quick, her calls were of a private
nature.   Nor were we always present, since, now that
my patient was out of danger, the Sergeant and I went
out riding a good deal — investigating Mur and its
surroundings.

It may be asked what they talked about on these
occasions.   I can only answer that, so far as I heard, the
general subject was the politics of Mur and its perpetual
war with the Fung.   Still, there must have been other
topics which I did not hear, since incidentally I discovered
that Orme was acquainted with many of Maqueda's
private affairs whereof he could only have learned from
her lips.

Thus when I ventured to remark that perhaps it was not
altogether wise for a young man in his position to become
so intimate with the hereditary ruler of an exclusive tribe
like the Abati, he replied cheerfully that this did not
in the least matter, as, of course, according to their ancient
laws, she could only marry with one of her own family, a
fact that made all complications impossible.   I inquired
which of her cousins, of whom I knew she had several,
was the happy man.   He replied:

"None of them.   As a matter of fact, I believe that she
is officially affianced to that fat uncle of hers, the fellow
who blows his own trumpet so much, but I need n't add
that this is only a form to which she submits in order to
keep the others off."

"Ah!" I said.   "I wonder if Prince Joshua thinks
it only a form?"

"Don't know what he thinks, and don't care," he
replied, yawning; "I only know that things stand as I
say, and that the porpoise-man has as much chance of

becoming the husband of Maqueda as you have of marrying the Empress of China. And now, to drop this matrimonial conversation and come to something more important, have you heard anything about Higgs and your son?"

"You are more in the way of learning state secrets than I am, Orme," I answered sarcastically, being rather irritated at the course of events and his foolishness. "What have you heard?"

"This, old fellow. I can't say how she knows it, but Maqueda says that they are both in good health and well treated. Only our friend Barung sticks to his word and proposes to sacrifice poor old Higgs on this day fortnight. Now, of course, that must be prevented somehow, and prevented it shall be if it costs me my life. Don't you suppose that I have been thinking about myself all the time, for it isn't so, only the trouble is that I can't find any plan of rescue which will hold water."

"Then what's to be done, Orme? I haven't spoken much of the matter before for fear of upsetting you when you were still weak, but now that you are all right again we must come to some decision."

"I know, I know," he answered earnestly; "and I tell you this, that rather than let Higgs die alone there, I will give myself up to Barung, and, if I can't save him, suffer with him, or for him if I can. Listen: there is to be a great council held by the Child of Kings on the day after to-morrow which we must attend, for it has only been postponed until I was well enough. At this council that rogue Shadrach is to be put upon his trial and will, I believe, be condemned to death. Also we are formally to return Sheba's ring which Maqueda lent to you to be used in proof of her story. Well, we may learn something then, or at any rate must make up our minds to definite action. And now I am to have my first ride, am I not? Come on, Pharaoh," he added to the dog, which had stuck to his bedside all through his illness so closely that it was difficult to entice him away even to eat; "we are going for a ride, Pharaoh; do you hear that, you faithful beast?"

CHAPTER IX

THE SWEARING OF THE OATH

TWO or three days after this conversation, I forget exactly which it was, Maqueda held her council in the great hall of the palace. When we entered the place in charge of a guard, as though we were prisoners, we found some hundreds of Abati gathered there who were seated in orderly rows upon benches. At the farther end, in an apse-shaped space, sat the Child of Kings herself on a gilded or perhaps a golden chair of which the arms terminated in lions' heads. She was dressed in a robe of glittering silver, and wore a ceremonial veil embroidered with stars, also of silver, and above it, set upon her dark hair, a little circlet of gold, in which shone a single gem that looked like a ruby. Thus attired, although her stature is small, her appearance was very dignified and beautiful, especially as the gossamer veil added mystery to her face.

Behind the throne stood soldiers armed with spears and swords, and at its sides and in front of it were gathered her court to the number of a hundred or more, including her waiting-ladies, who in two companies were arranged to the right and left. Each member of this court was gorgeously dressed according to his profession.

There were the generals and captains with Prince Joshua at the head of them in their Norman-like chain armour. There were judges in black robes and priests in gorgeous garments; there were territorial lords, of whose attire I remember only that they wore high boots, and men who were called Market-masters, whose business it was to regulate the rate of exchange of products, and with them the representatives of other trades.

In short, here was gathered all the aristocracy of the little population of the town and territory of Mur, every one of whom, as we found afterwards, possessed some high-sounding title answering to those of our dukes and lords and Right Honourables and knights, to say nothing of the Princes of the Blood, of whom Joshua was the first.

Really, although it looked so fine and gay, the spectacle was, in a sense, piteous, being evidently but a poor mockery and survival of the pageantry of a people that had once been great. The vast hall in which they were assembled showed this, since, although the occasion was one that excited public interest, it was after all but a quarter filled by those who had a right to be present.

With much dignity and to the sound of music we were marched up the broad nave, if I may describe it thus, for the building, with its apse and supporting cedar columns, bore some resemblance to a cathedral, till we reached the open space in front of the throne, where our guards prostrated themselves in their Eastern fashion, and we saluted its occupant in our own. Then, chairs having been given to us, after a pause a trumpet blew, and from a side chamber was produced our late guide, Shadrach, heavily manacled and looking extremely frightened.

The trial that followed I need not describe at length. It took a long while, and the three of us were called upon to give evidence as to the quarrel between our companion, the Professor, and the prisoner about the dog Pharaoh and other matters. The testimony, however, that proclaimed the guilt of Shadrach was that of his companion guides, who, it appeared, had been threatened with floggings unless they told the truth.

These men swore, one after the other, that the abandonment of Higgs was a preconceived plan. Several of them added that Shadrach was in traitorous communication with the Fung, whom he had warned of our advent by firing the reeds, and had even contrived to arrange that we were to be taken while he and the other Abati with the camels laden with our rifles and goods, which they hoped to steal, passed through in safety.

In defence Shadrach boldly denied the whole story, and especially that he had pushed the Gentile, Higgs, off his dromedary, as was alleged, and mounted it himself because his own beast had broken down or been injured.

However, his lies availed him little, since, after consultation with the Child of Kings, presently one of the black-robed judges condemned him to suffer death in a very cruel fashion which was reserved for traitors. Further, his possessions were to be forfeited to the State, and his wife and children and household to become public slaves, which meant that the males would be condemned to serve as soldiers, and the females allotted to certain officials in the order of their rank.

Several of those who had conspired with him to betray us to the Fung were also deprived of their possessions and condemned to the army, which was their form of penal servitude.

Thus amidst a mighty wailing of those concerned and of their friends and relatives ended this remarkable trial, of which I give some account because it throws light upon the social conditions of the Abati. What hope is there for a people when its criminals are sent, not to jail, but to serve as soldiers, and their womenfolk, however innocent, are doomed to become the slaves of the judges or whoever these may appoint? Be it added, however, that in this instance Shadrach and his friends deserved all they got, since, even allowing for a certain amount of false evidence, undoubtedly, for the purposes of robbery and private hate, they did betray those whom their ruler had sent them to guide and protect.

When this trial was finished and Shadrach had been removed, howling for mercy and attempting to kiss our feet, like the cur he was, the audience who had collected to hear it and to see us, the Gentile strangers, dispersed, and the members of the Privy Council, if I may call it so, were summoned by name to attend to their duties. When all had gathered, we three were requested to advance and take seats which had been placed for us among the councillors.

Then came a pause, and, as I had been instructed that I should do, I advanced and laid Sheba's ring upon a cushion held by one of the court officers, who carried it to Maqueda.

"Child of Kings," I said, "take back this ancient token which you lent to me to be a proof of your good faith and mine. Know that by means of it I persuaded our brother who is captive, a man learned in all that has to do with the past, to undertake this mission, and through him the Captain Orme who stands before you, and his servant, the soldier."

She took it and, after examination, showed it to several of the priests by whom it was identified.

"Though I parted from it with fear and doubt, the holy ring has served its purpose well," she said, "and I thank you, Physician, for returning it to my people and to me in safety."

Then she replaced it on the finger from which it had been withdrawn when she gave it to me many months before.

There, then, that matter ended.

Now an officer cried:

"Walda Nagasta speaks!" whereon every one repeated, "Walda Nagasta speaks," and was silent.

Then Maqueda began to address us in her soft and pleasant voice.

"Strangers from the Western country called England," she said, "be pleased to hear me. You know our case with the Fung — that they surround us and would destroy us. You know that in our extremity I took advantage of the wandering hither of one of you a year ago to beg him to go to his own land and there obtain fire-stuffs and those who understand them, with which to destroy the great and ancient idol of the Fung. For that people declare that if this idol is destroyed they will leave the land they dwell in for another, such being their ancient prophecy."

"Pardon, O Child of Kings," interrupted Orme, "but you will remember that only the other day Barung, Sultan of the Fung, said that in this event his nation would still live on to avenge their god, Harmac. Also he said that of all the Abati he would leave you alive alone."

Now at these ill-omened words a shiver and a murmur went through the Council. But Maqueda only shrugged her shoulders, causing the silver trimmings on her dress to tinkle.

"I have told you the ancient prophecy," she answered, "and for the rest words are not deeds. If the foul fiend, Harmac, goes I think that the Fung will follow him. Otherwise, why do they make sacrifice to earthquake as the evil god they have to fear? And when some five centuries ago, such an earthquake shook down part of the secret city in the bowels of the mountains that I will show to you afterwards, why did they fly from Mur and take up their abode in the plain, as they said, to protect the god?"

"I do not know," answered Oliver. "If our brother were here, he whom the Fung have captured, he might know, being learned in the ways of idol-worshipping, savage peoples."

"Alas! O Son of Orme," she said, "thanks to that traitor whom but now we have condemned, he is not here and, perhaps, could tell us nothing if he were. At least, the saying runs as I have spoken it, and for many generations, because of it, we Abati have desired to destroy the idol of the Fung to which so many of us have been offered in sacrifice through the jaws of their sacred lions. Now I ask," and she leaned forward, looking at Oliver, "will you do this for me?"

"Speak of the reward, my niece," broke in Joshua in his thick voice when he saw that we hesitated what to answer, "I have heard that these Western Gentiles are a very greedy people, who live and die for the gold which we despise."

"Ask him, Captain," exclaimed Quick, "if they despise land also, since yesterday afternoon I saw one of them try to cut the throat of another over a piece not bigger than a large dog-kennel."

"Yes," I added, for I confess that Joshua's remarks nettled me, "and ask him whether the Jews did not despoil the Egyptians of their ornaments of gold in the old days, and whether Solomon, whom he claims as a forefather, did not trade in gold to Ophir, and lastly whether he knows that most of his kindred in other lands make a very god of gold."

So Orme, as our spokesman, put these questions with great gusto to Joshua, whom he disliked intensely, whereat some of the Council, those who were not of the party of the Prince, smiled or even laughed, and the silver ornaments upon Maqueda's dress began to shake again as though she also were laughing behind her veil.

Still, she did not seem to think it wise to allow Joshua to answer — if he could — but did so herself, saying:

"The truth is, O my friends, that here we set small store by gold because, being shut in and unable to trade, it is of no use to us save as an ornament. Were it otherwise, doubtless we should value it as much as the rest of the world, Jew or Gentile, and shall do so when we are freed from our foes who hem us in. Therefore, my uncle is wrong to claim as a virtue that which is only a necessity, especially when, as your servant says," and she pointed to the Sergeant, "our people make land their gold and will spend their lives in gaining more of it, even when they have enough."

"Then do the Gentiles seek no reward for their services?" sneered Joshua.

"By no means, Prince," answered Oliver, "we are soldiers of fortune, since otherwise why should we have come here to fight your quarrel (laying an unpleasant emphasis on the "your") against a chief who, if half savage, to us seems to have some merits, those of honour and courage, for instance? If we risk our lives and do our work, we are not too proud to take whatever we can earn. Why should we be, seeing that some of us need wealth and that our brother, who is as good as dead yonder, owing to the treachery of those who were sent to guard him, has relatives in England who are poor and should be compensated for his loss?"

"Why, indeed?" ejaculated Maqueda. "Listen, now, my friends. In my own name and that of the Abati people I promised to you as many camel-loads of this gold as you can carry away from Mur, and before the day is done I will show it to you if you dare follow me to where it lies hid."

"First the work, then the pay," said Oliver. "Now tell us, Child of Kings, what is that work?"

"This, O Son of Orme. You must swear — if this is not against your consciences as Christians — that for the space of one year from to-day you will serve me and fight for me and be subject to my laws, striving all the while to destroy the idol Harmac by your Western skill and weapons, after which you shall be free to go whither you will with your reward."

"And if we swear, Lady," asked Oliver after reflection, "tell us what rank shall we hold in your service?"

"You shall be my chief captain for this enterprise, O Son of Orme, and those with you shall serve under you in such positions as you may please."

At these words a murmur of dissatisfaction arose from the mail-clad generals in the council.

"Are we, then, to obey this stranger, O Child of Kings?" queried Joshua as their spokesman.

"Aye, my uncle, so far as this great enterprise is concerned, as I have said. Can you handle the fire-stuffs of which they alone have the secret? Could any three of you have held the gate of Harmac against the armies of the Fung and sent it flying skyward?"

She paused and waited in the midst of a sullen silence.

"You do not answer because you cannot," continued Maqueda. "Then for this purpose be content to serve a while under the command of those who have the skill and power which you lack."

Still there was no answer.

"Lady," said Orme in this ominous quiet, "you are so good as to make me a general among your soldiers, but will they obey me? And who are your soldiers? Does every man of the Abati bear arms?"

"Alas! no," she replied, fixing upon his latter question perhaps because she could not answer the first. "Alas! no. In the old days it was otherwise, when my great ancestresses ruled, and then we did not fear the Fung.

But now the people will not serve as soldiers. They say it takes them from their trades and the games they love; they say they cannot give the time in youth; they say that it degrades a man to obey the orders of those set over him; they say that war is barbarous and should be abolished, and all the while the brave Fung wait without to massacre our men and make our women slaves. Only the very poor and the desperate, and those who have offended against the laws will serve in my army, except it be as officers. Oh! and therefore are the Abati doomed," and, throwing back her veil, suddenly, she burst into tears before us all.

I do not know that I ever remember seeing a sight more pathetic in its way than that of this beautiful and high-spirited young woman weeping in the presence of her Council over the utter degeneracy of the race she was called upon to rule. Being old and accustomed to these Eastern expressions of emotion, I remained silent, however; but Oliver was so deeply affected that I feared lest he should do something foolish. He went red, he went white, and was rising from his seat to go to her, had I not caught him by the arm and pulled him back. As for Quick, he turned his eyes to the ceiling, as though engaged in prayer, and I heard him muttering:

"The Lord help the poor thing, the Lord help her; the one pearl in the snout of all these gilded swine! Well, I understand I am a bit of a general now, and if I don't make 'em sit up for her sake my name ain't Samuel Quick."

Meanwhile there was much consternation and indignant murmuring amongst the Court, which felt that reflections had been thrown upon it collectively and individually. At such a crisis, as usual, Prince Joshua took the lead. Rising from his seat, he knelt, not without difficulty, before the throne, and said:

"O Child of Kings, why do you distress us with such words? Have you not the God of Solomon to protect you?"

"God protects those who protect themselves," sobbed Maqueda.

"And have you not many brave officers?"

"What are officers without an army?"

"And have you not me, your uncle, your affianced, your lover?" and he laid his hand where he conceived his heart to be, and stared up at her with his rolling, fish-like eyes. "Had it not been for the interference of these Gentiles, in whom you seem to put such trust," he went on, "should I not have taken Barung captive the other day, and left the Fung without a head?"

"And the Abati without such shreds of honour as still belong to them, my uncle."

"Let us be wed, O Bud of the Rose, O Flower of Mur, and soon I will free you from the Fung. We are helpless because we are separate, but together we shall triumph. Say, O Maqueda, when shall we be wed?"

"When the idol Harmac is utterly destroyed, and the Fung have departed for ever, my uncle," she answered impatiently. "But is this a time to talk of marriage? I declare the Council closed. Let the priests bring the rolls that these strangers from the West may take the oath, and then pardon me if I leave you."

Now from behind the throne appeared a gorgeous gentleman arrayed in a head-dress that reminded me faintly of a bishop's mitre, and wearing over his robes a breastplate of precious stones roughly polished, which was half hidden by a very long white beard.

This person, who it seemed was the high priest, carried in his hand a double roll of parchment written over with characters which we afterward discovered were bastard Hebrew, very ancient and only decipherable by three or four of the Abati, if indeed any of them could really read it. At least it was said to be the roll of the law brought by their forefathers centuries ago from Abyssinia, together with Sheba's ring and a few other relics, among them the cradle (a palpable forgery) in which the child of Solomon and Maqueda, or Belchis, the first known Queen of Sheba, was traditionally reported to have been rocked. This roll of the law, which for generations had been used at all important ceremonies among the Abati, such as the swearing-in of their queens and chief officers, was now tendered to us to hold and kiss while we took the oath of obedience and allegiance in the names of Jehovah and of Solomon (a strange mixture, it struck us), solemnly vowing to perform those things which I have already set out.

"This seems a pretty wide promise," said Oliver, after it had been read to us and translated by me to Quick. "Do you think that we ought to take it on?"

I answered "Yes," that was from my point of view, since otherwise I saw no chance of achieving the object that had caused me to enter upon this adventure. Then, being especially requested to do so, the Sergeant, after reflecting a while, gave his considered opinion.

"Sir," he said to Orme, "we are three white men here consorting with a mob of quarter-bred African Jews and one real lady. It seems to me that we had best swear anything they want us to, trusting to the lady to see us through the mess, since otherwise we shall be mere filibusters in the country without official rank, and liable therefore to be shot on sight by the enemy, or any mutineers who get the upper hand here. Also, we have the Professor and the Doctor's son to think of. Therefore I say: Swear to anything in reason, reserving allegiance to the Crown of Great Britain, and trust to luck. You see, Captain, we are in their power anyway, and this oath may help, but can't hurt us, while to refuse it must give offence to all these skunks, and perhaps to the lady also, which is of more consequence."

"I think you are probably right, Sergeant," said Orme. "Anyway, in for a penny, in for a pound."

Then he turned to Maqueda, who had been watching this conference in an unknown tongue with some anxiety, or so it seemed to me, and added in Arabic:

"O Child of Kings, we will take your oath, although it is wide, trusting to your honour to protect us from any pitfalls which it may cover, for we would ask you to remember that we are strangers in your land who do not understand its laws and customs. Only we stipulate that we retain our allegiance to our own ruler far away, remaining the subjects of that monarch with all rights thereto appertaining. Also, we stipulate that before we enter on our duties, or at any rate during those duties, we shall be at full liberty to attempt the rescue of our friend and companion, now a prisoner in the hands of the Fung, and of the son of one of us who is believed to be a slave to them, and that we shall have all the assistance which you can give us in this matter. Moreover, we demand that if we should be tried for any offence under this oath, you to whom we swear allegiance shall be our judge alone, none others intermeddling in the trial. If you accept these terms we will swear the oath; otherwise we swear nothing, but will act as occasion may arise."

Now we were requested to stand back while the Child of Kings consulted with her advisers, which she did for a considerable time, since evidently the questions raised involved differences of opinion. In the end, however, she and those who supported her seemed to overrule the objectors, and we were called up and told that our terms had been accepted and engrossed upon the form of the oath, and that everything there included would be faithfully observed by the Ruler and Council of the Abati.

So we signed and swore, kissing the book, or rather the roll, in the civilized fashion. Afterwards, very tired, for all this business had been anxious, we were conducted back to our own quarters to lunch, or rather to dine, for the Abati ate their heaviest meal at midday, taking a siesta after it according to the common Eastern custom.

About four o'clock of that afternoon I was awakened from my nap by the growls of Pharaoh, and looked up to see a man crouching against the door, evidently in fear of the dog's fangs. He proved to be a messenger from Maqueda, sent to ask us if we cared to accompany her to a place that we had never seen. Of course we answered "Yes," and were at once led by the messenger to a disused and dusty hall at the back of the palace, where presently Maqueda and three of her ladies joined us, and with them a number of men who carried lighted lamps, gourds of oil, and bundles of torches.

"Doubtless, friends," said Maqueda, who was unveiled and appeared to have quite recovered from her outburst of the morning, "you have seen many wonderful places in this Africa and other lands, but now I am about to show you one that, I think, is stranger than them all."

Following her, we came to a door at the end of the hall which the men unbolted and shut again behind us, and thence passed into a long passage cut in the rock, that sloped continually downwards and at length led through another doorway to the vastest cave that we had ever heard of or seen. So vast was it, indeed, that the feeble light of our lamps did not suffice to reach the roof, and only dimly showed to right and left the outlines of what appeared to be shattered buildings of rock.

"Behold the cave city of Mur," said Maqueda, waving the lamp she held. "Here it was that the ancients whom we believe to have been the forefathers of the Fung, had their secret stronghold. These walls were those of their granaries, temples, and places of ceremonial, but, as I told you, centuries ago an earthquake shattered them, leaving them as they are now. Also, it broke down much of the cave itself, causing the roof to fall, so that there are many parts where it is not safe to enter. Come now and see what is left."

We followed her into the depth of the wonderful place, our lanterns and torches making little stars of light in that great blackness. We saw the ruins of granaries still filled with the dust of what I suppose had once been corn, and came at length to a huge, roofless building of which the area was strewn with shattered columns, and among them overthrown statues, covered so thick by dust that we could only discover that most of them seemed to be shaped like sphinxes.

"If only Higgs were here," said Oliver with a sigh, and passed on to Maqueda, who was calling him to look at something else.

Leaving the temple in which it was unsafe to walk, she led us to where a strong spring, the water supply of the place, bubbled up into a rock basin, and overflowing thence through prepared openings, ran away we knew not whither.

"Look, this fountain is very ancient," said Maqueda, pointing to the lip of the basin that was worn away to the depth of several inches where those who drew water had for many generations rested their hands upon the hard rock.

"How did they light so vast a cavern?" asked Oliver.

"We do not know," she answered, "since lamps would scarcely have served them. It is a secret of the past which none of the Abati have cared to recover, and another is how the air is always kept fresh so deep in the bowels of the mountain. We cannot even say whether this place is natural, as I think, or hollowed out by men."

"Both, I expect," I answered. "But tell me, Lady, do the Abati make any use of this great cave?"

"Some corn is still stored here in pits in case of siege," she replied, adding sadly, "but it is not enough to be of real service, since almost all of it comes from the estates of the Child of Kings. In vain have I prayed the people to contribute, if only a hundredth part of their harvest, but they will not. Each says that he would give if his neighbour gave, and so none give. And yet a day may come when a store of corn alone would stand between them and death by hunger — if the Fung held the valley, for instance," and she turned impatiently and walked forward to show us the stables where the ancients kept their horses and the marks of their chariot wheels in the stone floor.

"Nice people, the Abati, sir," said Quick to me. "If it were n't for the women and children, and, above all, for this little lady whom I am beginning to worship like my master, as in duty bound, I 'd like to see them do a bit of hungering."

"There is one more place to show you," said Maqueda, when we had inspected the stables and argued as to what possible cause could have induced the ancients to keep horses underground, "which perhaps you will think worth a visit, since it holds the treasures that are, or shall be, yours. Come!"

We started forward again along various passages, the last of which suddenly widened into a broad and steep incline of rock, which we followed for quite fifty paces, till it ended in what seemed to be a blank wall.

Here Maqueda bade her ladies and attendants halt, which indeed they seemed very anxious to do, though at the moment we did not know why. Then she went to one end of the wall where it joined that of the passage, and, showing us some loose stones, asked me to pull them out, which I did, not without difficulty. When an aperture had been made large enough for a man to creep through, she turned to her people and said:

"You, I know, believe this place to be haunted, nor would the bravest of you enter it save by express command. But I and these strangers have no such fears. Therefore give us a gourd of oil and some torches and bide where you are till we return, setting a lamp in the hole in the wall to guide us in case our own should become extinguished. No, do not reason but obey. There is no danger, for though hot, the air within is pure, as I know who have breathed it more than once."

Then she gave her hand to Oliver, and with his assistance crept through the hole. We followed, to find ourselves in another cavern, where, as she had said, the temperature was much hotter than that without.

"What is this place?" asked Orme in a low voice, for its aspect seemed to awe him.

"The tomb of the old kings of Mur," she replied. "Presently you shall see," and once more she took his hand, for the slope was sharp and slippery.

On we went, always descending, for perhaps four hundred yards, our footfalls echoing loudly in the intense silence and our lamps, round which the bats circled in hundreds, making four stars of light in the utter blackness, till at length the passage widened out into what appeared to be a vast circular arena, with a lofty dome-like roof of rock. Maqueda turned to the right, and, halting before some objects that glimmered whitely, held up her light, saying, "Look!"

This was what we saw: A great stone chair and, piled upon its seat and upon its base, human bones. Amongst these was a skull, and on it, grotesquely tilted, a crown of gold, while other ornaments — sceptres, rings, necklaces, weapons and armour — were mingled with the bones. Nor was this all, for in a wide circle round the chair were other skeletons, fifty or more of them, and amongst them the ornaments that their owners had worn.

Also, in front of each stood a tray of some metal, which we afterwards discovered to be silver or copper, and heaped upon it every kind of valuable, such as golden cups and vases, toilet utensils, necklaces, pectorals, bracelets, leglets, earrings, and beads that seemed to be cut from precious stones, piles of ring money, and a hundred other things such as have been prized by mankind since the beginning of civilization.

"You understand," said Maqueda, as we stared openmouthed at this awful and marvellous sight, "he in the chair was the king. Those about him were his officers, guards, and women. When he was buried they brought his household here, bearing his wealth, sat them down about him, and killed them. Blow away the dust, and you will see that the rock beneath is still stained with their blood; also, there are the sword-marks on their skulls, and neckbones."

Quick, who was of an inquiring mind, stepped forward and verified these statements.

"Golly!" he said, throwing down the skull of a man over whom the tired executioners had evidently bungled badly, "I'm glad I didn't serve the old kings of Mur. But the same game goes on in a small way to-day in Africa, for when I was campaigning on the West Coast I came across it not a fortnight old, only there they had buried the poor beggars living."

"Perhaps," said Maqueda, when the Sergeant's remarks had been translated to her. "Yet I do not think
the custom is one that my people would love," and she
laughed a little, then added, "forward, friends, there are
many more of these kings and oil does not burn for ever."

So we moved on, and at a distance of some twenty
paces found another chair with scattered bones on and
about the seat, lying where each had fallen as the dead
men decayed. Round it were the skeletons of the unfor-
tunates who had been doomed to accompany him upon
his last journey, every one of them behind his tray of
golden objects, or of simple treasure. In front of this
king's chair also were the bones of a dog with a jewelled
collar.

Again we proceeded to a third mortuary, if it may so
be called, and here Maqueda pointed out the skeleton of
a man, in front of which stood a tray piled up with what
evidently had been the medicine bottles of the period and
among them a number of rude surgical instruments.

"Say, O Physician Adams," she remarked with a
smile, "would you have wished to be court doctor to the
kings of Mur, if indeed that was then their city's name?"

"No, Lady," I answered; "but I do wish to examine
his instruments if I have your leave," and while she
hurried forward I stooped down and filled my pockets.
Here I may remark that upon subsequent inspection I
found among these instruments, manufactured I know
not what number of thousands of years ago — for on
that point controversy rages among the learned —
many that with modifications are still in use to-day.

Of that strange and dreadful sepulchre there is little
more to tell. From monarch to monarch we marched on
till at length we grew weary of staring at bones and gold.
Even Quick grew weary, who had passed his early youth
in assisting his father, the parish sexton, and therefore,

like myself, regarded these relics with professional interest, though of a different degree. At any rate he remarked that this family vault was uncommonly hot, and perhaps, if it pleased her Majesty, as he called Maqueda, we might take the rest of the deceased gentlemen as read, like a recruit's attestation questions.

But just then we came to No. 25, according to my counting, and were obliged to stop to wonder, for clearly this king had been the greatest of them all, since round him lay about two or three times the average number of dead, and an enormous quantity of wealth, some of it in the form of little statues of men and women, or perhaps of gods. Yet, oddly enough, he was a hunchback with a huge skull, almost a monstrosity indeed. Perhaps his mind partook of the abnormal qualities of his body, since no less than eleven little children had been sacrificed at his obsequies, two of whom, judging from their crooked bones, must have been his own.

One wonders what chanced in Mur and the surrounding territories which then acknowledged its sway when King Hunchback ruled. Alas! history writes no record.

CHAPTER X

QUICK LIGHTS A MATCH

"HERE we begin to turn, for this cave is a great circle," said Maqueda over her shoulder. But Oliver, whom she addressed, had left her side and was engaged in taking observations behind the hunchback's funeral chair with an instrument which he had produced from his pocket.

She followed him and asked curiously what this thing might be, and why he made use of it here.

"We call it a compass," he answered, "and it tells me that beyond us lies the east, where the sun rises; also it shows at what height we stand above the sea, that great water which you have never seen, O Child of Kings. Say now, if we could walk through this rock, what should we find out yonder?"

"The lion-headed idol of the Fung, I have been told," she answered. "That which you saw before you blew up the gate of the city Harmac. But how far off it may be I do not know, for I cannot see through stone. Friend Adams, help me to refill the lamps, for they burn low, and all these dead would be ill company in the dark. So at least my people think, since there is not one of them that dares enter this place. When first we found it only a few years ago and saw the company it held, they fled, and left me to search it alone. Look, yonder are my footsteps in the dust."

So I refilled the shallow hand-lamps, and while I did

so Orme took some hasty observations of which he jotted down the results in his pocket-book.

"What have you learned?" she asked, when at last he rejoined us somewhat unwillingly, for she had been calling to him to come.

"Not so much as I should have done if you could have given me more time," he replied, adding in explanation, "Lady, I was brought up as an engineer, that is, one who executes works, and to do so takes measurements and makes calculations. For instance, those dead men who hollowed or dressed these caves must have been engineers and no mean ones."

"We have such among us now," she said. "They raise dams and make drains and houses, though not so good as those which were built of old. But again I ask — what have you learned, O wise Engineer?"

"Only that here we stand not so very far above the city Harmac, of which I chanced to take the level, and that behind yonder chair there was, I think, once a passage which has been built up. But be pleased to say nothing of the matter, Lady, and to ask me no more questions at present, as I cannot answer them with certainty."

"I see that you are discreet as well as wise," she replied with some sarcasm. "Well, since I may not be trusted with your counsel, keep it to yourself."

Oliver bowed and obeyed this curt instruction.

Then we began our return journey, passing many more groups of skeletons which now we scarcely troubled to look at, perhaps because the heavy air filled with dust that once had been the flesh of men, was telling on our energies. Only I noticed, or rather the observant Quick called my attention to the fact, that as we went the kings in their chairs were surrounded by fewer and fewer attendants and women, and that the offerings placed at their feet were of an ever-lessening value. Indeed, after we had passed another five or six of them, their murdered retinues dwindled to a few female skeletons, doubtless those of favourite wives who had been singled out for this particular honour.

At length there were none at all, the poor monarchs, who now were crowded close together, being left to explore the shades alone, adorned merely with their own jewellery and regalia. Ultimately even these were replaced by funeral gold-foil ornaments, and the trays of treasure by earthenware jars which appeared to have contained nothing but food and wine, and added to these a few spears and other weapons. The last of the occupied chairs, for there were empty ones beyond, contained bones which, from their slenderness and the small size of the bracelets among them, I saw at once had belonged to a woman who had been sent to the grave without companions or any offerings at all.

"Doubtless," said Maqueda, when I pointed this out to her, "at that time the ancients had grown weak and poor, since after so many kings they permitted a woman to rule over them and had no wealth to waste upon her burial. That may have been after the earth-quake, when only a few people were left in Mur before the Abati took possession of it."

"Where, then, are those of your own house buried?" asked Oliver, staring at the empty chairs.

"Oh! not in this place," she answered; "I have told you it was discovered but a few years ago. We rest in tombs outside, and for my part I will sleep in the simple earth, so that I may live on in grass and flowers, if in no other way. But enough of death and doom. Soon, who can tell how soon? we shall be as these are," and she shuddered. "Meanwhile we breathe, so let us make the best of breath. You have seen your fee, say, does it content you?"

"What fee?" he asked. "Death, the reward of Life? How can I tell until I have passed its gate?"

Here this philosophical discussion was interrupted by the sudden decease of Quick's lamp.

"Thought there was something wrong with the blooming thing," said the Sergeant, "but could n' t turn it up, as it has n't got a screw, without which these old-fashioned colza oils never were no good. Hullo! Doctor, there goes yours," and as he spoke, go it did.

"The wicks!" exclaimed Maqueda, "we forgot to bring new wicks, and without them of what use is oil? Come, be swift; we are still far from the mouth of this cave, where none except the high priests will dare to seek us," and, taking Oliver by the hand, she began to run, leaving us two to follow as best we could.

"Steady, Doctor," said Quick, "steady. In the presence of disaster comrades should always stick together, as it says in the Red-book presented by the Crown to warrant officers, but paid for out of their deferred allowance. Take my arm, Doctor. Ah! I thought so, the more haste the less speed. Look there," and he pointed to the flying shapes ahead, now a long way off, and with only one lamp between them.

Next instant Maqueda turned round holding up this remaining lamp and calling to us. I saw the faint light gleam upon her beautiful face and glitter down the silver ornaments of her dress. Very wild and strange she looked in that huge vault, seen thus for a single moment, then seen no more, for presently where the flame had been was but a red spark, and then nothing at all.

"Stop still till we come back to you," cried Oliver, "and shout at intervals."

"Yes, sir," replied Quick, and instantly let off a fearful yell, which echoed backward and forward across the vault till I was quite bewildered.

"All right, coming," answered Oliver, and his voice sounded so far to the left that Quick thought it wise to yell again.

Well, to cut a long story short, we next heard him on our right and then behind us.

"Can't trust sounds here, sir, echoes are too uncertain," said the Sergeant; "but come on, I think I've placed them now," and calling to *them* not to move, we headed in what we were sure was the right direction.

The end of that adventure was that presently I tripped up over a skeleton and found myself lying half stunned amidst trays of treasure, affectionately clasping a skull under the impression that it was Quick's boot. Well, he hauled me up again somehow, and, as we did not know what to do, we sat down amidst the dead and listened. By now the others were apparently so far off that the sound of Oliver's calling only reached us in faint, mysterious notes that came from we knew not whence.

"As, like idiots, we started in such a hurry that we forgot to bring any matches with us, there is nothing to be done, except wait," I said. "No doubt in due course those Abati will get over their fear of ghosts and come to look for us."

"Wish I could do the same, sir. I did n't mind deaders in the light, but the dark's a different matter. Can't you hear them rattling their shanks and talking all round us?"

"Certainly I do hear something," I answered, "but I think it must be the echo of our own voices."

"Well, let us hold our jaw, sir, and perhaps they will hold theirs, for this kind of conversation ain't nice."

So we were silent, but the strange murmuring still went on, coming apparently from the wall of the cave behind us, and it occurred to me that I had once heard something like it before, though at the time I could not

think where.   Afterwards I remembered that it was when,
as a boy, I had been taken to see the Whispering Gallery
in St. Paul's Cathedral in London.

Half an hour or so went by in this fashion, and still
there were no signs of the Abati or of our missing pair.
Quick began to fumble among his clothes. I asked
him what he was doing.

"Can't help thinking I've got a wax match somewhere,
Doctor.   I remember feeling it in one of the pockets of
this coat on the day before we left London, and thinking
afterward it was n't safe to have had it packed in a box
marked 'Hold.'   Now if only I could find that match,
we have got plenty of torches, for I 've stuck to my
bundle all through, although I never thought of them
when the lamps were going out.

Having small belief in the Sergeant's match, I made no
answer, and the search went on till presently I heard him
ejaculate:

"By Jingo, here it is, in the lining.   Yes, and the head
feels all right.   Now, Doctor, hold two of the torches
toward me; make ready, present, fire!" and he struck
the match and applied it to the heads of the resinous
torches.

Instantly these blazed up, giving an intense light in that
awful darkness. By this light, for one moment only,
we saw a strange and not unattractive spectacle. I think
I forgot to say that in the centre of this vault stood
a kind of altar which until that moment indeed I had not
seen. This altar, which doubtless had been used for
ceremonial purposes at the funerals of the ancient kings,
consisted of a plain block of black stone, whereon was
cut the symbol of a human eye, the stone being approached
by steps and supported upon carved and crouching
sphinxes.

On the lowest of these steps, near enough to enable

us to see them quite clearly, were seated Oliver Orme and Maqueda, Child of Kings. They were seated very close together; indeed, if I must tell the truth, Oliver's arm was about Maqueda's waist, her head rested upon his shoulder, and apparently he was engaged in kissing her upon the lips.

"Right about face," hissed the Sergeant, in a tone of command, "and mark time!"

So we right-abouted for a decent period, then, coughing loudly — because of the irritant smoke of the torches — advanced to cross the cavern, and by accident stumbled upon our lost companions. I confess that I had nothing to say, but Quick rose to the occasion nobly.

"Glad to see you, Captain," he said to Oliver. "Was getting very anxious about you, sir, until by good luck I found a match in the lining of my coat. If the Professor had been here he'd have had plenty, which is an argument in favour of continuous smoking even when ladies are present. Ah! no wonder her Majesty is faint in this hot place, poor young thing. It's lucky you didn't leave hold of her, sir. Do you think you could manage to support her, sir, as we ought to be moving. Can't offer to do so myself, as I have lamed my foot with the tooth of a dead king, also my arms are full of torches. But if you prefer the Doctor — what do you say, sir? That you *can* manage? There is such an echo in this vault that it is difficult to hear — very well, let us go on, for these torches won't last for ever, and you wouldn't like us to have to spend a whole night here with the lady in such a delicate condition, would you, especially as those nasty-tempered Abati might say that you had done it on purpose? Take her Majesty's arm, Doctor, and let us trek. I'll go ahead with the torches."

To all this artless harangue Oliver answered not a single word, but glared at us suspiciously over the shape of

Maqueda, who apparently had fainted. Only when I
ventured to offer her some professional assistance she
recovered, and said that she could get on quite well
alone, which meant upon Orme's arm.

Well, the end of it was that she got on, and so did we,
for the torches lasted until we reached the narrow, sloping passage, and, rounding the corner, saw the lantern
burning in the hole in the wall, after which, of course,
things were easy.

"Doctor," said Oliver to me in a voice of studied
nonchalance that night, as we were preparing to turn in,
"did you notice anything in the Vault of Kings this
afternoon?"

"Oh, yes," I answered, "Lots! Of course, myself,
I am not given to archæology, like poor Higgs, but the
sight struck me as absolutely unique. If I were inclined
to moralize, for instance, what a contrast between those
dead rulers and their young and beautiful successor,
full of life and love" — here he looked at me sharply —
"love of her people, such as I have no doubt in their
day ——"

"Oh, shut it, Adams! I don't want a philosophical
lecture with historical comparisons. Did you notice
anything except bones and gold when that unutterable
ass, Quick, suddenly turned on the lights — I mean
struck the match which unfortunately he had with him."

Now I gave it up and faced the situation.

"Well, if you want the truth," I said, "not *very* much
myself, for my sight is n't as good as it used to be. But the
Sergeant, who has extraordinary sharp eyes, thought that
he saw you kissing Maqueda, a supposition that your
relative attitudes seemed to confirm, which explains,
moreover, some of the curious sounds we heard before
he lit the torches. That's why he asked me to turn my

back. But, of course, we may have been mistaken. Do I understand you to say that the Sergeant was mistaken?"

Oliver consigned the Sergeant's eyes to an ultimate fate worse than that which befell those of Peeping Tom; then, in a burst of candour, for subterfuge never was his forte, owned up:

"You made no mistake," he said, "we love each other, and it came out suddenly in the dark. I suppose that the unusual surroundings acted on our nerves."

"From a moral point of view I am glad that you love each other," I remarked, "since embraces that are merely nervous cannot be commended. But from every other, in our circumstances, the resulting situation strikes me as little short of awful, although Quick, a most observant man, warned me to expect it from the first."

"Curse Quick," said Oliver again, with the utmost energy. "I'll give him a month's notice this very night."

"Don't," I said, "for then you will oblige him to take service with Barung, where he would be most dangerous. Look here, Orme, to drop chaff, this is a pretty mess."

"Why? What's wrong about it, Doctor?" he asked indignantly. "Of course, she's a Jew of some diluted sort or other, and I'm a Christian; but those things adapt themselves. Of course, too, she's my superior, but after all hers is a strictly local rank, and in Europe we should be on much the same footing. As for her being an Eastern, what does that matter? Surely it is not an objection which should have weight with *you*. And for the rest, did you ever see her equal?"

"Never, never, *never!*" I answered with enthusiasm. "The young lady to whom any gentleman has just engaged himself is always absolutely unequalled, and, let me admit at once that this one is perhaps the most original and charming that I have ever met in all Central Africa. Only, whatever may be the case with you, I don't know whether this fact will console me and Quick when our throats are being cut. Look here, Orme," I added, "did n't I tell you long ago that the one thing you must *not* do was to make love to the Child of Kings?"

"Did you? Really, I forget; you told me such a lot of things, Doctor," he answered coolly enough, only unfortunately the colour that rose in his cheeks betrayed his lips.

At this moment, Quick, who had entered the room unobserved, gave a dry cough, and remarked:

"Don't blame the Captain, Doctor, because he don't remember. There's nothing like shock from an explosion for upsetting the memory. I've seen that often in the Boer war, when, after a big shell had gone off somewhere near them, the very bravest soldiers would clean forget that it was their duty to stand still and not run like rabbits; indeed, it happened to me myself."

I laughed, and Oliver said something which I could not hear, but Quick went on imperturbably.

"Still, truth is truth, and if the Captain has forgotten, the more reason that we should remind him. That evening at the Professor's house in London, you did warn him, sir, and he answered that you need n't bother your head about the fascinations of a nigger woman ——"

"Nigger woman," broke out Oliver. "I never used such words; I never even thought them, and you are an impertinent fellow to put them into my mouth. Nigger woman! Good heavens! It's desecration."

"Very sorry, Captain, now I come to think of it I believe you said black woman, speaking in your haste. Yes, and I begged you not to brag, seeing that if you did we might live to see you crawling after her, with myself, Samuel Quick bringing up the rear. Well, there it is we are, and the worst of it is that I can't blame you, being as anticipated in the prophecy — for that's what it was though I didn't know it at the time — exactly in the same state myself, though, of course, at a distance, bringing up the rear respectfully, as said."

"You don't mean that you are in love with the Child of Kings?" said Oliver, staring at the Sergeant's grim and battered figure.

"Begging your pardon, Captain, that is exactly what I do mean. If a cat may look at a queen, why may n't a man love her? Howsoever, my kind of love ain't likely to interfere with yours. My kind means sentry-go and perhaps a knife in my gizzard; yours — well, we saw what yours means this afternoon, though what it will all lead to, we didn't see. Still, Captain, speaking as one who has n't been keen on the sex heretofore, I say — sail in, for it 's worth it, even if you 've got to sink afterwards, for this lady, although she is half a Jew and I never could abide Jews, is the sweetest and the loveliest and the best and the bravest little woman that ever walked God's earth."

At this point Oliver seized his hand and shook it warmly, and I may mention that I think some report of Quick's summary of her character must have reached Maqueda's ears. At any rate, thenceforward until the end she always treated the old fellow with what the French call the "most distinguished consideration."

But, as I was not in love, no one shook my hand, so, leaving the other two to discuss the virtues and graces of the Child of Kings, I went off to bed filled with the gloomiest forebodings. What a fool I had been not to insist that whatever expert accompanied Higgs should be a married man. And yet, now when I came to think of it, that might not have bettered matters, and perhaps would only have added to the transaction a degree of moral turpitude which at present was lacking, since even married men are sometimes weak.

The truth was that Maqueda's attractions were extraordinarily great. To her remarkable beauty she added a wonderful charm of manner and force of mind. Also her situation must touch the heart and pity of any man, so helpless was she in the midst of all her hollow grandeur, so lonely amongst a nation of curs whom she strove in vain to save, and should she escape destruction with them, doomed to so sad and repulsive a fate, namely, to become the wife of a fat poltroon who was her own uncle. Well, we know to what emotion pity is akin, and the catastrophe had occurred a little sooner than I had expected, that was all.

Doubtless to her, in comparison with the men to whom she was accustomed and allowed by etiquette to take as her associates, this brave and handsome young Englishman, who had come into her care sick and shattered after the doing of a great deed, must have seemed a veritable fairy prince. And she had helped to nurse him, and he had shown himself grateful for her kindness and condescension, and — the rest followed, as surely as the day follows the night.

But how would it end? Sooner or later the secret must come out, for already the Abati nobles, if I may call them so for want of a better name, and especially Joshua, were bitterly jealous of the favour their lady showed to the foreigner, and watched them both. Then what — what would happen? Under the Abati law it was death for anyone outside of the permitted degree of relationship to tamper with the affections of the Child of Kings. Nor was this wonderful, since that person held her seat in virtue of her supposed direct descent from Solomon and the first Maqueda, Queen of Sheba, and therefore the introduction of any alien blood could not be tolerated.

Moreover, Orme, having sworn an oath of allegiance,

had become subject to those laws.   Lastly, I could not in the least hope from the character of the pair concerned that this was but a passing flirtation.

Oh! without a doubt these two had signed their own death-warrant yonder in the Cave of Death, and incidentally ours also.   This must be the end of our adventure and my long search for the son whom I had lost.

CHAPTER XI

THE RESCUE FAILS

OUR breakfast on the following morning was a somewhat gloomy meal. By common consent no allusion was made to the events of the previous day, or to our conversation at bedtime.

Indeed, there was no talk at all to speak of, since, not knowing what else to do, I thought I could best show my attitude of mind by preserving a severe silence, while Quick seemed to be absorbed in philosophical reflections, and Orme looked rather excited and dishevelled, as though he had been writing poetry, as I daresay was the case. In the midst of this dreary meal a messenger arrived, who announced that the Walda Nagasta would be pleased to see us all within half an hour.

Fearing lest Orme should say something foolish, I answered briefly that we would wait upon her, and the man went, leaving us wondering what had happened to cause her to desire our presence.

At the appointed time we were shown into the small audience room, and, as we passed its door, I ventured to whisper to Oliver:

"For your own sake and hers, as well as that of the rest of us, I implore you to be careful. Your face is watched as well as your words."

"All right, old fellow," he answered, colouring a little. "You may trust me."

"I wish I could," I muttered.

Then we were shown in ceremoniously, and made our bows to Maqueda, who was seated, surrounded by some of the judges and officers, among them Prince Joshua, and talking to two rough-looking men clad in ordinary brown robes. She greeted us, and after the exchange of the usual compliments, said:

"Friends, I have summoned you for this reason. This morning when the traitor Shadrach was being led out to execution at the hands of these men, the officers of the law, he begged for a delay. When asked why, as his petition for reprieve had been refused, he said that if his life was spared he could show how your companion, he whom they call Black Windows, may be rescued from the Fung."

"How?" asked Orme and I in one breath.

"I do not know," she answered, "but wisely they spared the man. Let him be brought in."

A door opened, and Shadrach entered, his hands bound behind his back and shackles on his feet. He was a very fearful and much chastened Shadrach, for his eyes rolled and his teeth chattered with terror, as, having prostrated himself to the Walda Nagasta, he wriggled round and tried to kiss Orme's boot. The guards pulled him to his feet again, and Maqueda said:

"What have you to tell us, traitor, before you die?"

"The thing is secret, O Bud of the Rose. Must I speak before so many?"

"Nay," she answered, and ordered most of those present to leave the room, including the executioners and soldiers.

"The man is desperate, and there will be none left to guard him," said Joshua nervously.

"I 'll do that, your Highness," answered Quick in his bad Arabic, and stepping up behind Shadrach he added in English, "Now then, Pussy, you behave, or it will be the worse for you."

When all had gone again Shadrach was commanded to speak and say how he could save the Englishman whom he had betrayed into the hands of the Fung.

"Thus, Child of Kings," he answered, "Black Windows, as we know, is imprisoned in the body of the great idol."

"How do you know it, man?"

"O Lady, I do know it, and also the Sultan said so, did he not? Well, I can show a secret road to that idol whence he may be reached and rescued. In my boyhood I, who am called Cat, because I can climb so well, found that road, and when the Fung took me afterward and threw me to the lions, where I got these scars upon my face, by it I escaped. Spare me, and I will show it to you."

"It is not enough to show the road," said Maqueda. "Dog, you must save the foreign lord whom you betrayed. If you do not save him you die. Do you understand?"

"That is a hard saying, Lady," answered the man. "Am I God that I should promise to save this stranger who perchance is already dead? Yet I will do my best, knowing that if I fail you will kill me, and that if I succeed I shall be spared. At any rate, I will show you the road to where he is or was imprisoned, although I warn you that it is a rough one."

"Where you can travel we can follow," said Maqueda. "Tell us now what we must do."

So he told her, and when he had done the prince Joshua intervened, saying that it was not fitting that the Child of Kings in her own sacred person should undertake such a dangerous journey. She listened to his remonstrances and thanked him for his care for her.

"Still I am going," she said, "not for the sake of the stranger who is called Black Windows, but because, if there is a secret way out of Mur I think it well that I should know that way. Yet I agree with you, my uncle, that on such a journey I ought not to be unprotected, and therefore I pray that you will be ready to start with us at noon, since I am sure that then we shall all be safe."

Now Joshua began to make excuses, but she would not listen to them.

"No, no," she said, "you are too modest. The honour of the Abati is involved in this matter, since, alas! it was an Abati that betrayed Black Windows, and an Abati — namely, yourself — must save him. You have often told me, my uncle, how clever you are at climbing rocks, and now you shall make proof of your skill and courage before these foreigners. It is a command, speak no more," and she rose, to show that the audience was finished.

That same afternoon Shadrach, by mountain paths that were known to him, led a little company of people to the crest of the western precipice of Mur. Fifteen hundred feet or more beneath us lay the great plains upon which, some miles away, could be seen the city of Harmac. But the idol in the valley we could not see, because here the precipice bent over and hid it from our sight.

"What now, fellow," said Maqueda, who was clad in the rough sheepskin of a peasant woman, which somehow looked charming upon her. "Here is the cliff, there lies the plain; I see no road between the two, and my wise uncle, the Prince, tells me that he never heard of one."

"Lady," answered the man, "now I take command, and you must follow me. But first let us see that nobody nd nothing are lacking."

Then he went round the company and numbered them. In all we were sixteen; Maqueda, and Joshua, we three

Englishmen, armed with repeating rifles and revolvers, our guide Shadrach, and some picked mountaineers chosen for their skill and courage. For even in Mur there were brave men left, especially among the shepherds and huntsmen, whose homes were on the cliffs. These sturdy guides were laden with ropes, lamps, and long, slender ladders that could be strapped together.

When everything had been checked and all the ladders and straps tested, Shadrach went to a clump of bushes which grew feebly on the wind-swept crest of the precipice. In the midst of these he found and removed a large flat stone, revealing what evidently had once been the head of a stair, although now its steps were much worn and crumbled by the water that in the wet season followed this natural drain to the depths below.

"This is that road the ancients made for purposes of their own," explained Shadrach, "which, as I have said, I chanced to discover when I was a boy. But let none follow it who are afraid, for it is steep and rough."

Now Joshua, who was already weary with his long ride and walk up to the crest of the precipice, implored Maqueda almost passionately to abandon the idea of entering this horrid hole, while Oliver backed up his entreaties with few words but many pleading glances, for on this point, though for different reasons, the Prince and he were at one.

But she would not listen.

"My uncle," she said, "with you, the experienced mountaineer, why should I be afraid? If the Doctor here, who is old enough to be the father of either of us" (so far as Joshua was concerned this remark lacked truth), "is willing to go, surely I can go also? Moreover, if I remained behind, you would wish to stay to guard me, and never should I forgive myself if I deprived

you of such a great adventure. Also, like you, I love
climbing. Come, let us waste no more time.''

So we were roped up. First went Shadrach, with
Quick next to him, a position which the Sergeant insisted
upon occupying as his custodian, and several of the
mountaineers, carrying ladders, lamps, oil, food and
other things. Then in a second gang came two more
of these men, Oliver, Maqueda, myself, and next to me,
Joshua. The remaining mountaineers brought up the
rear, carrying spare stores, ladders, and so forth. When
all was ready the lamps were lit, and we started upon a
very strange journey.

For the first two hundred feet or so the stairs, though
worn and almost perpendicular, for the place was
like the shaft of a mine, were not difficult to descend, to
any of us except Joshua, whom I heard puffing and groaning behind me. Then came a gallery running eastward
at a steep slope for perhaps fifty paces, and at the end
of it a second shaft of about the same depth as the first,
but with the stairs much more worn, apparently by the
washing of water, of which a good deal trickled out of the
sides of the shaft. Another difficulty was that the air
rushing up from below made it hard to keep the lamps
alight.

Toward the bottom of this section there was scarcely
any stair left, and the climbing became very dangerous.
Here, indeed, Joshua slipped, and with a wail of terror
slid down the shaft and landed with his legs across my
back in such fashion that had I not happened to have
good hand and foot hold at the time, he would have
propelled me on to Maqueda and we must all have rolled
down headlong, probably to our deaths.

As it was, this fat and terrified fellow cast his arms
about my neck, to which he clung, nearly choking me,
until, just when I was about to faint beneath his weight

and pressure, the mountaineers in the third party arrived and dragged him off. When they had got him in charge, for I refused to move another step while he was immediately behind me, we descended by a ladder which the first party had set up, to the second level, where began another long, eastward-sloping passage that ended at the mouth of a third pit.

Here arose the great question as to what was to be done with the prince Joshua who vowed that he could go no farther, and demanded loudly to be taken back to the top of the cliff, although Shadrach assured him that thenceforward the road was much easier. At length we were obliged to refer the matter to Maqueda, who settled it in very few words.

"My uncle," she said, "you tell us that you cannot come on, and it is certain that we cannot spare the time and men to send you back. Therefore, it seems that you must stop where you are until we return, and if we should not return, make the best of your own way up the shaft. Farewell, my uncle, this place is safe and comfortable, and if you are wise you will rest a while."

"Heartless woman!" gobbled Joshua, who was shaking like a jelly with fear and rage. "Would you leave your affianced lord and lover alone in this haunted hole while you scramble down rocks like a wild cat with strangers? If I must stay, do you stay with me."

"Certainly not," replied Maqueda with decision. "Shall it be said that the Child of Kings is afraid to go where her guests can travel?"

Well, the end of it was that Joshua came on in the centre of the third body of mountaineers, who were practically obliged to carry him.

Shadrach was right, since for some reason or other the stairs thenceforward remained more perfect. Only they seemed almost endless, and before we reached our goal

I calculated that we must have descended quite twelve hundred feet into the bowels of the rock. At length, when I was almost tired out and Maqueda was so breathless that she was obliged to lean on Oliver, dragging me behind her like a dog on a string, of a sudden we saw a glimmer of daylight that crept into the tunnel through a small hole. By the mouth of yet another pit or shaft we found Shadrach and the others waiting for us. Saluting, he said that we must unrope, leave our lamps behind, and follow him. Oliver asked him whither this last shaft led.

"To a still lower level, lord," he answered, "but one which you will scarcely care to explore, since it ends in the great pit where the Fung keep their sacred lions."

"Indeed," said Oliver, much interested for reasons of his own, and he glanced at Quick, who nodded his head and whistled.

Then we all followed Shadrach to find ourselves presently upon a plateau about the size of a racquet court which, either by nature or by the hand of man, had been recessed in the face of that gigantic cliff. Going to the edge of this plateau, whereon grew many tree-ferns and some thick green bushes that would have made us invisible from below even had there been anyone to see us, we saw that the sheer precipice ran down beneath for several hundred feet. Of these yawning depths, however, we did not at the moment make out much, partly because they were plunged in shadow and partly for another reason.

Rising out of the gulf below was what we took at first to be a rounded hill of black rock, oblong in shape, from which projected a gigantic shaft of stone ending in a kind of fretted bush that alone was of the size of a cottage. The point of this bush-like rock was exactly opposite the little plateau on to which we had emerged and distant from it not more than thirty, or at most forty feet.

"What is that?" asked Maqueda, of Shadrach, pointing in front of her, as she handed back to one of the mountaineers a cup from which she had been drinking water.

"That, O Walda Nagasta," he answered, "is nothing else than the back of the mighty idol of the Fung, which is shaped like a lion. The great shaft of rock with the bush at the end of it is the tail of the lion. Doubtless this platform on which we stand is a place whence the old priests, when they owned Mur as well as the land of the Fung, used to hide themselves to watch whatever it was they wanted to see. Look," and he pointed to certain grooves in the face of the rock, "I think that here there was once a bridge which could be let down at will on to the tail of the lion-god, though long ago it has rotted away. Yet ere now I have travelled this road without it."

We stared at him astonished, and in the silence that followed I heard Maqueda whisper to Oliver:

"Perhaps that is how he whom we call Cat escaped from the Fung; or perhaps that is how he communicates with them as a spy."

"Or perhaps he is a liar, my Lady," interrupted Quick, who had also overheard their talk, a solution which, I confess, commended itself to me.

"Why have you brought us here?" asked Maqueda presently.

"Did I not tell you in Mur, Lady — to rescue Black Windows? Listen, now, it is the custom of the Fung to allow those who are imprisoned within the idol to walk unguarded upon its back at dawn and sunset. At least, this is their custom with Black Windows — ask me not how I know it; it is truth, I swear it on my life, which is at stake. Now this is my plan. We have with us a ladder that will reach from where we stand to the tail of the idol. Should the foreign lord appear upon the back of the god, which, if he still lives, as I believe he does, he is almost sure to do at sundown, as a man who dwells in the dark all day will love the light and air when he can get them, then some of us must cross and bring him back with us. Perhaps it had best be you, my lord Orme, since if I went alone, or even with these men, after what is past Black Windows might not altogether trust me."

"Fool," broke in Maqueda, "how can a man do such a thing?"

"O Lady, it is not so difficult as it looks. A few steps across the gulf, and then a hundred feet or so along the tail of the lion which is flat on the top and so broad that one may run down it if careful to follow the curves, that is on a still day — nothing more. But, of course, if the lord Orme is afraid, which I did not think who have heard so much of his courage ——" and the rogue shrugged his shoulders and paused.

"Afraid, fellow," said Oliver, "well, I am not ashamed to be afraid of such a journey. Yet if there is need I will make it, though not before I see my brother alone yonder on the rock, since all this may be but a trick of yours to deliver me to the Fung, among whom I know that you have friends."

"It is madness; you shall not go," said Maqueda. "You will fall and be dashed to pieces. I say that you shall not go."

"Why should he not go, my niece?" interrupted Joshua. "Shadrach is right; we have heard much of the courage of this Gentile. Now let us see him do something."

She turned on the Prince like a tiger.

"Very good, my uncle, then you shall go with him. Surely one of the ancient blood of the Abati will not shrink from what a 'Gentile' dares."

On hearing this Joshua relapsed into silence, and I

have no clear memory of what he did or said in connection with the rest of that thrilling scene.

Now followed a pause in the midst of which Oliver sat down and began to take off his boots.

"Why do you undress yourself, friend?" asked Maqueda nervously.

"Because, Lady," he answered, "if I have to walk yonder road it is safer to do so in my stockings. Have no fear," he added gently, "from boyhood I have been accustomed to such feats, and when I served in my country's army, it was my pleasure to give instruction in them, although it is true that this one surpasses all that ever I attempted."

"Still I do fear," she said.

Meanwhile Quick had sat down and begun to take off *his* boots.

"What are you doing, Sergeant?" I asked.

"Getting ready to accompany the Captain upon forlorn hope, Doctor."

"Nonsense," I said, "you are too old for the game, Sergeant. If any one goes, I should, seeing that I believe my son is over there, but I can't try it, as I know my head would give out, and I should fall in a second, which would only upset everybody."

"Of course," broke in Oliver, who had overheard us, "I'm in command here, and my orders are that neither of you shall come. Remember, Sergeant, that if anything happens to me it is your business to take over the stores and use them if necessary, which you alone can do. Now go and see to the preparations, and find out the plan of campaign, for I want to rest and keep quiet. I daresay the whole thing is humbug, and we shall see nothing of the Professor; still, one may as well be prepared."

So Quick and I went to superintend the lashing of two of the light ladders together and the securing of some

planks which we had brought with us upon the top of
the rungs, so as to make these ladders easy to walk on.   I
asked who would be of the party besides Shadrach and
Orme, and was told no one, as all were afraid.
Ultimately, however, a man named Japhet, one of the
mountaineers, volunteered upon being promised a grant
of land from the Child of Kings herself, which grant she
proclaimed before them all was to be given to his relatives
in the event of his death.

At length everything was ready, and there came another
spell of silence, for the nerves of all of us were so strained
that we did not seem able to talk.   It was broken by a
sound of sudden and terrible roaring that arose from
the gulf beneath.

"It is the hour of the feeding of the sacred lions which
the Fung keep in the pit about the base of the idol,"
explained Shadrach.   Then he added, "Unless he should
be rescued, I believe that Black Windows will be given
to the lions to-night, which is that of full moon and a
festival of Harmac, though may be he will be kept till
next full moon when all the Fung come up to worship."

This information did not tend to raise any one's spirits,
although Quick, who always tried to be cheerful, remarked
that it was probably false.

The shadows began to gather in the Valley of Harmac,
whereby we knew that the sun was setting behind the
mountains.   Indeed, had it not been for a clear and
curious glow reflected from the eastern sky, the gulf would
have been plunged in gloom.   Presently, far away upon a
rise of rock which we knew must be the sphinx head of
the huge idol, a little figure appeared outlined against the
sky, and there began to sing.   The moment that I heard
the distant voice I went near to fainting, and indeed
should have fallen had not Quick caught me.

"What is it, Adams?" asked Oliver, looking up from

where he and Maqueda sat whispering to each other
while the fat Joshua glowered at them in the background,
"Has Higgs appeared?"

"No," I answered, "but, thank God, my son still lives.
That is his voice. Oh! if you can, save him too."

Now there was much suppressed excitement, and
some one thrust a pair of field-glasses into my hand, but
either they were wrongly set or the state of my nerves
would not allow me to see through them. So Quick
took them and reported.

"Tall, slim figure wearing a white robe, but at the
distance in this light can't make out the face. One might
hail him, perhaps, only it would give us away. Ah! the
hymn is done and he's gone; seemed to jump into a
hole in the rock, which shows that he's all right, anyway, or he couldn't jump. So cheer up, Doctor, for you
have much to be thankful for."

"Yes," I repeated after him, "much to be thankful
for, but oh! I would that I had more after all these years
of search. To think that I should be so close to him and
he know nothing of it."

After the ceasing of the song and the departure of my
son, there appeared upon the back of the idol three
Fung warriors, fine fellows clad in long robes and armed
with spears, and behind them a trumpeter who carried
a horn or hollowed elephant's tusk. These men marched
up and down the length of the platform from the rise of
the neck to the root of the tail, apparently to make an
inspection. Having found nothing, for, of course, they
could not see us hidden behind the bushes on our little
plateau, of which no doubt they did not even know the
existence, and much less that it was connected with the
mountain plain of Mur, the trumpeter blew a shrill blast
upon his horn, and before the echoes of it had died away,
vanished with his companions.

"Sunset tour of inspection. Seen the same kind of things at Gib," said the Sergeant. "Oh! by Jingo! Pussy is n't lying after all — there he is," and he pointed to a figure that rose suddenly out of the black stone of the idol's back just as the guards had done.

It was Higgs, Higgs without a doubt; Higgs wearing his battered sun-helmet and his dark spectacles, Higgs smoking his big meerschaum pipe, and engaged in making notes in a pocket-book as calmly as though he sat before a new object in the British Museum.

I gasped with astonishment, for somehow I had never expected that we should really see him, but Orme, rising very quietly from his seat beside Maqueda, only said:

"Yes, that's the old fellow right enough. Well, now for it. You, Shadrach, run out your ladder and cross first that I may be sure you play no trick."

"Nay," broke in Maqueda, "this dog shall not go, for never would he return from his friends the Fung. Man," she added, addressing Japhet, the mountaineer to whom she had promised land, "go you over first and hold the end of the ladder while this lord crosses. If he returns safe your reward is doubled."

Japhet saluted, the ladder was run out and its end set upon the roughnesses in the rock that represented the hair of the sphinx's tail. The mountaineer paused a moment with face and hands uplifted; evidently he was praying. Then bidding his companions hold the hither end of the ladder, and having first tested it with his foot and found that it hung firm, calmly he walked across, being a brave fellow, and presently was seen seated on the opposing mass of rock.

Now came Oliver's turn. He nodded to Maqueda, who went white as a sheet, muttering some words to her that did not reach me. Then he turned and shook my hand.

"If you can, save my son also," I whispered.

"I 'll do my best if I can get hold of him," he answered. "Sergeant, if anything happens to me you know your duty."

"I 'll try and follow your example, Captain, under all circumstances, though that will be hard," replied Quick in a rather shaky voice.

Oliver stepped out on to the ladder. I reckoned that twelve or fourteen short paces would take him across, and the first half of these he accomplished with quiet certainty. When he was in the exact middle of the passage, however, the end of one of the uprights of the ladder at the farther side slipped a little, notwithstanding the efforts of Japhet to keep it straight, with the result that the plank bound on the rungs lost its level, sinking an inch or so to the right, and nearly causing Oliver to fall from it into the gulf. He wavered like a wind-shaken reed, attempted to step forward, hesitated, stopped, and slowly sank on to his hands and knees.

"*Ah!*" panted Maqueda.

"The Gentile has lost his head," began Joshua in a voice full of the triumph that he could not hide. "He — will ——"

Joshua got no further, for Quick, turning, threatened him savagely with his fist, saying in English:

"Stow your jaw if you don't want to follow him, you swine," whereon Joshua, who understood the gesture, if not the words, relapsed into silence.

Now the mountaineer on the farther side spoke, saying: "Have no fear, the ladder is safe."

For a moment Oliver remained in his crouching posture on the board, which was all that separated him from an awful death in the gulf beneath. Next, while we watched, agonized, he rose to his feet again, and with perfect calmness walked across to its other end.

"Well done our side!" said Quick, addressing Joshua, "why don't your Royal Highness cheer? No, you leave that knife alone, or presently there 'll be a hog the less in this world," and stooping down he relieved the Prince of the weapon which he was fingering with his round eyes fixed upon the Sergeant.

Maqueda, who had noted all, now interfered.

"My uncle," she said, "brave men are risking their lives yonder while we sit in safety. Be silent and cease from quarrelling, I pray you."

Next moment we had forgotten all about Joshua, being utterly absorbed in watching the drama in progress upon the farther side of the gulf. After a slight pause to recover his nerve or breath, Orme rose, and preceded by Japhet, climbed up the bush-like rock till he reached the shaft of the sphinx's tail. Here he turned and waved his hand to us, then following the mountaineer, walked, apparently with the utmost confidence, along the curves of the tail to where it sprang from the body of the idol. At this spot there was a little difficulty in climbing over the smooth slope of rock on to the broad, terrace-like back. Soon, however, they surmounted it, and vanishing for a few seconds into the hollow of the loins, which, of course, was a good many feet deep, re-appeared moving toward the shoulders. Between these we could see Higgs standing with his back toward us, utterly unconscious of all that was passing behind him.

Passing Japhet, Oliver walked up to the Professor and touched him on the arm. Higgs turned, stared at the pair for a moment, and then, in his astonishment, or so we guessed, sat down plump upon the rock. They pulled him to his feet, Orme pointing to the cliff behind, and evidently explaining the situation and what must be done. Then followed a short and animated talk. Through the glasses we could even see Higgs shaking his head. He

told them something, they came to a determination, for
now he turned, stepped forward a pace or two, and vanished, as I learned afterward, to fetch my son, without
whom he would not try to escape.

A while went by; it seemed an age, but really was under
a minute. We heard the sound of shouts. Higgs's white
helmet reappeared, and then his body, with two Fung
guards clinging on to him. He yelled out in English and
the words reached us faintly:

"Save yourself! I'll hold these devils. Run, you
infernal fool, run!"

Oliver hesitated, although the mountaineer was pulling
at him, till the heads of more Fung appeared. Then,
with a gesture of despair, he turned and fled. First ran
Oliver, then Japhet, whom he had outpaced, and after
them came a number of priests or guards, waving knives,
while in the background Higgs rolled on the rock with
his captors.

The rest was very short. Orme slid down the rump
of the idol on to the tail, followed by the mountaineer, and
after them in single file came three Fung, who apparently
thought no more of the perilous nature of their foothold
than do the sheiks of the Egyptian pyramids when they
swarm about those monuments like lizards. Nor, for
the matter of that, did Oliver or Japhet, who doubled
down the tail as though it were a racetrack. Oliver
swung himself on to the ladder, and in a second was
half across it, we holding its other end, when suddenly
he heard his companion cry out. A Fung had got hold
of Japhet by the leg and he lay face downward on
the board.

Oliver halted and slowly turned round, drawing his
revolver as he did so. Then he aimed and fired, and the
Fung, leaving go of Japhet's leg, threw up his arms and
plunged headlong into the gulf beneath. The next thing

I remember is that they were both among us, and somebody shouted, "Pull in the ladder."

"No," said Quick, "wait a bit."

Vaguely I wondered why, till I perceived that three of
those courageous Fung were following across it, resting
their hands upon each other's shoulders, while their companions cheered them.

"Now pull, brothers, pull!" shouted the Sergeant, and
pull we did. Poor Fung! they deserved a better fate.

"Always inflict loss upon the enemy when you get
a chance," remarked the Sergeant, as he opened fire
with his repeating rifle upon other Fung who by now
were clustering upon the back of the idol. This
position, however, they soon abandoned as untenable,
except one or two of them who remained there, dead
or wounded.

A silence followed, in the midst of which I heard Quick
saying to Joshua in his very worst Arabic:

"Now does your Royal Highness think that we Gentiles
are cowards, although it is true those Fung are as good
men as we any day?"

Joshua declined argument, and I turned to watch
Oliver, who had covered his face with his hands, and
seemed to be weeping.

"What is it, O friend, what is it?" I heard Maqueda
say in her gentle voice — a voice full of tears, tears of
gratitude I think. "You have done a great deed; you
have returned safe; all is well."

"Nay," he answered, forgetting her titles in his distress,
"all is ill. I have failed, and to-night they throw my
brother to the lions. He told me so."

Maqueda, finding no answer, stretched out her hand
to the mountaineer, his companion in adventure, who
kissed it.

"Japhet," she said, "I am proud of you; your reward

is fourfold, and henceforth you are a captain of my Mountaineers."

"Tell us what happened," I said to Oliver.

"This," he answered: "I remembered about your son, and so did Higgs. In fact, he spoke of him first — they seem to have become friends. He said he would not escape without him, and could fetch him in a moment, as he was only just below. Well, he went to do so, and must have found the guard instead, who, I suppose, had heard us talking. You know as much about the rest as I do. To-night, when the full moon is two hours high, there is to be a ceremony of sacrifice, and poor Higgs will be let down into the den of lions. He was writing his will in a note-book when we saw him, as Barung had promised to send it to us."

"Doctor," said the Sergeant, in a confidential voice, when he had digested this information, "would you translate for me a bit, as I want to have a talk with Cat there, and my Arabic don't run to it?"

I nodded, and we went to that corner of the plateau where Shadrach stood apart, watching and listening.

"Now, Cat," said the Sergeant (I give his remarks in his own language, leaving out my rendering), "just listen to me, and understand that if you tell lies or play games, either you or I don't reach the top of this cliff again alive. Do you catch on?"

Shadrach replied that he caught on.

"Very well. You've told us that once you were a prisoner among the Fung and thrown to these holy lions, but got out. Now just explain what happened."

"This, O Quick. After ceremonies that do not matter, I was let down in the food basket into the feeding den, and thrown out of the basket like any other meat. Then the gates were lifted up by the chains, and the lions came in to devour me according to their custom."

"And what happened next, Shadrach?"

"What happened? Why, of course I hid myself in the shadow as much as possible, right against the walls of the precipice, until a satan of a she-lion snuffled me out and gave a stroke at me. Look, here are the marks of her claws," and he pointed to the scars upon his face. "Those claws stung like scorpions; they made me mad. The terror which I had lost when I saw their yellow eyes came back to me. I rushed at the precipice as a cat that is hunted by a dog rushes at a wall. I clung to its smooth side with my nails, with my toes, with my teeth. A lion leaped up and tore the flesh of my leg, here, here," and he showed the marks, which we could scarcely see in that dim light. "He ran back for another spring. Above me I saw a tiny ledge, big enough for a hawk to sit on — no more. I jumped, I caught it, drawing up my legs so that the lion missed me. I made the effort a man makes once in his life. Somehow I dragged myself to that ledge; I rested one thigh upon it and pressed against the rock to steady myself. Then the rock gave, and I tumbled backward into the bottom of a tunnel. Afterward I escaped to the top of the cliff in the dark, O God of Israel! in the dark, smelling my way, climbing like a baboon, risking death a thousand times. It took me two whole days and nights, and the last of those nights I knew not what I did. Yet I found my way, and that is why my people name me Cat."

"I understand," said Quick in a new and more respectful voice, "and however big a rascal you may be, you've got pluck. Now say, remembering what I told you," and he tapped the handle of his revolver, "is that feeding den where it used to be?"

"I believe so, O Quick; why should it be changed? The victims are let down from the belly of the god, just there between his thighs where are doors. The feeding place lies in a hollow of the cliff; this platform on which we stand is over it.   None saw my escape, therefore none searched for the means of it, since they thought that the lions had devoured me, as they have devoured thousands. No one enters there, only when the beasts have fed full they draw back to their sleeping dens, and those who watch above let down the bars.   Listen," and as he spoke we heard a crash and a rattle far below. "They fall now, the lions having eaten.   When Black Windows and perhaps others are thrown to them bye-and-bye, they will be drawn up again."

"Is that hole in the rock still there, Shadrach?"

"Without doubt, though I have not been down to look."

"Then, my boy, you are going now," remarked Quick grimly.

CHAPTER XII

THE DEN OF LIONS

WE RETURNED to the others and told them everything that we had learned from Shadrach. "What's your plan, Sergeant?" asked Oliver when he had heard. "Tell me, for I have none; my head is muddled."

"This, Captain, for what it is worth; that I should go down through the hole that Cat here speaks of, and get into the den. Then when they let down the Professor, if they do, and pull up the gates, that I should keep back the lions with my rifle while he bolts to the ladder which is ready for him, and I follow if I can."

"Capital," said Orme, "but you can't go alone. I'll come too."

"And I also," I said.

"What schemes do you make?" asked Maqueda eagerly, for, of course, she could not understand our talk. We explained.

"What, my friend," she said to Oliver reproachfully, "would you risk your life again to-night? Surely it is tempting the goodness of God."

"It would be tempting the goodness of God if I left my friend to be eaten by lions, Lady," he answered.

Then followed much discussion. In the end it was agreed that we should descend to the level of the den, if this were possible; that Oliver and Quick should go down into the den with Japhet, who instantly volunteered to accompany them, and that I, with some of the mountaineers, should stop in the mouth of the hole as a reserve to cover their retreat from the lions. I pleaded to be allowed to take a more active part, but of this they would not hear, saying with some truth, that I was by far the best shot of the three, and could do much more to help them from above, if, as was hoped, the moon should shine brightly.

But I knew they really meant that I was too old to be of service in such an adventure as this. Also they desired to keep me out of risk.

Then came the question as to who should descend the last tunnel to the place of operations. Oliver wished Maqueda to return to the top of the cliff and wait there, but she said at once that she could not think of attempting the ascent without our aid; also that she was determined to see the end of the matter. Even Joshua would not go, I think that being an unpopular character among them, he distrusted the mountaineers, whose duty it would have been to escort him.

It was suggested that he should remain where he was until we returned, if we did return, but this idea commended itself to him still less than the other. Indeed he pointed out with much truth what we had overlooked, namely, that now the Fung knew of the passage and were quite capable of playing our own game, that is, of throwing a bridge across from the sphinx's tail and attempting the storm of Mur.

"And then what should I do if they found me here alone?" he added pathetically.

Maqueda answered that she was sure she did not know, but that meanwhile it might be wise to block the mouth of the tunnel by which we had reached the plateau in such a fashion that it could not easily be forced.

"Yes," answered Oliver, "and if we ever get out of

this, to blow the shaft in and make sure that it cannot be used."

"That shaft might be useful, Captain," said Quick doubtfully.

"There is a better way, Sergeant, if we want to mine under the sphinx; I mean through the Tomb of Kings. I took the levels roughly, and the end of it can't be far off. Anyhow this shaft is of no more use to us now the Fung have found it out."

Then we set to work to fill in the mouth of the passage with such loose stones as we could find. It was a difficult business, but in the end the mountaineers made a very fair job of it under our direction, piling the rocks in such a fashion that they could scarcely be cleared away in any short time without the aid of explosives.

While this work was going on, Japhet, Shadrach, and the Sergeant in charge of him, undertook to explore the last shaft which led down to the level of the den. To our relief, just as we had finished building up the hole, they returned with the news that now after they had removed a fallen stone or two it was quite practicable with the aid of ropes and ladders.

So, in the same order as before, we commenced its passage, and in about half an hour, for it was under three hundred feet in depth, arrived safely at the foot. Here we found a bat-haunted place like a room that evidently had been hollowed out by man. As Shadrach had said, at its eastern extremity was a large, oblong boulder, so balanced that if even one person pushed on either of its ends it swung around, leaving on each side a passage large enough to allow a man to walk through in a crouching attitude.

Very silently we propped open this primeval door and looked out. Now the full moon was up, and her brilliant light had begun to flood the gulf. By it we saw a dense shadow, that reached from the ground to three hundred feet or so above us. This we knew to be that thrown by the flanks of the gigantic sphinx which projected beyond the mountain of stone whereon it rested, those flanks whence, according to Shadrach, Higgs would be lowered in the food basket. In this shadow and on either side of it, covering a space of quite a hundred yards square, lay the feeding den whence arose a sickly and horrible odour such as is common to any place frequented by cats, mingled with the more pungent smell of decaying flesh.

This darksome den was surrounded on three sides by precipices, and on the fourth, that toward the east, enclosed by a wall or barrier of rock pierced with several gates made of bars of metal, or so we judged by the light that flowed through them.

From beyond this eastern wall came dreadful sounds of roars, snarls, and whimperings. Evidently there the sacred lions had their home.

Only one more thing need be mentioned. On the rock floor almost immediately beneath us lay remains which, from their torn clothes and hair, we knew must be human. As somebody explained, I think it was Shadrach, they were those of the man whom Orme had shot upon the tail of the sphinx, and of his companions who had been tilted off the ladder.

For a while we gazed at this horrible hole in silence. Then Oliver took out his watch, which was a repeater, and struck it.

"Higgs told me," he said, "that he was to be thrown to the lions two hours after moonrise, which is within fifteen minutes or so. Sergeant, I think we had better be getting ready."

"Yes, Captain," answered Quick; "but everything

is quite ready, including those brutes, to judge by the noise they make, excepting perhaps Samuel Quick, who never felt less ready for anything in his life. Now then, Pussy, run out that ladder. Here's your rifle, Captain, and six reload clips of cartridges, five hollow-nosed bullets in each. You'll never want more than that, and it's no use carrying extra weight. In your right-hand pocket, Captain, don't forget. I've the same in mine. Doctor, here's a pile for you; laid upon that stone. If you lie there, you'll have a good light and rest for your elbow, and at this range ought to make very pretty shooting, even in the moonlight. Best keep your pistol on the safe, Captain; at least, I'm doing so, as we might get a fall, and these new-fangled weapons are very hair-triggered. Here's Japhet ready, too, so give us your marching orders, sir, and we will go to business; the Doctor will translate to Japhet."

"We descend the ladder," said Orme, "and advance about fifty paces into the shadow, where we can see without being seen; where also, according to Shadrach, the food basket is let down. There we shall stand and await the arrival of this basket. If it contains the Professor, he whom the Fung and the Abati know as Black Windows, Japhet, you are to seize him and lead, or if necessary carry him to the ladder, up which some of the mountaineers must be ready to help him. Your duty, Sergeant, and mine, also that of the Doctor firing from above, will be to keep off the lions as best we can, should any lions appear, retreating as we fire. If the brutes get one of us he must be left, since it is foolish that both lives should be sacrificed needlessly. For the rest, you, Sergeant, and you, Japhet, must be guided by circumstances and act upon your own discretion. Do not wait for special orders from me which I may not be able to give. Now come on. If we do not return, Adams, you

will see the Child of Kings safely up the shafts and conduct her to Mur. Good-bye, Lady."

"Good-bye," answered Maqueda in a brave voice;
I could not see her face in that darkness. "Presently,
I am sure, you will return with your brother."

Just then Joshua broke in.

"I will not be outdone in courage by these Gentiles,"
he said. "Lacking their terrible weapons I cannot advance into the den, but I will descend and guard the foot
of the ladder."

"Very well, sir," answered Orme in an astonished
voice, "glad to have your company, I am sure. Only
remember that you must be quick in going up it again,
since hungry lions are active, and let all take notice
that we are not responsible for anything that may happen
to you."

"Surely you had better stop where you are, my uncle,"
remarked Maqueda.

"To be mocked by you forever after, my niece?"
No, I go to face the lions," and very slowly he crept
through the hole and began to descend the ladder.
Indeed, when Quick followed after an interval he
found him only half-way down, and had to hurry his
movements by accidentally treading on his fingers.

A minute or two later, peeping over the edge, I saw
that they were all in the den, that is, except Joshua, who
had reascended the ladder to the height of about six
feet, and stood on it face outward, holding to the rock
on either side with his hands as though he had been
crucified. Fearing lest he should be seen there, even
in the shadow, I suggested to Maqueda that she should
order him either to go down or to return, which she did
vigorously, but without effect. So in the end we left
him alone.

Meanwhile the three had vanished into the shadow

of the sphinx, and we could see nothing of them. The great round moon rose higher and higher, flooding the rest of the charnel-house with light, and, save for an occasional roar or whimper from the lions beyond the wall, the silence was intense. Now I could make out the metal gates in this wall, and even dark and stealthy forms which passed and repassed beyond their bars. Then I made out something else also; the figures of men gathering on the top of the wall, though whence they came I knew not. By degrees their number increased till there were hundreds of them, for the wall was broad as a roadway.

Evidently these were spectators, come to witness the ceremony of sacrifice.

"Prince," I whispered to Joshua, "you must get down off the ladder or you will betray us all. Nay, it is too late to come up here again, for already the moonlight strikes just above your head. Go down, or we will cast the ladder loose and let you fall."

So he went down and hid himself among some ferns and bushes where we saw no more of him for a while, and, to tell the truth, forgot his existence.

Far, far above us, from the back of the idol I suppose, came a faint sound of solemn chanting. It sank, and we heard shouts. Then suddenly, it swelled again. Now Maqueda, who knelt near me, touched my arm and pointed to the shadow which gradually was becoming infiltrated with the moonlight flowing into it from either side. I looked, and high in the air, perhaps two hundred feet from the ground, saw something dark descending slowly. Doubtless it was the basket containing Higgs, and whether by coincidence or no, at this moment the lions on the farther side of the wall burst into peal upon peal of terrific roaring. Perhaps their sentries watching at the gates saw or smelt the familiar basket, and communicated the intelligence to their fellows.

Slowly, slowly it descended till it was within a few feet of the ground, when it began to sway backward and forward like a pendulum, at each swing covering a wider arc. Presently, when it hung over the edge of the shadow that was nearest to us it was let down with a run and overset, and out of it, looking very small in those vast surroundings and that mysterious light, rolled the figure of a man. Although at that distance we could see little of him, accident assured us of his identity, for as he rolled the hat he wore fell from him, and I knew it at once for Higgs's sun-helmet. He rose from the ground, limped very slowly and painfully after the helmet, picked it up, and proceeded to use it to dust his knees. At this moment there was a clanking sound.

"Oh! they lift the gates!" murmured Maqueda.

Then followed more sounds, this time of wild beasts raging for their prey, and of other human beasts shrieking with excitement on the wall above. The Professor turned and saw. For a moment he seemed about to run, then changed his mind, clapped the helmet on his head, folded his arms and stood still, reminding me in some curious way, perhaps, because of the shortness of his thick figure, of a picture I had seen of the great Napoleon contemplating disaster.

To describe what followed is extremely difficult, for we watched not one but several simultaneous scenes. For instance, there were the lions, which did not behave as might have been expected. I thought that they would rush through the doors and bound upon the victim, but whether it was because they had already been fed that afternoon or because they thought that a single human being was not worth the trouble, they acted differently.

Through the opened gates they came in two indolent yellow lines, male lions, female lions, half-grown lions, cub lions that cuffed each other in play, in all perhaps fifty or sixty of them. Of these only two or three looked toward the Professor, for none of them ran or galloped, while the rest spread all over the den, some of them vanishing into the shadow at the edge of the surrounding cliff where the moonlight could not reach.

Here one of them, at any rate, must have travelled fast enough, for it seemed only a few seconds later that we heard a terrific yell beneath us, and craning over the rock I saw the prince Joshua running up the ladder more swiftly than ever did any London lamplighter when I was a boy.

But quickly as he came, the long, thin, sinuous thing beneath came quicker. It reared itself on its hind legs, it stretched up a great paw — I can see the gleaming claws in it now — and struck or hooked at poor Joshua. The paw caught him in the small of the back, and seemed to pin him against the ladder. Then it was drawn slowly downward, and heaven! how Joshua howled. Up came the other paw to repeat the operation, when, stretching myself outward and downward, with an Abati holding me by the ankles, I managed to shoot the beast through the head so that it fell all of a heap, taking with it a large portion of Joshua's nether garments.

A few seconds later he was among us, and tumbled groaning into a corner where he lay in charge of some of the mountaineers, for I had no time to attend to him just then.

When the smoke cleared at length, I saw that Japhet had reached Higgs, and was gesticulating to him to run, while two lions, a male and a female, stood at a little distance regarding the pair in an interested fashion.

Higgs, after some brief words of explanation, pointed to his knee. Evidently he was lamed and could not run. Japhet, rising to the occasion, pointed to his back, and bent down. Higgs flung himself upon it, and was hitched up like a sack of flour. The pair began to advance toward the ladder, Japhet carrying Higgs as one schoolboy carries another.

The lion sat down like a great dog, watching this strange proceeding with mild interest, but the lioness, filled with feminine curiosity, followed sniffing at Higgs, who looked over his shoulder. Taking off his battered helmet, he threw it at the beast, hitting her on the head. She growled, then seized the helmet, played with it for a moment as a kitten does with a ball of wool, and next instant, finding it unsatisfying, uttered a short and savage roar, ran forward, and crouched to spring, lashing her tail. I could not fire, because a bullet that would hit her must first pass through Japhet and Higgs.

But, just when I thought that the end had come, a rifle went off in the shadow and she rolled over, kicking and biting the rock. Thereon the indolent male lion seemed to awake, and sprang, not at the men, but at the wounded lioness, and a hellish fight ensued, of which the details and end were lost in a mist of dust and flying hair.

The crowd upon the wall, becoming alive to the real situation, began to scream in indignant excitement which quickly communicated itself to the less savage beasts. These set up a terrible roaring, and ran about, keeping for the most part to the shadows, while Japhet and his burden made slow but steady progress toward the ladder.

Then from the gloom beneath the hindquarters of the sphinx rose a sound of rapid firing, and presently Orme and Quick emerged into the moonlight, followed by a

number of angry lions that advanced in short rushes.
Evidently the pair had kept their heads, and were acting
on a plan.

One of them emptied his rifle at the pursuing beasts,
while the other ran back a few paces, thrusting in a
fresh clip of cartridges as he went. Then he began
to fire, and his companion in turn retreated behind him.
In this way they knocked over a number of lions, for
the range was too short for them to miss often, and the
expanding bullets did their work very well, paralyzing
even when they did not kill. I also opened fire over
their heads, and, although in that uncertain light the
majority of my shots did no damage, the others disposed
of several animals which I saw were becoming dangerous.

So things went on until all four, that is, Japhet with
Higgs upon his back, and Orme and Quick, were within
twenty paces of the ladder, although separated from
each other by perhaps half the length of a cricket pitch.
We thought that they were safe, and shouted in our joy,
while the hundreds of spectators on the wall who fortunately dared not descend into the den because of the
lions, which are undiscriminating beasts, yelled with
rage at the imminent rescue of the sacrifice.

Then of a sudden the position changed. From every
quarter fresh lions seemed to arrive, ringing the men
round and clearly bent on slaughter, although the shouting and the sound of firearms, which they had never
heard before, frightened and made them cautious.

A half-grown cub rushed in and knocked over Japhet
and Higgs. I fired and hit it in the flank. It bit savagely at its wound, then sprang on to the prostrate pair,
and stood over them growling, but in such pain that it
forgot to kill them. The ring of beasts closed in — we
could see their yellow eyes glowing in the gloom. Orme
and Quick might have got through by the help of their

rifles, but they could not leave the others. The dreadful climax seemed at hand.

"Follow me," said Maqueda, who all this while had watched panting at my side, and rose to run to the ladder. I thrust her back.

"Nay," I shouted. "Follow me, Abati! Shall a woman lead you?"

Of how I descended that ladder I have no recollection, nor do I in the least know how the mountaineers came after me, but I think that the most of them rolled and scrambled down the thirty feet of rock. At least, to their honour be it said, they did come, yelling like demons and waving long knives in their hands.

The effect of our sudden arrival from above was extraordinary. Scared by the rush and the noise, the lions gave way, then bolted in every direction, the wounded cub, which could not, or would not move, being stabbed to death where it stood over Higgs and Japhet.

Five minutes more and all of us were safe in the mouth of the tunnel.

That was how we rescued Higgs from the den of sacred lions that guarded the idol of the Fung.

CHAPTER XIII

THE ADVENTURES OF HIGGS

A MORE weary and dishevelled set of people than that which about the hour of dawn finally emerged from the mouth of the ancient shaft on to the cliffs of Mur, it has seldom been my lot to behold. Yet with a single exception the party was a happy one, for we had come triumphant through great dangers, and actually effected our object — the rescue of Higgs, which, under the circumstances most people would have thought impossible. Yes, there he was in the flesh before us, having injured his knee and lost his hat, but otherwise quite sound save for a few trifling scratches inflicted by the cub, and still wearing what the natives called his "black windows."

Even the prince Joshua was happy, though wrapped in a piece of coarse sacking because the lion had taken most of his posterior clothing, and terribly sore from the deep cuts left by the claws.

Had he not dared the dangers of the den, and thus proved himself a hero whose fame would last for generations? Had I not assured him that his honourable wounds, though painful (as a matter of fact, after they had set, they kept him stiff as a mummy for some days, so that unless he stood upon his feet, he had to be carried, or lie rigid on his face) would probably not prove fatal? And had he not actually survived to reach the upper air again which was more than he ever expected to do? No wonder that he was happy.

I alone could not share in the general joy, since, although my friend was restored to me, my son still remained a prisoner among the Fung. Yet even in this matter things might have been worse, since I learned that he was well treated, and in no danger, But of that I will write presently.

Never shall I forget the scene after the arrival of Higgs in our hole, when the swinging boulder had been closed and made secure and the lamps lighted. There he sat on the floor, his red hair glowing like a torch, his clothes torn and bloody, his beard ragged and stretching in a Newgate frill to his ears. Indeed, his whole appearance, accentuated by the blue spectacles with wire gauze side-pieces, was more disreputable than words can tell; moreover, he smelt horribly of lion. He put his hand into his pocket, and produced his big pipe, which had remained unbroken in its case.

"Some tobacco, please," he said. (Those were his first words to us!) "I have finished mine, saved up the last to smoke just before they put me into that stinking basket."

I gave him some, and as he lit his pipe the light of the match fell upon the face of Maqueda, who was staring at him with amused astonishment.

"What an uncommonly pretty woman," he said. "What's she doing down here, and who is she?"

I told him, whereon he rose, or rather tried to, felt for his hat, which, of course, had gone, with the idea of taking it off, and instantly addressed her in his beautiful and fluent Arabic, saying how glad he was to have this unexpected honour, and so forth.

She congratulated him on his escape, whereon his face grew serious.

"Yes, a nasty business," he said, "as yet I can hardly remember whether my name is Daniel, or Ptolemy

Higgs." Then he turned to us and added, "Look here, you fellows, if I don't thank you it isn't because I am not grateful, but because I can't. The truth is, I'm a bit dazed. Your son is all right, Adams; he's a good fellow, and we grew great friends. Safe? Oh! yes, he's safe as a church! Old Barung, he's the Sultan, and another good fellow, although he did throw me to the lions—because the priests made him—is very fond of him, and is going to marry him to his daughter."

At that moment the men announced that everything was ready for our ascent, and when I had attended to Joshua with a heart made thankful by Higgs's news, we began that toilsome business, and, as I have already said, at length accomplished it safely. But even then our labours were not ended, since it was necessary to fill up the mouth of the shaft so as to make it impossible for it to be used by the Fung who now knew of its existence.

Nor was this a business that could be delayed, for as we passed the plateau whence Oliver and Japhet had crossed to the sphinx, we heard the voices of men on the farther side of the rough wall that we had built there. Evidently the priests, or idol guards, infuriated by the rescue of their victim, had already managed to bridge the gulf and were contemplating assault, a knowledge which caused us to hurry our movements considerably. If they had got through before we passed them, our fate would have been terrible, since at the best we must have slowly starved in the pit below.

Indeed, as soon as we reached the top and had blocked it temporarily, Quick, weary as he was, was sent off on horseback, accompanied by Maqueda, Shadrach, now under the terms of his contract once more a free man, and two mountaineers, to gallop to the palace of Mur, and fetch a supply of explosives. The rest of us, 'or Higgs declined to leave, and we had no means of carrying Joshua, remained watching the place, or rather, the Abati watched while we slept with our rifles in our hands. Before noon Quick returned, accompanied by many men with litters and all things needful.

Then we pulled out the stones, and Oliver, Japhet, and some others descended to the first level and arranged blasting charges. A while after he reappeared with his companions, looking somewhat pale and anxious, and shouted to us to get back. Following our retreat to a certain distance, unwinding a wire as he came, presently he stopped and pressed the button of a battery which he held in his hand. There was a muffled explosion and a tremor of the soil like to that of an earthquake, while from the mouth of the shaft stones leapt into the air.

It was over, and all that could be noted was a sinkage in the ground where the ancient pit had been.

"I am sorry for them," said Oliver presently, "but it had to be done."

"Sorry for whom?" I asked.

"For those Fung priests, or soldiers. The levels below are full of them, dead or alive. They were pouring up at our heels. Well, no one will travel that road again."

Later, in the guest-house at Mur, Higgs told us his story. After his betrayal by Shadrach, which, it appeared, was meant to include us all, for the Professor overheard the hurried talk between him and a Fung captain, he was seized and imprisoned in the body of the great sphinx, where many chambers and dungeons had been hollowed out by the primeval race that fashioned it. Here Barung the Sultan visited him and informed him of his meeting with the rest of us, to whom apparently he had taken a great liking, and also that we had refused to purchase a chance of his release at the price of being false to our trust.

"You know," said Higgs, "that when first I heard this, I was very angry with you, and thought you a set of beasts. But on considering things I saw the other side of it, and that you were right, although I never could come to fancy the idea of being sacrificed to a sphinx by being chucked like a piece of horse-flesh to a lot of holy lions. However, Barung, an excellent fellow in his way, assured me that there was no road out of the matter without giving grave offence to the priests, who are very powerful among the Fung, and bringing a fearful curse on the nation.

"Meanwhile, he made me as comfortable as he could. For instance, I was allowed to walk upon the back of the idol, to associate with the priests, a suspicious and most exclusive set, and to study their entire religious system, from which I have no doubt that of Egypt was derived. Indeed, I have made a great discovery which, if ever we get out of this, will carry my name down to all generations. The forefathers of these Fung were undoubtedly also the forefathers of the pre-dynastic Egyptians, as is shown by the similarity of their customs and spiritual theories. Further, intercourse was kept up between the Fung, who then had their headquarters here in Mur, and the Egyptians in the time of the ancient empire, till the Twentieth Dynasty, indeed if not later. My friends, in the dungeons in which I was confined there is an inscription, or, rather, a *graffite*, made by a prisoner extradited to Mur by Rameses II., after twenty years' residence in Egypt, which was written by him on the night before he was thrown to the sacred lions that even in those days were an established institution. And I have got a copy of that inscription in my pocket-book. I tell you," he added in a scream of triumph, "I've got a certified copy of that inscription, thanks to Shadrach, on whose dirty head be blessings!"

I congratulated him heartily upon this triumph, and before he proceeded to give us further archæological details, asked him for some information about my boy.

"Oh," said Higgs, "he is a very nice young man, and extremely good-looking. Indeed, I am quite proud to have such a godson. He was much interested to hear that you were hunting for him after so many years, quite touched indeed. He still talks English, though with a Fung accent, and, of course, would like to escape. Meanwhile, he is having a very good time, being chief singer to the god, for his voice is really beautiful, an office which carries with it all sorts of privileges. I told you, didn't I, that he is to be married to Barung's only legitimate daughter on the night of the next full moon but one. The ceremony is to take place in Harmac City, and will be the greatest of its sort for generations, a feast of the entire people in short. I should very much like to be present at it, but being an intelligent young man he has promised to keep notes of everything, which I hope may become available in due course."

"And is he attached to this savage lady?" I asked, dismayed.

"Attached? Oh, dear no, I think he said he had never seen her, and only knew that she was rather plain and reported to possess a haughty temper. He is a philosophical young man, however, as might be expected from one who has undergone so many vicissitudes, and, therefore, takes things as they come, thanking heaven that they are no worse. You see, as the husband of the Sultan's daughter, unless the pair quarrel very violently, he will be safe from the lions, and he could never quite say as much before. But we didn't go into these domestic matters very deeply as there were so many more important things to interest us both. He wanted to know all about you and our plans, and naturally I wanted to know all about the Fung and the ritual and traditions connected with the worship of Harmac, so that we were never dull for a single moment. In fact, I wish that we could have had longer together, for we became excellent friends. But whatever happens, I think that I have collected the cream of his information," and he tapped a fat note-book in his hands, adding:

"What an awful thing it would have been if a lion had eaten this. For myself it did not matter; there may be many better Egyptologists, but I doubt if any one of them will again have such opportunities of original research. However, I took every possible precaution to save my notes by leaving a copy of the most important of them written with native ink upon sheepskin in charge of your son. Indeed, I meant to leave the originals also, but fortunately forgot in the excitement of my very hurried departure."

I agreed with him that his chances had been unique and that he was a very lucky archæologist, and presently he went on, puffing at his pipe.

"Of course, when Oliver turned up in that unexpected fashion on the back of the idol, remembering your wishes and natural desire to recover your son, I did my best to rescue him also. But he was n't in the room beneath, where I thought I should find him. The priests were there instead, and they had heard us talking above, and you know the rest. Well, as it happens, it didn't matter, though that descent into the den of lions — there were two or three hundred feet of it, and the rope seemed worn uncommonly thin with use — was a trying business to the nerves."

"What did you think about all the time?" asked Oliver curiously.

"Think about? I didn't think much, was in too great a fright. I just wondered whether St. Paul had the same sensations when he was let down in a basket; wondered what the early Christian martyrs felt like in the arena; wondered whether Barung, with whom my parting was quite affectionate, would come in the morning and look for me as Darius did for Daniel; and how much he would find if he did; hoped that my specs would give one of those brutes appendicitis, and so forth. My word, it was sickening, especially that kind of school-treat swing and bump at the end. I never could bear swinging. Still, it was all for the best, as I should n't have gone a yard along that sphinx's tail without tumbling off, tight-rope walking not being in my line; and I'll tell you what, you are just the best three fellows in the whole world. Don't you think I forget that because I have n't said much. And now let's have your yarn, for I want to hear how things stand, which I never expected to do this side of Judgment-day."

So we told him all, while he listened open-mouthed. When we came to the description of the Tomb of the Kings his excitement could scarcely be restrained.

"You haven't touched them," he almost screamed; "don't say you have been vandals enough to touch them, for every article must be catalogued *in situ*, and drawings must be made. If possible, specimen groups with their surrounding offerings should be moved so that they can be set up again in museums. Why, there's six months' work before me, at least. And to think that if it had n't been for you, by now I should be in process of digestion by a lion, a stinking, mangy, sacred lion!"

Next morning I was woke up by Higgs limping into my room in some weird sleeping-suit that he had contrived with the help of Quick.

"I say, old fellow," he said, "tell me some more

about that girl, Walda Nagasta. What a sweet face she's got, and what pluck! Of course, such things ain't in my line, never looked at a woman these twenty years past hard enough to remember her next morning, but, by Jingo! the eyes of that one made me feel quite queer here," and he hit the sleeping-suit somewhere in the middle, "though perhaps it was only because she was such a contrast to the lions."

"Ptolemy," I answered in a solemn voice, "let me tell you that she is more dangerous to meddle with than any lion, and what's more, if you don't want to further complicate matters with a flaming row, you had better keep to your old habits and leave her eyes alone. I mean that Oliver is in love with her."

"Of course he is. I never expected anything else, but what's that got to do with it? Why shouldn't I be in love with her, too? Though I admit," he added sadly, contemplating his rotund form, "the chances are in his favour, especially as he's got the start."

"They are, Ptolemy, for she's in love with him," and I told him what we had seen in the Tombs of Kings.

First he roared with laughter, then on second thoughts grew exceedingly indignant.

"I call it scandalous of Oliver, compromising us all in this way — the lucky dog! These selfish, amorous adventures will let us in for no end of trouble. It is even probable, Adams, that you and I may come to a miserable end, solely because of this young man's erotic tendencies. Just fancy neglecting business in order to run after a pretty, round-faced Jewess, that is if she *is* a Jewess, which I doubt, as the blood must have got considerably mixed by now, and the first Queen of Sheba, if she ever existed, was an Ethiopian. As a friend almost old enough to be his father, I shall speak to him very seriously."

"All right," I called after him as he hobbled off to take his bath, "only if you are wise, you won't speak to Maqueda, for she might misinterpret your motives if you go on staring at her as you did yesterday."

That morning I was summoned to see the prince Joshua and dress his wounds, which, although not of a serious nature, were very painful. The moment that I entered the man's presence I noticed a change in his face. Like the rest of us I had always set this fellow down as a mere poltroon and windbag, a blower of his own trumpet, as Oliver had called him. Now I got an insight into his real nature which showed me that although he might be these things and worse, he was also a very determined and dangerous person, animated by ambitions which he meant to satisfy at all hazards.

When I had done what I could for him and told him that in my opinion he had no ill results to fear from his hurts, since the thick clothes he was wearing at the time had probably cleaned the lion's paws of any poison that might have been on them, he said,

"Physician, I desire private words with you."

I bowed, and he went on:

"The Child of Kings, hereditary ruler of this land, somewhat against the advice of her Council, has thought fit to employ you and your Gentile companions in order that by your skill and certain arts of which you are masters, you may damage its ancient enemies, the Fung, and in reward has promised to pay you well should you succeed in your endeavours. Now, I wish you to understand that though you think yourselves great men, and may for aught I know be great in your own country, here you are but servants like any other mercenaries whom it may please us to hire."

His tone was so offensive that though it might have been wiser to keep silent, I could not help interrupting him.

"You use harsh words, Prince," I said; "let me then explain what is the real pay for which we work and undergo some risks. Mine is the hope of recovering a son who is the slave of your enemies. That of the Captain Orme is the quest of adventure and war, since being a rich man in his own country he needs no further wealth. That of him whom you call Black Windows, but whose name is Higgs, is the pure love of learning. In England and throughout the West he is noted for his knowledge of dead peoples, their languages, and customs, and it is to study these that he has undertaken so terrible a journey. As for Quick, he is Orme's man, who has known him from childhood, an old soldier who has served with him in war and comes hither to be with the master whom he loves."

"Ah!" said Joshua, " a servant, a person of no degree, who yet dares to threaten me, the premier prince of the Abati, to my face."

"In the presence of death all men are equal, Prince. You acted in a fashion that might have brought his lord, who was daring a desperate deed, to a hideous doom."

"And what do I care about his lord's desperate deeds, Physician? I see that you set store by such things, and think those who accomplish them great and wonderful. Well, we do not. There is no savage among the barbarous Fung who would not do all that your Orme does, and more, just because he is a savage. We who are civilized, we who are cultivated, we who are wise, know better. Our lives were given us to enjoy, not to throw away or to lose at the sword's point, and, therefore, no doubt, you would call us cowards."

"Yet, Prince, those who bear that title of coward which

you hold one of honour, are apt to perish 'at the sword's point.' The Fung wait without your gates, O Prince."

"And, therefore, O Gentile, we hire you to fight the Fung. Still, I bear no grudge against your servant, Quick, who is himself but a white-skinned Fung, for he acted according to his nature, and I forgive him; only in the future let him beware! And now —for a greater matter. The Child of Kings is beautiful, she is young and high-spirited; a new face from another land may perchance touch her fancy. But," he added meaningly, "let the owner of that face remember who she is and what he is; let him remember that for any outside the circle of the ancient blood to lift his eyes to the daughter of Solomon is to earn death, death slow and cruel for himself and all who aid and abet him. Let him remember, lastly, that this high-born lady to whom, he, an unknown and vagrant Gentile, dares to talk as equal to equal, has from childhood been my affianced, who will shortly be my wife, although it may please her to seem to flout me after the fashion of maidens, and that we Abati are jealous of the honour of our women. Do you understand?"

"Yes, Prince," I answered, for by now my temper was roused. "But I would have you understand something also — that we are men of a high race whose arm stretches over half the world, and that we differ from the little tribe of the Abati, whose fame is not known to us, in this — that we are jealous of our own honour, and do not need to hire strangers to fight the foes we fear to face. Next time I come to attend to your wounds, O Prince, I trust they will be in front, and not behind. One word more, if you will be advised by me you will not threaten that Captain whom you call a Gentile and a mercenary, lest you should learn that it is not always well to be a coward, of blood however ancient."

Then, in a towering rage, I left him, feeling that I had made a thorough fool of myself. But the truth was that I could not sit still and hear men such as my companions, to say nothing of myself, spoken of thus by a bloated cur, who called himself a prince and boasted of his own poltroonery. He glowered at me as I went, and the men of his party who hung about the end of the great room and in his courts, glowered at me also. Clearly he was a very dangerous cur, and I almost wished that instead of threatening to slap his face down in the tunnel, Quick had broken his neck and made an end of him.

So did the others when I told them the story, although I think it opened their eyes, and especially those of Oliver, to the grave and growing dangers of the situation. Afterward he informed me that he had spoken of the matter with Maqueda, and that she was much frightened for our sakes, and somewhat for her own. Joshua, she said, was a man capable of any crime, who had at his back the great majority of the Abati; a jealous, mean, and intolerant race who made up in cunning for what they lacked in courage.

Yet, as I saw well, the peril of their situation did nothing to separate this pair or to lessen their love. Indeed, rather did it seem to bind them closer together, and to make them more completely one. In short, the tragedy took its appointed course, whilst we stood by and watched it helplessly.

On the afternoon of my angry interview with Joshua we were summoned to a meeting of the Council, whither we went, not without some trepidation, expecting trouble. Trouble there was, but of a different sort to that which we feared. Scarcely had we entered the great room where the Child of Kings was seated in her chair of state surrounded by all the pomp and ceremony of her mimic court, when the big doors at the end of it were opened, and through them marched three gray-bearded men in white robes whom we saw at once were heralds or ambassadors from the Fung. These men bowed to the veiled Maqueda and, turning toward where we stood in a little group apart, bowed to us also.

But of Joshua, who was there supported by two servants, for he could not yet stand alone, and the other notables and priests of the Abati, they took not the slightest heed.

"Speak," said Maqueda.

"Lady," answered the spokesman of the embassy, "we are sent by our Sultan, Barung, son of Barung, Ruler of the Fung nation. These are the words of Barung: O Walda Nagasta! 'By the hands and the wit of the white lords whom you have called to your aid, you have of late done much evil to the god Harmac and to me his servant. You have destroyed one of the gates of my city, and with it many of my people. You have rescued a prisoner out of my hands, robbing Harmac of his sacrifice and thereby bringing his wrath upon us. You have slain sundry of the sacred beasts that are the mouth of sacrifice, you have killed certain of the priests and guards of Harmac in a hole of the rocks. Moreover my spies tell me that you plan further ills against the god and against me. Now I send to tell you that for these and other offences I will make an end of the people of the Abati, whom hitherto I have spared. In a little while I marry my daughter to the white man, that priest of Harmac who is called Singer of Egypt, and who is said to be the son of the physician in your service, but after I have celebrated this feast and my people have finished the hoeing of their crops, I take up the sword in earnest, nor will I lay it down again until the Abati are no more.

"Learn that last night after the holy beasts had been

slain and the sacrifice snatched away, the god Harmac
spoke to his priests in prophecy. And this was his
prophecy: that before the gathering in of the harvest
his *head* should sleep above the Plain of Mur. We
know not the interpretation of the saying, but this I
know, that before the gathering of harvest I, or those
who rule after me, will lie down to sleep within my
city of Mur."

"Now, choose — surrender forthwith and, save for
the dog, Joshua, who the other day tried to entrap me
against the custom of peoples, and ten others whom I shall
name, I will spare the lives of all of you, though Joshua
and these ten I will hang, since they are not worthy to
die by the sword. Or resist, and by Harmac himself I
swear that every man among the Abati shall die save
the white lords whom I honour because they are brave,
and that servant of yours who stood with them last night
in the den of lions, and that every woman shall be made
a slave, save you, O Walda Nagasta, because of your
great heart. Your answer, O Lady of the Abati!"

Now Maqueda looked around the faces of her Council,
and saw fear written upon them all. Indeed, as we
noted, many of them shook in their terror.

"My answer will be short, ambassadors of Barung,"
she replied, "still, I am but one woman, and it is fitting
that those who represent the people should speak for the
people. My uncle, Joshua, you are the first of my
Council, what have you to say? Are you willing to
give up your life with ten others whose names I do
not know, that there may be peace between us and
the Fung?"

"What?" answered Joshua, with a splutter of rage,
"do I live to hear a Walda Nagasta suggest that the
first prince of the land, her uncle and affianced husband,
should be surrendered to our hereditary foes to be hanged

like a worn-out hound, and do you, O unknown ten, who
doubtless stand in this chamber, live to hear it also?"

"My uncle, you do not. I asked if such was your
wish, that is all."

"Then I answer that it is not my wish, nor the wish
of the ten, nor the wish of the Abati. Nay, we will
fight the Fung and destroy them, and of their beast-
headed idol Harmac we will make blocks to build our
synagogues and stones to pave our roads. Do you hear,
savages of the Fung?" and assisted by his two servants
he hobbled toward them, grinning in their faces.

The envoys looked him up and down with their quiet
eyes. "We hear and we are very glad to hear," their
spokesman answered, "since we Fung love to settle our
quarrels with the sword and not by treaty. But to you,
Joshua, we say: Make haste to die before we enter Mur,
since the rope is not the only means of death whereof
we know."

Then very solemnly the three envoys saluted, first
the Child of Kings and next ourselves, and turned to go.

"Kill them!" shouted Joshua, "they have threatened
and insulted me, the Prince!" but no one lifted a hand
against them, and they passed safely out of the palace
to the square, where an escort waited with their horses.

CHAPTER XIV

HOW PHARAOH MET SHADRACH

WHEN the ambassadors had gone, at first there was silence, a very heavy silence, since even the frivolous Abati felt that the hour was big with fate. Of a sudden, however, the members of the Council began to chatter like so many monkeys, each talking without listening to what his neighbour said, till at length a gorgeously dressed person, I understood that he was a priest, stepped forward and shouted down the others.

Then he spoke in an excited and venomous fashion. He pointed out that we Gentiles had brought all the trouble upon Mur, since before we came the Abati, although threatened, had lived in peace and glory — he actually used the word glory! — for generations. But now we had stung the Fung as a hornet stings a bull and made them mad, so that they wished to toss the Abati. He proposed, therefore, that we should at once be ejected from Mur.

At this point I saw Joshua whisper into the ear of a man, who called out:

"No, no, for then they would go to their friend, Barung, a savage like themselves, and having learned our secrets, doubtless use them against us. I say that they should be killed instantly," and he drew a sword and waved it.

Quick walked up to the fellow and clapped a pistol to his head.

"Drop that sword," he said, "or *you*'ll never hear the end of the story," and he obeyed, whereon Quick came back.

Now Maqueda began to speak, quietly enough, although I could see that she was quaking with passion.

"These men are our guests," she said, "come hither to serve us. Would you murder our guests? Moreover, of what use would that be? One thing alone can save us, the destruction of the god of the Fung, since, according to the ancient saying of that people, when the idol is destroyed the Fung will leave their city of Harmac. Moreover, as to this new prophecy of the priests of the idol, that before the gathering in of harvest, his head shall sleep above the plain of Mur, how can that be if it is destroyed unless indeed it means that Harmac shall sleep in the heavens. Therefore what have you to fear from threats built upon that which cannot happen? But can *you* destroy this false god Harmac, or dare *you* fight the Fung? You know that it is not so, for had it been so what need was there for me to send for these Westerns? And if you murder them, will Barung thereby be appeased? Nay, I tell you that being a brave and honourable man, although our enemy, he will become ten times more wroth with you than he was before, and exact a vengeance even more terrible. I tell you also, that you may find another Walda Nagasta to rule over you, since I, Maqueda, will do so no more."

"That is impossible," said some one, "you are the last woman of the true blood."

"Then you can choose one of blood that is not true, or elect a king, as the Jews elected Saul, for if my guests are butchered, then I shall die of very shame."

These words of hers seemed to cow the Council, one of whom asked, what then would she have them do?

"Do?" she replied, throwing back her veil, "why, be

men, raise an army of every male who can carry sword;
help the foreigners, and they will lead you to victory.
People of the Abati, would you be slaughtered, would you
see your women slaves and your ancient name blotted
out from the list of peoples?"

Now some of them cried, "No."

"Then save yourselves. You are still many, the
foreigners here have skill in war; they can lead if you will
follow. Be brave a while, and I swear to you that by
harvest the Abati shall sit in the city of Harmac and not
the Fung in Mur. I have spoken, now do what you will,"
and rising from her chair of state she left the chamber,
motioning to us to do likewise.

The end of all this business was that a peace was made
between us and the Council of the Abati. After their
pompous, pedantic fashion they swore solemnly on the
roll of the Law that they would aid us in every way to
overcome the Fung, and even obey such military orders
as we might give them, subject to the confirmation of
these orders by a small council of their generals. In
short, being very frightened, for a time they forgot their
hatred of us foreigners.

So a scheme of operations was agreed upon, and some
kind of law passed by the Council, the only governing
body among the Abati, for they possessed no representa-
tive institutions, under which law a kind of conscription
was established for a while. Let me say at once that it
met with the most intense opposition. The Abati were
agriculturists who loathed military service. From their
childhood they had heard of the imminence of invasion,
but no actual invasion had ever yet taken place. The
Fung were always without, and they were always within,
an inland isle, the wall of rock that they thought impassable being their sea which protected them from danger.

They had no experience of slaughter and rapine, their imaginations were not sufficiently strong to enable them to understand what these things meant; they were lost in the pettinesses of daily life and its pressing local interests. Their homes in flames, they themselves massacred, their women and children dragged off to be the slaves of the victors, a poor remnant left to die of starvation among the wasted fields or to become wild men of the rocks! All these things they looked upon as a mere tale, a romance such as their local poets repeated in the evenings of a wet season, dim and far-off events which might have happened to the Canaanites and Jebusites and Amalekites in the ancient days whereof the book of their Law told them, but which could never happen to *them*, the comfortable Abati. In that book the Israelites always conquered in the end, although the Philistines, alias Fung, sat at their gates, for it will be remembered that it includes no account of the final fall of Jerusalem and awful destruction of its citizens, of which they had little, if any knowledge.

So it came about that our recruiting parties, perhaps press gangs would be a better term, were not well received. I know it, for this branch of the business was handed over to me, of course, as adviser to the Abati captains, and on several occasions, when riding round the villages on the shores of their beautiful lake, we were met by showers of stones, and were even the object of active attacks which had to be put down with bloodshed. Still, an army of five or six thousand men was got together somehow, and formed into camps, whence desertions were incessant, once or twice accompanied by the murder of officers.

"It's 'opeless, downright 'opeless, Doctor," said Quick to me, dropping his h's, as he sometimes did in the excitement of the moment. "What can one do with a crowd of pigs, everyone of them bent on bolting to his own sty, or anywhere except toward the enemy. The sooner the Fung get them the better for all concerned, say I, and if it wasn't for our Lady yonder (Quick always called Maqueda "our Lady," after it had been impressed upon him that "her Majesty" was an incorrect title), my advice to the Captain and you gentlemen would be: Get out of this infernal hole as quick as your legs can carry you, and let's do a bit of hunting on the way home, leaving the Abati to settle their own affairs."

"You forget, Sergeant, that I have a reason for staying in this part of the world, and so perhaps have the others. For instance, the Professor is very fond of those old skeletons down in the cave," and I paused.

"Yes, Doctor, and the Captain is very fond of something much better than a skeleton, and so are we all. Well, we've got to see it through, but somehow I don't think that every one of us will have that luck, though it's true that when a man has lived fairly straight according to his lights a few years more or less don't matter much one way or the other. After all, except you gentlemen, who is there that will miss Samuel Quick?"

Then without waiting for an answer, drawing himself up straight as a ramrod he marched off to assist some popinjays of Abati officers, whom he hated and who hated him, to instil the elements of drill into a newly raised company, leaving me to wonder what fears or premonitions filled his honest soul.

But this was not Quick's principal work, since for at least six hours of every day he was engaged in helping Oliver in our great enterprise of driving a tunnel from the end of the Tomb of Kings deep into the solid rock that formed the base of the mighty idol of the Fung. The task was stupendous, and would indeed have been impossible had not Orme's conjecture that some passage had once run from the extremity of the cave toward the idol proved to be perfectly accurate. Such a passage indeed was found walled up at the back of the chair containing the bones of the hunchbacked king. It descended very sharply for a distance of several hundred yards, after which for another hundred yards or more its walls and roof were so riven and shaky that, for fear of accidents, we found it necessary to timber them as we went.

At last we came to a place where they had fallen in altogether, shaken down, I presume by the great earthquake which had destroyed so much of the ancient cave city. At this spot, if Oliver's instruments and calculations could be trusted, we were within about two hundred feet of the floor of the den of lions, to which it seemed probable that the passage once led, and of course the question arose as to what should be done.

A Council was held to discuss this problem, at which Maqueda and a few of the Abati notables were present. To these Oliver explained that even if that were possible it would be useless to clear out the old passage and at the end find ourselves once more in the den of lions.

"What, then, is your plan?" asked Maqueda.

"Lady," he answered, "I, your servant, am instructed to attempt to destroy the idol, Harmac, by means of the explosives which we have brought with us from England. First, I would ask you if you still cling to that design?"

"Why should it be abandoned?" inquired Maqueda. "What have you against it?"

"Two things, Lady. As an act of war the deed seems useless, since supposing that the sphinx is shattered and a certain number of priests and guards are destroyed, how will that advance your cause? Secondly, such destruction will be very difficult, if it can be done at all. The stuff we have with us, it is true, is of fearful strength, yet who can be sure that there is enough of it to move this mountain of hard rock, of which I cannot calculate the weight, not having the measurements or any knowledge of the size of the cavities within its bulk. Lastly, if the attempt is to be made, a tunnel must be hollowed of not less than three hundred feet in length, first downward and then upward into the very base of the idol, and if this is to be done within six weeks, that is, by the night of the marriage of the daughter of Barung, the work will be very hard, if indeed it can be completed at all, although hundreds of men labour day and night."

Now Maqueda thought a while, then looked up and said:

"Friend, you are brave and skilful, tell us all your mind. If you sat in my place, what would you do?"

"Lady, I would lead out every able-bodied man and attack the city of the Fung, say, on the night of the great festival when they are off their guard. I would blow in the gates of the city of Harmac, and storm it and drive away the Fung, and afterwards take possession of the idol, and if it is thought necessary, destroy it piecemeal from within."

Now Maqueda consulted with her councillors, who appeared to be much disturbed at this suggestion, and finally called us back and gave us her decision.

"These lords of the Council," she said, speaking with a ring of contempt in her voice, "declare that your plan is mad, and that they will never sanction it because the Abati could not be persuaded to undertake so dangerous an enterprise as an attack upon the city of Harmac, which would end, they think, in all of them being killed. They point out, O Orme, that the prophecy is that the Fung will leave the plain of Harmac when their god is destroyed and not before, and that therefore it must be destroyed. They say, further, O Orme, that for a year you and your companions are the sworn servants of the

Abati, and that it is your business to receive orders, not to give them, also that the condition upon which you earn your pay is that you destroy the idol of the Fung. This is the decision of the Council, spoken by the mouth ot the prince Joshua, who command further that you shall at once set about the business to execute which you and your companions are present here in Mur."

"Is that *your* command also, O Child of Kings?" answered Oliver, colouring.

"Since I also think that the Abati can never be forced to attack the city of the Fung, it is, O Orme, though the words in which it is couched are not my words."

"Very well, O Child of Kings, I will do my best. Only blame us not if the end of this matter is other than these advisers of yours expect. Prophecies are two-edged swords to play with, and I do not believe that a race of fighting men like the Fung will fly and leave you triumphant just because a stone image is shattered, if that can be done in the time and with the means which we possess. Meanwhile, I ask that you should give me two hundred and fifty picked men of the Mountaineers, not of the townspeople, under the captaincy of Japhet, who must choose them, to assist us in our work."

"It shall be done," she answered, and we made our bows and went. As we passed through the Council we heard Joshua say in a loud voice meant for us to hear:

"Thanks be to God, these hired Gentiles have been taught their place at last."

Oliver turned on him so fiercely that he recoiled, thinking that he was about to strike him.

"Be careful, Prince Joshua," he said, "that before this business is finished you are not taught yours, which I think may be lowly at last," and he looked meaningly at the ground.

Well, the labour began, and it was heavy indeed as well as dangerous. Fortunately, in addition to the picrate compounds that Quick called "azure stinging bees," we had brought with us a few cases of dynamite of which we now made use for blasting purposes. A hole was drilled in the face of the tunnel, and the charge inserted. Then all retreated back into the Tomb of Kings till the cartridge had exploded, and the smoke cleared off, which took a long while, when our people advanced with iron bars and baskets, and cleared away the débris, after which the process must be repeated.

Oh! the heat of that narrow hole deep in the bowels of the rock, and the reek of the stagnant air which sometimes was so bad that the lights would scarcely burn. Indeed, after a hundred feet had been completed, we thought that it would be impossible to proceed, since two men died of asphyxiation and the others, although they were good fellows enough, refused to return into the tunnel. At length, however, Orme and Japhet persuaded some of the best of them to do so, and shortly after this the atmosphere improved very much, I suppose because we cut some cranny or shaft which communicated with the open air.

There were other dangers also, notably that of the collapse of the whole roof where the rock was rotten, as we found it to be in places. Then it proved very hard to deal with the water, for once or twice we struck small springs impregnated with copper or some other mineral that blistered the feet and skin, since every drop of this acid water had to be carried out in wooden pails. That difficulty we overcame at last by sinking a narrow well down to the level of the ancient tunnel of which I have spoken as having been shaken in by the earthquake.

Thus we, or rather Oliver and Quick with the Mountaineers, toiled on. Higgs did his best, but after a while proved quite unable to bear the heat, which became too much for so stout a man. The end of it was that he devoted himself to the superintendence of the removal of the rubbish into the Tomb of Kings, the care of the stores, and so forth. At least that was supposed to be his business, but really he employed most of his time in drawing and cataloguing the objects of antiquity and the groups of bones that were buried there, and in exploring the remains of the underground city. In truth, this task of destruction was most repellent to the poor Professor.

"To think," he said to us, "to think that I, who all my life have preached the iniquity of not conserving every relic of the past, should now be employed in attempting to obliterate the most wonderful object ever fashioned by the ancients! It is enough to make a Vandal weep, and I pray heaven that you may not succeed in your infamous design. What does it matter if the Abati are wiped out, as lots of better people have been before them? What does it matter if we accompany them to oblivion so long as that noble sphinx is preserved to be the wonder of future generations. Well, thank goodness, at any rate I have seen it, which is more, probably, than any of you will ever do. There, another brute is dumping his rubbish over the skull of No. 14!"

Thus we laboured continually, each at his different task, for the work in the mine never stopped. Oliver being in charge during the day and Quick at night for a whole week, since on each Sunday they changed with their gangs, Quick taking the day shift and Oliver the night, or *vice versa*. Sometimes Maqueda would come down to inspect progress, always, I noticed, at those hours when Oliver happened to be off duty. Then on this pre-text or on that they would wander away together to inspect I know not what in the recesses of the underground city, or elsewhere. In vain did I warn them that their every step was dogged, and that their every word and action were noted by spies who crept after them continually, since twice I caught one of these gentry in the act. They were infatuated, and would not listen.

Nowadays Oliver only left the underground city twice or thrice a week to breathe the fresh air for an hour or two. In truth, he had no time. For this same reason he fitted himself up a bed in what had been a priest's chamber, or a sanctuary in the old temple, and slept there, generally with no other guard but the great dog, Pharaoh, his constant companion even in the recesses of the mine.

It was curious to see how this faithful beast accustomed itself to the darkness, and made its other senses, especially that of smell, serve the purpose of eyes as do the blind. By degrees, too, it learned all the details of the operations; thus, when the cartridge was in place for firing, it would rise and begin to walk out of the tunnel even before the men in charge.

One night the tragedy that I feared very nearly happened, and indeed must have happened had it not been for this same hound, Pharaoh. About six o'clock in the evening Oliver came off duty after an eight-hour shift in the tunnel, leaving Higgs in command for a little while until it was time for Quick to go on at eight. I had been at work outside all day in connection with the new conscript army, a regiment of which was in revolt, because the men, most of whom were what we should call small-holders, declared that they wanted to go home to weed their crops. Indeed, it had proved necessary for the Child of Kings herself to be summoned to plead with them and condemn some of the ringleaders to punishment.

When at length this business was over we left together

and the poor lady, exasperated almost to madness, sharply refusing the escort of any of her people, requested me to accompany her to the mine.

At the mouth of the tunnel she met Oliver, as probably she had arranged to do, and after he had reported progress to her, wandered away with him as usual, each of them carrying a lamp, into some recess of the buried city. I followed them at a distance, not from curiosity, or because I wished to see more of the wonders of that city whereof I was heartily sick, but because I suspected that they were being spied upon.

The pair vanished round a corner that I knew ended in a *cul-de-sac*, so extinguishing my lamp, I sat down on a fallen column and waited till I should see their light reappear, when I proposed to effect my retreat. Whilst I sat thus, thinking on many things and, to tell the truth, very depressed in mind, I heard a sound as of some one moving, and instantly struck a match. The light of it fell full upon the face of a man whom I recognized at once as a body-servant of the prince Joshua, though whether he was passing me toward the pair or returning from their direction I could not be sure.

"What are you doing here?" I asked.

"What is that to you, Physician?" he answered.

Then the match burnt out, and before I could light another he had vanished, like a snake into a stone wall.

My first impulse was to warn Maqueda and Oliver that they were being watched, but reflecting that the business was awkward, and that the spy would doubtless have given over his task for that day, I left it alone, and went down to the Tomb of the Kings to help Higgs. Just afterwards Quick came on duty, long before his time, the fact being that he had no confidence in the Professor as a director of mining operations. When he appeared Higgs and I retreated from that close and filthy tunnel, and, by way of recreation, put in an hour or so at the cataloguing and archæological research in which his soul delighted.

"If only we could get all this lot out of Mur," he said, with a sweep of his hand, "we should be the most famous men in Europe for at least three days, and rich into the bargain."

"Ptolemy," I answered, "we shall be fortunate if we get ourselves alive out of Mur, let alone these bones and ancient treasures," and I told him what I had seen that evening.

His fat and kindly face grew anxious.

"Ah!" he said. "Well, I don't blame him; should probably do the same myself if I got the chance, and so would you—if you were twenty years younger. No, I don't blame him, or her either, for the fact is that although their race, education, and circumstances are so different, they are one of Nature's pairs, and while they are alive nothing will keep them apart. You might as well expect a magnet and a bit of iron to remain separate on a sheet of notepaper. Moreover, they give themselves away, as people in that state always do. The pursuit of archæology has its dangers, but it is a jolly sight safer than that of woman, though it did land me in a den of lions. What's going to happen, old fellow?"

"Can't say, but I think it very probable that Oliver will be murdered, and that we shall follow the same road, or, if we are lucky, be only bundled out of Mur. Well, it's time for dinner; if I get a chance I will give them a hint."

So we made our way to the old temple in the great cave, where we kept our stores and Oliver had his head-quarters. Here we found him waiting for us and our meal ready, for food was always brought to us by the palace servants. When we had eaten and these men had cleared away, we lit our pipes and fed the dog Pharaoh upon the scraps that had been reserved for him. Then I told Oliver about the spy whom I had caught tracking him and Maqueda.

"Well, what of it?" he said, colouring in his tell-tale fashion; "she only took me to see what she believed to be an ancient inscription on a column in that northern aisle."

"Then she'd have done better to take me, my boy," said Higgs. "What was the character like?"

"Don't know," he answered guiltily. "She could not find it again."

An awkward silence followed, which I broke.

"Oliver," I said, "I don't think you ought to go on sleeping here alone. You have too many enemies in this place."

"Rubbish," he answered, "though it's true Pharaoh seemed uneasy last night, and that once I woke up and thought I heard footsteps in the court outside. I set them down to ghosts, in which I have almost come to believe in this haunted place, and went to sleep again."

"Ghosts be blowed!" said Higgs vulgarly, "if there were such things I have slept with too many mummies not to see them. That confounded Joshua is the wizard who raises your ghosts. Look here, old boy," he added, "let me camp with you to-night, since Quick must be in the tunnel, and Adams has to sleep outside in case he is wanted on the army business."

"Not a bit of it," he answered; "you know you are too asthmatical to get a wink in this atmosphere. I won't hear of such a thing."

"Then come and sleep with us in the guest-house."

"Can't be done; the Sergeant has got a very nasty job down there about one o'clock, and I promised to be handy in case he calls me up," and he pointed to the portable field telephone that fortunately we had brought with us from England, which was fixed close by, adding, "if only that silly thing had another few hundred yards of wire, I 'd come; but, you see, it has n't and I must be in touch with the work."

At this moment the bell tinkled, and Orme made a jump for the receiver through which for the next five minutes he was engaged in giving rapid and to us quite unintelligible directions.

"There you are," he said, when he had replaced the mouthpiece on its hook, "if I had n't been here they would probably have had the roof of the tunnel down and killed some people. No, no; I can't leave that receiver unless I go back to the mine, which I am too tired to do. However, don't you fret. With a pistol, a telephone, and Pharaoh I 'm safe enough. And now, good night; you fellows had better be getting home, as I must be up early to-morrow and want to sleep while I can."

On the following morning about five o'clock, Higgs and I were awakened by someone knocking at our door. I rose and opened it, whereon in walked Quick, a grim and grimy figure, for, as his soaked clothes and soiled face told us, he had but just left his work in the mine.

"Captain wants to see you as soon as possible, gentlemen," he said.

"What 's the matter, Sergeant?" asked Higgs, as we got into our garments.

"You 'll see for yourself presently, Professor," was the laconic reply, nor could we get anything more out of him.

Five minutes later we were advancing at a run through the dense darkness of the underground city, each of us carrying a lamp. I reached the ruins of the old temple first, for Quick seemed very tired and lagged behind, and in that atmosphere Higgs was scant of breath and could not travel fast. At the doorway of the place where he slept stood the tall form of Oliver holding a lamp aloft. Evidently he was waiting for us. By his side sat the big yellow dog, Pharaoh, that, when he smelt us, gambolled forward, wagging his tail in greeting.

"Come here," said Orme, in a low and solemn voice, "I have something to show you," and he led the way into the priest's chamber, or sanctuary, or whatever it may have been, where he slept upon a rough, native-made bedstead. At the doorway he halted, lowered the lamp he held, and pointed to something dark on the floor to the right of his bedstead, saying, "Look!"

There lay a dead man, and by his side a great knife that evidently had fallen from his hand. At the first glance we recognized the face which, by the way, was singularly peaceful, as though it were that of one plunged in deep sleep. This seemed odd, since the throat below was literally torn out.

"Shadrach!" we said, with one voice.

Shadrach it was; Shadrach, our former guide, who had betrayed us; Shadrach who, to save his own life, had shown us how to rescue Higgs, and for that service been pardoned, as I think I mentioned. Shadrach and no other!

"Pussy seems to have been on the prowl and to have met a dog," remarked Quick.

"Do you understand what has happened?" asked Oliver, in a dry, hard voice. "Perhaps I had best explain before anything is moved. Shadrach must have crept in here last night — I don't know at what time, for I slept through it all — for purposes of his own. But he forgot his old enemy Pharaoh, and Pharaoh killed him. See his throat? When Pharaoh bites he doesn't growl, and, of course, Shadrach could say nothing, or, as he had dropped his knife, for the matter of that, do anything either. When I was woke up about an hour ago by the telephone bell the dog was fast asleep, for he is accustomed to that bell, with his head resting upon the body of Shadrach. Now, why did Shadrach come into my room at night with a drawn knife in his hand?"

"Doesn't seem a difficult question to answer," replied Higgs, in the high voice which was common to him when excited. "He came here to murder you, and Pharaoh was too quick for him, that's all. That dog was the cheapest purchase you ever made, friend Oliver."

"Yes," answered Orme, "he came here to murder me — you were right about the risk, after all — but what I wonder is, who sent him?"

"And so you may go on wondering for the rest of your life, Captain," exclaimed Quick. "Still, I think we might guess if we tried."

Then news of what had happened was sent to the palace, and within little over an hour Maqueda arrived, accompanied by Joshua and several other members of her Council. When she saw and understood everything she was horrified, and sternly asked Joshua what he knew of this business. Of course, he proved to be completely innocent, and had not the slightest idea of who had set the murderer on to work this deed of darkness. Nor had anybody else, the general suggestion being that Shadrach had attempted it out of revenge, and met with the due reward of his crime.

Only that day poor Pharaoh was poisoned. Well, he had done his work, and his memory is blessed.

CHAPTER XV

SERGEANT QUICK HAS A PRESENTIMENT

FROM this time forward all of us, and especially Oliver, were guarded night and day by picked men who it was believed could not be corrupted. As a consequence, the Tsar of Russia scarcely leads a life more irksome than ours became at Mur. Of privacy there was none left to us, since sentries and detectives lurked at every corner, while tasters were obliged to eat of each dish and drink from each cup before it touched out lips, lest our fate should be that of Pharaoh, whose loss we mourned as much as though the poor dog had been some beloved human being.

Most of all was it irksome, I think, to Oliver and Maqueda, whose opportunities of meeting were much curtailed by the exigencies of this rigid espionage. Who can murmur sweet nothings to his adored when two soldiers armed to the teeth have been instructed never to let him out of their sight? Particularly is this so if the adored happens to be the ruler of those soldiers to whom the person guarded has no right to be making himself agreeable. For when off duty even the most faithful guardians are apt to talk. Of course, the result was that the pair took risks which did not escape observation. Indeed, their intimate relations became a matter of gossip throughout the land.

Still, annoying as they might be, these precautions succeeded, for none of us were poisoned or got our throats cut, although we were constantly the victims of mysterious accidents. Thus, a heavy rock rolled down upon us when we sat together one evening upon the hill-side, and a flight of arrows passed between us while we were riding along the edge of a thicket, by one of which Higgs's horse was killed. Only when the mountain and the thicket were searched no one could be found. Moreover, a great plot against us was discovered, in which some of the lords and priests were implicated, but such was the state of feeling in the country that, beyond warning them privately that their machinations were known, Maqueda did not dare to take proceedings against these men.

A little later on things mended so far as we were concerned, for the following reason: One day two shepherds arrived at the palace with some of their companions, saying that they had news to communicate. On being questioned, these peasants averred that while they were herding their goats upon the western cliffs many miles away, suddenly on the top of the hills appeared a body of fifteen Fung, who bound and blindfolded them, telling them in mocking language to take a message to the Council and to the white men.

This was the message: That they had better make haste to destroy the god Harmac, since otherwise his head would move to Mur according to the prophecy, and that when it did so, the Fung would follow as they knew how to do. Then they set the two men on a rock where they could be seen, and on the following morning were in fact found by some of their fellows, those who accompanied them to the Court and corroborated this story.

Of course, the matter was duly investigated, but as I know, for I went with the search party, when we got to the place no trace of the Fung could be found, except one of their spears, of which the handle had been driven into the earth and the blade pointed toward Mur, evidently in threat or defiance. No other token of them remained, for, as it happened, a heavy rain had fallen and obliterated their footprints, which in any case must have been faint on this rocky ground.

Notwithstanding the most diligent search by skilled men, their mode of approach and retreat remained a mystery, as, indeed, it does to this day. The only places where it was supposed to be possible to scale the precipice of Mur were watched continually, so that they could have climbed up by none of these. The inference was, therefore, that the Fung had discovered some unknown path, and, if fifteen men could climb that path, why not fifteen thousand?

Only, where was this path? In vain were great rewards in land and honours offered to him who should discover it, for although such discoveries were continually reported, on investigation these were found to be inventions or mares' nests, since nothing but a bird could have travelled by such roads.

Then at last we saw the Abati thoroughly frightened, for, with additions, the story soon passed from mouth to mouth till the whole people talked of nothing else. It was as though we English learned that a huge foreign army had suddenly landed on our shores and, having cut the wires and seized the railways, was marching upon London. The effect of such tidings upon a nation that always believed invasion to be impossible may easily be imagined, only I hope that we should take them better than did the Abati.

Their swagger, their gay self-confidence, their talk about the "rocky walls of old Mur," evaporated in an hour. Now it was only of the disciplined and terrible regiments of the Fung, among whom every man was trained to war, and of what would happen to them, the civilized and domesticated Abati, a peace-loving people who rightly enough, as they declared, had refused all martial burdens, should these regiments suddenly appear in their midst. They cried out that they were betrayed — they clamoured for the blood of certain of the Councillors. That carpet knight, Joshua, lost popularity for a time, while Maqueda, who was known always to have been in favour of conscription and perfect readiness to repel attack, gained what he had lost.

Leaving their farms, they crowded together into the towns and villages, where they made what in South Africa are called laagers. Religion, which practically had been dead among them, for they retained but few traces of the Jewish faith if, indeed, they had ever really practised it, became the craze of the hour. Priests were at a premium; sheep and cattle were sacrificed; it was even said that after the fashion of their foes the Fung, some human beings shared the same fate. At any rate the Almighty was importuned hourly to destroy the hated Fung and to protect His people — the Abati —from the results of their own base selfishness and cowardly neglect.

Well, the world has seen such exhibitions before to-day, and will doubtless see more of them in the instance of greater peoples who allow luxury and pleasure-seeking to sap their strength and manhood.

The upshot of it all was that the Abati became obsessed with the saying of the Fung scouts to the shepherds, which, after all, was but a repetition of that of their envoys delivered to the Council a little while before: that they should hasten to destroy the idol Harmac, lest he should move himself to Mur. How an idol of such proportions, or even its head, could move at all they did not stop to inquire. It was obvious to them, however, that if it was destroyed there would be nothing to move and, further, that we Gentiles were the only persons who could possibly effect such destruction. So we also became popular for a little while. Everybody was pleasant and flattered us — everybody, even Joshua, bowed when we approached, and took a most lively interest in the progress of our work, which many deputations and prominent individuals urged us to expedite.

Better still, the untoward accidents such as those I have mentioned, ceased. Our dogs, for we had obtained some others, were no longer poisoned; rocks that appeared fixed did not fall; no arrows whistled among us when we went out riding. We even found it safe occasionally to dispense with our guards, since it was every one's interest to keep us alive — for the present. Still, I for one was not deceived for a single moment, and in season and out of season warned the others that the wind would soon blow again from a less favourable quarter.

We worked, we worked, we worked! Heaven alone knows how we did work. Think of the task, which, after all, was only one of several. A tunnel must be bored, for I forget how far, through virgin rock, with the help of inadequate tools and unskilled labour, and this tunnel must be finished by a certain date. A hundred unexpected difficulties arose, and one by one were conquered. Great dangers must be run, and were avoided, while the responsibility of this tremendous engineering feat lay upon the shoulders of a single individual, Oliver Orme, who, although he had been educated as an engineer, had no great practical experience of such enterprises.

Truly the occasion makes the man, for Orme rose to it in a way that I can only call heroic. When he was not actually in the tunnel he was labouring at his calculations, of which many must be made, or taking levels with such instruments as he had. For if there proved to be the slightest error all this toil would be in vain, and result only in the blowing of a useless hole through a mass of rock. Then there was a great question as to the effect which would be produced by the amount of explosive at his disposal, since terrible as might be the force of the stuff, unless it were scientifically placed and distributed, it would assuredly fail to accomplish the desired end.

At last, after superhuman efforts, the mine was finished. Our stock of concentrated explosive, about four full camel-loads in all, was set in as many separate chambers, each of them just large enough to receive the charge, hollowed in the primeval rock from which the idol had been hewn.

These chambers were about twenty feet from each other, although if there had been time to prolong the tunnel, the distance should have been at least forty in order to give the stuff a wider range of action. According to Oliver's mathematical reckoning, they were cut in the exact centre of the base of the idol, and about thirty feet below the actual body of the crouching sphinx. As a matter of fact this reckoning was wrong in several particulars, the charges having been set farther toward the east or head of the sphinx and higher up in the base than he supposed. When it is remembered that he had found no opportunity of measuring the monument which practically we had only seen once from behind, under conditions not favourable to accuracy in such respects, or of knowing its actual length and depth, these trifling errors were not remarkable.

What was remarkable is that his general plan of operations, founded upon a mere hypothetical estimate, should have proved as accurate as it did.

At length all was prepared, and the deadly cast-iron flasks had been packed in sand, together with dynamite cartridges, the necessary detonators, electric wires, and so forth, an anxious and indeed awful task executed entirely in that stifling atmosphere by the hands of Orme and Quick. Then began another labour, that of the filling in of the tunnels. This, it seems, was necessary, or so I understood, lest the expanding gases, following the line of least resistance, should blow back, as it were, through the vent-hole. What made that task the more difficult was the need of cutting a little channel in the rock to contain the wires, and thereby lessen the risk of the fracture of these wires in the course of the building-up process. Of course, if by any accident this should happen, the circuit would be severed, and no explosion would follow when the electric battery was set to work.

The arrangement was that the mine should be fired on the night of that full moon on which we had been told, and spies confirmed the information, the feast of the marriage of Barung's daughter to my son would be celebrated in the city of Harmac. This date was fixed because the Sultan had announced that so soon as that festivity, which coincided with the conclusion of the harvest, was ended, he meant to deliver his attack on Mur.

Also, we were anxious that it should be adhered to for another reason, since we knew that on this day but a small number of priests and guards would be left in charge of the idol, and that my son could not be among them. Now, whatever may have been the views of the Abati, we as Christians who bore them no malice, did not at all desire to destroy an enormous number of innocent Fung, as might have happened if we had fired our mine when the people were gathered to sacrifice to their god.

The fatal day had arrived at last. All was completed, save for the blocking of the passage which still went on.

or, rather, was being reinforced by the piling up of loose rocks against its mouth, at which a hundred or so of men laboured incessantly. The firing wires had been led into that little chamber in the old temple where the dog Pharaoh tore out the throat of Shadrach, and no inch of them was left unguarded for fear of accident or treachery.

The electric batteries—two of them, in case one should fail — had been tested but not connected with the wires. There they stood upon the floor, looking innocent enough, and we four sat round them like wizards round their magic pot, who await the working of some spell. We were not cheerful; who could be under so intense a strain? Orme, indeed, who had grown pale and thin with continuous labour of mind and body, seemed quite worn out. He could not eat or smoke, and with difficulty I persuaded him to drink some of the native wine. He would not even go to look at the completion of the work or to test the wires.

"You can see to it," he said; "I have done all I can. Now things must take their chance."

After our midday meal he lay down and slept quite soundly for several hours. About four o'clock those who were labouring at the piling up of débris over the mouth of the tunnel completed their task, and, in charge of Quick, were marched out of the underground city.

Then Higgs and I took lamps and went along the length of the wires which lay in a little trench covered over with dust, removing the dust and inspecting them at intervals. Discovering nothing amiss, we returned to the old temple, and at its doorway met the mountaineer, Japhet, who throughout all these proceedings had been our prop and stay. Indeed, without his help and that of his authority over the Abati, the mine could never have been completed, at any rate within the time.

The light of the lamp showed that his face was very anxious.

"What is the matter?" I asked.

"O Physician," he answered, "I have words for the ear of the Captain Orme. Be pleased to lead me to him."

We explained that he slept and could not be disturbed, but Japhet only answered as before, adding:

"Come you with me, my words are for your ears as well as his."

So we went into the little room and awoke Oliver, who sprang up in a great fright, thinking that something untoward had happened at the mine.

"What's wrong?" he asked of Japhet. "Have the Fung cut the wires?"

"Nay, O Orme, a worse thing; I have discovered that the prince Joshua has laid a plot to steal away 'Her-whose-name-is-high.'"

"What do you mean? Set out all the story, Japhet," said Oliver.

"It is short, lord. I have some friends, one of whom — he is of my own blood but ask me not his name—is in the service of the Prince. We drank a cup of wine together which I needed, and I suppose it loosed his tongue. At any rate, he told me, and I believed him. This is the story. For his own sake and that of the people the Prince desires that you should destroy the idol of the Fung, and therefore he has kept his hands off you of late. Yet should you succeed, he does not know what may happen. He fears lest the Abati in their grati-tude should set you up as great men."

"Then he is an ass!" interrupted Quick; "for the Abati have no gratitude."

"He fears," went on Japhet, "other things also. For instance, that the Child of Kings may express that gratitude by a mark of her signal favour toward one of you," and he stared at Orme, who turned his head aside. "Now, the Prince is affianced to this great lady, whom he desires to wed for two reasons: First, because this marriage will make him the chief man among the Abati, and, secondly, because of late he has come to think that he loves her whom he is afraid that he may lose. So he has set a snare."

"What snare?" asked one of us, for Japhet paused.

"I don't know," answered Japhet, "and I do not think that my friend knew either, or, if he did, he would not tell me. But I understand the plot is that the Child of Kings is to be carried off to the prince Joshua's castle at the other end of the lake, six hours' ride away, and there be forced to marry him at once."

"Indeed," said Orme, "and when is all this to happen?"

"I don't know, lord. I know nothing except what my friend told me, which I thought it right to communicate to you instantly. I asked him the time, however, and he said that he believed the date was fixed for one night after next Sabbath."

"Next Sabbath is five days hence, so that this matter does not seem to be very pressing," remarked Oliver with a sigh of relief. "Are you sure that you can trust your friend, Japhet?"

"No, lord, I am not sure, especially as I have always known him to be a liar. Still, I thought that I ought to tell you."

"Very kind of you, Japhet, but I wish that you had let me have my sleep out first. Now go down the line and see that all is right, then return and report."

Japhet saluted in his native fashion and went.

"What do you think of this story?" asked Oliver, as soon as he was out of hearing.

"All bosh," answered Higgs; "the place is full of talk and rumours, and this is one of them."

He paused and looked at me.

"Oh!" I said, "I agree with Higgs. If Japhet's friend had really anything to tell he would have told it in more detail. I daresay there are a good many things Joshua would like to do, but I expect he will stop there, at any rate, for the present. If you take my advice you will say nothing of the matter, especially to Maqueda."

"Then we are all agreed. But what are you thinking of, Sergeant?" asked Oliver, addressing Quick, who stood in a corner of the room, lost apparently in contemplation of the floor.

"I, Captain," he replied, coming to attention. "Well, begging their pardon, I was thinking that I don't agree with these gentlemen, except in so far that I should say nothing of this job to our Lady, who has plenty to bother her just now, and won't need to be frightened as well. Still, there may be something in it, for though that Japhet is stupid, he's honest, and honest men sometimes get hold of the right end of the stick. At least, he believes there is something, and that's what weighs with me."

"Well, if that's your opinion, what's best to be done, Sergeant? I agree that the Child of Kings should not be told, and I shan't leave this place till after ten o'clock to-night at the earliest, if we stick to our plans, as we had better do, for all that stuff in the tunnel wants a little time to settle, and for other reasons. What are you drawing there?" and he pointed to the floor, in the dust of which Quick was tracing something with his finger.

"A plan of our Lady's private rooms, Captain. She told you she was going to rest at sundown, didn't she, or earlier, for she was up most of last night, and wanted to get a few hours' sleep before — something happens. Well, her bed-chamber is there, is n't it? with another before it, in which her maids sleep, and nothing behind except a high wall and a ditch that cannot be climbed."

"That's quite right," interrupted Higgs. "I got leave to make a plan of the palace, only there is a passage six feet wide and twenty long leading from the guard-chamber to the ladies' anteroom."

"Just so, Professor, and that passage has a turn in it, if I remember right, so that two well-armed men could hold it against quite a lot. Supposing now that you and I, Professor, should go and take a nap in that guard-room, which will be empty, for the watch is set at the palace gate. We shan't be wanted here, since if the Captain can't touch off that mine, no one can, with the Doctor to help him just in case anything goes wrong, and Japhet guarding the line. I daresay there's nothing in this yarn, but who knows? There might be, and then we should blame ourselves. What do you say, Professor?"

"I? Oh, I'll do anything you wish, though I should rather have liked to climb the cliff and watch what happens."

"You'd see nothing, Higgs," interrupted Oliver, "except perhaps the reflection of a flash in the sky; so, if you don't mind, I wish you would go with the Sergeant. Somehow, although I am quite certain that we ought not to alarm Maqueda, I am not easy about her, and if you two fellows were there I should know she was all right, and it would be a weight off my mind."

"That settles it," said Higgs; "we'll be off presently. Look here, give us that portable telephone, which is of no use anywhere else now. The wire will reach to the palace, and if the machine works all right we can talk to you and tell each other how things are going on."

Ten minutes later they had made their preparations. Quick stepped up to Oliver and stood at attention, saying:

"Ready to march.   Any more orders, Captain?"

"I think not, Sergeant," he answered, lifting his eyes from the little batteries that he was watching as though they were live things. "You know the arrangements. At ten o'clock — that is about two hours hence — I touch this switch. Whatever happens it must not be done before, for fear lest the Doctor's son should not have left the idol, to say nothing of all the other poor beggars. The spies say that the marriage feast will not be celebrated until at least three hours after moonrise."

"And that's what I heard when I was a prisoner," interrupted Higgs.

"I daresay," answered Orme; "but it is always well to allow a margin in case the procession should be delayed, or something. So until ten o'clock I've got to stop where I am, and you may be sure, Doctor, that under no circumstances shall I fire the mine before that hour, as indeed you will be here to see. After that I can't say what will happen, but if we don't appear, you two had better come to look for us — in case of accidents, you know. Do your best at your end according to circumstances; the Doctor and I will do our best at ours. I think that is all, Sergeant. Report yourselves by the telephone if the wire is long enough and it will work, which I daresay it won't, and, anyway, look out for us about half-past ten. Good-bye!"

"Good-bye, Captain," answered Quick, then stretched out his hand, shook that of Orme, and without another word took his lamp and left the chamber.

An impulse prompted me to follow him, leaving Orme

and Higgs discussing something before they parted. When we had walked about fifty yards in the awful silence of that vast underground town, of which the ruined tenements yawned on either side of us, the Sergeant stopped and said suddenly.

"You don't believe in presentiments, do you, Doctor?"

"Not a bit," I answered.

"Glad of it, Doctor. Still, I have got a bad one now, and it is that I shan't see the Captain or you any more."

"Then that's a poor look-out for us, Quick."

"No, Doctor, for me. I think you are both all right, and the Professor, too. It's my name they are calling up aloft, or so it seems to me. Well, I don't care much, for, though no saint, I have tried to do my duty, and if it is done, it's done. If it's written, it's got to come to pass, hasn't it? For everything is written down for us long before we begin, or so I've always thought. Still, I'll grieve to part from the Captain, seeing that I nursed him as a child, and I'd have liked to know him well out of this hole, and safely married to that sweet lady first, though I don't doubt that it will be so."

"Nonsense, Sergeant," I said sharply; "you are not yourself; all this work and anxiety has got on your nerves."

"As it well might, Doctor, not but I daresay that's true. Anyhow, if the other is the true thing, and you should all see old England again with some of the stuff in that dead-house, I've got three nieces living down at home whom you might remember. Don't say nothing of what I told you to the Captain till this night's game is played, seeing that it might upset him, and he'll need to keep cool up to ten o'clock, and afterwards, too, perhaps. Only if we shouldn't meet again, say that Samuel Quick sent him his duty and God's blessing. And the same on yourself, Doctor, and your son, too. And now here comes the Professor, so good-bye!"

A minute later they had left me, and I stood watching them until the two stars of light from their lanterns vanished into the blackness.

CHAPTER XVI

HARMAC COMES TO MUR

SLOWLY and in very bad spirits I retraced my steps to the old temple, following the line of the telephone wire which Higgs and Quick had unreeled as they went. In the Sergeant's prognostications of evil I had no particular belief, as they seemed to me to be born of the circumstances which surrounded us, and in different ways affected all our minds, even that of the buoyant Higgs.

To take my own case, for instance. Here I was about to assist in an act which for aught I knew might involve the destruction of my only son. It was true we believed that this was the night of his marriage at the town of Harmac, some miles away, and that the tale of our spies supported this information. But how could we be sure that the date, or the place of the ceremony, had not been changed at the last moment? Supposing, for instance, that it was held, not in the town, as arranged, but in the courts of the idol, and that the fearful activities of the fiery agent which we were about to wake to life should sweep the celebrants into nothingness.

The thought made me turn cold, and yet the deed must be done; Roderick must take his chance. And if all were well, and he escaped that danger, were there not worse behind? Think of him, a Christian man, the husband of a savage woman who worshipped a stone image with a lion's head, bound to her and her tribe, a state prisoner, trebly guarded, whom, so far as I could see, there would be no hope of rescuing. It was awful. Then there were other complications. If the plan succeeded and the idols were destroyed, my own belief was that the Fung must thereby be exasperated. Evidently they knew some road into this stronghold. It would be used. They would pour their thousands up it, a general massacre would follow, of which, justly, we should be the first victims.

I reached the chamber where Oliver sat brooding alone, for Japhet was patrolling the line.

"I am not happy about Maqueda, Doctor," he said to me. "I am afraid there is something in that story. She wanted to be with us; indeed, she begged to be allowed to come almost with tears. But I would n't have it, since accidents may always happen; the vibration might shake in the roof or something; in fact, I don't think you should be here. Why don't you go away and leave me?"

I answered that nothing would induce me to do so, for such a job should not be left to one man.

"No, you 're right," he said; "I might faint or lose my head or anything. I wish now that we had arranged to send the spark from the palace, which perhaps we might have done by joining the telephone wire on to the others. But, to tell you the truth, I'm afraid of the batteries. The cells are new but very weak, for time and the climate have affected them, and I thought it possible that the extra distance might make the difference and that they would fail to work. That 's why I fixed this as the firing point. Hullo, there 's the bell. What have they got to say?"

I snatched the receiver, and presently heard the cheerful voice of Higgs announcing that they had arrived safely in the little anteroom to Maqueda's private apartments.

"The palace seems very empty," he added; "we only met one sentry, for I think that everybody else, except Maqueda and a few of her ladies, have cleared out, being afraid lest rocks should fall on them when the explosion occurs."

"Did the man say so?" I asked.

"Yes, something of that sort; also he wanted to forbid us to come here, saying that it was against the prince Joshua's orders that we Gentiles should approach the private apartments of the Child of Kings. Well, we soon settled that, and he bolted. Where to? Oh! I don't know; to report, he said."

"How's Quick?" I asked.

"Much the same as usual. In fact, he is saying his prayers in the corner, looking like a melancholy brigand with rifles, revolvers, and knives stuck all over him. I wish he wouldn't say his prayers," added Higgs, and his voice reached me in an indignant squeak; "it makes me feel uncomfortable, as though I ought to join him. But not having been brought up a Dissenter or a Moslem, I can't pray in public as he does. Hullo! Wait a minute, will you?"

Then followed a longish pause, and after it Higgs's voice again.

"It's all right," it said. "Only one of Maqueda's ladies who had heard us and come to see who we were. When she learns I expect she will join us here, as the girl says she's nervous and can't sleep."

Higgs proved right in his anticipations, for in about ten minutes we were rung up again, this time by Maqueda herself, whereon I handed the receiver to Oliver and retired to the other end of the room.

Nor, to tell the truth, was I sorry for the interruption, since it cheered up Oliver and helped to pass the time.

The next thing worth telling that happened was that,

an hour or more later, Japhet arrived, looking very frightened. We asked him our usual question: if anything was wrong with the wires. With a groan he answered "No," the wires seemed all right, but he had met a ghost.

"What ghost, you donkey?" I said.

"The ghost of one of the dead kings, O Physician, yonder in the burial cave. It was he with the bent bones who sits in the farthest chair. Only he had put some flesh on his bones, and I tell you he looked fearful, a very fierce man, or rather ghost."

"Indeed, and did he say anything to you, Japhet?"

"Oh! yes, plenty, O Physician, only I could not understand it all, because his language was somewhat different to mine, and he spat out his words as a green log spits out sparks. I think that he asked me, however, how my miserable people dared to destroy his god, Harmac. I answered that I was only a servant and did not know, adding that he should put his questions to you."

"And what did he say to that, Japhet?"

"I think he said that Harmac would come to Mur and settle his account with the Abati, and that the foreign men would be wise to fly fast and far. That's all I understood; ask me no more, who would not return into that cave to be made a prince."

"He's got hold of what Barung's envoys told us," said Oliver, indifferently, "and no wonder, this place is enough to make anybody see ghosts. I'll repeat it to Maqueda; it will amuse her."

"I wouldn't if I were you," I answered, "for it isn't exactly a cheerful yarn, and perhaps she's afraid of ghosts too. Also," and I pointed to the watch that lay on the table beside the batteries, "it is five minutes to ten."

Oh! that last five minutes! It seemed as many centuries. Like stone statues we sat, each of us lost in his own thoughts, though for my part the power of clear thinking appeared to have left me. Visions of a sort flowed over my mind without sinking into it, as water flows over marble. All I could do was to fix my eyes on the face of that watch, of which in the flickering lamp-light the second-hand seemed to my excited fancy to grow enormous and jump from one side of the room to the other.

Orme began to count aloud, "One, two, three, four, five — *now!*" and almost simultaneously he touched the knob first of one battery and next of the other. Before his finger pressed the left-hand knob I felt the solid rock beneath us surge — no other word conveys its movement. Then the great stone cross-piece, weighing several tons, that was set as a transom above the tall door of our room, dislodged itself, and fell quite gently into the doorway, which it completely blocked.

Other rocks fell also at a distance, making a great noise, and somehow I found myself on the ground, my stool had slid away from me. Next followed a muffled, awful roar, and with it came a blast of wind blowing where wind never blew before since the beginning of the world, that with a terrible wailing howled itself to silence in the thousand recesses of the cave city. As it passed our lamps went out. Lastly, quite a minute later I should think, there was a thud, as though something of enormous weight had fallen on the surface of the earth far above us.

Then all was as it had been; all was darkness and utter quietude.

"Well, that's over," said Oliver, in a strained voice which sounded very small and far away through that thick darkness; "all over for good or ill. I needn't have been anxious; the first battery was strong enough, for I felt the mine spring as I touched the second. I wonder," he went on, as though speaking to himself, "what amount of damage nearly a ton and a half of that

awful *azo-imide* compound has done to the old sphinx.
According to my calculations it ought to have been
enough to break the thing up if we could have spread
the charge more.   But, as it is, I am by no means certain.
It may only have driven a hole in its bulk, especially if
there were hollows through which the gases could run.
Well, with luck, we may know more about it later.
Strike a match, Adams, and light those lamps. Why,
what's that? Listen!"

As he spoke, from somewhere came a series of tiny
noises, that, though they were so faint and small, suggested rifles fired at a great distance. Crack, crack,
crack! went the infinitesimal noises.

I groped about, and finding the receiver of the field
telephone, set it to my ear. In an instant all grew
plain to me. Guns were being fired near the other end
of the wire, and the transmitter was sending us the
sound of them. Very faintly but with distinctness. I
could hear Higgs's high voice saying, "Look out, Sergeant, there's another rush coming!" and Quick answering, "Shoot low, Professor; for the Lord's sake shoot low.
You are empty, sir. Load up, load up! Here's a clip
of cartridges. Don't fire too fast. Ah! that devil got
me, but I've got him; he'll never throw another spear."

"They are being attacked!" I exclaimed. "Quick
is wounded. Now Maqueda is talking to you. She says,
'Oliver, come! Joshua's men assail me. Oliver, come!'"

Then followed a great sound of shouting answered
by more shots, and just as Orme snatched the receiver
from my hand the wire went dead. In vain he called
down it in an agonized voice. As well might he have
addressed the planet Saturn.

"The wire's cut," he exclaimed, dashing down the
receiver and seizing the lantern which Japhet had just
ᴜcceeded in re-lighting; "come on, there's murder

being done," and he sprang to the doorway, only to stagger back again from the great stone with which it was blocked.

"Good God!" he screamed, "we're shut in. How can we get out? How can we get out?" and he began to run round and round the room, and even to spring at the walls like a frightened cat. Thrice he sprang, striving to climb to the coping, for the place had no roof, each time falling back, since it was too high for him to grasp. I caught him round the middle, and held him by main force, although he struck at me.

"Be quiet," I said; "do you want to kill yourself? You will be no good dead or maimed. Let me think."

Meanwhile Japhet was acting on his own account, for he, too, had heard the tiny, ominous sounds given out by the telephone and guessed their purport. First he ran to the massive transom that blocked the doorway and pushed. It was useless; not even an elephant could have stirred it. Then he stepped back, examining it carefully.

"I think it can be climbed, Physician," he said. "Help me now," and he motioned to me to take one end of the heavy table on which the batteries stood. We dragged it to the doorway, and, seeing his purpose, Oliver jumped on to it with him. Then at Japhet's direction, while I supported the table to prevent its oversetting, Orme rested his forehead against the stone, making what schoolboys call "a back," up which the mountaineer climbed actively until he stood upon his shoulders, and by stretching himself was able to grasp the end of the fallen transom. Next, while I held up the lamp to give him light, he gripped the roughnesses of the hewn stone with his toes, and in a few moments was upon the coping of the wall, twenty feet or more above the floor line.

The rest was comparatively easy, for, taking off his

linen robe, Japhet knotted it once or twice, and let it down to us. By the help of this improvised rope, with Orme supporting me beneath, I, too, was dragged to the coping of the wall. Then both of us pulled up Oliver, who, without a word, swung himself over the wall, hanging to Japhet's arms, and loosing his hold, dropped to the ground on the farther side. Next came my turn. It was a long fall, and had not Oliver caught me I think that I should have hurt myself. As it was, the breath was shaken out of me. Lastly, Japhet swung himself down, landing lightly as a cat. The lamps he had already dropped to us, and in another minute they were all lighted, and we were speeding down the great cavern.

"Be careful," I cried; "there may be fallen rocks about."

As it happened I was right, for at that moment Oliver struck his legs against one of them and fell, cutting himself a good deal. In a moment he was up again, but after this our progress grew slow, for hundreds of tons of stone had been shaken from the roof and blocked the path. Also whole buildings of the ancient and underground city had been thrown down, although these were mostly blown inward by the rush of air. At length we came to the end of the cave, and halted dismayed, for here, where the blast of the explosion had been brought to a full stop, the place seemed to be crowded with rocks which it had rolled before it.

"My God! I believe we are shut in," exclaimed Oliver in despair.

But Japhet, lantern in hand, was already leaping from block to block, and presently, from the top of the débris, called to us to come to him.

"I think there is a road left, though a bad one, lords," he said, and pointed to a jagged, well-like hole blown out, as I believe, by the recoil of the blast. With difficulty and danger, for many of the piled-up stones were loose, we climbed down this place, and at its bottom squeezed ourselves through a narrow aperture on to the floor of the cave, praying that the huge door which led to the passage beyond might not be jammed, since if it were, as we knew well, our small strength could not avail to move it. Happily, this fear at least proved groundless, since it opened outward, and the force of the compressed air had torn it from its massive stone hinges and thrown it shattered to the ground.

We scrambled over it, and advanced down the passage, our revolvers in our hands. We reached the audience hall, which was empty and in darkness. We turned to the left, crossing various chambers, and in the last of them, through which one of the gates of the palace could be approached, met with the first signs of the tragedy, for there were bloodstains on the floor.

Orme pointed to them as he hurried on, and suddenly a man leapt out of the darkness as a buck leaps from a bush, and ran past us, holding his hands to his side, where evidently he had some grievous hurt. Now we entered the corridor leading to the private apartments of the Child of Kings, and found ourselves walking on the bodies of dead and dying men. One of the former I observed, as one does notice little things at such a moment, held in his hand the broken wire of the field telephone. I presume that he had snatched and severed it in his death pang at the moment when communication ceased between us and the palace.

We rushed into the little antechamber, in which lights were burning, and there saw a sight that I for one never shall forget.

In the foreground lay more dead men, all of them wearing the livery of Prince Joshua. Beyond was Sergeant Quick, seated on a chair. He seemed to be literally hacked to pieces. An arrow that no one had attempted to remove was fast in his shoulder; his head, which Maqueda was sponging with wet cloths — well, I will not describe his wounds.

Leaning against the wall near by stood Higgs, also bleeding, and apparently quite exhausted. Behind, besides Maqueda herself, were two or three of her ladies, wringing their hands and weeping. In face of this terrible spectacle we came to a sudden halt. No word was spoken by any one, for the power of speech had left us.

The dying Quick opened his eyes, lifted his hand, upon which there was a ghastly sword-cut, to his forehead, as though to shade them from the light — ah! how well I recall that pathetic motion — and from beneath this screen stared at us a while. Then he rose from the chair, touched his throat to show that he could not speak, as I suppose, saluted Orme, turned and pointed to Maqueda, and with a triumphant smile sank down and — died.

Such was the noble end of Sergeant Quick.

To describe what followed is not easy, for the scene was confused. Also shock and sorrow have blurred its recollection in my mind. I remember Maqueda and Orme falling into each other's arms before everybody. I remember her drawing herself up in that imperial way of hers, and saying, as she pointed to the body of Quick.

"There lies one who has shown us how to die. This countryman of yours was a hero, O Oliver, and you should hold his memory in honour, since he saved me from worse than death."

"What's the story?" asked Orme of Higgs.

"A simple one enough," he answered. "We got here all right, as we told you over the wire. Then Maqueda talked to you for a long while until you rang off, saying you wanted to speak to Japhet.   After that, at ten o'clock precisely, we heard the thud of the explosion.   Next, as we were preparing to go out to see what had happened, Joshua arrived alone, announced that the idol Harmac had been destroyed, and demanded that the Child of Kings 'for State reasons,' should accompany him to his own castle. She declined and, as he insisted, I took it upon myself to kick him out of the place.   He retired, and we saw no more of him, but a few minutes later there came a shower of arrows down the passage, and after them a rush of men, who called, 'Death to the Gentiles.   Rescue the Rose.'

"So we began to shoot and knocked over a lot of them, but Quick got that arrow through his shoulder.   Three times they came on like that, and three times we drove them back.   At last our cartridges ran low, and we only had our revolvers left, which we emptied into them. They hung a moment, but moved forward again, and all seemed up.

"Then Quick went mad.   He snatched the sword of a dead Abati and ran at them roaring like a bull.   They hacked and cut at him, but the end of it was that he drove them right out of the passage, while I followed, firing past him.

"Well, those who were left of the blackguards bolted, and when they had gone the Sergeant tumbled down. The women and I carried him back here, but he never said another word, and at last you turned up.   Now he's gone, God rest him, for if ever there was a hero in this world he was christened Samuel Quick!" and, turning aside, the Professor pushed up the blue spectacles he always wore on to his forehead, and wiped his eyes with the back of his hand.

With grief more bitter than I can describe we lifted up the body of the gallant Quick and, bearing it into

Maqueda's private apartment, placed it on her own bed, for she insisted that the man who had died to protect her should be laid nowhere else. It was strange to see the grim old soldier, whose face, now that I had washed his wounds, looked calm and even beautiful, laid out to sleep his last sleep upon the couch of the Child of Kings. That bed, I remember, was a rich and splendid thing, made of some black wood inlaid with scrolls of gold, and having hung about it curtains of white net embroidered with golden stars, such as Maqueda wore upon her official veil.

There upon the scented pillows and silken coverlet we set our burden down, the work-worn hands clasped upon the breast in an attitude of prayer, and one by one, bid our farewell to this faithful and upright man, whose face, as it chanced, we were never to see again, except in the glass of memory. Well, he had died as he had lived and would have wished to die — doing his duty and in war. And so we left him. Peace be to his honoured spirit!

In the bloodstained anteroom, while I dressed and stitched up the Professor's wounds, a sword-cut on the head, an arrow-graze along the face, and a spear-prick in the thigh, none of them happily at all deep or dangerous, we held a brief council.

"Friends," said Maqueda, who was leaning on her lover's arm, "it is not safe that we should stop here. My uncle's plot has failed for the moment, but it was only a small and secret thing. I think that soon he will return again with a thousand at his back and then——"

"What is in your mind?" asked Oliver. "To fly from Mur?"

"How can we fly?" she answered, "when the pass is guarded by Joshua's men, and the Fung wait for us without? The Abati hate you, my friends, and now that you have done your work I think that they will kill you if they can, whom they bore with only till it was done. Alas! alas! that I should have brought you to this false and ungrateful country," and she began to weep, while we stared at each other, helpless.

Then Japhet, who all this while had been crouched on the floor, rocking himself to and fro and mourning in his Eastern fashion for Quick, whom he had loved, rose, and, coming to the Child of Kings, prostrated himself before her.

"O Walda Nagasta," he said, "hear the words of your servant. Only three miles away, near to the mouth of the pass, are encamped five hundred men of my own people, the Mountaineers, who hate Prince Joshua and his following. Fly to them, O Walda Nagasta, for they will cleave to you and listen to me whom you have made a chief amongst them. Afterwards you can act as may seem wisest."

Maqueda looked at Oliver questioningly.

"I think that is good advice," he said. "At any rate, we can't be worse off among the Mountaineers than we are in this undefended place. Tell your women to bring cloaks that we can throw over our heads, and let us go."

Five minutes later, a forlorn group filled with fears, we had stolen over the dead and dying in the passage, and made our way to the side gate of the palace that we found open, and over the bridge that spanned the moat beyond, which was down. Doubtless Joshua's ruffians had used it in their approach and retreat. Disguised in the long cloaks with monk-like hoods that the Abati wore at night or when the weather was cold and wet, we hurried across the great square. Here, since we could not escape them, we mingled with the crowd that was gathered at its farther end, all of them — men, women and children — chattering like monkeys in the tree-tops, and pointing to the cliff at the back of the palace, beneath which, it will be remembered, lay the underground city.

A band of soldiers rode by, thrusting their way through the people, and in order to avoid them we thought it wise to take refuge in the shadow of a walk of green-leaved trees which grew close at hand, for we feared lest they might recognize Oliver by his height. Here we turned and looked up at the cliff, to discover what it was at which every one was staring. At that moment the full moon, which had been obscured by a cloud, broke out, and we saw a spectacle that under the circumstances was nothing less than terrifying.

The cliff behind the palace rose to a height of about a hundred and fifty feet, and, as it chanced just there a portion of it jutted out in an oblong shape, which the Abati called the Lion Rock, although personally, heretofore, I had never been able to see in it any great resemblance to a lion. Now, however, it was different, for on the very extremity of this rock, staring down at Mur, sat the head and neck of the huge lion-faced idol of the Fung. Indeed, in that light, with the promontory stretching away behind it, it looked as though it were the idol itself, moved from the valley upon the farther side of the precipice to the top of the cliff above.

"Oh! oh! oh!" groaned Japhet, "the prophecy is fulfilled — the head of Harmac has come to sleep at Mur."

"You mean that we have sent him there," whispered Higgs. "Don't be frightened, man; can't you understand that the power of our medicine has blown the head off the sphinx high into the air, and landed it where it sits now."

"Yes," I put in, "and what we felt in the cave was the shock of its fall."

"I don't care what brought him," replied Japhet, who seemed quite unstrung by all that he had gone through. "All I know is that the prophecy is fulfilled, and Harmac has come to Mur, and where Harmac goes the Fung follow."

"So much the better," said the irreverent Higgs. "I may be able to sketch and measure him now."

But I saw that Maqueda was trembling, for she, too, thought this occurrence a very bad omen, and even Oliver remained silent, perhaps because he feared its effect upon the Abati.

Nor was this wonderful since, from the talk around us, clearly that effect was great. Evidently the people were terrified, like Japhet. We could hear them foreboding ill, and cursing us Gentiles as wizards, who had not destroyed the idol of the Fung as we promised, but had only caused him to fly to Mur.

Here I may mention that as a matter of fact they were right. As we discovered afterwards, the whole force of the explosion, instead of shattering the vast bulk of the stone image, had rushed up through the hollow chambers in its interior till it struck against the solid head. Lifting this as though it were a toy, the expanding gas had hurled that mighty mass an unknown distance into the air, to light upon the crest of the cliffs of Mur, where probably it will remain for ever.

"Well," I said, when we had stared a while at this extraordinary phenomenon, "thank God it did not travel farther, and fall upon the palace."

"Oh! had it done so," whispered Maqueda, in a tearful voice, "I think you might have thanked God indeed, for then at least I should be free from all my troubles. Come, friends, let us be going before we are discovered."

CHAPTER XVII

I FIND MY SON

OUR road toward the pass ran through the camping ground of the newly created Abati army, and what we saw on our journey thither told us more vividly than any words or reports could do, how utter was the demoralization of that people. Where should have been sentries were no sentries; where should have been men were groups of officers talking with women; where should have been officers were camp followers drinking.

Through this confusion and excitement we made our way unobserved, or at any rate, unquestioned, till at length we came to the regiment of Mountaineers, who, for the most part, were goat-herds, poor people who lived upon the slopes of the precipices that enclosed the land of Mur. These folk, having little to do with their more prosperous brethren of the plain, were hardy and primitive of nature, and therefore retained some of the primeval virtues of mankind, such as courage and loyalty.

It was for the first of these reasons, and, indeed, for the second also, that they had been posted by Joshua at the mouth of the pass, which he knew well they alone could be trusted to defend in the event of serious attack. Moreover, it was desirable, from his point of view, to keep them out of the way while he developed his plans against the person of the Child of Kings, for whom these simple-minded men had a hereditary and almost a superstitious reverence.

As soon as we were within the lines of these Mountaineers we found the difference between them and the rest of the Abati. The other regiments we had passed unchallenged, but here we were instantly stopped by a picket. Japhet whispered something into the ear of its officer that caused him to stare hard at us. Then he saluted the veiled figure of the Child of Kings and led us to where the commander of the band and his subordinates were seated near a fire debating together. At some sign or word that did not reach us, this commander, an old fellow with a long gray beard, rose and said:

"Your pardon, but be pleased to show your faces."

Maqueda threw back her hood and turned so that the light of the moon fell full upon her, whereon the man dropped to his knee, saying:

"Your commands, O Walda Nagasta."

"Summon your regiment and I will give them," she answered, and seated herself on a bench by the fire, we three and Japhet standing behind her.

The commander issued orders to his captains, and presently the Mountaineers formed up on three sides of a square about us, to the number of a little over five hundred men. When all were gathered Maqueda mounted the bench upon which she had been sitting, threw back her hood so that every one could see her face in the light of the fire, and addressed them.

"Men of the mountain-side, this night just after the idol of the Fung had been destroyed, the prince Joshua, my uncle, came to me demanding my surrender to him, whether to kill me or to imprison me in his castle beyond the end of the lake, for reasons of state as he said, or for other vile purposes, I do not know."

At these words a murmur rose from the audience.

"Wait," said Maqueda, holding up her hand, "there is worse to come. I told my uncle, the prince Joshua, that he was a traitor and had best be gone. He went, threatening me, and, when I do not know, withdrew the guards that should be stationed at my palace gates. Now, some rumour of my danger had reached the foreigners in my service, and two of them, he who is called Black Windows, whom we rescued from the Fung, and the soldier named Quick, came to watch over me, while the Lord Orme and the Doctor Adams stayed in the cave to send out that spark of fire which should destroy the idol. Nor did they come without need, for presently arrived a band of Prince Joshua's men to take me.

"Then Black Windows and the soldier his companion fought a great fight, they two holding the narrow passage against many, and slaying a number of them with their terrible weapons. The end of it was, men of the mountains, that the warrior Quick, charging down the passage, drove away those servants of Joshua who remained alive. But in so doing he was wounded to the death. Yes, that brave man lies dead, having given his life to save the Child of Kings from the hands of her own people. Black Windows also was wounded — see the bandages about his head. Then came the Lord Orme and the Doctor Adams, and with them your brother Japhet, who had barely escaped with their lives from the cave city, and knowing that I was no longer safe in the palace, where even my sleeping-room has been drenched with blood, with them I have fled to you for succour. Will you not protect me, O men of the mountain-side?"

"Yes, yes," they answered with a great shout. "Command and we obey. What shall we do, O Child of Kings?"

Now Maqueda called the officers of the regiment apart and consulted with them, asking their opinions, one by one. Some of them were in favour of finding out where Joshua might be, and attacking him at once. "Crush the snake's head and its tail will soon cease wriggling!" these said, and I confess this was a view that in many ways commended itself to us.

But Maqueda would have none of it.

"What!" she exclaimed, "shall I begin a civil war among my people when for aught I know the enemy is at our gates?" adding aside to us, "also, how can these few hundred men, brave though they be, hope to stand against the thousands under the command of Joshua?"

"What, then, would you do?" asked Orme.

"Return to the palace with these Mountaineers, O Oliver, and by help of that garrison, hold it against all enemies."

"Very well," he replied. "To those who are quite lost one road is as good as another; they must trust to the stars to guide them."

"Quite so," echoed Higgs; "and the sooner we go the better, for my leg hurts, and I want a sleep."

So Maqueda gave her commands to the officers, by whom they were conveyed to the regiment, which received them with a shout, and instantly began to strike its camp.

Then it was, coming hot-foot after so much sorrow, loss and doubt, that there followed the happiest event of all my life. Utterly tired out and very despondent, I was seated on an arrow-chest awaiting the order to march, idly watching Oliver and Maqueda talking with great earnestness at a little distance, and in the intervals trying to prevent poor Higgs at my side from falling asleep. While I was thus engaged, suddenly I heard a disturbance, and by the bright moonlight caught sight of a man being led into the camp in charge of a guard of Abati soldiers, whom from their dress I knew to belong to a company that just then was employed in watching the lower gates of the pass.

I took no particular heed of the incident, thinking only that they might have captured some spy, till a murmur of astonishment, and the general stir, warned me that something unusual had occurred. So I rose from my box and strolled toward the man, who now was hidden from me by a group of the Mountaineers. As I advanced this group opened, the men who composed it bowing to me with a kind of wondering respect that impressed me, I did not know why.

Then for the first time I saw the prisoner. He was a tall, athletic young man, dressed in festal robes with a heavy gold chain about his neck, and I wondered vaguely what such a person could be doing here in this time of national commotion. He turned his head so that the moonlight showed his dark eyes, his somewhat oval-shaped face ending in a peaked black beard, and his finely cut features. In an instant I knew him.

It was my son Roderick!

Next moment, for the first time for very many years, he was in my arms.

The first thing that I remember saying to him was a typically Anglo-Saxon remark, for however much we live in the East or elsewhere, we never really shake off our native conventions, and habits of speech. It was, "How are you, my boy, and how on earth did you come here?" to which he answered, slowly, it is true, and speaking with a foreign accent.

"All right, thank you, Father. I ran upon my legs."

By this time Higgs hobbled up, and was greeting my son warmly, for, of course, they were old friends.

"Thought you were to be married to-night, Roderick?"
he said.

"Yes, yes," he answered, "I am half married according
to Fung custom, which counts not to my soul. Look,
this is the dress of marriage," and he pointed to his fine
embroidered robe and rich ornaments.

"Then, where's your wife?" asked Higgs.

"I do not know and I do not care," he answered,
"for I did not like that wife. Also it is all nothing as
I am not quite married to her. Fung marriage between
big people takes two days to finish, and if not finished
does not matter. So she marry some one else if she like,
and I, too."

"What happened then?" I asked.

"Oh, this, Father. When we had eaten the marriage
feast, but before we pass before priest, suddenly we
hear a thunder and see a pillar of fire shoot up into sky,
and sitting on top of it head of Harmac, which vanish
into heaven and stop there. Then everybody jump up
and say:

"'Magic of white man! Magic of white man! White
man kill the god who sit there from beginning of world,
now day of Fung finished according to prophecy. Run
away, people of Fung, run away!'

"Barung the Sultan tear his clothes, too, and say —
'Run away, Fung,' and my wife, she tear *her* clothes
and say nothing, but run like antelope. So they all run
toward east, where great river is, and leave me alone.
Then I get up and run, too — toward west, for I know
from Black Windows," and he pointed to Higgs, "when
we shut up together in belly of god before he let down
to lions, what all this game mean, and therefore not
frightened. Well, I run, meeting no one in night, till
I come to pass, run up it, and find guards, to whom
I tell story, so they not kill me, but let me through, and

at last I come here, quite safe, without Fung wife, thank God, and that end of tale."

"I am afraid you are wrong there, my boy," I said, "out of the frying pan into the fire, that's all."

"Out of frying pan into fire," he repeated. "Not understand; father must remember I only little fellow when Khalifa's people take me, and since then speak no English till I meet Black Windows. Only he give me Bible-book that he have in pocket when he go down to be eat by lions." (Here Higgs blushed, for no one ever suspected him, a severe critic of all religions, of carrying a Bible in his pocket, and muttered something about "ancient customs of the Hebrews.")

"Well," went on Roderick, "read that book ever since, and, as you see, all my English come back."

"The question is," said Higgs, evidently in haste to talk of something else, "will the Fung come back?"

"Oh! Black Windows, don't know, can't say. Think not. Their prophecy was that Harmac move to Mur, but when they see his head jump into sky and stop there, they run every man toward the sunrise, and I think go on running."

"But Harmac has come to Mur, Roderick," I said; "at least his head has fallen on to the cliff that overlooks the city."

"Oh! my father," he answered, "then that make great difference. When Fung find out that head of Harmac has come here, no doubt they come after him, for head his most holy bit, especially as they want hang all the Abati whom they not like."

"Well, let's hope that they won't find out anything about it," I replied, to change the subject. Then taking Roderick by the hand I led him to where Maqueda stood a yard or two apart, listening to our talk, but of course, understanding very little of it, and introduced him to her,

explaining in a few words the wonderful thing that had
happened. She welcomed him very kindly, and congratulated me upon my son's escape. Meanwhile, Roderick
had been staring at her with evident admiration. Now
he turned to us and said in his quaint broken English.

"Walda Nagasta most lovely woman! No wonder
King Solomon love her mother. If Barung's daughter,
my wife, had been like her, think I run through great
river into rising sun with Fung."

Oliver instantly translated this remark, which made
us all laugh, including Maqueda herself, and very grateful we were to find the opportunity for a little innocent
merriment upon that tragic night.

By this time the regiment was ready to start, and had
formed up into companies. Before the march actually
began, however, the officer of the Abati patrol, in whose
charge Roderick had been brought to us, demanded his
surrender that he might deliver his prisoner to the Com-
mander-in-Chief, Prince Joshua. Of course, this was
refused, whereon the man asked roughly:

"By whose order?"

As it happened, Maqueda, of whose presence he was
not aware, heard him, and acting on some impulse,
came forward, and unveiled.

"By mine," she said. "Know that the Child of
Kings rules the Abati, not the prince Joshua, and
that prisoners taken by her soldiers are hers, not his.
Be gone back to your post!"

The captain stared, saluted, and went with his companions, not to the pass, indeed, as he had been ordered,
but to Joshua. To him he reported the arrival of the
Gentile's son, and the news he brought that the
nation of the Fung, dismayed by the destruction of their
god, were in full flight from the plains of Harmac, purposing to cross the great river and to return no more.

This glad tidings spread like wildfire; so fast, indeed, that almost before we had begun our march, we heard the shouts of exultation with which it was received by the terrified mob gathered in the great square. The cloud of terror under which they had lived for weeks was suddenly lifted from them. They went mad in their delight; they lit bonfires, they drank, they feasted, they embraced each other and boasted of their bravery that had caused the mighty nation of the Fung to flee away forever.

Meanwhile, our advance had begun, nor in the midst of the general jubilation was any particular notice taken of us till we were in the middle of the square of Mur and within half a mile of the palace, when we saw by the moonlight that a large body of troops, two or three thousand of them, were drawn up in front of us, apparently to bar our way. Still we went on till a number of officers rode up, and addressing the commander of the regiment of Mountaineers, demanded to know why he had left his post, and whither he went.

"I go whither I am ordered," he answered, "for there is one here greater than I."

"If you mean the Gentile Orme and his fellows, the command of the prince Joshua is that you hand them over to us that they may make report to him of their doings this night."

"And the command of the Child of Kings is," replied the captain of the Mountaineers, "that I take them with her back to the palace."

"It has no weight," said the spokesman insolently, "not being endorsed by the Council. Surrender the Gentiles, hand over to us the person of the Child of Kings of whom you have taken possession, and return to your post till the pleasure of the prince Joshua be known."

Then the wrath of Maqueda blazed up.

"Seize those men!" she said, and it was done instantly. "Now, cut the head from him who dared to demand the surrender of my person and of my officers, and give it to his companions to take back to the prince Joshua as my answer to his message."

The man heard, and being a coward like all the Abati, flung himself upon his face before Maqueda, trying to kiss her robe and pleading for mercy.

"Dog!" she answered, "you were one of those who this very night dared to attack my chamber. Oh! lie not, I knew your voice and heard your fellow-traitors call you by your name. Away with him!"

We tried to interfere, but she would not listen, even to Orme.

"Would you plead for your brother's murderer?" she asked, alluding to Quick. "I have spoken!"

So they dragged him off behind us, and presently we saw a melancholy procession returning whence they came, carrying something on a shield. It reached the opposing ranks, whence there arose a murmur of wrath and fear.

"March on!" said Maqueda, "and gain the palace."

So the regiment formed into a square, and, setting Maqueda and ourselves in the centre of it, advanced again.

Then the fight began. Great numbers of the Abati surrounded us and, as they did not dare to make a direct attack, commenced shooting arrows, which killed and wounded a number of men. But the Highlanders also were archers and carried stronger bows. The square was halted, the first ranks kneeling and the second standing behind them. Then, at a given word, the stiff bows which these hardy people used against the lion and the buffalo upon their hills were drawn to the ear and loosed again and again with terrible effect.

On that open place it was almost impossible to miss the mobs of the Abati who, having no experience of war, were fighting without order. Nor could the light mail they wore withstand the rush of the heavy barbed arrows which pierced them through and through. In two minutes they began to give, in three they were flying back to their main body, those who were left of them, a huddled rout of men and horses. So the French must have fled before the terrible longbows of the English at Crécy and Poictiers, for, in fact, we were taking part in just such a mediæval battle.

Oliver, who was watching intently, went to Japhet and whispered something into his ear. He nodded and ran to seek the commander of the regiment. Presently the result of that whisper became apparent, for the sides of the hollow square wheeled outward and the rear moved up to strengthen the centre.

Now the Mountaineers were ranged in a long, double or triple line, behind which were only about a dozen soldiers, who marched round Maqueda, holding their shields aloft in order to protect her from stray arrows. With these, too, came our four selves, a number of camp-followers and others, carrying on their shields those of the regiment who were too badly wounded to walk.

Leaving the dead where they lay, we began to advance, pouring in volleys of arrows as we went. Twice the Abati tried to charge us, and twice those dreadful arrows drove them back. Then at the word of command the Highlanders slung their bows upon their backs, drew their short swords, and in their turn charged.

Five minutes afterwards everything was over. Joshua's soldiers threw down their arms, and ran or galloped to right and left, save a number of them who fled through the gates of the palace, which they had opened, and across the drawbridge into the courtyards within. After them, or, rather, mixed up with them, followed the Mountaineers, killing all whom they could find, for they were out of hand and would not listen to the commands of Maqueda and their officers, that they should show mercy.

So, just as the dawn broke this strange moonlit battle ended, a small affair, it is true, for there were only five hundred men engaged upon our side and three or four thousand on the other, yet one that cost a great number of lives and was the beginning of all the ruin that followed.

Well, we were safe for a while, since it was certain, after the lesson which he had just learned, that Joshua would not attempt to storm the double walls and fosse of the palace without long preparation. Yet even now a new trouble awaited us, for by some means, we never discovered how, that wing of the palace in which Maqueda's private rooms were situated suddenly burst into flames.

Personally, I believe that the fire arose through the fact that a lamp had been left burning near the bed of the Child of Kings upon which was laid the body of Sergeant Quick. Perhaps a wounded man hidden there overturned the lamp; perhaps the draught blowing through the open doors brought the gold-spangled curtains into contact with the wick.

At any rate, the wood-panelled chambers took fire, and had it not happened that the set of the wind was favourable, the whole palace might have been consumed. As it was, we succeeded in confining the conflagration to this particular part of it, which within two hours had burnt out, leaving nothing standing but the stark, stone walls.

Such was the funeral pyre of Sergeant Quick, a noble one, I thought to myself, as I watched it burn.

When the fire was so well under control, for we had pulled down the connecting passage where Higgs and Quick fought their great fight, that there was no longer any danger of its spreading, and the watches had been set, at length we got some rest.

Maqueda and two or three of her ladies, one of them, I remember, her old nurse who had brought her up, for her mother died at her birth, took possession of some empty rooms, of which there were many in the palace, while we lay, or rather fell, down in the guest-chambers, where we had always slept, and never opened our eyes again until the evening.

I remember that I woke thinking that I was the victim of some wonderful dream of mingled joy and tragedy. Oliver and Higgs were sleeping like logs, but my son Roderick, still dressed in his bridal robes, had risen and sat by my bed staring at me, a puzzled look upon his handsome face.

"So you are here," I said, taking his hand. "I thought I dreamed."

"No, Father," he answered in his odd English, "no dream; all true. This a strange world, Father. Look at me! For how many years — twelve — fourteen, slave of savage peoples for whom I sing, priest of Fung idol, always near death but never die. Then Sultan Barung take fancy to me, say I come of white blood and must be his daughter's husband. Then your brother Higgs made prisoner with me and tell me that you hunt me all these years. Then Higgs thrown to lions and you save him. Then yesterday I married to Sultan's daughter, whom I never see before but twice at feast of idol. Then Harmac's head fly off to heaven, and all Fung people run away, and I run too, and find you. Then battle, and many killed, and arrow scratch my neck but not hurt me," and he pointed to a graze just over his jugular

vein, "and now we together. Oh! Father, very strange
world! I think there God somewhere who look after us!"

"I think so, too, my boy," I answered, "and I hope
that He will continue to do so, for I tell you we are in
a worse place than ever you were among the Fung."

"Oh, don't mind that, Father," he answered gaily,
for Roderick is a cheerful soul. "As Fung say, there
no house without door, although plenty people made
blind and can't see it. But we not blind, or we dead
long ago. Find door by and by, but here come man
to talk to you."

The man proved to be Japhet, who had been sent
by the Child of Kings to summon us, as she had news
to tell. So I woke the others, and after I had dressed
the Professor's flesh wounds, which were stiff and sore,
we joined her where she sat in the gateway tower of
the inner wall. She greeted us rather sadly, asked Oliver
how he had slept and Higgs if his cuts hurt him. Then
she turned to my son, and congratulated him upon his
wonderful escape and upon having found a father if he
had lost a wife.

"Truly," she added, "you are a fortunate man to be
so well loved, O son of Adams. To how many sons are
given fathers who for fourteen long years, abandoning
all else, would search for them in peril of their lives,
enduring slavery and blows and starvation and the
desert's heat and cold for the sake of a long-lost face?
Such faithfulness is that of my forefather David for his
brother Jonathan, and such love it is that passes the love
of women. See that you pay it back to him, and to his
memory until the last hour of your life, child of Adams."

"I will, indeed, I will, O Walda Nagasta," answered
Roderick, and throwing his arms about my neck he embraced me before them all. It is not too much to say that
this kiss of filial devotion more than repaid me for all I

had undergone for his beloved sake. For now I knew that I had not toiled and suffered for one of no worth, as is so often the lot of true hearts in this bitter world.

Just then some of Maqueda's ladies brought food, and at her bidding we breakfasted.

"Be sparing," she said with a melancholy little laugh, "for I know not how long our store will last. Listen! I have received a last offer from my uncle Joshua. An arrow brought it — not a man; I think that no man would come lest his fate should be that of the traitor of yesterday," and she produced a slip of parchment that had been tied to the shaft of an arrow and, unfolding it, read as follows:

"O Walda Nagasta, deliver up to death the Gentiles who have bewitched you and led you to shed the blood of so many of your people, and with them the officers of the Mountaineers, and the rest shall be spared. You also I will forgive and make my wife. Resist, and all who cling to you shall be put to the sword, and to yourself I promise nothing.

"Written by order of the Council,

"JOSHUA, PRINCE OF THE ABATI."

"What answer shall I send?" she asked, looking at us curiously.

"Upon my word," replied Orme, shrugging his shoulders, "if it were not for those faithful officers I am not sure but that you would be wise to accept the terms. We are cooped up here, but a few surrounded by thousands, who, if they dare not assault, still can starve us out, as this place is not victualled for a siege."

"You forget one of those terms, O Oliver!" she said slowly, pointing with her finger to the passage in the letter which stated that Joshua would make her his wife, "Now do you still counsel surrender?"

"How can I?" he answered, flushing, and was silent.

"Well, it does not matter what you counsel," she went on with a smile, "seeing that I have already sent my answer, also by arrow. See, here is a copy of it," and she read:

"To my rebellious People of the Abati:

"Surrender to me Joshua, my uncle, and the members of the Council who have lifted sword against me, to be dealt with according to the ancient law, and the rest of you shall go unharmed. Refuse, and I swear to you that before the night of new moon has passed there shall be such woe in Mur as fell upon the City of David when the barbarian standards were set upon her walls. Such is the counsel that has come to me, the Child of Solomon, in the watches of the night, and I tell you that it is true. Do what you will, people of the Abati, or what you must, since your fate and ours are written. But be sure that in me and the Western lords lies your only hope.

"WALDA NAGASTA."

"What do you mean, O Maqueda," I asked, "about the counsel that came to you in the watches of the night?"

"What I say, O Adams," she answered calmly. "After we parted at dawn I slept heavily, and in my sleep a dark and royal woman stood before me, whom I knew to be my great ancestress, the beloved of Solomon. She looked on me sadly, yet as I thought with love. Then she drew back, as it were, a curtain of thick cloud that hid the future and revealed to me the young moon riding the sky and beneath it Mur, a blackened ruin, her streets filled with dead. Yes, and she showed to me other things, though I may not tell them, which also shall come to pass, then held her hands over me as if in blessing, and was gone."

"Old Hebrew prophet business! Very interesting,"

I heard Higgs mutter below his breath, while in my own heart I set the dream down to excitement and want of food. In fact, only two of us were impressed, my son very much, and Oliver a little, perhaps because everything that Maqueda said was gospel to him.

"Doubtless all will come to pass as you say, Walda Nagasta," said Roderick with conviction. "The day of the Abati is finished."

"Why do you say that, Son?" I asked.

"Because, Father, among the Fung people from a child I have two offices, that of Singer to the God and that of Reader of Dreams. Oh! do not laugh. I can tell you many that have come true as I read them; thus the dream of Barung which I read to mean that the head of Harmac would come to Mur, and see, there it sit," and, turning, he pointed through the doorway of the tower to the grim lion-head of the idol crouched upon the top of the precipice, watching Mur as a beast of prey watches the victim upon which it is about to spring. "I know when dreams true and when dreams false; it my gift, like my voice. I know that this dream true, that all," and as he ceased speaking I saw his eyes catch Maqueda's, and a very curious glance pass between them.

As for Orme, he only said:

"You Easterns are strange people, and if you believe a thing, Maqueda, there may be something in it. But you understand that this message of yours means war to the last, a very unequal war," and he looked at the hordes of the Abati gathering on the great square.

"Yes," she answered quietly, "I understand, but however sore our straits, and however strange may seem the things that happen, have no fear of the end of that war, O my friends."

CHAPTER XVIII

THE BURNING OF THE PALACE

ORME was right. Maqueda's defiance did mean war, "an unequal war." This was our position. We were shut up in a long range of buildings, of which one end had been burned, that on account of their moat and double wall, if defended with any vigour, could only be stormed by an enemy of great courage and determination, prepared to face a heavy sacrifice of life. This was a circumstance in our favour, since the Abati were not courageous, and very much disliked the idea of being killed, or even injured.

But here our advantage ended. Deducting those whom we had lost on the previous night, the garrison only amounted to something over four hundred men, of whom about fifty were wounded, some of them dangerously. Moreover, ammunition was short, for they had shot away most of their arrows in the battle of the square, and we had no means of obtaining more. But, worst of all, the palace was not provisioned for a siege, and the Mountaineers had with them only three days' rations of sundried beef or goat's flesh, and a hard kind of biscuit made of Indian corn mixed with barley meal. Thus, as we saw from the beginning, unless we could manage to secure more food our case must soon grow hopeless.

There remained yet another danger. Although the palace itself was stone-built, its gilded domes and ornamental turrets were of timber, and therefore liable to be fired, as indeed had already happened. The roof also was of ancient cedar beams, thinly covered with concrete, while the interior contained an enormous quantity of panels, or rather boarding, cut from some resinous wood.

The Abati, on the other hand, were amply supplied with every kind of store and weapon, and could bring a great force to blockade us, though that force was composed of a timid and undisciplined rabble.

Well, we made the best preparations that we could, although of these I did not see much, since all that day my time was occupied in attending to the wounded with the help of my son and a few rough orderlies, whose experience in doctoring had for the most part been confined to cattle. A pitiful business it proved without the aid of anæsthetics or a proper supply of bandages and other appliances. Although my medicine chest had been furnished upon a liberal scale, it proved totally inadequate to the casualties of battle. Still, I did my best and saved some lives, though many cases developed gangrene and slipped through my fingers.

Meanwhile Higgs, who worked nobly, notwithstanding his flesh wounds, which pained him considerably, and Orme were also doing their best with the assistance of Japhet and the other officers of the highland regiment. The palace was thoroughly examined, and all weak places in its defences were made good. The available force was divided into watches and stationed to the best advantage. A number of men were set to work to manufacture arrow shafts from cedar beams, of which there were plenty in the wooden stables and outhouses that lay at the back of the main building, and to point and wing the same from a supply of iron barbs and feathers which fortunately was discovered in one of the guard-houses. A few horses that remained in a shed were killed and salted down for food, and so forth.

Also every possible preparation was made to repel attempts to storm, paving stones being piled up to throw upon the heads of assailants and fires lighted on the walls to heat pitch and oil and water for the same purpose.

But, to our disappointment, no direct assault was delivered, such desperate methods not commending themselves to the Abati. Their plan of attack was to take cover wherever they could, especially among the trees of the garden beyond the gates, and thence shoot arrows at anyone who appeared upon the walls, or even fire them in volleys at the clouds, as the Normans did at Hastings, so that they might fall upon the heads of persons in the courtyards. Although these cautious tactics cost us several men, they had the advantage of furnishing us with a supply of ammunition which we sorely needed. All the spent arrows were carefully collected and made use of against the enemy, at whom we shot whenever opportunity offered. We did them but little damage, however, since they were extremely careful not to expose themselves.

In this fashion three dreary days went past, unrelieved by any incident except a feint, for it was scarcely more, which the Abati made upon the second night, apparently with the object of forcing the great gates under cover of a rainstorm. The advance was discovered at once, and repelled by two or three volleys of arrows and some rifle-shots. Of these rifles, indeed, whereof we possessed about a score, the Abati were terribly afraid. Picking out some of the most intelligent soldiers we taught them how to handle our spare guns, and though, of course, their shooting was extremely erratic, the result of it, backed up by our own more accurate markmanship, was to force the enemy to take cover. Indeed, after one or two experiences of the effect of bullets, not a man would show himself in the open within five hundred yards until night had fallen.

On the third afternoon we held a council to determine what must be done, since for the last twenty-four hours it had been obvious that things could not continue as they were. To begin with, we had only sufficient food left to keep our force from starvation for two more days. Also the spirits of our soldiers, brave men enough when actual fighting was concerned, were beginning to flag in this atmosphere of inaction. Gathered into groups, they talked of their wives and children, and of what would happen to them at the hands of Joshua; also of their cattle and crops, saying that doubtless these were being ravaged and their houses burned. In vain did Maqueda promise them fivefold their loss when the war was ended, for evidently in their hearts they thought it could only end one way. Moreover, as they pointed out, she could not give them back their children if these were killed.

At this melancholy council every possible plan was discussed, to find that these resolved themselves into two alternatives — to surrender, or to take the bull by the horns, sally out of the palace at night and attack Joshua. On the face of it this latter scheme had the appearance of suicide, but, in fact, it was not so desperate as it seemed. The Abati being such cowards it was quite probable that they would run in their thousands before the onset of a few hundred determined men, and that, if once victory declared itself for the Child of Kings, the bulk of her subjects would return to their allegiance. So we settled on it in preference to surrender, which we knew meant death to ourselves, and for Maqueda a choice between that last grim solution of her troubles and a forced marriage.

But there were others to be convinced, namely, the Mountaineers. Japhet, who had been present at the council, was sent to summon all of them except those actually on guard, and when they were assembled in the large inner court Maqueda went out and addressed them.

I do not remember the exact words of her speech, and I made no note of them, but it was extremely beautiful and touching. She pointed out our plight, and that we could halt no longer between two opinions, who must either fight or yield. For herself she said she did not care, since, although she was young and their ruler, she set no store upon her life, and would give it up gladly rather than be driven into a marriage which she considered shameful, and forced to pass beneath the yoke of traitors.

But for us foreigners she did care. We had come to her country at her invitation, we had served her nobly, one of us had given his life to protect her person, and now, in violation of her safeguard and that of the Council, we were threatened with a dreadful death. Were they, her subjects, so lacking in honour and hospitality that they would suffer such a thing with no blow struck to save us?

Now the majority of them shouted "No," but some were silent, and one old captain advanced, saluted, and spoke.

"Child of Kings," he said, "let us search out the truth of this matter. Is it not because of your love for the foreign soldier, Orme, that all this trouble has arisen? Is not that love unlawful according to our law, and are you not solemnly affianced to the prince Joshua?"

Maqueda considered a while before she replied, and said slowly:

"Friend, my heart is my own, therefore upon this point answer your question for yourself. As regards my uncle Joshua, if there existed any abiding contract between us it was broken when a few nights ago he sent his servants armed to attack and drag me off I know not whither. Would you have me marry a traitor and a coward? I have spoken."

"No," again shouted the majority of the soldiers.

Then in the silence that followed the old captain replied, with a canniness that was almost Scotch:

"On the point raised by you, O Child of Kings, I give no opinion, since you being but a woman, if a high-born one, would not listen to me if I did, but will doubtless follow that heart of yours of which you speak, to whatever end is appointed. Settle the matter with your betrothed Joshua as you will. But we also have a matter to settle with Joshua, who is a toad with a long tongue that if he seems slow yet never misses his fly. We took up your cause, and have killed a great number of his people, as he has killed some of ours. This he will not forget. Therefore it seems to me that it will be wise that we should make what we can of the nest that we have built, since it is better to die in battle than on the gallows. For this reason, then, since we can stay here no longer, for my part I am willing to go out and fight for you this night, although Joshua's people, being so many and ours so few, I shall think myself fortunate if I live to see another sun."

This hard and reasoned speech seemed to appeal to the dissentients, with the result that they withdrew their opposition, and it was agreed that we should attempt to break our way through the besieging army about one hour before the dawn, when they would be heavily asleep and most liable to panic.

Yet, as it chanced, that sortie was destined never to take place, which perhaps was fortunate for us, since I am convinced that it would have ended in failure. It is true that we might have forced our way through Joshua's army, but afterwards those of us who remained alive would have been surrounded, starved out, and, when our strength and ammunition were exhausted, taken prisoners or cut down.

However that may be, events shaped a different course

for us, perhaps because the Abati got wind of our intention and had no stomach for a pitched battle with desperate men. As it happened, this night from sunset on to moonrise was one of a darkness so remarkable that it was impossible to see anything even a foot away, also a wind blowing from the east made sounds very inaudible. Only a few of our men were on guard, since it was necessary that they should be rested till it was time for them to prepare for their great effort. Also, we had little fear of any direct attack.

About eight o'clock, however, my son Roderick, one of the watch stationed in the gateway towers, who was gifted with very quick ears, reported that he thought he heard people moving on the farther side of the massive wooden doors beyond the moat. Accordingly some of us went to listen, but could distinguish nothing, and concluded therefore that he was mistaken. So we retired to our posts and waited patiently for the moon to rise. But as it chanced no moon rose, or rather we could not see her, because the sky was completely covered by thick banks of thunder-clouds presaging the break-up of a period of great heat. These, as the wind had now died down, remained quite stationary upon the face of the sky, blotting out all light.

Perhaps another hour had passed when, chancing to look behind me, I saw what I thought was a meteor falling from the crest of the cliff against which the palace was built, that cliff whither the head of the idol Harmac had been carried by the force of the explosion.

"Look at that shooting star," I said to Oliver, who was at my side.

"It is not a shooting star, it is fire," he replied in a startled voice, and, as he spoke, other streaks of light, scores of them, began to rain down from the brow of the cliff and land upon the wooden buildings to the rear of the palace that were dry as tinder with the drought, and, what was worse, upon the gilded timber domes of the roof.

"Don't you understand the game?" he went on. "They have tied firebrands to arrows and spears to burn us out. Sound the alarm. Sound the alarm!"

It was done, and presently the great range of buildings began to hum like a hive of bees. The soldiers still half asleep, rushed hither and thither shouting. The officers also, developing the characteristic excitement of the Abati race in this hour of panic, yelled and screamed at them, beating them with their fists and swords till some kind of control was established.

Then attempts were made to extinguish the flames, which by this time had got hold in half a dozen places. From the beginning the effort was absolutely hopeless. It is true that there was plenty of water in the moat, which was fed by a perennial stream that flowed down the face of the precipice behind; but pumping engines of any sort were quite unknown to the Abati, who, if a building took fire, just let it burn, contenting themselves with safeguarding those in its neighbourhood. Moreover, even in the palace, such articles as pails, jugs, or other vessels were comparatively few and far between.

Those that we could find, however, were filled with water and passed by lines of men to the places in most danger — that is, practically everywhere — while other men tried to cut off the advance of the flames by pulling down portions of the building.

But as fast as one fire was extinguished, others broke out for the rain of burning darts and of lighted pots or lamps filled with oil descended continuously from the cliff above. A strange and terrible sight it was to see them flashing down through the darkness, like the fiery darts that shall destroy the wicked in the day of Armageddon.

Still, we toiled on despairingly. On the roof we four

white men and some soldiers, under the command of
Japhet, were pouring water on to several of the gilded
domes, which now were well alight. Close by, wrapped
in a dark cloak and attended by some of her ladies, stood
Maqueda. She was quite calm, although sundry burning
arrows and spears, falling with great force from the cliff
above, struck the flat roofs close to where she stood.

Her ladies, however, were not calm. They wept and
wrung their hands, while one of them went into violent
hysterics in her very natural terror. Maqueda turned
and bade them descend to the courtyard of the gateway,
where she said she would join them presently. They
rushed off, rejoicing to escape the sight of those burning
arrows, one of which had just pierced a man and set his
clothes and hair on fire, causing him to leap from the roof
in his madness.

At Oliver's request I ran to the Child of Kings to lead
her to some safer place, if it could be found. But she
would not stir.

"Let me be, O Adams," she said. "If I am to die,
I will die here. But I do not think that is fated," and with
her foot she kicked aside a burning spear that had struck
the cement roof, and, rebounding, fallen quite close to her.
"If my people will not fight," she went on, with bitter
sarcasm, "at least they understand the other arts of war,
for this trick of theirs is clever. They are cruel also.
Listen to them mocking us in the square. They ask
whether we will roast alive or come out and have our
throats cut. Oh!" she went on, clenching her hands, "oh!
that I should have been born the head of such an accursed
race. Let Sheol take them all, for in the day of their
tribulation no finger will I lift to save them."

She was silent for a moment, and down below, near the
gateway, I heard some brute screaming, "Pretty pigeons!
Pretty pigeons, are your feathers singeing? Come then

into our pie, pretty pigeons, pretty pigeons!" followed by shouts of ribald laughter.

But it chanced it was this hound himself who went into the "pie." Presently, when the flames were brighter, I saw him, in the midst of a crowd of his admirers, singing his foul song, another verse of it about Maqueda, which I will not repeat, and by good fortune managed to put a bullet through his head. It was not a bad shot considering the light and circumstances, and the only one I fired that night. I trust also that it will be the last I shall ever fire at any human being.

Just as I was about to leave Maqueda and return with her message to Orme, to the effect that she would not move, the final catastrophe occurred. Amongst the stables was a large shed filled with dry fodder for the palace horses and camels. Suddenly this burst into a mass of flame that spread in all directions. Then came the last, hideous panic. From every part of the palace the Mountaineers, men and officers together, rushed down to the gateway. In a minute, with the single exception of Japhet we four and Maqueda were left alone upon the roof, where we stood overwhelmed, not knowing what to do. We heard the drawbridge fall; we heard the great doors burst open beneath the pressure of a mob of men; we heard a coarse voice — I thought it was that of Joshua — yell:

"Kill whom you will, my children, but death to him who harms the Child of Kings. She is my spoil!"

Then followed terrible sights and sounds. The cunning Abati had stretched ropes outside the doors; it was the noise they made at this work which had reached Roderick's ears earlier during the darkness. The terrified soldiers, flying from the fire, stumbled and fell over these ropes, nor could they rise again because of those who pressed behind. What happened to them all I am sure I do not know, but doubtless many were crushed to death and many more killed by Joshua's men. I trust, however, that some of them escaped, since, compared to the rest of the Abati, they were as lions are to cats, although, like all their race, they lacked the stamina to fight an uphill game.

It was at the commencement of this terrific scene that I shot the foul-mouthed singer.

"You shouldn't have done that, old fellow," screamed Higgs in his high voice striving to make himself heard above the tumult, "as it will show those swine where we are."

"I don't think they will look for us here, anyway," I answered.

Then we watched a while in silence.

"Come," said Orme at length, taking Maqueda by the hand.

"Where are you going, O Oliver?" she asked, hanging back. "Sooner will I burn than yield to Joshua."

"I am going to the cave city," he answered; "we have nowhere else to go, and little time to lose. Four men with rifles can hold that place against a thousand. Come."

"I obey," she answered, bowing her head.

We went down the stairway that led from the roof on which the inhabitants of the palace were accustomed to spend much of their day, and even to sleep in hot weather, as is common in the East. Another minute and we should have been too late. The fire from one of the domes had spread to the upper story, and was already appearing in fierce little tongues of flame mingled with jets of black smoke through cracks in the crumbling partition wall.

As a matter of fact this wall fell in just as my son Roderick, the last of us, was passing down the stairs. With the curiosity of youth he had lingered for a few moments to watch the sad scene below, a delay which nearly cost him his life.

On the ground floor we found ourselves out of immediate

danger, since the fire was attacking this part of the palace from above and burning downward. We had even time to go to our respective sleeping-places and collect such of our possessions and valuables as we were able to carry. Fortunately, among other things, these included all our notebooks, which to-day are of priceless value. Laden with these articles, we met again in the audience hall which, although it was very hot, seemed as it had always been, a huge, empty place whereof the roof painted with stars was supported upon thick cedar columns, each of them hewn from a single tree.

Passing down that splendid apartment, which an hour later had ceased to exist, lamps in hand, for these we had found time to collect and light, we reached the mouth of the passage that led to the underground city without meeting a single human being.

Had the Abati been a different race they could perfectly well have dashed in and made us prisoners, for the draw-bridge was still intact. But their cowardice was our salvation, for they feared lest they should be trapped by the fire. So I think at least, but justice compels me to add that, on the spur of the moment, they may have found it impossible to clear the gateways of the mass of fallen or dead soldiers over which it would have been difficult to climb.

Such, at any rate, was the explanation that we heard afterwards.

We reached the mouth of the vast cave in perfect safety, and clambered through the little orifice which was left between the rocks rolled thither by the force of the explosion, or shaken down from the roof. This hole, for it was nothing more, we proceeded to stop with a few stones in such a fashion that it could not be forced without much toil and considerable noise, only leaving one little tortuous channel through which, if necessary, a man could creep.

The labour of rock-carrying, in which even Maqueda shared, occupied our minds for a while, and induced a kind of fictitious cheerfulness. But when it was done, and the silence of that enormous cave, so striking in comparison with the roar of the flames and the hideous human tumult which we had left without, fell upon us like sudden cold and blinding night upon a wanderer in windy, sunlit mountains, all our excitement perished. In a flash we understood our terrible position, we who had but escaped from the red fire to perish slowly in the black darkness.

Still we strove to keep up our spirits as best we could. Leaving Higgs to watch the blocked passage, a somewhat superfluous task, since the fire without was our best watchman, the rest of us threaded our way up the cave, following the telephone wire which poor Quick had laid on the night of the blowing-up of the god Harmac, till we came to what had been our headquarters during the digging of the mine. Into the room which had been Oliver's, whence we had escaped with so much difficulty after that event, we could not enter because of the transom that blocked the doorway. Still, there were plenty of others at hand in the old temple, although they were foul with the refuse of the bats that wheeled about us in thousands, for these creatures evidently had some unknown access to the open air. One of these rooms had served as our store-chamber, and after a few rough preparations we assigned it to Maqueda.

"Friends," she said, as she surveyed its darksome entrance, "it looks like the door of a tomb. Well, in the tomb there is rest, and rest I must have. Leave me to sleep, who, were it not for you, O Oliver, would pray that I might never wake again.

"Man," she added passionately, before us all, for now in face of the last peril every false shame and wish to

conceal the truth had left her; "man, why were you born
to bring woe upon my head and joy to my heart? Well,
well, the joy outweighs the woe, and even if the angel
who led you hither is named Azrael, still I shall bless him
who has revealed to me my soul. Yet for you I weep, and
if only your life could be spared to fulfil itself in happiness
in the land that bore you, oh! for you I would gladly die."

Now Oliver, who seemed deeply moved, stepped to her
and began to whisper into her ear, evidently making some
proposal of which I think I can guess the nature. She
listened to him smiling sadly, and made a motion with
her hand as though to thrust him away.

"Not so," she said, "it is nobly offered, but did I accept,
through whatever universes I may wander, those who
came after would know me by my trail of blood, the blood
of him who loved me. Perhaps, too, by that crime I
should be separate from you for ever. Moreover, I tell
you that though all seems black as this thick darkness, I
believe that things will yet end well for you and me — in
this world or another."

Then she was gone, leaving Orme staring after her like
a man in a trance.

"I daresay they will," remarked Higgs *sotto voce* to me,
"and that's first-rate so far as they are concerned. But
what I should jolly well like to know is how they are
going to end for *us* who haven't got a charming lady to
see us across the Styx."

"You needn't puzzle your brain over that," I answered
gloomily, "for I think there will soon be a few more skeletons in this beastly cave, that's all. Don't you see that
those Abati will believe we were burned in the palace?"

CHAPTER XIX

STARVATION

I WAS right. The Abati did think that we had been burned. It never occurred to them that we might have escaped to the underground city. So at least I judged from the fact that they made no attempt to seek us there until they learned the truth in the fashion that I am about to describe. If anything, this safety from our enemies added to the trials of those most hideous days and nights. Had there been assaults to repel and the excitement of striving against overwhelming odds, at any rate we should have found occupation for our minds and remaining energies.

But there were none. By turns we listened at the mouth of the passage for the echo of footsteps that never came. Nothing came to break a silence so intense that at last our ears, craving for sound, magnified the soft flitter of the bats into a noise as of an eagle's wings, till at last we spoke in whispers, because the full voice of man seemed to affront the solemn quietude, seemed intolerable to our nerves.

Yet for the first day or two we found occupation of a sort. Of course our first need was to secure a supply of food, of which we had only a little originally laid up for our use in the chambers of the old temple, tinned meats that we had brought from London and so forth, now nearly all consumed. We remembered that Maqueda had told us of corn from her estates which was stored annually in pits to provide against the possibility of a siege of Mur, and asked her where it was.

She led us to a place where round stone covers with rings attached to them were let into the floor of the cave, not unlike those which stop the coal-shoots in a town pavement, only larger. With great difficulty we prized one of these up; to me it did not seem to have been moved since the ancient kings ruled in Mur and, after leaving it open for a long while for the air within to purify, lowered Roderick by a rope we had to report its contents. Next moment we heard him saying, "Want to come up, please. This place not pleasant."

We pulled him out and asked what he had found.

"Nothing good to eat," he answered, "only plenty of dead bones and one rat that ran up my leg."

We tried the next two pits with the same result — they were full of human bones. Then we cross-examined Maqueda, who, after reflection, informed us that she now remembered that about five generations before a great plague had fallen on Mur, which reduced its population by one-half. She had heard, also, that those stricken with the plague were driven into the underground city in order that they might not infect the others, and supposed that the bones we saw were their remains. This information caused us to close up those pits again in a great hurry, though really it did not matter whether we caught the plague or no.

Still, as she was sure that corn was buried somewhere, we went to another group of pits in a distant chamber, and opened the first one. This time our search was rewarded, to the extent that we found at the bottom of it some mouldering dust that years ago had been grain. The other pits, two of which had been sealed up within three years as the date upon the wax showed, were quite empty.

Then Maqueda understood what had happened.

"Surely the Abati are a people of rogues," she said. "See now, the officers appointed to store away my corn which I gave them have stolen it! Oh! may they live to lack bread even more bitterly than we do to-day."

We went back to our sleeping-place in silence. Well might we be silent, for of food we had only enough left for a single scanty meal. Water there was in plenty, but no food. When we had recovered a little from our terrible disappointment we consulted together.

"If we could get through the mine tunnel," said Oliver, "we might escape into the den of lions, which were probably all destroyed by the explosion, and so out into the open country."

"The Fung would take us there," suggested Higgs.

"No, no," broke in Roderick, "Fung all gone, or if they do, anything better than this black hole, yes, even my wife."

"Let us look," I said, and we started.

When we reached the passage that led from the city to the Tomb of Kings, it was to find that the wall at the end of it had been blown bodily back into the parent cave, leaving an opening through which we could walk side by side. Of course the contents of the tomb itself were scattered. In all directions lay bones, objects of gold and other metals, or overturned thrones. The roof and walls alone remained as they had been.

"What vandalism!" exclaimed Higgs, indignant even in his misery. "Why wouldn't you let me move the things when I wanted to, Orme?"

"Because they would have thought that we were stealing them, old fellow. Also those Mountaineers were superstitious, and I did not want them to desert. But what does it matter, any way? If you had, they would have been burned in the palace."

By this time we had reached that end of the vast tomb where the hunchbacked king used to sit, and saw at once that our quest was vain. The tunnel which we had dug beyond was utterly choked with masses of fallen rock that we could never hope to move, even with the aid of explosives, of which we had none left.

So we returned, our last hope gone.

Also another trouble stared us in the face; our supply of the crude mineral oil which the Abati used for lighting purposes was beginning to run low. Measurement of what remained of the store laid up for our use while the mine was being made, revealed the fact that there was only enough left to supply four lamps for about three days and nights: one for Maqueda, one for ourselves, one for the watchman near the tunnel mouth, and one for general purposes.

This general-purpose lamp, as a matter of fact, was mostly made use of by Higgs. Truly, he furnished a striking instance of the ruling passion strong in death. All through those days of starvation and utter misery, until he grew too weak and the oil gave out, he trudged backward and forward between the old temple and the Tomb of Kings carrying a large basket on his arm. Going out with this basket empty, he would bring it back filled with gold cups and other precious objects that he had collected from among the bones and scattered rubbish in the Tomb. These objects he laboriously catalogued in his pocket-book at night, and afterwards packed away in the empty cases that had contained our supplies of explosive and other goods, carefully nailing them down when filled.

"What on earth are you doing that for, Higgs?" I asked petulantly, as he finished off another case, I think it was his twentieth.

"I don't know, Doctor," he answered in a thin voice,

for like the rest of us he was growing feeble on a water-diet. "I suppose it amuses me to think how jolly it would be to open all these boxes in my rooms in London after a first-rate dinner of fried sole and steak cut thick," and he smacked his poor, hungry lips. "Yes, yes," he went on, "to take them out one by one and show them to ———— and ————," and he mentioned certain officials of the British and other Museums with whom he was at war, "and see them tear their hair with rage and jealousy, while they wondered in their hearts if they could not manage to seize the lot for the Crown as treasure-trove, or do me out of them somehow," and he laughed a little in his old, pleasant fashion.

"Of course I never shall," he added sadly, "but perhaps one day some other fellow will find them here and get them to Europe, and if he is a decent chap, publish my notes and descriptions, of which I have put a duplicate in each box, and so make my name immortal. Well, I'm off again. There are four more cases to fill before the oil gives out, and I must get that great gold head into one of them, though it is an awful job to carry it far at a time. Doctor, what disease is it that makes your legs suddenly give way beneath you, so that you find you self sitting in a heap on the floor without knowing how you came there? You don't know? Well, no more do I, but I've got it bad. I tell you I'm downright sore behind from continual and unexpected contact with the rock."

Poor old Higgs! I did not like to tell him that his disease was starvation.

Well, he went on with his fetching and carrying and cataloguing and packing, I remember that the last load he brought in was the golden head he had spoken of, the wonderful likeness of some prehistoric king which has since excited so much interest throughout the world.

The thing being too heavy for him to carry in his weakened state, for it is much over life-size, he was obliged to roll it before him, which accounts for the present somewhat damaged condition of the nose and semi-Egyptian diadem.

Never shall I forget the sight of the Professor as he appeared out of the darkness, shuffling along upon his knees where his garments were worn into holes, and by the feeble light of the lamp that he moved from time to time, painfully pushing the great yellow object forward, only a foot or so at each push.

"Here it is at last," he gasped triumphantly, whilst we watched him with indifferent eyes. "Japhet, help me to wrap it up in the mat and lift it into the box. No, no, you donkey — face upward — so. Never mind the corners, I 'll fill them with ring-money and other trifles," and out of his wide pockets he emptied a golden shower, amongst which he sifted handfuls of dust from the floor and anything else he could find to serve as packing, finally covering all with the goat's-hair blanket which he took from his bed.

Then very slowly he found the lid of the box and nailed it down, resting between every few strokes of the hammer whilst we watched him in our intent, but idle, fashion, wondering at the strange form of his madness.

At length the last nail was driven, and seated on the box he put his hand into his inner pocket to find his notebook, then incontinently fainted. I struggled to my feet and sprinkled water over his face till he revived and rolled on to the floor, where presently he sank into sleep or torpor. As he did so the first lamp went out.

"Light it, Japhet," said Maqueda, "it is dark in this place."

"O Child of Kings," answered the man, "I would obey if I could, but there is no more oil."

Half an hour later the second lamp went out. By the light that remained we made such arrangements as we could, knowing that soon darkness would be on us. They were few and simple: the fetching of a jar or two of water, the placing of arms and ammunition to our hands, and the spreading out of some blankets on which to lie down side by side upon what I for one believed would be our bed of death.

While we were thus engaged, Japhet crawled into our circle from the outer gloom. Suddenly I saw his haggard face appear, looking like that of a spirit rising from the grave.

"My lamp is burned out," he moaned; "it began to fail whilst I was on watch at the tunnel mouth, and before I was half way here it died altogether. Had it not been for the wire of the 'thing-that-speaks' which guided me, I could never have reached you. I should have been lost in the darkness of the city and perished alone among the ghosts."

"Well, you are here now," said Oliver. "Have you anything to report?"

"Nothing, lord, or at least very little. I moved some of the rocks that we piled up, and crept down the hole till I came to a place where the blessed light of day fell on me, only one little ray of it but still the light of day. I think that something has fallen upon the tunnel and broken it, perhaps one of the outer walls of the palace. At least I looked through a crack and saw everywhere ruins — ruins that still smoke. From among them I heard the voices of men shouting to each other.

"One of them called to his companion that it was strange, if the Gentiles and the Child of Kings had perished in the fire, that they had not found their bones which would be known by the guns they carried His friend answered that it was strange indeed, but being magicians, perhaps they had hidden away somewhere. For his part he hoped so, as then sooner or later they would be found and put to death slowly, as they deserved, who had led astray the Child of Kings and brought so many of the heaven-descended Abati to their death. Then, fearing lest they should find and kill me, for they drew near as I could tell by their voices, I crept back again, and that is all my story."

We said nothing; there seemed to be nothing to say, but sat in our sad circle and watched the dying lamp. When it began to flicker, leaping up and down like a thing alive, a sudden panic seized poor Japhet.

"O Walda Nagasta," he cried, throwing himself at her feet, "you have called me a brave man, but I am only brave where the sun and the stars shine. Here in the dark amongst so many angry spirits, and with hunger gnawing at my bowels, I am a great coward; Joshua himself is not such a coward as I. Let us go out into the light while there is yet time. Let us give ourselves up to the Prince. Perhaps he will be merciful and spare our lives, or at least he will spare yours, and if we die, it will be with the sun shining on us."

But Maqueda only shook her head, whereon he turned to Orme, and went on:

"Lord, would you have the blood of the Child of Kings upon your hands? Is it thus that you repay her for her love? Lead her forth. No harm will come to her who otherwise must perish here in misery."

"You hear what the man says, Maqueda?" said Orme heavily. "There is some truth in it. It really does not matter to us whether we die in the power of the Abati or here of starvation; in fact, I think that we should prefer the former end, and doubtless no hand will be laid on you. Will you go?"

"Nay," she answered passionately. "A hand would be laid on me, the hand of Joshua, and rather than that he should touch me I will die a hundred deaths. Let fate take its course, for as I have told you, I believe that then it will open to us some gate we cannot see. And if I believe in vain, why, there is another gate which we can pass together, O Oliver, and beyond that gate lies peace. Bid the man be silent, or drive him away. Let him trouble me no more."

The lamp flame sank low. It flickered, once, twice, thrice, each time showing the pale, drawn faces of us six seated about it, like wizards making an incantation, like corpses in a tomb.

Then it went out.

How long were we in that place after this? At least three whole days and nights, I believe, if not more, but of course we soon lost all count of time. At first we suffered agonies from famine, which we strove in vain to assuage with great draughts of water. No doubt these kept us alive, but even Higgs, who it may be remembered was a teetotaller, confessed to me that he has loathed the sight and taste of water ever since, and indeed now drinks beer and claret like other people. It was torture; we could have eaten anything. In fact, the Professor did manage to catch and eat a bat that got entangled in his red hair. He offered me a bite of it, I remember, and was most grateful when I declined.

The worst of it was also that we had a little food, a few hard ship's biscuits, which we had saved up for a purpose, namely, to feed Maqueda. This was how we managed it. At certain intervals I would announce that it was time to eat, and hand Maqueda her biscuit. Then we would all pretend to eat also, saying how much we felt refreshed by the food and how we longed for more, and smacking our lips and biting on a bit of wood so that she could not help hearing us.

This piteous farce went on for forty-eight hours or more until at last the wretched Japhet, who was quite demoralized and in no mood for acting, betrayed us, exactly how I cannot remember. After this Maqueda would touch nothing more, which did not greatly matter as there was only one biscuit left. I offered it to her, whereon she thanked me and all of us for our courtesy toward a woman, took it, and gave it to Japhet, who ate it like a wolf.

It was some time afterwards that we discovered Japhet to be missing; at least we could no longer touch him, nor did he answer when we called. Therefore, we concluded that he had crept away to die and, I am sorry to say, thought little more about it for, after all, what he suffered, or had suffered, we suffered also.

I recall that before we were overtaken by the last sleep, a strange fit came upon us. Our pangs passed away, much as these do when mortification follows a wound, and with them that horrible craving for nutriment. We grew cheerful and talked a great deal. Thus Roderick gave me the entire history of the Fung people and of his life among them and other savage tribes. Further, he explained every secret detail of their idol worship to Higgs, who was enormously interested, and tried to make some notes by the aid of our few remaining matches. When even that subject was exhausted, he sang to us in his beautiful voice — English hymns and Arab songs. Oliver and Maqueda also chatted together quite gaily, for I heard them laughing, and gathered that he was engaged in trying to teach her English.

The last thing that I recollect is the scene as it was revealed by the momentary light of one of the last matches. Maqueda sat by Oliver. His arm was about her waist, her head rested upon his shoulder, her long hair flowed loose, her large and tender eyes stared from her white, wan face up toward his face, which was almost that of a mummy.

Then on the other side was my son, supporting himself against the wall of the room, and beyond him Higgs, a shadow of his former self, feebly waving a pencil in the air and trying, apparently, to write a note upon his Panama straw hat which he held in his left hand, as I suppose, imagining it to be a pocket-book. The incongruity of that sun-hat in a place where no sun had ever come, made me laugh, and as the match went out I regretted that I had forgotten to look at his face to ascertain whether he was still wearing his smoked spectacles.

"What is the use of a straw hat and smoked spectacles in kingdom-come?" I kept repeating to myself, while Roderick, whose arm I knew was about me, seemed to answer:

"The Fung wizards say that the sphinx Harmac once wore a hat, but, my father, I do not know if he had spectacles."

Then a sensation as of being whirled round and round in some vast machine, down the sloping sides of which I sank at last into a vortex of utter blackness, whereof I knew the name was death.

Dimly, very dimly, I became aware that I was being carried. I heard voices in my ears, but what they said I could not understand. Then a feeling of light struck upon my eyeballs which gave me great pain. Agony ran all through me as it does through the limbs of one who is being brought back from death by drowning. After this something warm was poured down my throat, and I went to sleep.

When I awoke again it was to find myself in a large room that I did not know. I was lying on a bed, and by the light of sunrise which streamed through the window-places, I saw the three others, my son Roderick, Orme and Higgs lying on other beds, but they were still asleep.

Abati servants entered the room bringing food, a kind of rough soup with pieces of meat in it of which they gave me a portion in a wooden bowl that I devoured greedily. Also they shook my companions until they awoke and almost automatically ate up the contents of similar bowls, after which they went to sleep again, as I did, thanking heaven that we were all still alive.

Every few hours I had a vision of these men entering with the bowls of soup or porridge, until at last life and reason came back to me in earnest, and I saw Higgs sitting up on the bed opposite and staring at me.

"I say, old fellow," he said, "are we alive, or is this Hades?"

"Can't be Hades," I answered, "because there are Abati here."

"Quite right," he replied. "If the Abati go anywhere, it's to hell, where they have n't whitewashed walls and four-post beds. Oliver, wake up. We are out of that cave, anyway."

Orme raised himself on his hand and stared at us.

"Where's Maqueda?" he asked, a question to which of course, we could give no answer, till presently Roderick woke also and said:

"I remember something. They carried us all out of the cave; Japhet was with them. They took the Child of Kings one way and us another, that is all I know."

Shortly afterwards the Abati servants arrived, bearing food more solid than the soup, and with them came one of their doctors, not that old idiot of a court physician, who examined us, and announced that we should all recover, a fact which we knew already. We asked many questions of him and the servants, but could get no answer, for evidently they were sworn to silence. However, we persuaded them to bring us water to wash in. It came, and with it a polished piece of metal, such as the Abati used for a looking-glass, in which we saw our faces, the terrible, wasted faces of those who have gone within a hair's breadth of death by starvation in the dark.

Yet although our gaolers would say nothing, something in their aspect told us that we were in sore peril of our lives. They looked at us hungrily, as a terrier looks at rats in a wire cage of which the door will presently be opened. Moreover, Roderick, who, as I think I have said, has very quick ears, overheard one of the attendants whisper to another:

"When does our service on these hounds of Gentiles come to an end?" to which his fellow answered, "The Council has not decided, but I think to-morrow or the next day, if they are strong enough. It will be a great show."

Also that evening, about sunset, we heard a mob shouting outside the barrack in which we were imprisoned, for that was its real use, "Give us the Gentiles! Give us the Gentiles! We are tired of waiting," until at length some soldiers drove them away.

Well, we talked the thing over, only to conclude that there was nothing to be done. We had no friend in the place except Maqueda, and she, it appeared, was a prisoner like ourselves, and therefore could not communicate with us. Nor could we see the slightest possibility of escape.

"Out of the frying-pan into the fire," remarked Higgs gloomily. "I wish now that they had let us die in the cave. It would have been better than being baited to death by a mob of Abati."

"Yes," answered Oliver with a sigh, for he was thinking of Maqueda, "but that 's why they saved us, the vindictive beasts, to kill us for what they are pleased to call high treason."

"High treason!" exclaimed Higgs. "I hope to goodness their punishment for the offence is not that of mediæval England; hanging is bad enough — but the rest ——!"

"I don't think the Abati study European history," I broke in; "but it is no use disguising from you that they have methods of their own. Look here, friends," I added, "I have kept something about me in case the worst should come to the worst," and I produced a little bottle containing a particularly swift and deadly poison done up into tabloids, and gave one to each of them. "My advice is," I added, "that if you see we are going to be exposed to torture or to any dreadful form of death, you should take one of these, as I mean to do, and cheat the Abati of their vengeance."

"That is all very fine," said the Professor as he pocketed his tabloid, "but I never could swallow a pill without water at the best of times, and I don't believe those beasts will give one any. Well, I suppose I must suck it, that's all. Oh! if only the luck would turn, if only the luck would turn!"

Three more days went by without any sign of Higgs's aspiration being fulfilled. On the contrary, except in one respect, the luck remained steadily against us. The exception was that we got plenty to eat and consequently regained our normal state of health and strength more rapidly than might have been expected. With us it was literally a case of "Let us eat and drink, for to-morrow we die."

Only somehow I don't think that any of us really believed that we should die, though whether this was because we had all, except poor Quick, survived so much, or from a sneaking faith in Maqueda's optimistic dreams, I cannot say. At any rate we ate our food with appetite, took exercise in an inner yard of the prison, and strove to grow as strong as we could, feeling that soon we might need all our powers. Oliver was the most miserable among us, not for his own sake, but because, poor fellow, he was haunted with fears as to Maqueda and her fate, although of these he said little or nothing to us. On the other hand, my son Roderick was by far the most cheerful. He had lived for so many years upon the brink of death that this familiar gulf seemed to have no terrors for him.

"All come right somehow, my father," he said airily. "Who can know what happen? Perhaps Child of King drag us out of mud-hole, for after all she very strong cow, or what you call it, heifer, and I think toss Joshua if he drive her into corner. Or perhaps other thing occur."

"What other thing, Roderick?" I asked.

"Oh! don't know, can't say, but I think Fung thing. Believe we not done with Fung yet, believe they not run far. Believe they take thought for morrow and come back again. Only," he added sadly, "hope my wife not come back, for that old girl too full of lofty temper for me. Still, cheer up, not dead yet by long day's march, and meanwhile food good and this very jolly rest after beastly underground city. Now I tell Professor some more stories about Fung religion, den of lions, and so forth."

On the morning after this conversation a crisis came. Just as we had finished breakfast the doors of our chamber were thrown open and in marched a number of soldiers wearing Joshua's badge. They were headed by an officer of his household, who commanded us to rise and follow him.

"Where to?" asked Orme.

"To take your trial before the Child of Kings and her

Council, Gentile, upon the charge of having murdered certain of her subjects," answered the officer sternly.

"That's all right," said Higgs with a sigh of relief. "If Maqueda is chairman of the Bench we are pretty certain of an acquittal, for Orme's sake if not for our own."

"Don't you be too sure of that," I whispered into his ear. "The circumstances are peculiar, and women have been known to change their minds."

"Adams," he replied, glaring at me through his smoked spectacles, "if you talk like that we shall quarrel. Maqueda change her mind, indeed! Why, it is an insult to suggest such a thing, and if you take my advice you won't let Oliver hear you. Don't you remember, man, that she's in love with him?"

"Oh, yes," I answered, "but I remember also that Prince Joshua is in love with her, and that she is his prisoner."

CHAPTER XX

THE TRIAL AND AFTER

THEY set us in a line, four ragged-looking fellows, all of us with beards of various degrees of growth, that is, all the other three, for mine had been an established fact for years, and everything having been taken away from us, we possessed neither razor nor scissors.

In the courtyard of our barrack we were met by a company of soldiers, who encircled us about with a triple line of men, as we thought to prevent any attempt at escape. So soon as we passed the gates I found, however, that this was done for a different reason, namely, to protect us from the fury of the populace. All the way from the barrack to the courthouse whither we were being taken now that the palace was burned, the people were gathered in hundreds, literally howling for our blood. It was a strange, and, in a way, a dreadful sight to see even the brightly dressed women and children shaking their fists and spitting at us with faces distorted by hate.

"Why they love you so little, Father, when you do so much for them?" asked Roderick, shrugging his shoulders and dodging a stone that nearly hit him on the head.

"For two reasons," I answered. "Because their Lady loves one of us too much, and because through us many of their people have lost their lives. Also they hate strangers, and are by nature cruel, like most cowards, and now that they have no more fear of the Fung, they think it will be safe to kill us."

"Ah!" said Roderick; "yet Harmac has come to Mur," and he pointed to the great head of the idol seated on the cliff, "and I think where Harmac goes, Fung follow, and if so they make them pay plenty for my life, for I great man among Fung; Fung myself, husband of Sultan's daughter. These fools, like children, because they see no Fung, think there are no Fung. Well, in one year, or perhaps one month, they learn."

"I daresay, my boy," I answered, "but I am afraid that won't help us."

By now we were approaching the courthouse where the Abati priests and learned men tried civil and some criminal cases. Through a mob of nobles and soldiers who mocked us as we went, we were hustled into the large hall of judgment that was already full to overflowing.

Up the centre of it we marched to a clear space reserved for the parties to a cause, or prisoners and their advocates, beyond which, against the wall, were seats for the judges. These were four members of the Council, one of whom was Joshua, while in the centre as President of the Court, and wearing her veil and beautiful robes of ceremony, sat Maqueda herself.

"Thank God, she's safe!" muttered Oliver with a gasp of relief.

"Yes," answered Higgs, "but what's she doing there? She ought to be in the dock, too, not on the Bench."

We reached the open space, and were thrust by armed soldiers with swords to where we must stand, and although each of us bowed to her, I observed that Maqueda took not the slightest notice of our salutations; she only turned her head and said something to Joshua on her right, which caused him to laugh.

Then with startling suddenness the case began. A kind of public prosecutor stood forward and droned out the charge against us. It was that we, who were in the employ of the Abati, had traitorously taken advantage of our position as mercenary captains to stir up a civil war, in which many people had lost their lives, and some been actually murdered by ourselves and our companion who was dead. Moreover, that we had caused their palace to be burned and, greatest crime of all, had seized the sacred person of the Walda Nagasta, Rose of Mur, and dragged her away into the recesses of the underground city whence she was only rescued by the chance of an accomplice of ours, one Japhet, betraying our hiding-place.

This was the charge which, it will be noted, contained no allusion whatever to the love entanglement between Maqueda and Oliver. When it was finished the prosecutor asked us what we pleaded, whereon Oliver answered as our spokesman that it was true there had been fighting and men killed, also that we had been driven into the cave, but as to all the rest the Child of Kings knew the truth, and must speak for us as she wished.

Now the audience began to shout, "They plead guilty! Give them to death!" and so forth, while the judges, rising from their seats, gathered round Maqueda and consulted her.

"By heaven! I believe she is going to give us away!" exclaimed Higgs, whereon Oliver turned on him fiercely and bade him hold his tongue, adding:

"If you were anywhere else you should answer for that slander!"

At length the consultation was finished; the judges resumed their seats, and Maqueda held up her hand. Thereon an intense silence fell upon the place. Then she began to speak in a cold, constrained voice:

"Gentiles," she said, addressing us, "you have pleaded guilty to the stirring up of civil war in Mur, and to the slaying of numbers of its people, facts of which there is no need for evidence, since many widows and fatherless children can testify to them to-day. Moreover, you did, as alleged by my officer, commit the crime of bearing off my person into the cave and keeping me there by force to be a hostage for your safety."

We heard and gasped, Higgs ejaculating, "Good gracious, what a lie!" But none of the rest of us said anything.

"For these offences," went on Maqueda, "you are all of you justly worthy of a cruel death." Then she paused and added, "Yet, as I have power to do, I remit the sentence. I decree that this day you and all the goods that remain to you which have been found in the cave city, and elsewhere, together with camels for yourselves and your baggage, shall be driven from Mur, and that if any one of you returns hither, he shall without further trial be handed over to the executioners. This I do because at the beginning of your service a certain bargain was made with you, and although you have sinned so deeply I will not suffer that the glorious honour of the Abati people shall be tarnished even by the breath of suspicion. Get you gone, Wanderers, and let us see your faces no more forever!"

Now the mob gathered in the hall shouted in exultation, though I heard some crying out, "No, kill them! Kill them!"

When the tumult had died down Maqueda spoke again saying:

"O noble and generous Abati, you approve of this deed of mercy; you who would not be held merciless in far lands, O Abati, where, although you may not have heard of them, there are, I believe, other peoples who think themselves as great as you. You would not have it whispered, I say, that we who are the best of the world, we, the children of Solomon, have dealt harshly even with stray dogs that wandered to our gates? Moreover, we called these dogs to hunt a certain beast for us, the lion-headed beast called Fung, and, to be just to them, they hunted well. Therefore spare them the noose, though they may have deserved it, and let them run hence with their bone, say you, the bone which they think that they have earned. What does a bone more or less matter to the rich Abati, if only their holy ground is not defiled with the blood of Gentile dogs?"

"Nothing at all! Nothing at all!" they shouted. "Tie it to their tails and let them go!"

"It shall be done, O my people! And now that we have finished with these dogs, I have another word to say to you. You may have thought or heard that I was too fond of them, and especially of one of them," and she glanced toward Oliver. "Well, there are certain dogs who will not work unless you pat them on the head. Therefore I patted this one on the head, since, after all, he is a clever dog who knows things that we do not know; for instance, how to destroy the idol of the Fung O great Abati, can any of you really have believed that I, of the ancient race of Solomon and Sheba, I, the Child of Kings, purposed to give my noble hand to a vagrant Gentile come hither for hire? Can you really have believed that I, the solemnly betrothed to yonder Prince of Princes, Joshua, my uncle, would for a moment even in my heart have preferred to him such a man as that?" And once again she looked at Oliver, who made a wild motion, as though he were about to speak. But before he could so much as open his lips Maqueda went on:

"Well, if you believed, not guessing that all the while I was working for the safety of my people, soon shall you be undeceived, since to-morrow night I invite you to the great ceremony of my nuptials, when, according to the ancient custom, I break the glass with him whom on the following night I take to be my husband," and, rising, she bowed thrice to the audience, then stretched out her hand to Joshua.

He, too, rose, puffing himself out like a great turkey cock, and, taking her hand, kissed it, gobbling some words which we did not catch.

Wild cheering followed, and in the momentary silence which followed Oliver spoke.

"Lady," he said, in a cold and bitter voice, "we 'Gentiles' have heard your words. We thank you for your kind acknowledgment of our services, namely, the destruction of the idol of the Fung at the cost of some risk and labour to ourselves. We thank you also for your generosity in allowing us, as the reward of that service, to depart from Mur, with insult and hard words, and such goods as remain to us, instead of consigning us to death by torture, as you and your Council have the power to do. It is indeed a proof of your generosity, and of that of the Abati people which we shall always remember and repeat in our own land, should we live to reach it. Also we trust that it will come to the ears of the savage Fung, so that at last they may understand that true nobility and greatness lie not in brutal deeds of arms, but in the hearts of men. But now, Walda Nagasta, I have a last request to make of you, namely, that I may see your face once more to be sure that it is you who have spoken to us, and not another beneath your veil, and that if this be so, I may carry away with me a faithful picture of one so true to her country and noble to her guests as you have shown yourself this day."

She listened, then very slowly lifted her veil, revealing such a countenance as I had never seen before. It was

Maqueda without doubt, but Maqueda changed. Her face was pale, which was only to be expected after all she had gone through; her eyes glowed in it like coals, her lips were set. But it was her expression, at once defiant and agonized, which impressed me so much that I never shall forget it. I confess I could not read it in the least, but it left upon my mind the belief that she was a false woman, and yet ashamed of her own falsity. This was the greatest triumph of her art, that in those terrible circumstances she should still have succeeded in conveying to me, and to the hundreds of others who watched, this conviction of her own turpitude.

For a moment her eyes met those of Orme, but although he searched them with pleading and despair in his glance, I could trace in hers no relenting sign, but only challenge not unmixed with mockery. Then with a short, hard laugh she let fall her veil again and turned to talk with Joshua. Oliver stood silent a little while, long enough for Higgs to whisper to me:

"I say, isn't this downright awful? I'd rather be back in the den of lions than live to see it."

As he spoke I saw Oliver put his hand to where his revolver usually hung, but, of course, it had been taken from him. Next he began to search in his pocket, and finding that tabloid of poison which I had given him, lifted it toward his mouth. But just as it touched his lips, my son, who was next to him, saw also. With a quick motion he struck it from his fingers, and ground it to powder on the floor beneath his heel.

Oliver raised his arm as though to hit him, then without a sound fell down senseless. Evidently Maqueda noted all this also, for I saw a kind of quiver go through her, and her hands gripped the arms of her chair till the knuckles showed white beneath the skin. But she only said:

"This Gentile has fainted because he is disappointed with his reward. Take him hence and let his companion, the Doctor Adams, attend to him. When he is recovered, conduct them all from Mur as I have decreed. See that they go unharmed, taking with them plenty of food lest it be said that we only spared their lives here in order that they might starve without our gates."

Then waving her hand to show that the matter was done with, she rose and, followed by the judges and officers, left the court by some door behind them.

While she spoke a strong body of guards had surrounded us, some of whom came forward and lifted the senseless Oliver on to a stretcher. They carried him down the court, the rest of us following.

"Look," jeered the Abati as he passed, "look at the Gentile pig who thought to wear the Bud of the Rose upon his bosom. He has got the thorn now, not the rose. Is the swine dead, think you?"

Thus they mocked him and us.

We reached our prison in safety, and there I set to work to revive Oliver, a task in which I succeeded at length. When he had come to himself again he drank a cup of water, and said quite quietly:

"You fellows have seen all, so there is no need for talk and explanations. One thing I beg of you, if you are any friends of mine, and it is that you will not reproach or even speak of Maqueda to me. Doubtless she had reasons for what she did; moreover, her bringing up has not been the same as ours, and her code is different. Do not let us judge her. I have been a great fool, that is all, and now I am paying for my folly, or, rather, I have paid. Come, let us have some dinner, for we don't know when we shall get another meal."

We listened to this speech in silence only I saw Roderick turn aside to hide a smile and wondered why he smiled.

Scarcely had we finished eating, or pretending to eat, when an officer entered the room and informed us roughly that it was time for us to be going. As he did so some attendants who had followed him threw us bundles of clothes, and with them four very beautiful camel-hair cloaks to protect us from the cold. With some of these garments we replaced our rags, for they were little more, tying them and the rest of the outfit up into bundles.

Then, clothed as Abati of the upper class, we were taken to the gates of the barrack, where we found a long train of riding camels waiting for us. The moment that I saw these beasts I knew that they were the best in the whole land, and of very great value. Indeed, that to which Oliver was conducted was Maqueda's own favourite dromedary, which upon state occasions she sometimes rode instead of a horse. He recognized it at once, poor fellow, and coloured to the eyes at this unexpected mark of kindness, the only one she had vouchsafed to him.

"Come, Gentiles," said the officer, "and take count of your goods, that you may not say that we have stolen anything from you. Here are your firearms and all the ammunition that is left. These will be given to you at the foot of the pass, but not before, lest you should do more murder on the road. On those camels are fastened the boxes in which you brought up the magic fire. We found them in your quarters in the cave city, ready packed, but what they contain we neither know nor care. Full or empty, take them, they are yours. Those," and he pointed to two other beasts, "are laden with your pay which the Child of Kings sends to you, requesting that you will not count it till you reach Egypt or your own land, since she wishes no quarrelling with you as to the amount. The rest carry food for you to eat; also, there are two spare beasts. Now, mount and begone."

So we climbed into the embroidered saddles of the kneeling dromedaries, and a few minutes later were riding through Mur toward the pass, accompanied by our guard and hooting mobs that once or twice became threatening, but were driven off by the soldiers.

"I say, Doctor," whispered Higgs to me excitedly, "do you know that we have got all the best of the treasure of the Tomb of Kings in those five and twenty cases? I have thought since that I was crazy when I packed them, picking out the most valuable and rare articles with such care, and filling in the cracks with ring money and small curiosities, but now I see it was the inspiration of genius. My subliminal self knew what was going to happen, and was on the job, that's all. Oh! if only we can get it safe away, I shall not have played Daniel and been nearly starved to death for nothing. Why, I'd go through it all again for that golden head alone. Shove on, shove on, before they change their minds; it seems too good to be true."

Just then a rotten egg thrown by some sweet Abati youth landed full on the bridge of his nose, and dispersing itself into his mouth and over his smoked spectacles, cut short the Professor's eloquence, or rather changed its tenor. So absurd was the sight that in spite of myself I burst out laughing, and with that laugh felt my heart grow lighter, as though our clouds of trouble were lifting at length.

At the mouth of the pass we found Joshua himself waiting for us, clad in all his finery and chain armour, and looking more like a porpoise on horseback than he had ever done.

"Farewell, Gentiles," he said, bowing to us in mockery,

"we wish you a quick journey to Sheol, or wherever such swine as you may go. Listen, you Orme. I have a message for you from the Walda Nagasta. It is that she is sorry she could not ask you to stop for her nuptial feast, which she would have done had she not been sure that, if you stayed, the people would have cut your throat, and she did not wish the holy soil of Mur to be defiled with your dog's blood. Also she bids me say that she hopes that your stay here will have taught you a lesson, and that in future you will not believe that every woman who makes use of you for her own ends is therefore a victim of your charms. To-morrow night and the night after, I pray you think of our happiness and drink a cup of wine to the Walda Nagasta and her husband. Come, will you not wish me joy, O Gentile?"

Orme turned white as a sheet and gazed at him steadily. Then a strange look came into his gray eyes, almost a look of inspiration.

"Prince Joshua," he said in a very quiet voice, "who knows what may happen before the sun rises thrice on Mur? All things that begin well do not end well, as I have learned, and as you also may live to learn. At least, soon or late, your day of reckoning must come, and you, too, may be betrayed as I have been. Rather should you ask me to forgive your soul the insults that in your hour of triumph you have not been ashamed to heap upon one who is powerless to avenge them," and he urged his camel past him.

As we followed I saw Joshua's face turn as pale as Oliver's had done, and his great round eyes protrude themselves like those of a fish.

"What does he mean?" said the Prince to his companions. "Pray God he is not a prophet of evil. Even now I have a mind — no, let him go. To break my marriage vow might bring bad luck upon me. Let him go!" and he glared after Oliver with fear and hatred written on his coarse features.

That was the last we ever saw of Joshua, uncle of Maqueda, and first prince among the Abati.

Down the pass we went and through the various gates of the fortifications, which were thrown open as we came and closed behind us. We did not linger on that journey. Why should we when our guards were anxious to be rid of us and we of them? Indeed, so soon as the last gate was behind us, either from fear of the Fung or because they were in a hurry to return to share in the festivities of the approaching marriage, suddenly the Abati wheeled round, bade us farewell with a parting curse, and left us to our own devices.

So, having roped the camels into a long line, we went on alone, truly thankful to be rid of them, and praying, every one of us, that never in this world or the next might we see the face or hear the voice of another Abati.

We emerged on to the plain at the spot where months before we had held our conference with Barung, Sultan of the Fung, and where poor Quick had forced his camel on to Joshua's horse and dismounted that hero. Here we paused awhile to arrange our little caravan and arm ourselves with the rifles, revolvers, and cartridges which until now we had not been allowed to touch.

There were but four of us to manage the long train of camels, so we were obliged to separate. Higgs and I went ahead, since I was best acquainted with the desert and the road, Oliver took the central station, and Roderick brought up the rear, because he was very keen of sight and hearing and from his long familiarity with them, knew how to drive camels that showed signs of obstinacy or a wish to turn.

On our right lay the great city of Harmac. We noted

that it seemed to be quite deserted. There, rebuilt now, frowned the gateway through which we had escaped from the Fung after we had blown so many of them to pieces, but beneath it none passed in or out. The town was empty, and although they were dead ripe the rich crops had not yet been reaped. Apparently the Fung people had left the land.

Now we were opposite to the valley of Harmac, and saw that the huge sphinx still sat there as it had done for unknown thousands of years. Only its head was gone, for that had "moved to Mur," and in its neck and shoulders appeared great clefts, caused by the terrific force of the explosion. Moreover, no sound came from the enclosures where the sacred lions used to be. Doubtless every one of them was dead.

"Don't you think," suggested Higgs, whose archæological zeal was rekindling fast, "that we might spare half an hour to go up the valley and have a look at Harmac from the outside? Of course, both Roderick and I are thoroughly acquainted with his inside, and the den of lions, and so forth, but I would give a great deal just to study the rest of him and take a few measurements. You know one must camp somewhere, and if we can't find the camera, at dawn one might make a sketch."

"Are you mad?" I asked by way of answer, and Higgs collapsed, but to this hour he has never forgiven me.

We looked our last on Harmac, the god whose glory we had destroyed, and went on swiftly till darkness overtook us almost opposite to that ruined village where Shadrach had tried to poison the hound Pharaoh, which afterwards tore out his throat. Here we unloaded the camels, no light task, and camped, for near this spot there was water and a patch of maize on which the beasts could feed.

Before the light quite faded Roderick rode forward for a little way to reconnoitre, and presently returned announcing shortly that he had seen no one.   So we ate of the food with which the Abati had provided us, not without fear lest it should be poisoned, and then held a council of war.

The question was whether we should take the old road towards Egypt, or now that the swamps were dry, strike up northward by the other route of which Shadrach had told us.   According to the map this should be shorter, and Higgs advocated it strongly, as I discovered afterwards because he thought there might be more archæological remains in that direction.

I, on the other hand, was in favour of following the road we knew, which, although long and very wearisome, was comparatively safe, as in that vast desert there were few people to attack us, while Oliver, our captain, listened to all we had to say, and reserved his opinion.

Presently, however, the question was settled for us by Roderick, who remarked that if we travelled to the north we should probably fall in with the Fung.   I asked what he meant, and he replied that when he made his reconnaissance an hour or so before, although it was true that he had seen no one, not a thousand yards from where we sat he had come across the tracks of a great army.   This army, from various indications, he felt sure was that of Barung, which had passed there within twelve hours.

"Perhaps my wife with them, so I no want go that way, Father," he added with sincere simplicity.

"Where could they be travelling?" I asked.

"Don't know," he answered, "but think they go round to attack Mur from other side, or perhaps to find new land to north."

"We will stick to the old road," said Oliver briefly. "Like Roderick I have had enough of all the inhabitants of this country.   Now let us rest a while; we need it."

About two o'clock we were up again and before it was

dawn on the following morning we had loaded our camels and were on the road. By the first faint light we saw that what Roderick had told us was true. We were crossing the track of an army of many thousand men who had passed there recently with laden camels and horses. Moreover, those men were Fung, for we picked up some articles that could have belonged to no other people, such as a head-dress that had been lost or thrown away, and an arrow that had fallen from a quiver.

However, we saw nothing of them, and, travelling fast, to our great relief by midday reached the river Ebur, which we crossed without difficulty, for it was now low. That night we camped in the forest-lands beyond, having all the afternoon marched up the rising ground at the foot of which ran the river.

Toward dawn Higgs, whose turn it was to watch the camels, came and woke me.

"Sorry to disturb you, old fellow," he said, "but there is a most curious sky effect behind us which I thought you might like to see."

I rose and looked. In the clear, starlight night I could just discern the mighty outline of the mountains of Mur. Above them the firmament was suffused with a strange red glow. I formed my own conclusion at once, but only said:

"Let us go tell Orme," and led the way to where he had lain down under a tree.

He was not sleeping; indeed, I do not think he had closed his eyes all night, the night of Maqueda's marriage. On the contrary, he was standing on a little knoll staring at the distant mountains and the glow above them.

"Mur is on fire," he said solemnly. "Oh, my God, Mur is on fire!" and turning he walked away.

Just then Roderick joined us.

"Fung got into Mur," he said, "and now cut throat of all Abati. We well out of that, but pig Joshua have very warm wedding feast, because Barung hate Joshua who try to catch him not fairly, which he never forget, often talk of it."

"Poor Maqueda!" I said to Higgs, "what will happen to her?"

"I don't know," he answered, "but although once, like everybody else, I adored that girl, really as a matter of justice she deserves all she gets, the false-hearted little wretch. Still it is true," he added, relenting, "she gave us very good camels, to say nothing of their loads."

But I only repeated, "Poor Maqueda!"

That day we made but a short journey, since we wished to rest ourselves and fill the camels before plunging into the wilderness, and feeling sure that we should not be pursued, had no cause to hurry. At night we camped in a little hollow by a stream that ran at the foot of a rise. As dawn broke we were awakened by the voice of Roderick, who was on watch, calling to us in tones of alarm to get up, as we were followed. We sprang to our feet, seizing our rifles.

"Where are they?" I asked.

"There, there," he said, pointing toward the rise behind us.

We ran round some intervening bushes and looked, to see upon its crest a solitary figure seated on a very tired horse, for it panted and its head drooped. This figure, which was entirely hidden in a long cloak with a hood, appeared to be watching our camp just as a spy might do. Higgs lifted his rifle and fired at it, but Oliver, who was standing by him, knocked the barrel up so that the bullet went high, saying.

"Don't be a fool. If it is only one man there's no need to shoot him, and if there are more you will bring them on to us."

Then the figure urged the weary horse and advanced slowly, and I noticed that it was very small. "A boy," I thought to myself, "who is bringing some message."

The rider reached us, and slipping from the horse, stood still.

"Who are you?" asked Oliver, scanning the cloaked form.

"One who brings a token to you, lord," was the answer, spoken in a low and muffled voice. "Here it is," and a hand, a very delicate hand, was stretched out, holding between the fingers a ring.

I knew it at once; it was Sheba's ring which Maqueda had lent to me in proof of her good faith when I journeyed for help to England. This ring, it will be remembered, we returned to her with much ceremony at our first public audience. Oliver grew pale at the sight of it.

"How did you come by this?" he asked hoarsely "Is she who alone may wear it dead?"

"Yes, yes," answered the voice, a feigned voice as I thought. "The Child of Kings whom you knew is dead, and having no more need for this symbol of her power, she bequeathed it to you whom she remembered kindly at the last."

Oliver covered his face with his hands and turned away.

"But," went on the speaker slowly, "the woman Maqueda whom once it is said you loved ——"

He dropped his hands and stared.

"—— the woman Maqueda whom once it is said you — loved — still lives."

Then the hood slipped back, and in the glow of the rising sun we saw the face beneath.

It was that ôf Maqueda herself!

A silence followed that in its way was almost awful.

"My lord Oliver," asked Maqueda presently, "do you accept my offering of Queen Sheba's ring?"

NOTE BY MAQUEDA

Once called Walda Nagasta and Takla-Warda, that is, Child of Kings and Bud of the Rose, once also by birth Ruler of the Abati people, the Sons of Solomon and Sheba.

I, MAQUEDA, write this by the command of Oliver, my lord, who desires that I should set out certain things in my own words.

Truly all men are fools, and the greatest of them is Oliver, my lord, though perhaps he is almost equalled by the learned man whom the Abati called Black Windows, and by the doctor, Son of Adam. Only he who is named Roderick, child of Adam, is somewhat less blind, because having been brought up among the Fung and other peoples of the desert, he has gathered a little wisdom. This I know because he has told me that he alone saw through my plan to save all their lives, but said nothing of it because he desired to escape from Mur, where certain death waited on him and his companions. Perhaps, however, he lies to please me.

Now, for the truth of the matter, which not being skilled in writing I will tell briefly.

I was carried out of the cave city with my lord and the others, starving, starving, too weak to kill myself, which otherwise I would have done rather than fall into the hands of my accursed uncle, Joshua. Yet I was stronger than the rest, because as I have learned, they tricked me about those biscuits, pretending to eat when they were not eating, for which never will I forgive them. It was Japhet, a gallant man on one side, but a coward on the other like the rest of the Abati, who betrayed us, driven thereto by

emptiness within, which, after all, is an ill enemy to fight.
He went out and told Joshua where we lay hid, and then,
of course, they came.

Well, they took away my lord and the others, and me
too they bore to another place and fed me till my strength
returned, and oh! how good was that honey which
first I ate, for I could touch nothing else. When I was
strong again came Prince Joshua to me and said, "Now
I have you in my net; now you are mine."

Then I answered Joshua, "Fool, your net is of air; I
will fly through it."

"How?" he asked. "By death," I answered, "of
which a hundred means lie to my hand. You have robbed
me of one, but what does that matter when so many
remain? I will go where you and your love cannot pursue
me."

"Very well, Child of Kings," he said, "but how about
that tall Gentile who has caught your eyes, and his companions? They, too, have recovered, and they shall die
every one of them after a certain fashion (which, I
Maqueda, will not set down, since there are some things
that ought not to be written). If you die, they die;
as I told you, they die as a wolf dies that is caught by the
shepherds; they die as a baboon dies that is caught by
the husbandman."

Now I looked this way and that, and found that there
was no escape. So I made a bargain.

"Joshua," I said, "let these men go and I swear upon
the name of our mother, she of Sheba, that I will marry
you. Keep them and kill them, and you will have none
of me."

Well, in the end, because he desired me and the power
that went with me, he consented.

Then I played my part. My lord and his companions
were brought before me, and in presence of all the people I

mocked them; I spat in their faces, and oh! fools, fools, fools, they believed me! I lifted my veil, and showed them my eyes, and they believed also what they seemed to see in my eyes, forgetting that I am a woman who can play a part at need. Yes, they forgot that there were others to deceive as well, all the Abati people, who, if they thought I tricked them, would have torn the foreigners limb from limb. That was my bitterest morsel, that I should have succeeded in making even my lord believe that of all the wicked women that ever trod this world, I was the most vile. Yet I did so, and he cannot deny it, for often we have talked of this thing till he will hear of it no more.

Well, they went with all that I could give them, though I knew well that my lord cared nothing for what I could give, nor the doctor, Child of Adam, either, who cared only for his son that God had restored to him. Only Black Windows cared, not because he loves wealth, but because he worships all that is old and ugly, for of such things he fashions up his god.

They went, for their going was reported to me, and I, I entered into hell because I knew that my lord thought me false, and that he would never learn the truth, namely, that what I did I did to save his life, until at length he came to his own country, if ever he came there, and opened the chests of treasure, if ever he opened them, which perhaps he would not care to do. And all that while he would believe me the wife of Joshua, and — oh! I cannot write of it. And I, I should be dead; I, I could not tell him the truth until he joined me in that land of death, if there men and women can talk together any more.

For this and no other was the road that I had planned to walk. When he and his companions had gone so far that they could not be followed, then I would tell Joshua and the Abati all the truth in such language as should never be forgotten for generations, and kill myself before their eyes, so that Joshua might lack a wife and the Abati a Child of Kings.

I sat through the Feast of Preparation and smiled and smiled. It passed and the next day passed, and came the night of the Feast of Marriage. The glass was broken, the ceremony was fulfilled. Joshua rose up to pledge me before all the priests, lords, and headmen. He devoured me with his hateful eyes, me, who was already his. But I, I handled the knife in my robe, wishing, such was the rage in my heart, that I could kill him also.

Then God spoke, and the dream that I had dreamed came true. Far away there rose a single cry, and after it other cries, and the sounds of shouting and of marching feet. Far away tongues of fire leaped into the air, and each man asked his neighbour, "What is this?" Then from all the thousands of the feasting people rose one great scream, and that scream said, "Fung! Fung! The Fung are on us! Fly, fly, fly!"

"Come," shouted Joshua, seizing me by the arm, but I drew my dagger on him and he let go. Then he fled with the other lords, and I remained in my high seat beneath the golden canopy alone.

The people fled past me without fighting; they fled into the cave city, they fled to the rocks; they hid themselves among the precipices, and after them came the Fung, slaying and burning, till all Mur went up in flames. And I, I sat and watched, waiting till it was time for me to die also.

At last, I know not how long afterward, appeared before me Barung, a red sword in his hand, which he lifted to me in salute.

"Greeting, Child of Kings," he said. "You see Harmac is come to sleep at Mur."

"Yes," I answered, "Harmac is come to sleep at Mur, and many of those who dwelt there sleep with him. What of it? Say, Barung, will you kill me, or shall I kill myself?"

"Neither, Child of Kings," he answered in his high fashion. "Did I not make you a promise yonder in the Pass of Mur, when I spoke with you and the Western men, and does a Fung Sultan break his word? I have taken back the city that was ours, as I swore to do, and purified it with fire," and he pointed to the raging flames. "Now I will rebuild it, and you shall rule under me."

"Not so," I answered; "but in place of that promise I ask of you three things."

"Name them," said Barung.

"They are these: First, that you give me a good horse and five days' food, and let me go where I will. Secondly, that if he still lives you advance one Japhet, a certain mountaineer who befriended me and brought others to do likewise, to a place of honour under you. Thirdly, that you spare the rest of the Abati people."

"You shall go whither you desire, and I think I know where you will go," answered Barung. "Certain spies of mine last night saw four white men riding on fine camels toward Egypt, and reported it to me as I led my army to the secret pass that Harmac showed me, which you Abati could never find. But I said, 'Let them go; it is right that brave men who have been the mock of the Abati, should be allowed their freedom.' Yes, I said this, although one of them was my daughter's husband, or near to it. But she will have no more of him who fled to his father rather than with her, so it was best that he should go also, since, if I brought him back it must be to his death."

"Yes," I answered boldly, "I go after the Western men; I who have done with these Abati. I wish to see new lands."

"And find an old love who thinks ill of you just now," he said, stroking his beard. "Well, no wonder, for here has been a marriage feast. Say, what were you about to do, O Child of Kings? Take the fat Joshua to your breast?"

"Nay, Barung, I was about to take *this* husband to my breast," and I showed him the knife that was hidden in my marriage robe.

"No," he said, smiling, "I think the knife was for Joshua first. Still, you are a brave woman who could save the life of him you love at the cost of your own. Yet, bethink you, Child of Kings, for many a generation your mothers have been queens, and under me you may still remain a queen. How will one whose blood has ruled so long endure to serve a Western man in a strange land?"

"That is what I go to find out, Barung, and, if I cannot endure, then I shall come back again, though not to rule the Abati, of whom I wash my hands for ever. Yet, Barung, my heart tells me I shall endure."

"The Child of Kings has spoken," he said, bowing to me. "My best horse awaits her, and five of my bravest guards shall ride with her to keep her safe till she sights the camp of the Western men. I say happy is he of them who was born to wear the sweet-scented Bud of the Rose upon his bosom. For the rest, the man Japhet is in my hands. He yielded himself to me who would not fight for his own people because of what they had done to his friends, the white men. Lastly, already I have given orders that the slaying shall cease, since I need the Abati to be my slaves, they who are cowards, but cunning in many arts. Only one more man shall die," he added sternly, "and that is Joshua, who would have taken me by a trick in the mouth of the pass. So plead not for him, for by the head of Harmac, it is in vain."

Now hearing this I did not plead, fearing lest I should anger Barung, and but waste my breath.

At daybreak I started on the horse, having with me the five Fung captains. As we crossed the market place I met those that remained alive of the Abati, being driven in hordes like beasts, to hear their doom. Among them was Prince Joshua, my uncle, whom a man led by a rope about his neck, while another man thrust him forward from behind, since he knew that he went to his death and the road was one which he did not wish to travel. He saw me, and cast himself down upon the ground, crying to me to save him. I told him that I could not, though it is the truth, I swear it before God, that, notwithstanding all the evil he had worked toward me, toward Oliver my lord, and his companions, bringing to his end that gallant man who died to protect me, I would still have saved him if I could. But I could not, for although I tried once more, Barung would not listen. So I answered:

"Plead, O Joshua, with him who has the power in Mur to-day, for I have none. You have fashioned your own fate, and must travel the road you chose."

"What road do you ride, mounted on a horse of the plains, Maqueda? Oh! what need is there for me to ask? You go to seek that accursed Gentile whom I would I had killed by inches, as I would that I could kill you."

Then, calling me by evil names, Joshua sprang at me as though to strike me down, but he who held the rope about his neck jerked him backward, so that he fell and I saw his face no more.

But oh! it was sad, that journey across the great square, for the captive Abati by hundreds — men, women, and children together — with tears and lamentations, cried to me to preserve them from death or slavery at the hands of the Fung. But I answered:

"Your sins against me and the brave foreign men who fought so well for you I forgive, but search your hearts, O Abati, and say if you can forgive yourselves? If you had listened to me and to those whom I called in to help us, you might have beaten back the Fung, and remained free for ever. But you were cowards; you would not learn to bear arms like men, you would not even watch your mountain walls, and soon or late the people who refuse to be ready to fight must fall and become the servants of those who are ready."

And now, my Oliver, I have no more to write, save that I am glad to have endured so many things, and thereby win the joy that is mine to-day. Not yet have I, Maqueda, wished to reign again in Mur, who have found another throne.

THE END

e ५ ४
25'